Praise for *Left on Rancho:*

"With a gripping narrative, snappy dialogue, and obvious familiarity with the cannabis industry and immigration issues at the Southern border, Paola crafts a masterful tale. I couldn't rest till I knew how all the pieces tied together. A blend of intrigue and relevance makes *Left on Rancho* a must-read."

—Jude Berman, author of *The Die* and *The Vow*

"Paola's all-too-realistic narrative dives head first into the dark underbelly of the cannabis industry. As we follow the protagonist deeper into the ethical quagmire, the bodies pile up in this page-turning debut."

—Mike Trigg, author of *Burner* and *Bit Flip*

"As someone who has been on the ground floor of cannabis policy in California, *Left on Rancho* masterfully captures the good, the bad, the legal, and the not so legal perspectives of the California cannabis world and weaves them into an enthralling and satisfying thriller, with dead-on, well-developed characters that are only found in the Wild West of California cannabis."

—Niccoló De Luca, Vice President of Townsend Public Affairs

"*Left on Rancho* is a mystery proximal to California's legal recreational cannabis industry. Add immigration and the result is an intense, savvy, intelligent, and informative whodunnit. The reader is treated to vivid descriptions of southern California and the Mojave Desert, with characters that are nuanced and realistic, enhancing the realism of the story."

—Elizabeth R. Aden, PhD, author of *The Goldilocks Genome*

LEFT ON RANCHO

LEFT ON RANCHO

A NOVEL

FRANCESCO PAOLA

Published by SparkPress, a BookSparks imprint,
A division of SparkPoint Studio, LLC
Phoenix, Arizona, USA, 85007
www.gosparkpress.com

Published 2025
Printed in the United States of America
Print ISBN: 978-1-68463-292-3
E-ISBN: 978-1-68463-293-0
Library of Congress Control Number: 2024916277

Formatting by Kiran Spees

To
Jackie

"*Nel mezzo del cammin di nostra vita*
mi ritrovai per una selva oscura,
ché la diritta via era smarrita."

"Midway in our life's journey
I found myself in a dark forest,
for the straight path had been lost."
—Dante Alighieri, *La Divina Commedia*

CHAPTER 1

Friday, October 18, 2019

"I need your help, Andy."

"Charlie? What's it been . . . ten years? Since that bender in Boston?"

"Something like that."

"I missed that entire conference because of you." The lost weekend had gone on for three days: wine "tasting" from the Côte d'Or, food from Chinatown holes-in-the-wall, and nightcaps in the old Combat Zone.

"Listen—"

"How'd that restaurant work out?"

"That lasted six months. I'm doing something new," Charlie said.

"What, you opening an Italian joint and need my help?" Andrew laughed, not at his wit, but because he was genuinely happy his friend had called him.

"Funny guy. The restaurant business is for shit. I'm in cannabis now. You heard of gummies?"

"Candy?"

"Edibles make cannabis accessible to everyone, from Gen Z to octogenarians. No stigma of being a pothead, no need to inhale. Massive potential!" He sounded amped up, but that was Charlie.

"How's a tech entrepreneur going to help with a weed company?"

He was intrigued but played it cool. He'd heard from his venture buddies that cannabis was a hot investment—a game changer, the next wealth creator. And importantly for Andrew, it wasn't tech.

"*Cannabis.*"

"Right, cannabis. Because it's legal now."

Charlie laughed a strange, nervous laugh. "Come to SoCal. Check out the factory, see what you think."

"You're in SoCal?" Andrew walked to the window and stared down the hill. Alcatraz was faintly visible through the thickening fog. "If I'd known I would have come down to see you."

"Well, now's your chance. We're in a rut. We need adult supervision." His friend was pitching him hard. He sounded like an impetuous tech bro—a myopic twenty-something who couldn't discern a business plan from a restaurant menu. But this was Charlie—his best friend from high school, the star athlete. The one who always got the girl.

"I'm a software guy. I know nothing about manufacturing."

"It's not rocket science, Andy."

Other than his dad, Charlie was the only person who called him Andy. "This is quite a change from white tablecloths and fine dining."

"We'll have some fun together. Like old times."

Charlie was also the friend Andrew could never say no to.

Three days later, Andrew crossed the Cajon Pass. He shifted into fourth and watched the parched San Bernardino mountains fade in the rearview mirror. The Mojave Desert lay before him, a barren, rock-strewn landscape dotted with nothing but forlorn Joshua trees and stunted creosote bushes.

He'd packed all his belongings, minus what he had put in storage, into his midnight-blue 993. Golf clubs, with the driver and three wood out of the bag, lay across the back seat because being a proper Porsche, there was no trunk. A Tumi roller and a backpack were on the passenger's seat, his hand pushing them out of the way every time he shifted into sixth gear.

He passed signs for Hesperia and Victorville, and at the next exit, merged onto the 395. Occasional signs of life dotted an infinite dust bowl: strip malls with the essentials of the desert economy; the Mojave Desert Truckstop providing gas, food, showers and more; a minor league stadium with the bleachers in disrepair. He drove by the towering welcome sign that loomed over a solitary Joshua tree: ADELANTO: THE CITY WITH UNLIMITED POSSIBILITIES.

At the next intersection, he took a left on Rancho Road.

What Andrew construed from his research was that Adelanto, located in the Inland Empire, was an isolated California backwater, an afterthought built by a desperate populace trying to sustain itself on the edges of an infertile desert. The extreme summer heat had worsened as the years passed, volatile easterly winds whipped up debris in the fall months, and frigid winter temperatures limited outdoor activities.

Adelanto had two primary economic contributors: incarceration, anchored in a US Immigration and Customs Enforcement (ICE) detention center managed by the Federal Detention Network Group (FDN), three state and federal prisons, and a local jail; and cannabis, with multiple grow, manufacture, and distribution facilities spread across the desert. This was not the Southern California one read about or saw on TV or in the movies. This was not the California Dream.

He continued on Rancho, slaloming around potholes and slowing as he eased over crevices in the asphalt, protecting the low-riding car. A solitary bus stop kiosk stood at an otherwise deserted intersection, the empty, flat, oiled road extending north and south into infinity. He drove by incongruous signs advertising warehouse facilities and immigration services. Some were nailed to telegraph poles, others sprouted out of the desert floor, like native flora.

He passed a sprawling, single-story structure with spartan wings that radiated like octopus tentacles. The entire complex was protected by two concentric chain-link fences topped with razor wire. A couple of uniformed men stood at attention by its entrance, where a placard impaled in the desert read: DESERT SANDS, A CORRECTIONAL FACILITY, aka an immigration detention center. Besides cannabis, FDN was the only other reason to take a left on Rancho.

He swerved to avoid another crater and coasted up to the factory. Isolated, it rose alone out of the desert, a twenty-foot-tall structure enclosed in Mondrianesque siding painted an assortment of grays. A chain-link fence topped with both barbed *and* razor wire enclosed the property: Kannawerks, his new employer.

Andrew drove through the open gate and pulled in past two Ford Explorers marked San Bernardino County Sheriff taking up both visitor parking spaces. He hesitated. What did he know? Maybe this was the norm? He parked next to a solitary black Prius and sat for a few moments listening to the engine idle.

When Charlie had called him, Andrew had been about to hop on a plane back to Thailand, which he would have considered home if "home" were his thing. He'd hit bottom after he was forced to shut down his last company. Silicon Valley had given him sustenance for the last twenty years, but he couldn't deal with it anymore. Or "it" couldn't deal with him.

"And bring your clubs," Charlie had added. "You can stay at the corporate rental; it's on a golf course. It's not the Royal Hua Hin, but it's got its own desert charm."

Charm.

Andrew considered the blighted wilderness of the Mojave and thought of another desert, the Sonoran, where his father had recently retired. Tucson, in the Catalina foothills, teemed with hundred-year-old saguaros mingling with forests of jumping chollas and ocotillos that bloomed overnight after the first monsoon rain. Mesquites reached for the sun along dry riverbeds, innumerable cactus species stood stalwart—barrel, organ pipe, buckhorn. *That's* fucking charm. But here? Not one saguaro—just Martian dust.

Andrew lifted his backpack over the gear shift and stepped out of the car. A pungent, skunk-like musk hung in the air with intermittent wind gusts intensifying the scent. He walked over to the main entrance, which had two large green letters—KW—floating above it, and pressed the buzzer.

A short, bald man opened the door. He wore a light-blue gown, and his half smile revealed a missing eyetooth. He glanced behind Andrew, his eyes widening at the sight of the Porsche. "*¿De qué año es?*"

"Ninety-six," Andrew said.

The man's smile broadened. He introduced himself as Álvaro and motioned for Andrew to come in.

"*Tenemos un problema,*" he said, his smile fading.

"I see that."

"*Espera aquí.*"

Álvaro rapped his knuckles on another door. A man stepped out into the brightly lit foyer, quickly closing the door behind him. He had a slight limp.

"Everything is fine," the man said, as if attempting to forestall questions. "A couple of officers from Victor Valley Station just got here. They need to check up on a few things . . . it has nothing to do with us." His accent was cleaner, more polished than Álvaro's. So was his handshake. "I am Miguel. Call me Mike."

Mike was thin, one of those men who would never carry an extra pound of flesh, with a full head of black hair neatly parted to the left, gray-streaked temples, and a trimmed moustache. Andrew pegged him to be in his early forties, a couple of years younger than himself.

"I guess you should come in." Mike gave Andrew a once over. "They'll be more comfortable talking to you."

"Do you want to tell me what's going on?"

"Welcome to the High Desert," Mike said. He opened the door and introduced Andrew as the new boss to the waiting officers.

Andrew stifled his surprise at the word "boss" as the two officers stared him down. In one corner stood a tall man in uniform. He had a military crewcut and wore olive-green slacks, a khaki collared shirt with various insignia, and a deputy sheriff's star pinned above the left pocket. He held a cap in his hands. In the opposite corner, a woman sat in a swivel chair. She was dressed in a blue blazer, a white polo shirt, jeans, and black cowboy boots, with a shiny badge clipped to her belt. She stared at a six-by-four grid of video feeds on a fifty-inch console. They both had semi-automatics holstered on their belts.

The woman said to Andrew, "I'm Sheriff's Detective Morales— Rachel Morales. Homicide Detail. The body of an escaped FDN detainee was found a few clicks from here on Friday morning. Massive head trauma." She returned her gaze to the console. "Just another day in Adelanto."

Andrew glanced at Mike expectantly, who shrugged.

She continued, "This factory is on a direct line between the FDN facility and where the body was found. We're here to review footage from your external cameras to see if we find anything of relevance. Coroner says he died sometime between midnight and 2:00 a.m."

Mike walked over to the video console and scrolled through the camera inventory. He selected one of the five external cameras, jumped to 11:30 p.m. from the prior Thursday's feed, and clicked play. The images were clear, considering that the system looked like it belonged in a museum. He stopped the playback just after the timer reached 2:30 a.m. Nothing unusual. He selected another camera and repeated the process. Nothing.

After two hours, they had gone through all of the external cameras, with the exception of camera number four. It was the only camera that faced north into the barren desert behind the factory, and it was out of commission.

"Well, let's see what the coroner comes back with. I'll let you know if we need anything else." The detective motioned to the uniformed officer, and as she stepped out the door, said to Andrew, "And get the cameras fixed. The BCC won't like that."

Mike and Andrew watched on the video feeds as the officers got in their cars and drove away. Then Mike fell into his swivel chair and mumbled, "¿Qué chingados?"

"What's the BCC?"

"Bureau of Cannabis Control. It is the main state regulator. We must keep all video for ninety days. If not, they can fine us . . . shut us down."

"What about these other cameras? They're out, too."

The chair creaked as Mike leaned forward. "Some of the internal camera feeds in the factory. This system is old. No one knows how to work the thing."

"Why not?"

"I do not know. You are the IT guy."

Andrew ignored the slight. "We should get them fixed."

"I will put it on the list," Mike said, staring at his laptop.

Andrew let it go. He'd have plenty of time to learn the business and to address the issues that had to be dealt with. He went to the large window that exposed the factory production line. Polished machinery was organized in neat rows extending across the floor, void of personnel. A large digital display with the date, time, and other unknown measurements presided over the line.

"So, should we be concerned?" Andrew asked Mike.

"Concerned about what?"

"The dead guy. Just another day in Adelanto?"

Mike picked up a stack of papers and nonchalantly tapped them on the desk. "None of our business. A *coyote* probably had something to do with it."

"Coyote?"

"Smuggler." He seemed irritated. "The inmates bribe the guards and hire a coyote to get them away from here. The same way migrants hire a coyote to get them across the border. Sometimes they get caught, sometimes they make a life for themselves. The coyote probably asked for more money and the guy ran. It is dark, cold—they cannot get far."

"Where's Charlie?" Andrew asked, changing the subject.

"At the Vegas facility. He will be back in a few days."

"I thought he'd be here to meet me."

Mike shrugged. He rummaged through papers on his desk, picked up a business card, and handed it to Andrew. "He left this for you, address and access code for the corporate rental, in Helendale."

The front of the card read, MIGUEL VARGAS, VICE PRESIDENT, FACTORY MANAGER. Barely legible letters and numbers were scribbled on the back in Charlie's familiar lefty scrawl.

Álvaro was hovering in wait when they left the factory. He'd removed his gown, revealing dense tattoos covering his thick arms. Mike and he exchanged words in Spanish. Álvaro seemed nervous, which made Andrew wonder if his arrival had also offended him.

Mike considered Andrew for a moment. "Álvaro wants to know if he can check out your car."

Andrew nodded at Álvaro. They walked to the Porsche, and Andrew opened the back panel, revealing the spotless, air-cooled engine. Álvaro leaned over and inspected the machine, and not daring to touch anything, moved his head over the clustered pipes, fan, and vents, smiling. He then slipped into the bucket seat and caressed the blue leather steering wheel.

Andrew took a few pictures of Álvaro, his head poking out the window, a boyish grin on his face, as though he'd just crossed the finish line at the checkered flag in Monte Carlo.

A warm gust of wind intensified the skunk scent. "That smell . . . does it ever go away?" Andrew asked Mike.

"From the cannabis extraction facilities down the road. When the wind blows from their direction, there is no escaping it. Do not worry, you will not get high." Mike stepped into the black Prius and took off.

When Álvaro was done, Andrew tossed his backpack on the passenger's seat and sat down. He pulled the business card out of his pocket to type the address into the nav app. He read the card more closely this time and smiled.

The access code was 1988.

The year he'd moved to Thailand and met Charlie.

CHAPTER 2

Andrew—Andrea on his birth certificate—was born in Italy and had grown up as a nomad. His father was a US cultural attaché in Rome, and his mother was the youngest of three siblings from an upper-crust Roman family. They met during one of the social diplomatic events that his father organized in Rome in the early seventies. His mother teased that she'd fallen for the embodiment of the prototypical American—six-four, a sharp, sculpted face, blond hair, dark, honest eyes. But really it had been for his curiosity, one that matched hers.

Andrea was three when his father's posting in Rome ended. He had negotiated to be sent to Southeast Asia, as he was keen to take advantage of the potential in the region to refine and redefine American influence now that the war was over.

If his mother was crestfallen to leave her family, she never showed it. His father's subsequent posting was Kuala Lumpur, then Singapore, and finally in 1988, when Andrea was thirteen, Andrea's father settled them in Bangkok, Thailand. His father had no family left in the States, so Andrea spent his summers in Italy with his mother and her family, and the rest of the year in the country they resided in at the time. Andrea never visited his father's native country until he went to university.

With his father often gone for days on diplomatic errands, Andrea's mother embraced the expat life—the travel and cultural diversity, something foreign to her sisters, all still living within a two-block radius of their parents. His mother's curiosity and adventurous spirit were contagious. Coupled with the need to adapt to new schools, make new friends, and absorb new cultures, Andrea acquired a chameleon-like ability to immerse himself and trust these new worlds and make them his own, as if he'd always been a part of them.

Andrea met Charlie on his first day of eighth grade while they waited for the bus to take them to the International School of Bangkok—ISB. They both lived at the Royal Garden Towers, a twelve-story apartment complex on Sukhumvit Soi Sawatdi—Charlie on the ninth floor, Andrea right below him in apartment 8C. Andrea had introduced himself as "Andrew," which he had always done in English-speaking environments.

"Mind if I call you Andy?" Charlie had asked. Andrew *did* mind, but he wasn't going to tell his new friend that.

They became inseparable—in class, little league, at the pool after school, or at the shack to grab *cha yen* (iced tea), sour *mamuang* (mango), or diced *saparot* (pineapple) served in plastic bags with a rubber band tied around one corner.

Charlie introduced Andrew to American sports: the Patriots, Red Sox, and Celtics. They watched VHS tapes sent by Charlie's sister in the States: Al Michaels, Frank Gifford, commercials and all. He even taught Andrew how to play baseball.

It seemed that the only time they were not together was when Andrew was doing his homework. Andrew's mother ensured that he stayed the course and made the grades to enter an American university because there was no future for him in Italy. She knew better after having left the chaos of her home country and saw how the rest of the world lived, thanks to Andrew's father.

The friends' interests diverged in the last two years of high school. Charlie smoked more and more weed, got marginal grades, and failed to find direction, while Andrew continued to excel on his disciplined path. *His* priorities were clear.

However, he and Charlie always found time to hang out, with Charlie sometimes materializing at Andrew's door after another shouting match with his dad. And there was baseball. Charlie, the talented southpaw, Andrew behind the plate catching his fast balls, sliders, and curves. Both averaged over .450 in their last two seasons and won the pennant both times.

Andrew merged onto the 395 and let the Porsche fly, the g-forces pushing him back into the bucket seat as the air-cooled motor hummed. He admired the contrast of the long, black roads with the bare desert. The endless roads were a connection with the external world, which let him know he could escape at any time—if he wanted to.

As he crossed Air Expressway, the cars ahead slowed down. He downshifted into second gear. A construction worker flagged traffic. A trip that should have taken him twenty minutes took him an hour.

He finally turned left on Eucalyptus Parkway, slowing down as he passed the man-made lakes and the clusters of single-family homes. Trees lining a fairway partially obscured a green—a welcome sight amidst the arid desert.

At the end of the cul-de-sac, he pulled into the driveway of 1897 Camino del Celador. Andrew stepped out of the car and yawned as he surveyed the surroundings. The single-story home was bordered by freshly manicured landscaping, comprised of nonnative cacti interspersed with mesquites and cottonwoods. Red gravel obscured the brown dust. A black motorcycle with gleaming chrome exhausts stood in the solitary parking spot abutting the fairway.

He took his driver and three wood out of the back seat, followed by his golf bag, and recomposed the set. With the clubs slung over his shoulder, he made his way up the walkway, with his Tumi trailing behind. The metal gate squealed as he pushed it open. Lizards scampered into the bushes. He punched the code into the keypad.

The house had a terracotta floor dotted with Navajo rugs and fourteen-foot vaulted ceilings hovering over an open floor plan. A masonry fireplace decorated the corner, and a sliding glass door opened up to a patio, while tall windows bathed the rooms in natural light. He wasn't surprised with the home's elegance and charm; Charlie did have expensive tastes.

He left his clubs in the foyer, found the guest room, and dropped his bags before laying down. The phone rang just as he'd shut his eyes.

Diana. He threw his phone on the bed. He'd made it clear that it was over. Maybe she was just checking up on him, making sure he had arrived safely . . . He had told her, repeatedly, that he did not want the responsibility; that he could barely take care of himself; that he did not want to—no—could not be tied down. He had told her he needed separation to regroup and recharge. Her priorities were not aligned with his; they never had been. *And why subject offspring to the inevitable suffering caused by catastrophes we created and continued to propagate?*

He took several slow, deep breaths.

When that didn't help, he headed to the living room and rummaged through the cabinets in the bar nook. He found several bottles of wine—Chardonnay, Bordeaux . . . Chianti? That was unexpected. Charlie was a Francophile, had been since he graduated from that hospitality school in Geneva. The restaurants he managed and owned were all French—Le Metropole, a chain of Bistro Le Jardin. The mystery continued in the kitchen, where Andrew unearthed bags of pasta from Gragnano, and cans of San Marzano tomatoes, Italian staples that Charlie—who never strayed from Gallic cuisine—referred to as "peasant food." But the large bottle of extra virgin olive oil was sacrilege. An Italian in the mix. A woman?

He poured himself a generous glass of Chianti and walked out to the patio, the setting sun looming large behind the long, dense branches of a mesquite tree. The patio lights came on. A few feet over the low stucco wall was a fairway mottled yellow and green and surrounded by parched rough, a small lake visible to his left. He savored the wine for a moment, wondering what or whom had incited Charlie to expand his culinary horizons.

He headed back inside to the kitchen, gathered the peasant food, and went to work: pour oil in a saucepan, add the tomatoes, fill a stock pot with water, add salt, and wait.

He sipped the wine, finally starting to relax, and immediately caught a whiff of weed, or Mary Jane as Charlie used to call it. Had he left the outdoor light on? No, it had come on automatically when he'd gone outside earlier. . . He froze. A Black man the size of a mountain stared him down.

Andrew hesitated.

The man was clad in a loose-fitting linen shirt, black jeans, and black leather combat boots. He must have been six-foot-six with bleached curly hair that was all but incandescent against his skin. He had wide, almond-shaped eyes, a strong nose, and a large scar down his right temple. The man waved, the joint held high, amusement washing over his face, breaking the spell. He slid the door open.

"You're Andrew." He put the joint in an ashtray and held out his hand. "I'm Ish. Didn't mean to startle you. Charlie told me you'd be here."

Andrew, feeling the fragility of his hand in Ish's grip, nervously smiled.

"Want some?" Ish said.

Andrew stared at the smoldering joint. "I'll stick with alcohol."

"Suit yourself." Ish went back outside, took a couple of long hits, and smothered the joint, saving the roach for later. A cloud of smoke followed him inside. "Was on my way from Vegas and didn't have the energy to make it all the way to LA. I said to myself, 'Why not meet the new boss?'"

Again with *the boss*. "You're with Kannawerks, then?"

"On the front line. Sales, budtender relationships."

"Budtender?"

Ish examined him. "Do you know anything about weed? What we do?"

"Let's just say I've got a lot to learn."

"Oh right, you're from tech. Hope Charlie knows what he's doing. Anyway, a budtender is like a bartender or a barista, except the cannabis equivalent. They advise on what product is right for you. You want to chill? Unwind? Take the edge off? Relieve pain or anxiety? Sleep? Party? They'll recommend strains, form factors, and brands. Budtenders are cannabis consultants for both the novice and experienced user. Well, some of them anyway."

He went to the refrigerator, popped open a beer, and took a long swig, watching Andrew stir the sauce. "Smells good. What's that you're making?"

"Spaghetti al pomodoro minus the basil and garlic," Andrew said, refilling his glass and pouring some wine into the sauce.

"Enough for two?"

"And then some."

Ish sat on the couch in the living room, put his feet up on the coffee table, and sipped his beer. Andrew covered the sauce and joined Ish. The sun had set, the sky painted red and purple. Andrew, drawn to it, went to the window.

"Water's boiling," Ish said.

"Shit." Andrew ran back to the stove. As he was placing the pasta into the sputtering cauldron, the doorbell rang.

"What is this, Grand Central?" he muttered to himself. When it became clear that Ish had no intention of getting up, Andrew threw in the rest of the pasta and sprinted to the door.

"I hope I am not disturbing," Mike said, a bottle in hand.

"Mike!" Ish called out from the couch.

Mike acknowledged Ish with a nod. "Cazadores Añejo."

"My favorite," Ish said.

"No first day on the job should involve dead bodies, compadre," Mike said to Andrew.

"It *was* bizarre," Andrew said.

"Dead bodies?" Ish asked.

Mike told Ish about the body in the desert, Detective Morales, and the video review.

"Just another day in Adelanto," Ish said.

"That is what she said," Mike said.

"Join us for dinner?" Andrew asked Mike.

Mike's eyes rested forlornly on the tequila bottle. "It's my turn to help with the homework."

"You live in South Lake, like, two minutes from here," Ish said. "Call your wife, tell her *el nuevo jefe* insists."

"Sounds like a plan," Andrew said. Time to wear these guys down. They had every right to ignore an outsider. He may know nothing about weed, but this, he had covered. After growing up in Asia and especially while working on assignments *in* Asia over the years, he had learned relationships were built on trust, and trust was built outside the office, at dinner, in bars, in karaoke parlors lubricated by shochu and sake and whiskey—and a lot of it. Conversations would meander within loosely defined guard-rails—never about work—until the third or fourth drink and then transform into chaos. If you were in a karaoke bar, a pretty local girl would be waiting for you to sit back down after the crooning was over.

He'd make do without the singing and the pretty local girls tonight; he'd settle for the company and the tequila.

"Nice golf clubs," Mike said, heading to the kitchen, where he reached into a cupboard and pulled out three tumblers. He handed one to Andrew.

"The course seems nice—do you play?" Andrew asked.

"I prefer fútbol."

"The one with a proper round ball?"

"What other kind is there?"

Andrew raised his empty tumbler, and the two men held eyes—fútbol, the instant equalizer. Mike chuckled and opened the freezer, fetched some ice cubes, and dropped them into the tumblers, which signaled for Ish to join them. Mike poured healthy doses of golden liquid into each glass, being careful not to spill any.

"¡Salud!" They touched glasses. Andrew sipped the tequila, knowing how that would sit with the Chianti. Ish retreated to the couch and closed his eyes.

Mike sat on the lone stool in the kitchen, nursing his drink. "Do you play fútbol?"

"Not anymore, but I watch. It's in my blood."

"What kind of blood?"

"Italian."

"You are Italian?" This seemed to surprise him.

"I prefer the Premier League. Serie A pales in comparison."

"The English stuff is overrated," Mike said. "There is no creativity, no one dribbles the ball anymore. It is all run, press, tackle. There is no room for a good, old-fashioned número diez, you know what I mean?"

"Platini, Zidane, Messi—"

"Messi? Not that pendejo."

"How can you say that?"

"I have to. I am from Mexico. A Mexican never supports an Argentinian." He smiled.

"Like Italians and Swiss—oil and water."

Mike sipped his drink. "I used to play. I believed I could make it as a pro. All through high school and university, I played for a semipro team, until one day in the second year of university a *pinche culero* crushed my left ankle with a tackle, studs up. Two weeks in the hospital. Six months to rehabilitate. Fútbol career over, just like that." He snapped his fingers and took another sip of his tequila. "So I finished my university degree, got an entry-level job with Toyota, thanks to a cousin. I was lucky."

That explained the limp. Andrew bit into a strand of spaghetti he'd pulled from the pot—almost done.

"Ángel, my son, he just turned seven. He is crazy about fútbol. We are out every evening in the yard, after work, dribbling around cones, kicking tennis balls on the volley. Maybe he will make it, unlike his father." Mike took a swig, his eyes downcast.

"Sounds like he has a dedicated coach." Andrew drained the pasta, threw it in the sauce, and gave it one final stir.

They helped themselves to generous portions directly from the pan that Andrew had set on a dish pad on the dining table. Mike refilled everybody's glass, giving Andrew the more generous pour.

Silence ensued, while the guests used various techniques—all unacceptable ones, according to Andrew's mother—to get the spaghetti on their forks and in their stomachs. It seemed like they hadn't eaten in days.

"What's Ish short for?" Andrew asked, finally breaking the silence.

"Ishida."

Andrew set down his fork and gave him a once over.

"Lawrence Hiroshi Ishida. Father's Japanese. I was born in Japan. Came back here in third grade." He took a drink, then sat back, his plate empty. "This is fucking good. Where'd you learn to do this?"

"Summers in Italy, with my mom's side of the family," he said.

"You don't look Italian."

"What does *Italian* look like?"

Ish eyed Mike, who nodded. "Manuela."

"I knew there was an Italian somewhere. She work in the factory?"

"No," Ish said, as he scooped more pasta onto his plate.

"Manuela is Charlie's fiancée," Mike said. He topped Andrew's glass off.

"Charlie has a fiancée?"

"When he first took over, she would come and stay here with him," Mike said.

"A fiancée is not in Charlie's MO," Andrew said.

"Well, anyway, she hated it out here," Ish said.

Andrew didn't probe. He studied his glass, then glanced at Mike and decided that before he lost control of his faculties he'd make an exception to his rule and steered the conversation to work. "Charlie tells me that before he took over Kannawerks, the company was near bankruptcy less than nine months after raising money. I guess that kind of shit doesn't only happen in tech."

"Yeah, the Kannawerks founder was a bozo," Ish said. "I'm sure Charlie's filled you in."

Charlie's told me jack, Andrew didn't say.

"Charlie's helped us recover. Some," Ish said.

"Our brand saved us," Mike said. "The problem was execution. We had too many products, and we were not efficient in the factory."

"We fucked up our budtender and retailer relationships," Ish said. "Those are on the mend, but we're still only number three in market share in California edibles. We've made some progress, but not as much as one would hope. Right, Mike? Number one and two were upstarts a year ago. Now they're killing it."

"I do not understand why we are not doing better. This business is not that hard," Mike said.

Andrew, who'd been silently sipping his tequila while the two of them went back and forth, set down his tumbler and said, "Low barriers to entry."

Mike seemed confused, while Ish leaned in with a wry grin. "What do you mean?"

"You said the top two companies in the market are younger than Kannawerks, which tells me it doesn't take much to enter this space. But how you sustain and grow is critical to success. Is it distribution? Scale? Innovation? Finding the right product-market fit? You're right Ish. What does a tech guy know about weed? I've never dealt with manufacturing a consumer good before. And I've never sold a physical commodity. But I have taken commodity *technology* services, like outsourcing, and created successful companies by focusing on a specific niche and investing in continuous innovation. It's not that hard."

Ish downed what remained of his tequila. "Sounds like you *will* figure it out." He patted Andrew on the back and disappeared into the darkened hallway.

The tequila was starting to hit Andrew. He walked to the kitchen and drank two glasses of water. Mike followed with his empty plate, muttering something about how his wife was going to kill him. "Amigo, sorry about today." He dropped his plate in the sink. "I was nervous—the police, a new boss."

"We'll make it work."

"Hey, look what I found." Ish held aloft a pair of women's panties. Black.

"Those aren't mine," Andrew deadpanned. "Where'd you find them?"

"Behind the toilet."

"Probably Manuela's," Mike said.

"I doubt it. They're a couple of sizes too big." Ish held them up for all to see.

"You will like her," Mike said to Andrew.

"They're too big," Ish insisted.

"I am telling you they are Manuela's," Mike said.

Ish twirled the panties on his finger, smiling. "They're not hers." He threw the panties in the trash.

Andrew let it go.

Mike reached for the bottle of Cazadores and emptied the contents in Andrew's glass before he could say no.

Ish opened the sliding doors, the cool breeze a welcome change from the interior air made stuffy by the revelatory conversation. "One last toke and then I'm going to crash in the other bedroom." Ish relit the roach. He seemed impervious to the cold.

"I'm calling it a night, too. Thanks for the food and the company, amigo," Mike said. They shook hands and said their goodbyes.

Andrew stared at the plates on the dining room table and the pans piled up in the sink. *Fuck it.* He ambled to the bedroom, stripped to his boxers, set the alarm for 6:00 a.m., and passed out.

CHAPTER 3

The roar of a motorcycle startled Andrew from a deep sleep. Where was he? His head throbbed. He sat up and placed his feet on the floor, the cool tiles counterbalancing the pain. He faced the mirror of the closet across the bed; the six-foot-three frame greeting him was not a welcome sight: sagging posture, disheveled auburn hair, dark bags under his eyes, vertical red scar on his abdomen— compliments of a recent operation—and pasta finding a permanent home. He stumbled to the bathroom.

At 6:30 a.m., there was a hint of twilight from the east, the desert not yet warmed by the sun. He sat in the bucket seat and fumbled for the key. He instinctively reached for the ignition on the right of the steering column. *Where'd it go?* He rubbed his head. *That's right*, he was not in a Volkswagen GTI, he was in a car that descended from models designed for a standing start at Le Mans—sprint across the track, jump in the car, and simultaneously turn the ignition with your left hand and strap on the seatbelt with your right hand. He inserted the key with his left hand and turned it. The engine started. He hadn't been sure that it would.

The Porsche had been an impulse buy, made possible in the late nineties by the dot-com euphoria. Armed with a computer science degree from Berkeley, it had been easy for Andrew to land a job at a startup in Silicon Valley, the recruiting pipelines overflowing with candidates as the Internet started to go mainstream. eBusiness. eCommerce. Employee number seven. After two years, he had written a $63,000 check—as if writing five-figure checks were a daily occurrence—for the midnight-blue 993 C4S. He purchased it from a colleague who was upgrading . . . everyone was upgrading, everyone was shitting money. Instant gratification was the norm.

Srini had warned him. He had taken a liking to Andrew and saw potential in him. When Andrew drove up to the office in the Porsche, Srini had walked him to a conference room and shut the door. He never shut the door.

"Andrew," he had said calmly. "I am not one to provide personal advice, but you need to think about . . ." He paused. "To plan for . . ." He paused again. "Your future."

He couldn't say more as the CEO of a public company, and Andrew understood. When the roller-coaster ride neared its apex, only a few had taken money off the table: the experienced executives, alumni of IBM, HP, and AT&T who had seen this movie before and liquidated as much as they could in early spring 2000 . . . and Andrew, while the others dreamed. When the bubble burst, the roller coaster began its rapid descent, accelerating downhill and falling off a precipice after the Twin Towers fell. The company had gone through a series of layoffs, merged with a competitor, and cut overhead. The company stock, now a penny stock, hovered at two cents a share—a stark contrast to the earlier promise of infinite riches that had been pervasive in the Valley.

The speech was short. Srini had announced the company was filing for Chapter 11. No sales, no revenues, we're done. That day was everyone's last; they were all out on the street. The following week Andrew flew to Thailand, telling his friends that he was spending time with his parents. He could afford to take time off thanks to Srini's prescient advice. He put his Porsche in storage, as he couldn't bear to sell it and was too ashamed to be seen in it—a stark reminder of what once was and what could have been.

He hadn't seen it again until he drove to Adelanto.

He found a different route to the factory: the National Trails Highway. The old Route 66. It was slightly out of the way, but it avoided the construction on the 395 and the more pleasant scenery made up for the added time: an arroyo bed flanked the road to its west, with verdant trees and cacti dotting the landscape, and contrasting red, rock-strewn hills to the east. Multimegawatt solar tracking installations permeated the scene, the panels shimmering with dew in the growing light, ready to engage, waiting for the sun to crest over the low hills. He passed a sign for Elmer's Bottle Tree Ranch. People kept themselves busy with any amusement they could find in the desolation.

The road was empty. He floored it and felt the car reach ninety, hearing the familiar, air-cooled hum. Considering it was almost twenty-five years old, the car ran well. He slowed down as he approached Oro Grande, the first visible signs of life, and crossed the Mojave River bridge onto Air Expressway. The riverbed was bone dry. A towering yellow sign with imposing black letters read: DO NOT PICK UP HITCHHIKERS, thus announcing the Federal Correctional Facility, which was different than FDN, one mile down the road. He passed by an isolated RV park, its perimeter demarcated by low-lying gray-and-brown shrubs, and took a left. He reached Kannawerks and found a space, although the lot was now full. The sun made its presence felt as he pressed the buzzer.

It was cold inside the factory, like walking into a meat locker. Mike handed Andrew a light-blue gown, surgical mask, and hairnet.

"This is a food-safe facility. Beyond this point we must wear full PPE."

Andrew had spent his entire career writing and deploying code and building software. He restrained himself from asking what PPE stood for, but his expression unmasked his ignorance. "Personal protective equipment. And if you are on the line, you must wear gloves." They stood in the staging area, separated from the production area by a sixteen-foot chain-link fence. Rhythmic hip-hop music blared from a speaker over the packing line, the operators swaying as they filled puck-sized tins with minuscule, orange, cubed candy: gummies. When Charlie had told Andrew they manufactured cannabis-infused gummies it had sounded so juvenile. Or maybe he was out of touch. Getting old.

The factory was a brightly lit cavernous box: the twenty-foot ceiling enclosed an assortment of machines; taped yellow lines on the polished cement floor demarcated various jurisdictions; PPE-clad operators focused on their tasks. A loud HVAC system droned in the background. The chain-link fence extended along the western perimeter surrounding an area filled with pallets of colored boxes stacked one upon the other near a loading dock. They stepped onto the floor. On the left was the packing line, and on the right were stacks of white plastic trays containing colored gummies.

"The production process is simple. We make candy, it just happens to be cannabis-infused gummies," Mike said, raising his voice to almost a shout. They walked by stainless steel mixers, past a long, square tunnel that was spitting out gummy-filled rubber molds—like modified muffin trays, but with a grid of about fifty small square cavities instead of the usual six or twelve—as operators grabbed them and stacked them on a metal table. The conveyor carrying the molds extended back into the jaws of a machine whose pistons furiously, yet elegantly, deposited red goo into the molds coming out of the tunnel. A slender pipe originating in a large cauldron fed the pistons. Two operators manned the cauldron and constantly checked the readings on a flashing monitor. The noise from the machines was deafening.

They stood by two large, stainless-steel vats. An operator punched buttons on a screen. "This is Ashlee. She is a supervisor and runs the cooking and depositing stations," Mike yelled. She acknowledged Andrew with a nod.

"The ingredients Kyle preps today are for the batches we will make tomorrow," Mike continued, gesturing at a lanky figure standing by the vats. "Before we start the cooking process, Kyle kits the raw materials, making sure we have the right ingredients and quantities, which vary based on what gummy we are producing. Most important are the active ingredients—the cannabis. It is Kyle's job to take the cannabis oil from the freezer to the cooking station on the day we produce. We pride ourselves on having the most accurate dosing in the industry."

Kyle was hard to miss. He was taller than Andrew, thin, and wore round professorial spectacles that framed his narrow, pallid, blue eyes.

"What's Kyle's role?"

"Quality and R and D. We got lucky."

"What do you mean?"

"We did not have real R and D when we started. Our formulation was created by amateurs. When we resumed production after the shutdown, we continued using the old formula. Sometimes the gummies would arrive at the retailers melted into one hard glob, even with refrigerated trucks. This was one of the many reasons why competitors began to replace us on shelves. We also started getting consumer complaints. We thought it was the fault of the distributors, but then we ran tests on our gummies against those of our competitors, and the melting point of our gummies was significantly lower. Then Charlie heard that one of our competitors, Akmana, who also made gummies, was being investigated by the BCC for selling expired vape cartridges on the illegal market. Their license was suspended pending an investigation. Charlie recruited both Ashlee and Kyle, who ran R and D at Akmana, and Kyle fixed the melting problem."

"What flavor are we making now?" Andrew asked over the hum of the motors.

"Pomegranate."

"And what's this?" Andrew asked, motioning to the machine with the hopper, pistons, and conveyor.

"This is the depositor," Mike said. "We began using it in June. Easy to operate and maintain. Great throughput. There is another one in storage. We did everything manually before. It was crazy. You can still see the old process—we still make the small, 'classic' gummies," he said, making air quotes. "But we will soon stop making those. For the new process, the cooker feeds the depositor, an operator manually places the molds onto the conveyor, and the machine does the rest by pumping three grams of the slurry into each depression as the molds go by." Andrew watched the molds disappear into the rectangular tunnel as they left the depositor.

"How many gummies can we make in a day?"

"In one eight-hour shift we can make up to four batches, and each batch contains five thousand units—in our case tins—with twenty gummies per tin. That is almost four hundred thousand gummies in a day. Now we are only making two, sometimes three batches per day. We are waiting for sales to pick up."

Mike continued, "After they are filled, the molds pass through a cooling chamber, and then over there the gummies are demolded." As an operator pulled the lever on a shiny box, gummies popped out of the mold into a white plastic tray. "Before we had the cooling chamber, and before we fixed the gummy formulation, we had to wait two hours before demolding the gummies, otherwise they were too soft. Now we put them into the tumblers right away without waiting."

They walked over to one of the large metal mixers. "We have had these tumblers for longer than the depositor. The last owners of Kannawerks were using cement mixers, and I mean actual cement mixers, to tumble the gummies. They were not food safe. I had these installed." Mike gently caressed the chrome surface of the tumbler. "The gummies are placed into the tumbler with sugar for thirty minutes, then transferred to trays to cure. You can see them stacked up here and on the other side. Twenty-four hours later they are ready to be packed. With the old methods, we had to cure them for three days."

"Sounds like you did a lot of fixing."

"I have done what I could. I have been here for almost two years. I started under the old owners. My good friend Manny hired me. He was trying to introduce automation. Back then they were cooking the gummies in large pots over an open flame and mixing the slurry with a huge wooden spatula. A real *chingadera*. And we were the number one gummy company in California." He shook his head and cast his gaze to the floor. "Then they fired Manny for reasons I still do not know . . . the founder did strange things. I had only been here for one month when it happened. With my visa, I could not really go anywhere else, so I stayed and tried to do what I could to bring efficiencies to the operations. I am just scratching the surface of what Charlie and his team inherited." He tapped his fingers on the tumbler. "We now go to the packing line."

The loud hip-hop music eclipsed the din of the machines. "Manny had good intentions." Mike had stopped shouting. "He started with the easiest thing to fix: the cooking. Then he proposed automating the depositing function. As I said, before we were pouring the slurry by hand out of pitchers into micro ice-cube molds that we bought online, molds that we can no longer source. So Manny proposed automating it, but Abe, the founder, refused. The 'classic' gummies, which weigh only one-and-a-half grams, are small enough that twenty of them fit into a tobacco dip-sized tin, which fits comfortably in your jeans pocket, making the tin an easy way to share gummies at a party. That was Abe's vision." Mike's voice rose again. "The smallest gummy the depositor can make while maintaining accurate dosage is two-and-a-half grams, you see. Bigger gummies meant new packaging, and how can you fit a larger tin or box or bag into the front pocket of your jeans? Abe always talked about building a 'house of brands,' the tin the first brand innovation in cannabis, and becoming the 'Coca-Cola of cannabis' . . . I have no idea what any of that meant. He forgot about the operational foundations of a business. The legend is that Abe started the company in his garage." He adjusted his hair net. "But it seems all he did after he raised a lot of money was to make the garage bigger." Andrew sensed a smile under Mike's mask.

A "Jobsian" reality distortion field. Andrew had seen this many times: a founder with an idea who makes the first big sale, raises a round of funding, and then gets caught up in the hubris. Surrounding himself with sycophants, the fool believes that he and he alone is the one who can lead the company to greatness, so he stymies dialogue and the exchange of ideas and slams the doors of innovation and growth shut. And what did this distorted, empire-building reality lead to? Bankruptcy.

Andrew reminded himself to ask Charlie or Ish about the founder: Abe. Kannawerks clearly had some serious baggage. Classic gummies? Like "technical debt," as they called it in software: instead of scrapping a buggy and decrepit piece of software and starting anew, developers piled new bad code on top of old bad code, thereby compounding the bugs and outages until the entire system crashed. Sometimes understanding the past was needed to make sense of the present. Sometimes you *had* to probe. If Andrew was going to contribute and succeed, then he didn't want any surprises.

"And here we are, the 'classic' process—Abe's dream in action." More air quotes from Mike. There were at least twenty operators sorting, weighing, and packing gummies. Álvaro, the packing lead, ambled down the line and patted an operator on the back. Mike caught his attention and waved him over.

"Hola," said Mike, as they fist-bumped.

"Hola, Señor."

"Are we on schedule?"

"Sí, we add operators to the line, we get extra batch packed no problem."

Mike continued, "We are packing the classic tangerine gummies. You can see the size of the gummies and the tin, very small, and it is all manual. The only change we made to the classic gummies was with the new formulation, so they do not melt."

Andrew asked Álvaro, "What about the larger gummies? How are we packing those?"

"Sí, tins wider, taller," Álvaro said, taking one out of his pocket. He grabbed one of the smaller tins from the packing line and held them next to each other. "We have to still do manual."

"I can fit *these* bigger tins in my pocket," Andrew said.

"So can I," Mike said.

An operator was placing barcode stickers onto boxes filled with sealed tins. "Are those UPC codes?" asked Andrew.

"METRC tags."

"Metric?"

"Marijuana enforcement, tracking, reporting, and compliance. Seed-to-sale tracking. It is how the government tracks marijuana in California. Every time the cannabis changes form—from plant to oil, oil to gummy, gummy to tin, tin to case—it is assigned a METRC tag. That way a tin of gummies can be traced back to the plant it came from, technically a seed. It is a way to ensure that all legal cannabis is accounted for and taxed. We even have to issue METRC tags for destroyed product."

"I get it. It's a way to prevent illegal stuff from being made and to make sure you can't skim off the top," Andrew said.

They passed through a double door. Floor-to-ceiling racks surrounded the perimeter. "All raw materials, packaging, everything except the cannabis, or 'active ingredient,' is stored here. We keep cannabis under lock and key in a freezer next to the R and D office because of the value . . . and because it is a Schedule 1 drug. Only Kyle and I have access."

"That's fucked up," Andrew said.

"What is?"

"The Cannabis Paradox: that cannabis is a Schedule 1 drug, deemed the most dangerous of the controlled substance levels. The US Government puts it in the same category as heroin, LSD, and ecstasy. Meanwhile Vicodin, oxycodone, cocaine, crystal meth, fentanyl, drugs that are killing people every day, are all a level below it in Schedule 2. The government has backward ideas about keeping us safe."

Mike took off his hairnet and mask and glanced at the digital display. "*Chingado.* We have to go."

"Go where?"

"Taco Tuesday, amigo. Ends in fifteen minutes."

They threw their PPE in the appropriate bins and went outside.

CHAPTER 4

The transition from the glacial factory air to the dry desert heat felt like stumbling into the path of a breathing dragon. Andrew and Mike walked across Holly Road to a food truck, a bright-orange, elongated van with a solitary green saguaro painted on its side and Bottom-Up Tacos hand painted in large white letters above the awning shading the windows. The menu hung on the side of the truck and was written in an elegant cursive script: *Asada, Chuleta, Adobada, Barbacoa, Cabeza, Lengua, Tripas, Pollo Asado.* The aromatic symphony of roast pork, braised lamb, cumin, and lime wafted in the air.

A group of people gathered off to the side waiting for their orders. Álvaro held court, exchanging pleasantries with the woman behind the serving window. Andrew and Mike joined the line behind Kyle as he placed his order. He was clad in a black T-shirt and black pants that contrasted with his pasty, milky-white skin. Moles dotted his forearms and shaved head. When he was done placing his order, he walked to the serving window without acknowledging either of them.

"What does the house recommend?" Andrew asked the woman in the window. She ripped a sheet from the order pad and placed it in the runner. "Tripe, tongue, head," she said and wrote down the order. "You're new," she continued.

"New to Adelanto."

She lifted her gaze. "You're not from around here."

"What gave it away?"

"How much time do you have?"

"Anything else you'd like to tell me about me?"

"You won't stay here long. No one does." She ran her hand through her short blond hair. "Name?"

"Andrew. I'm fine with the tripe and the tongue, but not so sure about the head."

"Lamb it is." She scribbled on her pad.

He noticed her eyes. They were a light shade of hazel.

"Bottom-Up Tacos?"

She seemed surprised that anyone would bother to ask. "The meat should be the centerpiece of a taco. We don't want to drown it in sauce and garnishes, so we build the taco upside down—salsa, garnish, meat—from the bottom up."

"Innovative. I'll let you know how it tastes."

"I know how it tastes," she said after a beat.

"You know my name, it's only fair I know yours."

"Renée." She smiled.

"Nice to meet you, Renée."

"We're here every Tuesday and Thursday, ten to eleven thirty."

"See you Thursday."

They sat at Mike's desk, tacos laid out on the paper bags. The beef tongue was crispy, and the tripe melted in his mouth. Renée was right; it didn't need any of the garnishes. "Not bad," Andrew said.

"The tacos or Renée?"

"Ha ha. Does she have a story?"

Mike took a bite of his taco, a dribble of salsa spilling on the table. He wiped it off with his napkin. "Not much, other than her tacos are fantastic."

"Nice compliment, coming from a Mexican."

"She has a steady schedule in Adelanto and Victorville with the other cannabis factories, and also FDN, but I do not think she likes to go there."

"Who would? Look at what happened to that poor guy."

Andrew studied the pixelated video screen. The operators were back on the floor, and Kyle's tall frame disappeared into the R and D office. "Any coffee around here?"

Mike crumpled the paper bags and threw them in the trash. "Come."

They walked down a bright corridor and entered a sub-zero lunchroom. A brewing machine sputtered in the corner. A woman took the cup from the holder and sat down. She was about five-six, her brown hair streaked with blue came down to her shoulders, with bangs over her forehead. A yellow T-shirt hugged prominent breasts. She had a faint smile on her face.

Mike opened a drawer filled with K-Cups and Andrew scrounged around and found the maximum caffeine kick: a Colombia Dark Roast. A long way from an espresso, but it was the caffeine that mattered.

"I'm Ashlee," the woman said, when she caught Andrew staring at her.

"I thought I recognized you." Shed of her PPE, she was attractive in her own way with round, green eyes and a small, button nose. They sat down at her table.

"How do you like working for Willy Wonka?" she asked.

"Willy Wonka with a twist," he responded, taking a sip. The coffee was watered down and bitter. "A lot to take in. I understand you've been at this for a while. You came from Akmana, right?"

She grimaced. "I was only there for nine months. That place was fucked up." She sipped her coffee and stared at the cup in her hands. "I've been doing the weed thing since the medical marijuana days."

"She is good," Mike said.

Ashlee motioned with her hand, belittling the comment.

"One of the few skilled people we have, in charge of the most important parts of the process, cooking and pouring. I mean depositing. If it was not for her, the dosage would not be within the plus/minus ten percent threshold mandated by the regulators. It is almost an art, even though we follow recipes."

"Any pointers for someone new?" Andrew asked Ashlee.

"Spend time on the floor."

"Anyone else besides Kyle come with you from Akmana?"

"We just filled the two positions," Mike said.

"No one else wanted to come over. Hard to convince them to stay out here. Middle of nowhere." She finished her coffee. "Have you spent time with Ish and Ethan yet?"

"Ish yes, Ethan no," he said.

"Go see them. You'll come up to speed *like that*." She snapped her fingers. "I need to go, we're doing one last run." She threw her cup in the bin and walked out of the room.

"She's nice. Sounds like she knows her stuff," Andrew said.

"Yes. I do not know how she does it, though, as a single mother, working in this business, taking care of a two-year-old daughter."

"Two-year-old, huh?"

"I heard her husband disappeared. Took everything except the baby."

Behind closed doors, Mike walked Andrew through the production schedule for the month. Riveting it was not. Andrew tried to stay engaged, asking questions where he could, but he soon realized it was better to just listen and then follow up with questions later. As they started discussing the product portfolio, they heard a commotion outside the office. The door burst open and Charlie entered the room, as if propelled by a sharp gust of wind.

"There you are, Andy."

They embraced, Andrew ready for his old pal's physicality, a bear hug that knocked the wind out of you and held on for one too many beats.

Andrew extricated himself and staggered backward.

His friend had barely aged in the last decade. The Middle Eastern features inherited from his father were softened by his mother's Boston Brahmin pedigree, which combined to give him the magnetic edge of a youth in a Caravaggio painting. He was slightly shorter than Andrew, with broad shoulders, black hair with a hint of curl, and brown hypnotic eyes.

"You haven't changed," Charlie said, smiling. "Is that your ride out there? The Porsche?"

"Yes."

"Nice." He nodded approvingly. "Let's take it for a spin. We can catch up along the way." Charlie walked to the door and said to Mike, "Don't forget about the investors on Friday. Let's put on a show for them. Make sure we have the line humming, the depositor on overtime, the tumblers cranking, and the packing line dancing!" His eyes gleamed. "Turn up that music, I want to hear those horns blaring. I want the investors to see we have a team that cares while having fun."

"Sure thing," Mike said.

Charlie said to Andrew, "And there's a party that same night at Kendall Ranch. You'll meet the executive team, sales and marketing, prospective investors, and partners."

They walked by an M6 that was parked in front of the entrance—Charlie's ride, Andrew assumed—and reached the Porsche. As Charlie lowered himself in the car, he whistled and said, "This is one bad ride. Not what I would have expected from you, Andy. You were always so serious. Low-key." He strapped on the belt and glanced at the back. "The fixed wing, the wide back. Smokin'. Do you race it? Track it?"

"No, I've never taken it out on a track. It's been in storage for the last seventeen years . . . never could get rid of it. Glad I didn't."

"*Seventeen years*? What the fuck, Andy?"

"Long story."

Charlie ran his hand along the leather dash. "No wonder it's in great shape. Retro, hard-to-find, a collector's item. These things go for six figures, in the one fifties. I'd be careful where you park around here. They'll load it on a tow truck and have it on a container headed to Asia before you know it's even gone."

"Says the man with the M6. You don't see many high-end BMWs on this side of the Cajon Pass." Andrew shifted into fourth.

"Cost of doing business in LA. Your car is a status symbol. The higher up you are or want to get, the more expensive or exotic your ride has to be if you're going to be accepted and respected, especially in the circles that I'm in. I like nice cars, but I'm no fanatic."

"What *circles* are you in?"

"Same as always. Hospitality, restaurants—high-end restaurants to be specific. I still have a large stake in La Closerie in Beverly Hills. I had others in Santa Monica and Pacific Palisades, but they didn't last long, not the right fit for those neighborhoods. We hired a Michelin-starred chef to run La Closerie. We get celebrities in there every night, and with social media and all that crap, it propels itself."

"What about the cannabis circle?" Andrew asked, as he took a right.

Charlie glanced behind him. "Why don't you stay on the 395? It's nice and straight."

"Construction up ahead. We'll take Route 66."

"You're a local already."

Andrew shifted into fifth gear and repeated, "How'd you enter the cannabis circle?"

"I was bored." Charlie sighed. "And I was tired of watching restaurants grow and then implode. Not to mention the margins suck. Yes, the high-end fare has better margins, but the revenue was not in line with the level of effort you needed to just open the damn thing." He fiddled with the radio knob. "A few years ago, I was introduced to Max Aurel. Old LA money. His family owns a bank, among other things. He became the primary investor in La Closerie. After the restaurant opened, he asked if I would be interested in helping him with a company his niece was starting: prepackaged, frozen vegan meals distributed through higher-end supermarket chains—Trader Joe's, Whole Foods, Bristol Farms. She was passionate, and she believed that if we didn't modify our food consumption habits, we as a species were fucked."

"We *are* fucked, and food alone isn't going to solve it. But go on." Andrew took a left on the National Trails Highway.

"I got involved as an advisor. It was a blast."

There was nobody on the road except for a few trucks heading south. Andrew double de-clutched into third and floored the gas. Charlie's head snapped back into the headrest.

"Shit, that's nice. Listen to that engine, a purring panther. Where'd you learn to do that?"

"My mom's vintage Fiat 500, summers in Italy. I told you to come and visit."

"Yeah, I know."

"The gearbox was so small, it fit into your pocket. You had to downshift by double de-clutching, otherwise you'd pulverize the gears. Not necessary now, but it feels good."

"I miss your mom," Charlie said.

"Me too."

They fell silent for a moment and watched the bare desert fly by.

"How's your dad?"

"Retired. He's in Tucson."

"Hard to picture that."

"The retired part or Tucson?"

"Both!" Charlie guffawed. The speakers crackled. Charlie reached over and switched off the radio.

"Anyway," Charlie said, "going back to the frozen vegan meals. Ultimately, it was all about distribution and shelf space, but with low barriers to entry, the big boys came in and we got crowded out." He paused. "I loved it, though. That's how I got involved in cannabis—Max liked what I did for his niece, so he connected me with Kannawerks. He's the lead investor in the company. I'll introduce you." He faced Andrew. "And when I do, I want you to impress him."

"I got it. Don't worry."

The road extended before them, a shimmering black line surrounded by rock-strewn dunes, platoons of Joshua trees, and yellow-and-brown dust . . . dust that morphed into the occasional dirt devil. Andrew kept his foot on the accelerator.

"After the vegan venture folded," Charlie continued, "I went back to running La Closerie full time, and one night a few weeks later, I had dinner with Max. He was in a foul mood. He had come from a Kannawerks board meeting where they had decided to liquidate the company. This was late November 2018. He said the company had burned through almost thirty million dollars raised earlier that year with little to show for it, except for brand recognition in California and Nevada, and a rapidly eroding market share. The management team wasn't that bright."

"Abe? I was going to ask you about him."

"Yeah, that knucklehead. He's Max's grandson—the only reason Max invested in a cannabis gummy venture. He likes more traditional investments: real estate and restaurants. He's old school. Anyway, when recreational marijuana was legalized in January 2018, Kannawerks became the number one edible company overnight. So they launched a CBD line—cannabidiol, derived from hemp—and tried to expand into the other states where recreational cannabis was already legal: Nevada, Colorado, Michigan, Massachusetts. But getting a license in those states was expensive, and there were few synergies from state-to-state. You can't transfer cannabis across state lines—it's a federal crime. California is the largest legal cannabis market in the world—stay focused there!"

Charlie leaned forward. "But their idea of investing in California was to over hire, pay above-market salaries, and buy as many billboard ads as they could. At two hundred and fifty thousand dollars a pop—for a salary or a billboard—they were vaporizing cash. And it demonstrates a fundamental ignorance about the business."

Charlie's eyes beamed. "See, you win in cannabis if you control the path to the customer by owning both distribution *and* the relationship with the budtenders."

Andrew nodded and smiled at the familiar intensity. "Ish mentioned that."

"The key is owning shelf space. It's that simple. You *must* have a recognized brand and a quality product with decent margins. You have to innovate by introducing new products at a rapid pace, and you need to understand and know the regulatory environment—but these are all table stakes. We're selling a commoditized product: a sugar-coated gummy. It all comes down to distribution and retail. If you don't master that, you are fucked. Just like Kannawerks was fucked when two upstarts, Caygata and Kativa, blew past them within the first nine months of legalization. *Poof!*" Charlie sat back. "Fuck, let's go back. I've got a dinner in LA I can't be late to."

At the next intersection, Andrew made a U-turn.

"Max was ready to throw in the towel, then we started talking about the similarities between the vegan play and Kannawerks," Charlie said. "Turns out everything that we'd learned could be applied to Kannawerks. Within two weeks, he'd corralled the original investors, recapitalized the company, fired the executive team—getting shit from Abe's mother in the process—and installed me as CEO. Almost a year later, we're number three in market share in California edibles, making decent gross margins, and we're in over four hundred dispensaries. And Nevada's doing well." He slouched and sighed.

"You don't sound enthusiastic."

"We're in a bit of a pickle."

"Go on."

"We've got enough cash in the bank to continue doing what we're doing for a while, but that's not going to be enough." He stared at the scattered rocks and isolated Joshua trees flying by. "The key to this business is distribution, right? Well, our competitors are outspending us, and we *can't* grow beyond where we are now. We're stuck. Our revenues have marginally increased over the last two quarters, but no matter how much we spend, how much we innovate, we're still number three. Max and the rest of the investors are getting antsy. That's why I asked you to come here . . . to run the company and keep the ship on course, while I find more investors and a merger candidate. We can't go it alone."

"I guess that's why I'm confused. I thought I was coming to help with automation and IT-related stuff. Now I know why everyone is calling me 'boss.'"

Charlie leaned closer to Andrew and, almost in a whisper, said, "I've been following you in your trade pubs for the last three months. Where am I going to find someone that understands how to run this kind of business?"

Andrew didn't respond.

"I can't tap into my hospitality network. They don't know shit other than opening, running, and shutting down restaurants. Plus, I don't trust them. You, on the other hand, have built and run successful companies from the ground up. You know the fundamentals. You know how to manage a team."

"I've also built and run a business that didn't fare so well—"

"Fuck that shit!" He sat back. "I trust you, Andy. Mike knows the operations inside and out, but he needs to be managed. Our sales and marketing teams are doing an OK job, but they need direction."

Andrew nodded. "I think I understand, Charlie."

"I've got a lot at stake in the business, Andy. The management team's compensation, your compensation, my compensation, is based on achieving specific revenue and profitability targets. We're not getting there. The only way out is to outspend the competition, build a broader distribution network, and diversify away from gummies. That's why we're considering a merger—flower, vape, extracts—with companies that have reach. I've got a pool of investors that believe in the market. They're ready to finance Kannawerks, but only if we can show we are no longer a one-trick pony and we can scale."

"What, exactly, do you want me to do?" Andrew was driving on autopilot, accelerating past eighty; he wasn't paying attention to the empty road ahead because he was trying to absorb as much information as possible from Charlie, who had worked himself into a near frenzy.

"Spend time with Mike. Learn all aspects of the manufacturing process. Fix our supply chain—I know we're overspending on raw materials and packaging. Uncrate the second depositor. Get it on the floor so it appears operational. Spend time with Ish and Ethan. Ish is an industry oracle. Ethan runs sales. Visit our key retailers. Get familiar with the financials. You'll meet everyone at the party on Friday. And—"

"Shit," Andrew said, hitting the brakes. They flew by an SUV with sheriff markings driving in the opposite direction. Too late. The SUV's lights flashed on and the siren blared. It made a U-turn in the middle of the highway and sped their way, a trail of dust in its wake. Andrew slowed down and pulled over. Not what he needed. He'd been doing ninety, thirty-five miles over the speed limit. His hands choked the steering wheel.

"Don't worry, out here if it's your first offense, they'll give you a warning and let you go."

Andrew reached over and found the registration in the glove compartment. He pulled his driver's license from his money clip and waited. The officer parked a few car lengths behind them. The cruiser lights flashed. No one came out.

"I'm fucked."

"I said don't worry."

Andrew tried the radio; all he got was static. He switched it off when he saw the officer get out of the car. He was tall, thin, and wore the standard issue deputy uniform. Andrew watched him approaching in the rearview mirror. He seemed familiar. The officer bent over and peered into the car. Detective Morales's sidekick. Andrew lowered the window. Up close he could read the name tag: JP Wyjrczyk. It did not compute. Deputy Buy-A-Vowel.

The deputy stared Andrew down, then glanced over at Charlie. Charlie sat impassively, with his eyes forward. "License and registration," the deputy said in a high-pitched twang, incongruent with his authority and height. Andrew handed him the documents. "Wait here," the deputy said mechanically. He walked back to the SUV, sat down, and shut the door.

"He was at the factory, yesterday, with a detective. Did you hear what happened?"

"Crazy fuckers. It's not the first time someone's escaped from that facility. But it's the first time an escapee has been found dead." Charlie sighed. "It's none of our business."

After several minutes, the deputy ambled over. "Sir, I clocked you over ninety. Under other circumstances we'd have to take you in and suspend your license. Consider this a warning." He handed back the license and registration. "Good afternoon." He touched the brim of his cap. Before the deputy could reach his SUV, Andrew was on his way.

"He must have recognized you." And then Charlie laughed and said, "I told you. They leave you alone if you contribute to their economy. Hell, if it wasn't for cannabis, Adelanto would go back to being a prison town. Talk about a one-trick pony!"

Andrew kept it under sixty the rest of the way. When they arrived back at the factory, Ashlee was standing by the entrance, clad in jeans and the yellow T-shirt, smoking a cigarette. The lot was empty, the operators having left for the day.

"Thanks for the ride, Andy. I think you have enough for now. Don't forget about the depositor." Charlie stepped out of the car. He gave Ashlee a one-armed hug reserved for an intimate acquaintance, and then they walked to the back of the building.

CHAPTER 5

Mike was still in his office. The digital display above the packing line read 3:00 p.m.

"Everyone clears out of here on the nose, don't they?" Andrew asked.

"There is no need to stay after two-thirty. We only run one shift, and people like to get home as soon as possible. These people work to live, they have families, other interests. Like Álvaro. He fixes and refurbishes classic muscle cars, which is why he liked your Porsche. He is working on a '69 Camaro and a '71 Ford Torino. That is his passion, but one cannot earn a living with it. This job provides a paycheck and health benefits. Transactional but honest." He gestured at the production schedule on the whiteboard. "Maybe someday we will have to run multiple shifts, but sales would have to triple, and we are nowhere near that. When that happens, we can deploy the second depositor and automate the packing line."

"Speaking of which, Charlie wants it on the floor by Friday."

"This Friday?"

"For the site visit."

"Why did he not tell me before?" Mike walked over to the window and eyed the factory floor. "I guess we can put it next to the other one. There is plenty of room. We can uncrate and start the installation tomorrow."

"I'll be here."

"Do not come too early, unless you want to meet the security guards."

"I was going to ask, what's the security setup like?"

"There are motion detectors situated at the entrances and on the factory floor connected directly to law enforcement and the alarm company. We must be careful. There have been break-ins at other cannabis factories nearby, mostly extraction facilities. The thieves are more interested in raw materials like biomass and processed oil. To better manage security and control access, no one is allowed in the factory before five in the morning and rarely after five in the afternoon. There must always be at least two people in the factory at any given time, no exceptions. We have a contract with a local agency for two night guards on a twelve-hour shift. They are built like gorillas. You would not want to get to know them."

"I'll see you tomorrow. Wait for me before you start with the depositor." Andrew headed to the car. The skunk odor lingered in the warm wind, and a nauseous pang hit him as he sat down. He cranked up the AC and took a few deep breaths. What the hell was he doing? He built and ran software companies at the forefront of innovation, working with brilliant, arrogant individuals solving complex problems and servicing large, enterprise customers. Contracts worth millions of dollars. And now? A candy company in a commoditized industry that was federally illegal and required gorillas guarding the facilities at night. A resume-killer. He put the car into first and headed out.

He stopped at the local supermarket to load up on wilted vegetables and unripe fruit. He picked up a piece of smoked cheddar, canned beans, yogurt, honey, and crackers—something to tide him over for a few days until he could find a more palatable alternative.

Stepping out of the supermarket, bags in hand, he passed an assortment of storefronts: a nail salon with scattered patrons, two workers arguing with each other as they installed an El Pollo Loco sign, and a near-empty diner. The sun's glare briefly blinded him, and as his eyes adjusted, a whisp of blue hair caught his eye. He smiled and waved. Ashlee returned the smile and wave from behind the diner window. She sat across from a rotund man with a prominent nose, an aggressive comb-over covering his bald pate, and a blank expression on his face.

It was past four when Andrew got back to the house with a couple of hours of daylight left—enough time to hit the range. He hadn't swung a club in weeks and was itching to get back into it, missing the routine and calm. He swapped his jeans and button-down for shorts, a golf shirt, and a hat, then loaded his clubs into the car, careful to take the driver and three wood out of the bag, gently placing them on top of the golf bag.

The clubhouse stood over a small lake and a sparsely filled parking lot with parched fairways extending radially. Andrew dropped his clubs outside the pro shop, where logoed shirts and windbreakers hung along the walls as did a placard with the latest-and-greatest driver, which guaranteed more distance off the tee. He made his way past a display of assorted putters and wedges and walked up to the registration desk. The AC blew on him and on a squat golf pro standing behind the counter typing away on a keyboard. He sported a standard-issue crew cut and goatee.

"Yes?" he said, barely acknowledging Andrew.

"I'd like to use the range."

"Are you a member?"

"I'm staying with a friend out on Celador."

"We don't allow unaccompanied guests to use the facilities."

"That's odd. I was told anyone staying on the property, including guests, could play."

"You were told wrong."

The pro hadn't stopped typing during the exchange. Andrew

drummed his fingers on the counter and considered the pro shop. He saw paint peeling off the walls, partly obscured by the placard and hanging polo shirts; stains on the carpet near the exit leading to the Grill; a nearly empty driving range through the window behind the pro, with one solitary golfer hitting balls; and a single lining up his putt on the eighteenth green. This was not the Olympic Club. This was the empty Crooked Ridge Country Club in the middle of the Mojave Desert, and this jackass wouldn't let him use the range. Andrew wanted to enlighten the fuck that the only reason this place existed, the only reason it was in business, the only reason they could give the fairways a semblance of green, was because of the mandatory fees that all the homes on the property had to pay to be a "member."

"Let me ask you this," Andrew said. "How much are green fees for *accompanied* guests?"

"One hundred dollars."

"Okay. How many guests do you typically get out here in this oasis?"

The pro studied Andrew. The typing stopped. "What's it to you?"

"Just asking."

"A couple a day during the week, a dozen or so on weekends."

"Tell you what. How about I give you twenty-five bucks to use the range for one hour, that's equivalent to one hour of a four-hour round." He pulled out his money clip and put two twenties on the counter. "Keep the change."

The pro glanced at both doors and laid his doughy, hairless hand on the twenties. "Balls are on the range. Closes at five-thirty." He pocketed the cash.

Andrew headed to the range. The solitary golfer, a middle-aged man of medium build, wore a spotless white, wide-brimmed golf hat with matching polo shirt and shorts. He was busy hacking at balls with an iron. Andrew went to the far-right side of the driving range and set down his bag.

The sun approached the horizon while the marker flags snapped in the warm gusts. He took out a sand wedge and aimed for the nearest flag. He swung easy and without thought. A half-swing, three-quarter swing, full swing, always aiming at a target, always shaping the shot, always holding the follow through, not thinking about mechanics.

"That's one hell of a swing."

The man in white stood behind him, smiling with an iron in his hand. "What's your handicap?"

"Three."

"Wow! Your swing is a rarity out here. I'm Zeke, by the way."

"Andrew," he said, extending his hand. "Played one year in college. Like riding a bike, you know, as long as your head cooperates."

"College, huh? Where?"

"Cal."

"Go Bears." Zeke tapped his iron on the grass. "I'll let you get back to it. The range is closing soon." He started to amble back. "Listen, when you're done, can I offer you a drink at the Grill?"

The guy seemed lonely. "Sure."

"It's just that we don't get a lot of—how can I say this—*educated* people out here." He wore a sheepish grin.

"I'll catch you there." Andrew proceeded to carve balls through the air, going through the clubs in his bag, from wedges to irons to woods.

Zeke placed the drinks and a basket of popcorn on the table. "Helendale's not exactly a golfing destination." He sat across from Andrew. "You don't look like someone who works for FDN or the prisons. And you're not military grade."

"Cannabis. Kannawerks."

"That would have been my guess."

"And you?"

"I'm a lawyer."

"Out here?"

"No, in San Diego. My sister's here. She likes the desert. She's not doing too well, so I come and spend time with her, mostly in the fall and winter months." He sipped his drink. "In fact, she used to work for the City of Adelanto. She needed help a few years ago to set up the regulations and taxation parameters for cannabis companies. The city wanted to diversify away from prisons."

"Go figure."

"Yeah, surprising," he laughed. "I had taken a sabbatical from my corporate job—legal counsel for a major commercial developer in SoCal. Data centers, industrial parks, warehouses. The growth was crazy—*is* crazy—with Amazon and Walmart and Microsoft all making massive investments. Compound that with the explosion of delivery services and cannabis legalization, and it's nonstop deals." He fanned himself with his hat. "I came here to help her write the regs and consulted with the city to onboard several of the early companies—growers, manufacturers, distributors, retailers."

"I came from that world: data centers, software, the cloud." Andrew started to peel the label from his bottle.

"From software to cannabis, the transition should be straightforward," Zeke said with a wry grin.

"It's all downhill."

"Yeah, downhill. . ." Zeke paused momentarily, as if lost in thought. Then he leaned forward and said, "My sister retired early because she couldn't deal with the corruption in city hall."

"Out here?"

Zeke took another sip and placed his glass on the table. "It's endemic in cannabis. The proposition that legalized recreational cannabis was enacted in a way that makes it nearly impossible to survive without paying someone off. Cities and counties in the Inland Empire are broke and need the money. Adelanto almost went bankrupt in 2014. They were ready to let San Bernardino County take over the city until they legalized cannabis, hoping for a revenue windfall. That never materialized. I mean, you've seen what it's like out here."

"Dust. Rocks. Said prisons."

"And poverty and misery. In Adelanto, there are no movie theaters, no gyms, no rec centers, no department stores. And there are multiple city council members, including a former mayor, awaiting trial for taking bribes to ensure favorable city ordinances for cannabis dispensaries, ensuring permits went to certain people. The FBI's even involved."

"The Feds?"

"And we're talking about paltry five-figure bribes. It's comical. Petty crooks. They deposited checks with the name of the entities doing the bribing into their own bank accounts! How dumb can you be? Right out of a Coen Brothers' movie. I mean, if you're going to take a bribe, at least get paid in cash. And corruption *is* endemic because Prop 64 fosters this behavior: the decision on where cannabis businesses can operate is determined by the cities and counties; it isn't centralized. Prop 64 has revived the Wild West. Anything goes, with no accountability." He finished his drink and leaned back in the chair. "Sorry. Didn't mean to go off."

"It's okay." Andrew sipped his beer and contemplated the desolation. The sun had almost set, and the wind had picked up, blowing dust and errant tumbleweeds across the fairways. "I should get going. Cannabis hours start before sunrise. I'll take you up on that round this weekend."

"See you Saturday," Zeke said. "And don't worry. Someone of your caliber should be able to navigate the cannabis mess."

Andrew went back to the house, showered, wished he'd picked up some vodka, and poured himself a glass of Chianti.

The story kept getting better. Corrupt officials. Resurrected bankrupt entities. What *was* he getting himself into? It wasn't only the industry, product, and location that were foreign to him. Now he was in the Wild West. Zeke thankfully had not asked Andrew what had brought him here, otherwise he would have answered that he had no choice: Diana was gone, no fixed domicile, a bank account running on fumes, alienated friends. He was searching for a way to reinvent himself, something his nomadic upbringing had enabled him to do over and over. Adapt. And this was it—cannabis, Adelanto. As far removed from the life of Andrew as possible.

CHAPTER 6

Andrew made his way down Rancho, daybreak an hour away, his car the lone vehicle on the road, the headlights carving a path through the desert. He passed the bus stop to infinity, and as he veered by a dormant San Bernardino County office, he slammed on the brakes. The car skidded in the dust and slowed to a crawl.

To his left was a bonfire and a large crowd. Some of the men and women in the crowd held placards, while others held dummies of a fat orange man hanging by a noose. One dummy hung upside down. A dozen cars, headlights on, enveloped the FDN facility in a hellish, yellow glow. Opposite the protesters stood a score of uniformed guards, clad in brown shirts and brown jackets with brass buttons shining in the headlights, arms folded across their chests. None of them were under six feet tall. Two sheriff SUVs flanked the officers, red and blue lights flashing.

A pair of headlights approached Andrew from the rear. He moved to the side and let a black Prius by. Mike. An arm extended out of the car, waved at the protesters, and formed a fist. Horns blared. A single voice, coming from a small woman brandishing a megaphone standing majestically on the hood of a pickup, called out, followed by a unified response from the crowd. At first Andrew couldn't make out what they were saying. He rolled down his window. *Queremos . . .*

justicia para Porfirio. Queremos . . . justicia para Porfirio. Over and over.

Andrew was not surprised. Pro and anti-immigration protests were common. The immigration "problem" had transmogrified into a vitriolic political issue. It was fanned by fools and zealots who listened to the rabid media, radio talking heads, and who sourced their online "news" from disreputable sources: Facebook feeds, YouTube channels, and Twitter handles whose content was provided by offshore troll farms, bots, and nation states trying to destabilize the United States. They were galvanized by the success of the 2016 election and the inability and unwillingness of the social media platforms to do anything to stop it. Andrew knew this. He had been in the bowels of the Valley, late-night discussions with colleagues, debating the pros and cons of the immigration issue into the wee hours. Concentrated Attention was the business model. The longer eyeballs were focused on a platform, the longer the platform controlled what they saw, the more ads served, the more money the platforms raked in, and the more the stock was worth. Algorithms ensured hate nurtured hate, xenophobia compounded xenophobia, and ignorance ran rampant. And beyond the damage done to the hungry, the poor, and the destitute, he couldn't hire talented, eager software engineers.

He rolled past the crowd. The protesters' gazes followed his car without breaking their rhythm. He just made out the signs as he passed. Some had a picture of a young man, with a smile that accentuated his overbite and a mass of curls atop his head. The signs were a bilingual assortment: Justicia. We are not criminals. FDN Mata. ICE = Asesinos. Shut down FDN.

Andrew parked, opened the Brivo app, and pressed the Kannawerks Front button. The door clicked open. Mike waited in the lobby for him.

"What was that all about?" Andrew asked as they stepped into the office.

"You should have kept going. Stopping is asking for trouble," Mike said.

"I can outrun them."

"Be careful. You do not look Latino, but they do not like rich white people, either. With your car and education, you are also part of the problem. You do not want to mess with those FDN *cabrones*."

Andrew thought he'd been referring to the protesters, but Mike continued, "They are the Good Guys, keeping America safe, preventing thieves from entering the country and stealing American jobs. They are making America great again. All *mierda*. The pro-FDN people say they bring jobs to Adelanto. Who cares about a job where you have to sell your soul to the devil?" He slammed his hands on the desk.

"FDN has applied for a permit with the City of Adelanto to expand their facility. That is what most of the protests have been about. But with the death of the inmate, the crowd is now bigger. Today it was twice the usual size. I hope the permit for FDN is not renewed in January, but Adelanto needs the jobs and the money."

The team had already transferred the crates containing the depositor from storage and started unpacking the components. The entire line was massive—cooker, depositor, and cooling chamber—taking up four large crates and several hours to assemble. By 10:30 a.m.—lunchtime—the depositor and its peripherals were connected, making the machine *appear* operational.

Andrew spent the next few hours with Ashlee learning the functional aspects of the cooking and depositing processes. Mike was right—she knew her stuff and navigated the machinery instinctively, like she was driving a car.

He spent time with Mike and Álvaro brainstorming on ways to automate the packing line. And lastly, he sat down with Kyle in the lab to learn more about the R and D process, the formulation changes, and how they were able to achieve such accurate dosing. Andrew took copious notes out of habit.

"The original formulation was junk," Kyle began. "Concocted by amateurs with no grounding in science or chemistry. I changed the recipe to a pectin-based one and reduced the amount of gelatin without impacting either the flavor or the mouthfeel of the gummies. Melting-point temperature went up, cooking and curing times went down. Basic stuff."

Basic. For him.

"To maintain accurate and consistent dosage, I came up with the great idea of using pre-measured, frozen cannabis ingots. You know, when you're doing the laundry, you throw a detergent pod into the machine, and it's done. Why not do the same with cannabis? Every one of our products has a fixed active ingredient ratio—cannabinol (CBN) to cannabidiol (CBD) to tetrahydrocannabinol (THC). So it was just a matter of premixing the ingots—pods—with the right ratio based on batch size, freezing them, and then adding the ingot to the cooker. That takes away the second guessing and the need to always have skilled resources mixing the active ingredients." Kyle sat back on the stool and crossed his arms. "Simple."

Too simple, Andrew didn't say.

The R and D lab was the size of a large conference room, where two machines resembling stacked LaserJet printers sat side by side on a wide, stainless-steel table. A red cabinet with a biohazard sign stood in a corner. A fume hood bolted to the wall hung opposite the table. Kyle continued his monologue.

"I sample the batches after each production run and measure the active ingredient dosage to ensure the batches are within spec. Out of spec, we can't sell them. That's what these machines are for." The LaserJets. "HPLCs. High Performance Liquid Chromatography machines like we had in chemistry class. Samples from the same batches are then sent to Green Valley Labs so that a third-party COA can be issued for the batch."

Andrew nodded, pretending to understand.

"Certificate of Analysis." Kyle grabbed a few papers from the table and handed them to Andrew. "Validates potency and ensures there are no pesticides, residual solvents, or any other contaminants. The COA guarantees that the product is pure and contains what's on the label." He stood, his lanky frame towering over Andrew and Mike. "One of the benefits of legalized cannabis is that you know what you're getting. You're not smoking, vaping, or ingesting crap, shit that can make you sick or kill you."

"What's in there?" Andrew asked. Multicolored gummies sat in petri dishes under the fume hood. There were more colors than the rainbow, each petri dish labeled with a flavor—elderberry, mango habanero, pink lemonade, blackberry lime, mangosteen lychee.

"R and D," Kyle told Andrew. He slid open the glass door and took out one of the petri dishes containing purple gummies. "I run small, undosed batches to test out new flavors. Once I lock in the flavor, I make a limited run of dosed gummies to dial in the active ingredient formulation." He held out the petri dish. "These are dosed dual-action elderberry gummies—part of the new Sleep line. And the mango habanero is the new Alta line. They'll be out in a month, just in time for Christmas. The beauty of these babies is that we're using new technology I perfected to accelerate the absorption of ingested cannabis—nanomolecular emulsion. Gets you high faster and lets you stay high or sleep longer."

"Nanomolecular emulsion," Andrew said. "So you've solved the problem of getting to a quicker high without sacrificing the long-lasting edible effects." Andrew had read about this in one of the articles Charlie had sent him. There was a difference in the high between inhaling and ingesting cannabis. He thought back to his college days when he would occasionally light up or partake in brownie fests.

With smoking, vaping, or dabbing, the cannabis was absorbed by the body faster and more directly through the lungs, enabling the user to reach a near-immediate high . . . potent but short-lived. When one ingested cannabis, there's a slower onset, but a longer-lasting high. The current Kannawerks gummy labels stated: "Wait seventy-five minutes to feel the full effects of one gummy."

"So this is our killer app. And we'll be first to market."

"Correct. We've tested these against our current product line and our competitors' edibles, and ninety percent of the test subjects reported feeling the onset in less than fifteen minutes instead of the usual seventy-five."

"Tested? As in—"

"Our sales and marketing teams are willing guinea pigs, as are budtenders."

"I should have known."

"You're still learning."

"You said they would be out in a month. When is the launch date? And Mike, are we set to produce these?"

"We're good," Mike said. He'd been quiet until now. "The manufacturing process is the same. We make the ingots with the new formulation, and we keep doing what we do."

"With the exception of adding the terpenes at the end," Kyle said. "The flavors, aromas, therapeutic properties. We use cannabis distillate: activated, concentrated, and purified THC suspended in soluble oils. But it's commodity cannabis that lacks the terpene profile that we're trying to recreate. To get the *entourage* effect we need to put them back in—"

"Entourage?" Andrew's head was spinning.

"The entourage effect is the combination of cannabinoids and terpenes designed to amplify and maintain a consistent experience for the consumer. Users can dial in the effect they want to achieve— be alert, chill, relax, and sleep. When you smoke flower, you can reach the desired effect naturally, depending on the strain. With our gummies we tried using full spectrum oil—cannabis with multiple cannabinoids and natural terpenes left in—but maintaining accurate dosage was a challenge. So, we recreate the entourage effect artificially. We just have to be careful not to denature the terpenes—high heat can do that—so we put them in at the end of the cooking process." He addressed Mike. "It took the cooking team quite a while to figure out the timing, otherwise we would have had these on the market months ago. How many batches did you go through before you got it right?"

Mike didn't answer.

Andrew, sensing the tension, thanked Kyle for the primer, and he and Mike walked out of the lab onto an empty floor.

"Where does that door lead to?" he asked Mike, nodding at the back-left corner of the factory.

"This entire building is two units. That door leads to the other unit, another thirty thousand square feet. Abe was given the option to seal it off, but he asked the landlord to leave the door. He thought that Kannawerks would need it for additional warehouse storage or for expansion. That one has its own entrance on Commerce Way. We cannot access the space. I think it is used as a storage facility. We occasionally see trucks pull up loading and unloading pallets. The landlord owns most of the cannabis facilities in Adelanto. We found out about Akmana through him."

Andrew glanced at the digital display above the packing line: a few minutes past three. "What's the other reading besides temperature?"

"Humidity. We have to keep the temperature and the humidity within a tight range, otherwise the gummies get too dry or too soft. I receive a notification on my phone if they go outside a specific range."

"Nice. The display and data are online then?"

"Yes, they call it I-O-T, I forgot what it stands for—"

"Internet of Things."

* * *

Back at the house, he limited himself to one martini and held off on the wine, hoping for a good night's sleep—a rarity. To unwind, he flipped through the Criterion Channel. He found an obscure film, *High Plains Drifter*, that he'd stumbled upon years before in college. He had come home from a party, room spinning, magnetized by the grainy picture on AMC when AMC still stood for American Movie Classics and the TCM—Turner Classic Movies—channel was cogitating in Ted Turner's head.

A man with no name rides into the frontier town of Lago and, like a parasite destroying its host, seduces the citizens, turns them against each other, literally has them paint the town red, and executes three returning gunslingers—men who had killed the town marshal the prior year—men intent on enacting revenge on the townsfolk who had made the men scapegoats in a conspiracy perpetrated by all . . . for the greater good of Lago.

"That's the price of progress," the town innkeeper says, as the man with no name rides off on his pale horse and dissolves into the high plain.

CHAPTER 7

He woke up craving Renée's tacos. *Barbacoa.* Let her suggest the rest. He drove by the FDN facility again. The site was empty, with remnants of the bonfire strewn along the road, the wind having obscured the tire marks with dust where the cars had idled the prior morning.

"They are not here," Mike said.

"Who's not here?"

"Álvaro, Ashlee. I called them. Ashlee said her daughter is sick. Álvaro did not answer." He paced the room. "They are the first ones here. Álvaro for sure. He likes to clock in his hours, then go home. And today we have to pack two batches and get the materials off the floor for the site visit."

"Don't we have backups?"

"Backups?" He smirked. "These people can only do basic things, they cannot do anything complicated other than counting to twenty, putting gummies in a tin, and closing the tin. Álvaro is the only guy who has any capability. I hired him; I trained him. It took months."

"Figure out the schedule for the day. Then let's plan out the site visit. We'll stay as late as we have to."

Mike let out a long sigh. "I am glad you are here. You can work in my office while I sort things out."

Andrew walked over to the lunchroom. Kyle was at a table, his gaze fixated on the cup in his hands, his shoulders hunched. The steam from the cup fogged up his glasses.

"Late night?" Andrew asked as he placed a cartridge in the machine.

"Couldn't sleep. Happens sometimes."

"You should have taken one of those elderberry gummies," Andrew said, pressing the brew button.

Kyle's blank expression didn't change.

"Everything OK?"

Kyle blinked, then forced a smile. The eyes opaque. "Just gotta catch up on some sleep, that's all."

"I hear you," Andrew said, picking up his coffee.

"Well, gotta hit the lab."

"I'll come by later to prep for the site visit," Andrew said.

"I've got it covered."

"I'd still like to prep."

"I said I've got it."

Andrew gave Kyle a hard stare. In his software days, demos with clients, investors, and prospects were a do-or-die situation—scripted scenarios, backups at the ready, contingency plans, practice runs. Until the demo ran on its own. "Call me paranoid, but I need to see a run-through. I'll stop by at seven."

"Whatever."

Andrew and Mike kept the investor demo simple and scheduled a small depositor run of the sour cherry gummies. This meant that timing was critical. They needed to start cooking the slurry exactly one hour before the depositor came into action, giving them about an hour of slack time to showcase the pistons pumping gummies into the molds. They would also show the packing line in action—not the most efficient process to showcase, but they could discuss their plans for introducing automation. And if Ashlee was a no-show, Mike would run the depositor.

Right before lunch, they met with Kyle, who was now more alert. He would walk the investors through the quality control processes, as well as go over the pillars of Kannawerks's growth strategy: the new Sleep and Alta lines. Kyle's confidence was not unfounded—his presentation was sleek, detailed, and informative.

After the prep sessions, Andrew headed out to the taco truck. As he waited in line, he shielded his face from an unpleasant, swirling, warm wind. It felt different . . . suffocating. The skunk odor was gone, the easterly wind dissipating the rancid smell. The same easterly wind that transformed into Santa Anas as it funneled over the mountains and accelerated through the passes, and dried out as it rolled down the hills and slopes, fueling fires before reaching the ocean. He remembered the scars of the Oakland and Berkeley Hills fires, which were still present when he'd arrived as a freshman at Cal in '93. The fires and destruction touched everyone at the university.

"You again," Renée said.

"The name's Andrew."

"My tacos must have made an impression. Was it the tongue or the tripe?" She grinned.

"What are you smiling at?"

"Are you going to order?"

"Right. *Barbacoa.* You pick the other two." He stepped to the side, flustered.

As he waited, he noticed Ashlee's battered Chevy Cruze pulling into the parking lot. She seemed haggard, her hair scrunched into a tight bun and wearing sweats as if she had just woken up. But as much as he wanted to go off on her about the tardiness, he was relieved and would let it slide for today.

A strong gust buffeted the awning over the serving window; the canvas slapped on the metal frame. "Hey, Andrew." Renée leaned out the window. "Would you mind untying and helping me roll up the awning? This wind is freaking me out. It's been at it all morning."

He untied the ropes on both sides of the frame as she pulled it up, securing the awning on a couple of hooks.

"Thanks," she said, stepping out of the truck.

He had only seen her from the waist up until now. She was five-foot-eight, maybe five-foot-nine. Up close, he noticed a small mole just above her lip. Elegant. Her jeans and white T-shirt gave her a pleasant, casual demeanor. Approachable.

"How do you like Adelanto?" she asked.

"Everything I dreamed of."

She smiled . . . a pleasant smile.

"I haven't had a chance to explore."

"There's nothing to explore."

"I'm staying at the company digs, out in Helendale, until I figure out where to settle."

"Not much to do out there." She stared at the ground, her foot toying with a pebble. "What brings you to the High Desert?"

"Helping out a friend."

"Charlie?"

"You know him?"

"We're catering the party Friday."

Andrew nodded in approval.

"And where did you come from?" she asked.

"San Fran." He hated the sound of it.

"Been there for work."

"Tacos?"

"A prior life."

"A prior life to tacos?"

She leaned back on the truck, a droll smile on her face.

"Andrew!" A brunette handed him his order.

He thanked her, opened the bag, and took in the aroma: roast pork and rosemary. It reminded him of the *porchetta* he'd devour during summers in Italy. "It's good you're doing the taco thing now." She opened the door of the truck. "We should get together sometime, you know, not out here."

"Sure."

"I'm in Claremont, near the colleges."

"I'll be in LA next week," he said. "Where are you off to now?" *What a lame thing to ask.*

"Muskrat. We have a faithful following there." She glanced over at the serving window, where the brunette was resting her head on her hands, smiling. "Andrew, meet Lina. Lina, Andrew," Renée said.

"Hola." Lina waved. Andrew smiled back.

"Well, I better go," he said to Renée. He noticed her hands. Her fingers were long, thin, and graceful, devoid of jewelry, but that didn't mean anything because she was in a kitchen all day. His mind was now in overdrive: *What did you do before tacos? How did you get into the taco gig? How long's the commute to Claremont? Where are you from?* He was sweating.

"Enjoy the tacos," she said.

He forgot to ask for her number.

As Andrew entered the foyer, Mike rushed out of his office. "They cannot find him."

"Find who?"

"Álvaro. I spoke to his wife." He took a deep breath. "He never came home, and she has not seen him since yesterday morning."

"Let's slow down. Is this unusual for him?"

"Yes. He is a dedicated family man and one of our most regular workers."

"Did his wife report him missing to the sheriff?"

"She does not speak English, and she does not like the law."

"Let's call the sheriff's office. What was that detective's name? Morales?"

"We cannot have the authorities here when we have important guests coming tomorrow."

"At least he'll be on their radar."

"It is too risky. And the operators get nervous when the authorities come. Everyone here can work legally, do not misunderstand me, but there has been an increase in harassment cases of Latinos. 'Routine traffic stops.' We are the *outsiders*. We have to be careful." His face was flushed.

"All right, let's keep this under wraps. If anyone asks, tell them that Álvaro is visiting a relative who got sick or something. After the site visit, we call the Victor Valley Station and report Álvaro missing. OK?"

"OK."

"One more thing. Ashlee. I saw her come in. She didn't look good."

"Yes, she needed to find someone else to take care of her daughter. She said her mom is sick. She usually babysits the girl."

"We need her to be *on* for the investor visit tomorrow."

"I will make sure of it."

CHAPTER 8

One of the few downsides of driving a vintage Porsche was that there was no Bluetooth connection for a mobile. There *was* a flip phone that came with the car, which sat in its case attached to the central console, but it was 1996 technology, and who knows if it could still send or receive signals. It did power up, though.

Andrew had to fumble with his phone while driving, which was not the safest way to have a conversation. He shifted into sixth gear and dialed Charlie's number, careful not to cross the double yellow line.

"I will be there by eight," Charlie said. "Investors arrive at ten. That will give us enough time to finalize the show."

"We're all set."

"Good. What else is going on?"

"I need to speak with you about personnel, staffing."

"Problems?"

"Nothing serious, just that one of the guys is MIA. I'm concerned about single points of failure and hiring challenges given the skill levels out here." Should he bother Charlie with this trivia?

"Who's MIA?"

"Álvaro. Packing lead."

"Probably drunk at home. He doesn't matter. I would worry if Kyle or Ashlee didn't show."

"Ashlee came in late, some problem with her kid."

Andrew waited for Charlie to say something.

"It was a babysitter issue," Andrew finally said.

"Look, I know we can't hire the right people in Adelanto, but we have a good enough team for what we need now, and the sooner we close this next round and find the right partner, we can kiss Adelanto goodbye. We can go back to civilization, Santa Rosa, Santa Barbara, LA, take your pick; I know we won't win if we stay where we are. So don't get too comfortable in Adelanto," Charlie chuckled.

"How can I? It's a wasteland out here. The stifling wind, the desolation, the isolation. You can't breathe."

"You're always so dramatic."

"We need an Adelanto exit strategy, Charlie."

"What do you think I've been working on?"

Andrew had been at the company for less than a week and prioritizing getting out of Adelanto already felt right . . . until he walked into Mike's office.

"Good morning, amigo," Mike said. He was seated at his desk, hair parted, trimmed moustache, and focused on the monitor. Andrew stared at Mike for a minute, wondering how he might feel about an exit strategy.

Andrew set two coffees down on the desk. "Mike, why are you here?"

"You mean in the factory?" Mike asked, reaching for the coffee.

"Here at Kannawerks in Adelanto in cannabis. Didn't you tell me you were in automotive for a while? Toyota?"

He took a sip and put down the cup. "Remember I told you Manny hired me? Well, I asked him for a job. I needed to get my family out of Mexico."

Andrew sat down, curious.

"I was with Toyota for a decade. I worked my way up from the line to supervisor. I was recruited out of Toyota by an OEM based in Jalisco, just outside of Guadalajara. I was hired as the quality manager. They used to send me as part of a delegation to visit our customers in the United States. Big customers. I would go with my boss and a few others to keep these relationships close.

"On one of these trips to Dallas, we were invited to a dinner at a steakhouse—private dining room, mahogany-paneled walls, white tablecloths, five-star service. Real nice. We had just renegotiated the contract and had extended the partnership for another five years. Massive for us *and* for the Americans.

"After the Wagyu steaks and too many bottles of red wine, the main partner guy, *el jefe*, insisted that we all join him at his favorite strip club. He would not stop talking about this *chica* and how beautiful she was, the lap dances, and the VIP lounges. He was drunk and loud, and we were in Texas. But I was done for the evening, and I do not like these places. Who needs them? I love my wife. So I said no, politely. El jefe went crazy, his big bald head and face red like a tomato. 'What kind of sissies are you bringing across the border, and why the hell don't you like strip clubs, and are you a fag?'"

"Jesus."

"He threatened to cancel the contract and find alternative partners who would not disrespect their hosts. He screamed at my boss to fire me. *Loco*. The *cabrón* was furious. He was a big man."

"What happened?"

"My boss ordered me to get in the car, go to that chingado strip club, and if we lost this contract, there would be problems for me."

"What did you do?"

"I had no choice. I went. I stayed long enough for one lap dance and watched el jefe bury his head in the chest of a big girl, my cue to get out of there. She was not even attractive; none of the girls were.

They were all well-built, you know what I mean? He had a fetish for young girls with large breasts."

"Crazy."

"No, that was not the crazy part. We went back to Mexico and everything became una mierda. I was demoted to supervisor. I was followed. Our neighbors did not want to be seen with us. I was pulled over by the police and made to sit in the car for hours while they 'checked my papers.' And then one day I received an envelope in the mail, containing bullets inscribed with the names of my children. That was when I called Manny. I got my NAFTA visa, and we moved to Adelanto. All because I did not want to go to a *pinche* titty bar in Texas."

"And you don't think you can go back?"

"I do not know. It has been almost two years. I go back to visit family—my mother is ninety. I have heard stories where you move to the other side of Mexico, get a new job, start a new life, and the next thing you know you are hanging by your feet from an overpass with your guts spilled onto the highway below. Adelanto is not perfect, but it is where my job is. And I know my family will be safe here in the middle of nowhere."

Charlie directed the show like a circus ringleader. The tour had started in the R and D lab, where the new lines of fast-acting gummies were well-received. Ashlee initiated the cooking process on the depositor before the investors reached the floor. With Swiss-watch timing, they approached the line as the pistons began depositing the red slurry into the molds, which moved into the cooling chamber, after which the operators removed the molds and demolded the gummies, the brightly colored candy falling into the white trays. The investors peppered Charlie with questions as Andrew and Mike stood to the side, watching the scene unfold.

Suddenly, a sharp screech like fingernails on a chalkboard burst from the depositor, followed by a loud bang. The pistons stopped, but the conveyor belt kept going, the molds half-filled. The hot slurry overflowed, oozing down the sides of the hopper and enveloping the pistons, pooling out across the conveyor and falling to the floor in a slow, steady cascade. Ashlee froze. Mike jumped to the console and slammed the emergency button, which only stopped the conveyor belt; the hopper kept overflowing. The cooking pump needed to be shut off.

Mike ran to the electrical panel, ran his finger down the row of fuses, and flipped a switch. The pump stopped.

Smoke emanated out of the pistons while vapor rose from the hopper. The melted gummy base formed a dark-red blob under the depositor, slowly expanding its footprint as if it had a life of its own.

Charlie came over to Mike with the investors left to themselves by the packing line where there was no Álvaro; he was still MIA.

"What the fuck happened? Ashlee, come here," Charlie said as he motioned to her frozen figure standing before the sputtering machine. "Why didn't you hit the abort button? You were right there."

She scowled at him, adjusted her hairnet, and put her hands in her pockets.

They all moved out of the way of the expanding blob.

"Get this thing cleaned up fast," Charlie hissed. "Andy, come with me."

Charlie reintroduced Andrew to the investors, telling them that Andrew was there to provide expert oversight over the operations so that situations like the one they had just witnessed could be avoided in the future. With their faces hidden behind surgical masks, it was hard to tell what the investors were thinking.

CHAPTER 9

The ranch came into view as Andrew coasted along the banks of the Mojave River, passing by the occasional verdant desert knoll and dry arroyo, the hills separating Victorville from Apple Valley exemplifying the contrasting aesthetic of the High Desert.

Charlie had offered to host the guests overnight in the suites, anticipating that they would be too drunk to drive home. He had hired an up-and-coming DJ who was popular on the LA club circuit. He had organized shuttles to and from LA, thereby ensuring that the right people got there on time. Current and prospective investors were invited, including the group who had witnessed the depositor fail that morning. And most importantly, he had extended invitations to a handful of potential M and A candidates, companies that he had been in discussion with—firms that had complementary products to Kannawerks's gummies and had what Kannawerks did not: a distribution network and deeper relationships with dispensaries.

Andrew drove through the iron-gated entrance, his wheels slowly crunching through the gravel, careful not to scratch the chassis or the midnight-blue paint. His headlights illuminated a two-story adobe structure with a tall mesquite tree arching over the courtyard at the end of the driveway. The food trucks were already there, and the smell of stewed lamb and pork belly wafted in the air.

He opened his door to find an acne-scarred valet who seemed no older than sixteen. "I'll park it, thank you," Andrew said, reconsidering. No way this child would know how to handle a stick shift. "Where should I put it?"

"You can park it on the lawn," the valet said.

Andrew fished out his money clip and handed the valet a ten-dollar bill. He moved the car onto the grass, finding a corner spot where dings and dents could be avoided. He pocketed the key. The sun had already set, but there was still enough light to observe the grounds. The main building was surrounded by a wide porch and a well-lit dining area on a raised platform, where tables were paired with standing heat lamps, which resembled blooming mushrooms. Tall grasses surrounded a pond. Cattle-grazing fields extended to the north. Joshua trees, mesquites, and even a few saguaros dotted the surroundings. An oasis in the High Desert, just like the website said.

Lights were strung in the courtyard, illuminating the facade. Two jack-o-lanterns, the features of their ghostly faces sharpened by dancing candles, greeted him as he walked up the wooden steps into the main hall. A staircase sat on the left while tall wood-beamed ceilings arched over the great room. A working grandfather clock stood in the corner, and portraits and black-and-white pictures depicting the ranch over the years hung on the adobe walls.

A handful of people stood around a bar that had been set up across from the entrance, a first stop for guests. Charlie held court in the huddle and when he saw Andrew, he waved him over.

The group greeted him, all with drinks in hand.

"This is Ethan, runs sales, knows the market inside and out." Charlie held each person's shoulder as he introduced them. "You've met Ish, knows where the bodies are buried. Claire, marketing savant. Orinda, finance, keeps us all in check. And Boris, our compliance and risk officer. What do you do Boris?" Charlie smiled. "Oh yeah, make sure we don't lose our license."

Andrew shook everyone's hand.

"This is Andy. Sorry, *Andrew*. I've known him for over thirty years, and as I've said to many of you, he's my proxy." He said to Andrew, "Have a drink, meet the team. Then come find me. We've got work to do."

"Let's go find a seat outside before it gets too cold," Ethan said. He was thin, with a delicate, sculpted face, light-blue eyes, and a blond man bun perched on his head. Andrew grabbed a beer, and together with Ish, they headed down an interior corridor and stepped out on the porch. They found some wicker chairs and organized them around a small table. The song of the crickets was calming . . . nice. A soft breeze touched the green fields extending into the low hills.

Ish pulled out a pre-rolled joint, lit it, and took a hit. The pungent smoke hovered above them. He offered it to Andrew.

"No thanks," he said.

Ish shrugged.

"I had a bad experience the last time I toked," Andrew said. "And I'm guessing this isn't your grandmother's pot, not the one I smoked in college anyway."

Ish grinned. "No, it isn't."

Ethan grabbed the joint from Ish, took a hit, and held the smoke in. "Bad experience, huh?" He exhaled slowly and handed the joint back to Ish.

"We've all done stupid shit," Ish said.

"Happened about a decade ago. An old college roommate threw a party the night before the Big Game. A bunch of us had been talking about a reunion, the timing worked out, and there were folks in town that we hadn't seen in a while. It was up in the Berkeley Hills, in the same house I had lived in my senior year.

"There were college buddies and work acquaintances—it was a great crowd. There was one woman . . . Amanda." He shook his head. "We hit it off, you know, one of those situations where everything clicks: the music, the crowd, the view, the whole fucking vibe. Then she offered me a joint." Andrew leaned over and put the beer on the table. "I hadn't smoked a joint since college, and I was never a big toker. She brought it to my lips; I couldn't resist. I proceeded to take one, two, three hits. Next thing I know I feel a nudge. I wake up in my old room, in my old bed. It was four in the morning. Amanda was gone." He stepped off the porch. "I couldn't remember a fucking thing. I don't trust myself on weed."

"Doesn't sound like a bad experience to me, you just got too high," Ish said. He crushed the roach between his fingers and threw it in the dirt as Ethan reached over with a tin of gummies. Ish grabbed a couple and popped them in his mouth. "You just need to know your limits . . . figure out the right dosage for the right kind of high," he said. "These gummies and the joint will get us through the evening relaxed. Take the edge off."

Andrew felt ignorant and curious. "Why did you just take gummies after the joint?"

"Lengthens the effect. The joint gets you high fast and the gummy keeps you high longer," Ish said.

"Right, right, I knew that, but I'd never put two and two together. So the new product lines we're releasing—Sleep and Alta—are an all-in-one solution?"

"Game changers," Ethan said. "No one else has anything that's close."

"We're going to kill it on 4/20," Ish said.

"What's so special about April twentieth?" Andrew asked.

"Think of it as the Cannabis New Year. We sell more product in the week leading up to 4/20 than in an entire month," Ethan said. "It started in the seventies with some high school kids in Nor Cal smoking weed at 4:20 p.m. every afternoon . . . 4/20 became a code for 'Let's go smoke some weed, dude.' When pot was illegal, it was a counterculture signal. Now that it's legal, it's a major marketing event. Not everyone's happy about it, but we sell a ton of shit during the High Holidays. Everyone sells a ton of shit."

Andrew smirked. "Kind of fucked up, but we're talking about weed."

"Why do you say that?"

"Because April twentieth is Hitler's birthday."

"As in Adolph?" Ish asked.

"Look it up."

"You're right. That is fucked up," Ish said. He scratched the stubble on his chin. "How do you know it's his birthday?"

"Relax. I'm a student of European History."

"That's right. Italian."

"We should get back inside and mingle." Ethan said to Andrew, "Come to LA and we'll give you the straight dope, explain the ins and outs—strains, dosage, actives—the works."

"Kyle schooled me on that."

Ish waved his hand disparagingly. "That was theory coming from a 'scientist.'" He used air quotes. "This is an art. I'm talking from the consumer's perspective, the street."

"His science did fix our products," Ethan said.

"Science. He was a grad student. He did *research* at UCLA. We're the ones in the trenches. Leave it to us for the schooling, Andrew. We'll show you what you need to know."

CHAPTER 10

The DJ booth was on the landing hovering over the great room. Tech house music pumped from the speakers, while bodies swayed on the dance floor. Guests, all with drinks in hand, some with cigarettes or joints that smelled like skunk, were scattered throughout the cavernous room, with more smokers on the porch and in the courtyard. The bar was the hub of the party, with guests lining up for their first, second, or third drink. The place was packed.

Andrew dropped the empty bottle into one of the bins and scanned the scene. Ish and Ethan were already at the food truck. He couldn't see Charlie anywhere but would find him after he picked up another drink.

He leaned on the counter to catch the bartender's attention.

"Nice Rolex."

Andrew glanced left, then scanned down. A man with a lightly tanned face, a strong, angular nose, ocean-blue eyes, and a head of thinning sandy-blond hair with graying whisps around his temples stood holding a whiskey, neat. The tumbler was half-full.

"Nice pour."

"I tip well," the man said, holding the drink up to the light. He lay the glass on the counter, his gaze resting on Andrew. Suddenly he grabbed Andrew's left wrist. "The textured dial, silver linen. Unique. Early seventies?"

Andrew nodded.

The man tightened his grasp on the wrist and inspected the clasp. "And in fine shape."

Andrew didn't mind the compliments on the watch. What he did mind was the abruptness with which the man had clutched his arm. He pulled his arm back and the grip loosened, but not completely.

"You have a golfer's hand," the man continued. He ran the tips of his fingers over the callouses on Andrew's palm. The cologne—spicy, sweet mandarin, and geranium—was overpowering. And probably expensive.

Andrew masked his discomfort by giving the man a once-over: he had a disarming smile and wore a crisp, white dress shirt open at the collar, the outfit completed by a navy-blue suit and shoes that weren't cheap—TOD'S or Ferragamo—Andrew couldn't tell in the light.

"Terence," the man said. "Terence Kayne." He let go of Andrew's wrist and picked up his glass. He had the trace of an English accent— not the Queen's English—North England, maybe.

"Andrew."

"*The* Andrew?"

"Depends on which one."

"Charlie's Andrew."

"That's me."

Terence patted Andrew's arm. "Sorry about the inquisition. I get excited by vintage and rare pieces." He pulled back his sleeve and showed Andrew his Patek: perpetual calendar chronograph, moon phases and all.

"Nice."

"We should play sometime," Terence said. "Come to my club, Shepherd Dunes. Classic layout, the greens are a bit deceptive. Know where that is?"

"Sure," Andrew said hesitantly. "As soon as I get settled—"

An arm suddenly slung around Andrew. "I see you've met the landlord," Charlie said. He said to Terence, "I need to talk to you. I left you several messages."

"We can chat Monday," Terence said. He raised his glass and excused himself. "Cheers, Andrew. Don't be a stranger." He handed Andrew his business card and disappeared into the crowd.

"What did he want?" Charlie asked as they walked away.

"He liked my watch."

They passed by a table stacked with Kannawerks hoodies—swag for the guests. Andrew grabbed one and put it on. "How does a Brit become a cannabis landlord?" he asked.

"I don't know how he ended up here. All I know is that he made a bunch of money in data centers before he switched to cannabis properties. Forget about him. Come on, there's someone I want you to meet."

"Let me grab some food."

"Hurry up, I'll be on the patio," Charlie said.

The food trucks were on opposite sides of the courtyard, and the orange-and-green taco truck sharply contrasted with the red-and-gold pasta truck: Cucina Trastevere serving Amatriciana, Gricia, Carbonara, and Pomodoro.

"How's it going in there?" Renée asked.

"You know . . . drugs, drinks, music," Andrew said.

She laughed a soft laugh that ended in a chortle. "What'll it be?"

"Surprise me."

The tacos were out in less than a minute, but Andrew held his plate, not ready to leave. "How long are you here for?"

"Until we run out of food."

"Hope you brought enough."

"Yeah," she laughed, "at this rate we may be out before midnight." She nodded at the line behind him, and that was his cue to leave, but not before he asked for her number.

He found Charlie on the patio, where people mingled at the tables, some eating pasta, some devouring the tacos, and others inhaling both. Bottles and glasses littered the tables, on which tins of gummies sat half empty waiting for the next taker. The drone of voices was broken by relaxed laughter. No one was on edge.

"Andy, I want you to meet Theo," Charlie said. "He runs Blue Savannah, one of the larger cannabis funds. Theo, this is Andy, the new executive I told you about. Fresh off the boat from San Francisco."

"Have a seat," Theo said, gesturing at a chair. Mid-forties, he had a marine's crew cut, a smattering of freckles, and he was fit: a black polo shirt hugged his sculpted biceps.

Andrew sat down. "You're not cold?"

"Cold is a state of mind."

"When you're done, Andy, come find me." Charlie excused himself.

Andrew asked Theo, "Do you mind if I eat?"

"Go right ahead."

Andrew took a bite. *Lengua. Good call, Renée.*

"So, Andy, what brings you to the world of cannabis?"

He finished swallowing and said, "I left the diminutive behind in high school. Call me Andrew."

"Why did *Andrew* come here all the way from the Bay Area?"

"How much time do you have?"

"I'm not going anywhere."

"Charlie called as I was shutting down my last company." Andrew put his half-eaten taco on the plate and realized he had left his beer at the bar. "And I was ready for a change."

"Serendipitous."

"You could say that."

"Change is also one way to describe what you went through."

Andrew studied Theo, confused.

"I know Srini. We've gone in together on a few investments. He told me what happened."

Andrew sat back. He hadn't thought about *what happened* since he'd arrived in the High Desert. He should call Srini, Andrew's first CEO during the dot-com boom and bust who, over the years, had become a mentor to Andrew, and who was also on the board of directors of his last startup. "Srini was there for me until the end. The voice of reason when it was all coming undone. There aren't many investors who would do what he did."

"No, there aren't," Theo said.

As Andrew took another bite, Ethan walked up and placed a beer on the table. "You must be thirsty."

"Thanks. Ethan, have you met Theo?"

"More than once," Ethan said, rearranging his man bun.

"Catch you later, Ethan?" Theo asked.

The two fist-bumped and Ethan joined a group of women the two men had been eyeing.

"Ethan and I have a few mutual acquaintances, some stranger than others," Theo said. "Inevitable in cannabis." Theo held up the tumbler and rattled the ice. "You just have to partner with the good ones."

"And Charlie's one of the good ones?" Andrew asked.

"He owes me the latest financials. We'll see."

"That doesn't sound like an endorsement."

He sipped his drink. "I came in when Max recapitalized the company. He introduced me to Charlie. I liked him and his vision. But a lot has happened in the two years since recreational legalization. The cannabis industry is slowing down—not the demand, which is rising. But there's a glut of companies in the market, all with 'me too' products. The fundamentals don't support the current valuations. The air has already started to come out of this bubble, and it's going to continue deflating. It's inevitable. We're in a protracted downturn in cannabis. The hype is fading and it's time for these companies to be run like real businesses."

This was the first time Andrew had heard about a slowdown or that valuations were too high. "What about the new Sleep and Alta lines?" he asked. "The fast-acting, long-lasting ones. I hear those are going to be hot."

"Promising, sure." Theo put down his tumbler. "All other competitive products, the *legal* products that purport to do the same, are bullshit. I know because we've had them tested. The formulation is the same as regular products but with different packaging. You could sue them for false advertising or report them to the BCC, but why?"

"Sleep, or lack thereof, is a global epidemic. Kannawerks is the only one with a fast-acting formulation, which will appeal to a much broader customer base. Why can't we be the ones to succeed?"

Theo leaned forward, moving his tumbler to the side. "I'm not saying the new Kannawerks lines won't succeed. I'm saying it's a *market* problem."

"What does that mean?"

"The market problem is that illegal cannabis dwarfs the legal market in California by more than three to one. Seventy percent. And it's not getting smaller. It's growing thanks to those bureaucratic idiots in Sacramento that can't get out of their own way. There are three," he held up his fingers, "three entities in California that regulate cannabis. The BCC, the CDPH, and the CDFA."

"I've heard of the Bureau of Cannabis Control."

"CDPH, California Department of Public Health, and the CDFA, the Department of Food and Agriculture. The governor is proposing a budget increase to consolidate cannabis regulation under one agency, but at the rate bills get passed, we'll be well into 2020, if not 2021."

Theo shifted out of heat-lamp range and continued. "Then there's the tax situation. If the state lowered the combined excise and cultivation taxes from an average of thirty-five percent down to fifteen percent, *and* enforced the law, *and* provided incentives to grow the legal market to Colorado levels, the state would make as much tax revenue as they make today. With room to grow. And when the feds legalize cannabis, they're going to want a piece of the pie. At the current tax levels, forget it. If the feds add eight or ten points on top of what California is taxing now, that means a tax rate north of fifty percent. Who will want to stay in the business? And I'm not even including the taxes levied by *cities* for retail, distribution, and manufacturing. Or Section 280E."

"280E?" Andrew asked.

"Doubles your effective income tax. You can't deduct most of your expenses—it's a racketeering law."

"Christ."

"Let's tax cannabis and bring in tax revenue—great! But if you're going to tax the shit out of the legal stuff, then *eradicate* the illegal crap that's cheap and dangerous, makes people sick, and kills. But there's no enforcement."

Peals of feminine laughter reached them. Two of the women had their arms around Ethan.

"Let's hope Ethan doesn't do irreparable damage," Theo said. He reached for his glass. "Prop 64 allowed recreational marijuana to flourish, but it also lowered the cost and risk of doing business in cannabis. The criminal penalty for illegal cannabis cultivation has gone from a felony punishable with jail time to a five-hundred-dollar misdemeanor *no matter how large the crop or haul.* So to bring a felony case that *might* shut down an illegal operation, prosecutors must find other charges."

Theo took a long sip and set the glass down. "Compound this with another beauty. The new law prohibits counties that do not permit commercial cannabis grow or manufacturing or distribution facilities from receiving state enforcement grants, so illegals set up shop there. Why? Because the local authorities have no budget and limited resources to police, raid, or shut down the illegal operations. There are so many unregulated grow operations, manufacturing facilities, and dispensaries all over California that it's like a game of Whac-A-Mole. It's an infestation of apocalyptic proportions. You can even find illegal dispensaries on Weedmaps and Yelp."

"If there are so many illegal operations in sight, and you can find illegal dispensaries on legit online platforms, why don't they go after them?"

"Because enforcement is unfunded and understaffed and the regulators have their heads up their ass. Instead of fostering and helping the legal entities succeed, the bureaucrats inspect *legal* grow operations, and *legal* manufacturers, and *legal* dispensaries, and make them spend hundreds of thousands of dollars on fees and improvements to their facilities to meet local and state requirements. Unless someone is injured, or fires a gun, or dies, nothing happens.

"But the real problem for Kannawerks, Andrew, is that there's already a product in the *illegal* market that is fast-acting and long-lasting—the same as your proprietary formula—and it works."

"What are you talking about?"

"It's called Pink Dot. At twice the THC dosage per gummy, you're paying a quarter of what you'd pay for an equivalent legit dose. It's been out for a while."

"No one on the team's mentioned this."

"They're either not paying attention or they don't care. It's hot shit."

This was a lot to process. He scanned the surroundings for Ish. Ethan's harem had expanded. Where the fuck was Charlie? He threw the crumpled napkin on the table. "So what's the point, Theo? Why are you even talking to us? Why would anyone want to be in legal cannabis?"

"Simple. First, California will become a six-billion-dollar market by 2021—the legal part alone—making it the largest *legal* cannabis market in the world. Second, multistate operators—MSOs—are expanding. They bring scale, and scale wins in this game. They'll either crush you or buy you, an easy payback for us as Kannawerks investors if the latter happens. Third, recreational cannabis use is becoming more socially acceptable, bringing in new demographics. And fourth, cannabis *will* be legalized at the federal level. This won't happen anytime soon, but the companies that are ready, those that have a platform and a brand, will reap the benefits. With the syco-phants in Washington, who knows when that's going to happen, but I am an optimist." He smiled.

"We'll be dead by then."

"It'll happen sooner than you think."

"Let's hope so." Andrew wondered about Kannawerks's viability. Charlie said they were bringing in just under two million dollars a month in revenue. He needed to review the numbers and see for himself.

Theo stood up. "Looks like Ethan needs some help."

"Thanks for the market primer."

"Anytime. And if you're ever in Santa Monica, swing by. There's an amazing Italian restaurant around the corner from my office where fresh pasta is flown in daily from Bologna. Something to do with the eggs."

A market slowdown. Illegal cannabis. Pink Dot. Federal legal-ization a mirage. Andrew went in search of something stronger than a beer. He stepped inside the main hall, the thumping music hit-ting him full force. Swaying bodies had carved out a virtual dance floor. Smoke wafted past the dimmed lights, shrouding the room in an electric haze, while joints floated around the party seemingly by themselves.

He squeezed past the weaving, sweating dancers and ordered a Belvedere and tonic. A thick hand swatted him on the back, almost spilling his drink. "Miss me?" Ish smiled.

"Just the person I wanted to see."

"I'll have the same," he said to the bartender. When the drink came, they navigated outside to an isolated firepit, the flames licking the night air. They sat down and warmed their hands over the fire.

Andrew pulled the hoodie over his head. "Have you heard of Pink Dot?"

"Yes."

"Have you tried it?"

"I've tried a lot of things."

"How is it?"

"Whoever's making it knows what they're doing. Works as well as our new line in terms of speed and duration."

"How come no one told me?"

"Who cares?"

"How can anyone succeed in this industry if a product on the illegal market anticipates a legal innovation?"

"It's a fact of life. The illegal market is not going away anytime soon."

"I'd like to get my hands on some."

"Pink Dot? What for?"

"I want to check out the packaging, have the product tested in a lab, see what's in it. Understand what we're up against."

"Waste of time. There's enough demand in the legal market. We should focus on that and not worry about what's sold under the counter." He was coherent for having smoked a joint and taken a few gummies.

"Still, can't hurt."

"Fine. Come to LA and we'll go find some." He pulled out a pack of cigarettes and lit one.

"I'd like to see legit dispensaries as well."

"Why don't you come down next week? We'll go on a ride-along, and then you can stay the night. We host budtender roundtables every other Tuesday. You can hang out and then party."

They heard a commotion behind them. A man stumbled out of the house and leaned against a post, as if he was preventing the house from falling. He opened his mouth, tried to say something, and fell off the porch into the dirt. The man lay there until he was picked up by a couple that had rushed out of the house. They carried him inside.

"Is it always like this?"

"I've seen worse," Ish said.

They exchanged phone numbers and Andrew headed to the patio. He saw the silhouettes of Ashlee and Kyle seated on the patio step, drinks in one hand and cigarettes in the other.

"Not your scene, is it?" Kyle asked, without a glance at Andrew.

Andrew ignored the comment and sat down next to them, which they didn't seem to appreciate.

"Have you seen Mike?"

"He was still at the factory when we left, inspecting the depositor," Ashlee said. "He thinks he can fix it himself, but I told him we'll need to call maintenance. The pistons are jammed."

"What do you think happened?"

"Wear and tear, I'm guessing. We run those things hard."

"Did the investors say anything about the fuckup?" Kyle asked.

"Charlie did damage control."

"Would be a shame if those investors didn't double down."

"After the spiel I just got from one of them, I'm not so sure. Illegal market dwarfing the legal market, competitive contraband stealing our thunder." He refrained from mentioning Pink Dot.

"The pie's big enough for everyone," Ashlee said. She flicked the cigarette butt away, and as she stood, her frame entered the light. She wore a red blouse, designer jeans, simple flats, and makeup that highlighted her round green eyes; nothing like the factory supervisor Andrew had interacted with that morning.

* * *

Charlie led Andrew on the schmoozing rounds. He introduced him to Zack, the Vapix CEO. They talked for a few minutes, promising to connect the following week in a more conducive setting. Andrew wasn't so sure about hooking up with a vape company after all the negative press, but he would go along with Charlie's strategy of finding a partner to unlock distribution.

They met Harold, a former Wall Street executive with an investment focus on emerging trends: renewables, electric vehicles, crypto, and now dipping his toes in cannabis.

"It's all about the data," he repeated. "You own the data, you build competitive advantage, you optimize shelf space by product, you know your customer, you introduce machine learning, you outsmart your competitors. With data. It's all about the data."

Sorry buddy, Andrew wanted to say, *we're not selling credit cards, we're selling marijuana-infused candy. People just want to get high.*

There was the ferret-faced, trust-fund baby who espoused investment in cannabis as a way to support equity license allocation and social justice movements: another white man atoning for his ancestors' sins.

As they walked away, Charlie said, "That guy'll never invest in cannabis. I've been talking to him for six months. He likes to hear himself talk and just wants to feel good about himself."

There were Whytt Thorburn III and Frost Johnson, Harvard MBAs. Charlie called them the Hardy Boys, wearing blazers, chinos, and topsiders, who had started with a grow operation in Oregon and were now in California, up north in Willits.

"It's all about the purity of the strain," they said, finishing each other's sentences. "We've engineered the highest yield cannabis plant ever. We've introduced the concept of terroir to cannabis. We're targeting the cannabis connoisseur, the cannasseur."

Andrew glanced at Charlie, who shrugged.

There were serious investors, too, not just cannabis idealists. Most of the existing investors were ready to double down on their Kannawerks bet, while established funds asked the hard questions, like Theo, on the financials, the impact of the illegal market, the industry slowdown, and the inflated valuations. Andrew listened and chimed in where he could, while Charlie did his best to convince the skeptics that Kannawerks was unique, and that the platform was the right one to scale beyond the California border.

Look at Nevada, after all.

Guests lined up at the valet with tickets in hand while a couple slow danced on the patio to imaginary music. Andrew sipped a vodka tonic, the firepit crackling in the cool, dry air. "Diverse bunch," he said.

Charlie nursed his tequila on the rocks. "I know we can count on the existing guys."

"I don't think that's enough to get us what we need. Who else is there? The large funds seem to have soured on cannabis."

"That's what they say now, but with enough momentum from the current investors, and if we can find the right partner, we'll get the scale we need to grow in and beyond California."

"Maybe. But it seems like it's going to be a slog."

"What do you mean?"

"This is not going to work like a tech play."

Charlie stared at him with a puzzled expression.

"The level of effort that has to be put in to make this work, it's not commensurate with the potential returns." Andrew put his glass on the ground and leaned in. "The level of effort, Charlie. With a tech play in software, for example, the effort you put in is in the design and development phases, but once you launch the product, it has legs—you build it once and sell copies that cost almost nothing . . . as long as you continue to innovate, find the right distribution strategy, and target a niche that will take the competition months or even years to penetrate, especially if you build a platform that can foster a perpetuating ecosystem. This industry and Kannawerks have none of that."

"That's above my pay grade, Andy."

"I was surprised at the size of the illegal market. I mean, I knew it *existed*, but seventy percent? And no enforcement? We're making candy. Anyone can make candy—"

"I didn't bring you here to be a naysayer."

"I heard a lot of skepticism from the veterans. Theo, for instance."

"Others are interested. And the new guys."

"They're naive, Charlie. They're like children who haven't done their homework. They're arriving late to the party just as the music is about to stop."

"You've been here for one week."

"I've seen this movie multiple times."

Charlie walked to the firepit, the light accentuating his features. "Andy, you're way smarter than I am, you've always been. I've been dealt this set of cards, and I'm playing them as best I can. You're coming down from tech to cannabis. I get it. But I'm moving up from hospitality. You see, this is way better than where I came from; it's got higher upside potential for me. It's all relative."

Andrew picked up a pebble and threw it in the fire.

"This industry is here to stay."

"Charlie, don't get me wrong. But this is a war, and we're only waging a battle—is it worth the effort? For us?"

"We raise the money, we merge with a partner, maybe even get acquired by an MSO, and we move on."

They stared at the flames in silence. Andrew thought about what Charlie had just said: it's all relative. Maybe cannabis was better for both of them, in different ways, regardless of the challenges. He walked over and put his arm around Charlie. "We'll make it work."

CHAPTER 11

It was a straight shot up Route 66 back to Helendale. The car was freezing, the problem with an air-cooled engine, which took its time to warm up the interior. He rubbed his hands together, the heat starting to blow only after he was back in Helendale pulling into the garage. He poured a generous glass of vodka and stumbled to the bedroom.

That's all he remembers.

It's dark. He's driving on a dirt road, the red taillights giving the billowing dust a macabre glow. He crawls past a wooden gate. The road is now paved. The stars are visible through branches and leaves of trees arching over the road with the moon peeking through, casting jagged shadows. He can't seem to reach a solitary light, but once he does, he sees that it's a single flickering candle, casting a pale glow on a tall, black door.

He hears voices inside. He walks into the room, the ceilings extending above him into an infinite domed cupola. He makes his way through the anonymous crowd, and it parts for him like the Red Sea did for Moses. Everyone is quiet now. He steps through a door, wooden steps creak under his feet. He sees two silhouettes seated on a manicured lawn, floodlights shining on them, their blond heads glowing in the light. He approaches the two shapes, and as he draws closer, he sees they are naked. He doesn't recognize the women. They wave him over, motioning for him to sit down. He tries to say something but can't. One of the women stands up, her blond hair cascading over her bare body. She reaches out to him and smiles.

Andrew jumped awake. Getting his bearings, he remembered he was in Helendale, in bed, shivering. He rubbed his face. A sawblade was grinding in his head. He walked to the bathroom, relieved himself, and grabbed a couple of Advil. The thermostat in the hall read sixty-one degrees. He upped it to seventy-three and poured himself a glass of water in the kitchen to down the Advil. The microwave clock read 3:11 a.m.—he'd only been asleep for two hours.

He needed to stop the late-night intake, even though he had already scaled back since the shutdown. The alcohol, the cyclical thoughts, and the lack of sleep culminated in lethargic starts to the mornings with slow fades in the afternoons. Combined with lack of exercise, it impacted his concentration, focus, and thought process. He wasn't getting any younger; he needed to slow it down. Eliminate it.

He knew that would never happen. But it was counterproductive—debilitating. It accentuated the anxiety, lightened the sleep, and spurred thoughts that perpetuated other, senseless, endless thoughts as if on a fly wheel, which led to anxious dreams and nightmares. He remembered that the German word for dream was *traum*. They were right. Dreams *are* traumatic. Fucking Freud. Wait, he was Austrian.

He stripped off his jeans and shirt and crawled back under the covers, where he fell into a deep sleep.

CHAPTER 12

The thing about snakes is their instinct to leave you alone. They're afraid of *you*, and they know *you* wouldn't make a good meal. But if *you* irk them, or annoy them, or step on them, they'll defend themselves, and they'll bite. If they are of the venomous kind, *you* will be in severe pain, and *you* may even die. The most dangerous kinds are the young ones because the adults know how to dose their venom when they attack their prey, whereas young snakes haven't had enough practice and don't have enough experience to know better. They go all in on their prey and deplete all the venom from their glands into their unknowing victim. *You.*

As he stepped outside to sip his morning coffee, Andrew found the molted skin of a baby rattler in the corner of the patio. He knew it was a baby rattler from its length, the diamond pattern on the dry skin, and the lack of a rattle at its end. There must be a nest nearby, as they didn't tend to venture far prior to reaching full maturity. The snake must have crawled through the drainage hole in the stucco wall bordering the golf course. He picked up a rock from the faux, dry riverbed and sealed the hole. It was late in the season for snakes, but the heat had been oppressive well into October, so no surprise to find evidence of rattler activity. He picked up the skin and threw it over the wall, and as he did so, he felt the hairs on the back of his neck rise up. He had an aversion to snakes ever since the day a viper dropped at his feet from a tree in Bangkok. That was the first time he remembered feeling helpless . . . that he wasn't in control.

Zeke scanned the cloudless sky. "Let's hope the wind doesn't start up again. This time of year, it can get nasty. I had to stop my round on Thursday because of the dust."

Andrew checked the scorecard. "What tees do you play from?"

"Golds. The greens are well protected. Makes for a good challenge."

Sixty-five hundred yards. Andrew pocketed the scorecard and secured his bag on the golf cart. Zeke hopped in and they headed to the first tee. There was no one else around.

Andrew's drive found the middle of the fairway. Zeke duffed his drive in the left rough. They hopped in the cart and drove out to Zeke's ball, where he took out a hybrid and wacked the ball onto the green. It rolled to within a few feet of the pin.

Andrew hit a pitching wedge to the left-center of the green, leaving himself a twelve-foot putt for birdie. His putt lipped out, and he tapped in for his par. Zeke made his birdie.

At the next tee Andrew asked, "Have you heard of Terence Kayne?"

"Yeah, I know him," Zeke said, surprised, and not pleasantly so.

"Figured, you being in data centers and all."

"I'd stay clear of him if I were you."

"Might be difficult. He's our landlord."

Zeke lined up his shot and ripped his drive down the middle. "I can't believe Kayne is still around."

Andrew remained quiet.

"Did he tell you why he's no longer in data centers?"

"No."

"Screw it, let's play. You're up. I don't want to spoil the round."

Zeke carded a forty-one and Andrew a thirty-seven on the front nine. They picked up a couple of sandwiches and proceeded with the back nine. They were still the only golfers on the course, likely because of the heat and the sustained wind.

Standing on the seventeenth tee, Zeke brought up Terence again. "He's a thief."

Andrew flared his tee shot into the bunker to the right of the green.

"He borrowed money to purchase data center properties by misrepresenting his assets and his net worth. He forged documents. I was working on one of these deals, and what I saw didn't compute. I brought in the regulators. They saw the same things I did."

"And?"

"When the regulators confronted Kayne, he pleaded ignorance. They investigated, but they couldn't find anything substantial. He got a slap on the wrist. Nothing else. He was—is—like a *mafia don*, two or three steps removed from any wrongdoing. Plausible deniability. Turns out he was broke. He was up to his neck in loans that he was close to defaulting on, so he needed to borrow more to cover his debts. After the ordeal, even though he wasn't convicted of any wrongdoing, he couldn't continue to do business in the industry—no one trusted him. So he liquidated everything and disappeared."

Andrew proceeded to balloon his sand shot over the green and into the thick rough.

"Everyone's moving to the cloud. Data centers are hot. But Kayne managed to screw that up." Zeke made his par putt. Andrew holed out for a double bogie.

Zeke stood over his ball. "Watch out, Andrew. I wouldn't be surprised if Kayne is in trouble with his current holdings. The cannabis market peaked late spring, early summer. It depends on when he got in, what his occupancy rates are, and how much he's levered. God knows who loaned him the money this time, but I am not surprised given the euphoria around cannabis after recreational legalization.

What happens to Kannawerks if he goes belly up?" He wacked the ball down the fairway.

The first thing he noticed on his car was the grime. It reminded him of the dust carried by the Scirocco winds out of Africa, blanketing Rome with a red film that encrusted surfaces after the rains fell in the summer afternoons. Except he wasn't in Rome, and there was no rain . . . just the wind and heat of late October in the High Desert, whose intense and voluminous dust shrouded his car in yellow filth that seemed impossible to eliminate.

He threw his clubs in the back, sat in the bucket seat, and slammed the door. His mind raced. *Theo's assessment of the industry. Terence, the landlord, is a thief? What if he goes bankrupt? And what did he and Charlie have to talk about?*

Maybe it was nothing; maybe he was still hungover. Or maybe this was a legitimate feeling he should listen to because he'd sworn never to work *with* a friend or *for* a friend again. The last time he intermingled the personal and professional, it didn't end well. It was one of the primary reasons he was now in the High Desert. He gunned the car out of the lot.

If you're going to have a heart attack, make sure it happens in a public place just before rush hour, preferably in front of a pharmacy with a cop one block away and San Francisco General a straight shot down the 101. Andrew's cofounder, Simon, had collapsed on the street from a massive heart attack. Dead. Or at least he had been dead. For a while.

The cop performed CPR less than one minute after the coronary, the pharmacist applied a defibrillator, the ambulance was there in five, but the blockage was so great that it took them twenty-two minutes to stabilize the heartbeat. Simon was placed in an induced coma for one week, prognosis negative. If he was going to come out of it, he'd be a vegetable unable to function. He'd need to be hand-fed, diapered, and cleaned. Daily.

The first words Simon uttered when he came out of the coma were, "Is Andrew near?" They'd worked hard to build the company, and whether they'd wanted to or not, they'd grown even closer throughout the process. Simon was home in three weeks. Andrew went to visit and left despondent: Simon's eyes were sunk back in his skull, like an addict's after a hit of fentanyl. Face gaunt and gaze ashen. He couldn't remember his password.

Simon recovered and was deemed "neurologically intact." It was a miracle, they said. After two months, he was back at work doing what he did best . . . what *they* did best. Andrew was relieved. They were gaining traction and winning deals.

And then one day Simon wanted Andrew out. They had met for lunch in San Mateo prior to a quarterly board meeting.

"You aren't CEO material," he had said. "You don't know how to scale the company. You're incompetent."

Andrew leaned in, incredulous. "Incompetent? *I* recruited the board, *I* raised the seed round *and* the Series A, *I* negotiated all the complex deals—"

"I'm taking this to the board. Today." Simon put down the menu and sat back.

"What are you going to tell them?"

"Everything, starting with the company financials. They're shit." He opened his laptop and started typing.

"We've been profitable for the last two quarters! The last deal alone—"

"We won that deal because *you* gave them something under the table." Simon was still typing, not making eye contact.

"You're fucking crazy. Where's the proof?"

"I don't need proof. And you hired that idiot COO without telling me."

"You interviewed him and gave him a thumbs up! He ran a company ten times the size of ours, *he* brings the expertise to scale!" Andrew threw a twenty on the table and stood up.

"Plus, the team can't stand you. And clients don't trust you."

The ordeal lasted one quarter. It consumed them at the expense of clients and their personal lives—Andrew's personal life.

If a heart stops beating for six minutes, there is the potential for severe and permanent brain damage, with the organs soon to follow. What happens when the brain is starved of oxygen for twenty-two minutes?

Simon had survived against all odds. But something had snapped within him, and an irreversible paranoia had set in.

The board voted to liquidate Simon, but he stood firm. They were at an impasse, or so they thought, until one day Simon walked away. It was over just like that. He resigned from the company and the board, signed away all his rights, which as a cofounder, he had many. The last Andrew heard was that Simon had moved to Anchorage, Alaska, and had found a consulting job at Elmendorf Airforce Base. Something involving revamping their search-and-rescue systems for downed aircraft and compromised vehicles in the Alaskan wilderness.

After three months of chaos, the company was in a downward spiral. Talent fled. Clients didn't renew their licenses. Competitors swooped in and won all the fifty-fifty deals, even the eighty-twenty deals.

And then came Ulrike. They met just as Andrew's personal, Diana, and professional, Simon, storms collided. Ulrike was an analyst with their largest client, who had committed to a multiyear, multimillion-dollar contract, thereby giving Andrew's company a lifeline. Ulrike was proactive, smart, young, and she had energy. She worked with Andrew on the platform deployment, knew how to navigate the organization, helped decipher the politics, and socialize the solution. Team lunches led to solo lunches, which led to drinks, which led to dinners, and then climaxed in breakfasts.

The client terminated the contract for cause, the tryst forbidden in the twenty-first century. Careless. But Andrew didn't care. He knew it was over. It was the last nail in the proverbial coffin. He tried to slow the downfall and scoured the Valley for funding alternatives, but after exhausting all cash-infusion options, after contributing all of his savings, including liquidating his Russian Hill condo, after enduring the talent and client exodus, and after discovering that the only prospective buyer was led by an alcoholic CEO with a string of bankruptcies on his resume, Andrew admitted defeat. He paid out one month's severance to the remaining employees, held onto enough cash to take care of future liabilities, returned what was left to investors, sold the intellectual property for one dollar to one of the investing venture capital funds, and shut down the company.

He never saw Ulrike again.

After he reviewed his scorecard over the first sips of a double vodka, he opened the sliding glass door and stepped out onto the patio. On the drive over, Charlie had left him a voicemail: "Dinner with Max on Wednesday. Be there with bells on." Andrew would confirm in the morning. As he nursed his drink and observed the waxing moon, the wind gusted, causing the mesquite to shed its feathery leaves on the ground. Andrew peered over the stucco wall. The rattler skin was gone.

CHAPTER 13

"How late were you at the party?" It had taken Andrew most of that Sunday morning to muster up enough courage to call Renée.

"We ran out of food at eleven-thirty. I looked for you before we left, but you were in an intense conversation. I didn't want to disturb."

"You should have." He leaned on the patio door and watched a golfer hack his ball out of a bunker.

She finally broke the silence. "What are you doing for lunch?"

"No plans."

"There's a great Ramen place in Claremont, round the corner. Or I can meet you halfway if it's too far—"

"I'll come there," he said, a bit too eagerly. "Gets me out of the High Desert. It will be the first decent dining experience since I got here." *With you*, he didn't add.

The wind seemed to carry the now-clean Porsche—he'd spent the morning carefully washing it—over the Cajon Pass and down the winding, split, 15 freeway with the Los Angeles Basin extending before him. Without a cloud on the horizon, there was a blinding glare bouncing off the unfolding tarmac. He eased into fourth gear and used the engine to slow into the curve and accelerate through its apex, his back pressed into the seat.

Renée was waiting for him outside the restaurant. Andrew leaned in and kissed her on the cheek. On instinct. He stepped back, uncertain, and she caressed his cheek with her hand, letting him know that was okay. Andrew held the door open, and she parted the silk curtains.

They sat in a booth. A red pitcher filled with ice water was on the table next to a stack of translucent plastic cups. A bento box filled with assorted jars and spices sat against the wall.

"The owner is from Hokkaido," she said. "One of the sons opened this location. He's the one in the kitchen standing over the finishing station and adding the accoutrements. They're known for their broth."

"Ramen's all about the broth," Andrew said.

"Spoken like a true expert."

"I spent a lot of time in Tokyo with my last company."

"I've always wanted to go to Japan."

"When you do visit Japan, you won't want to leave."

"From Japan to Adelanto. Why would you ever trade the Far East for the High Desert?"

"It's a long story."

"I've got time."

"Let's just say, I didn't have a choice." He reached for two plastic cups. "Charlie called me at the right time, as if he sensed I needed help."

"How'd you guys meet?"

"We were in high school together, in Bangkok."

"You worked in Japan, you lived in Thailand, I won't even guess where you were born."

"Rome."

She stared at him. "The plot thickens."

"What about you?" He didn't want to give her a chance to ask more questions.

"What about me?" She sat back.

"You're not from here."

"Why do you say that?"

"I don't know. I can sense you're not a SoCal native."

"There aren't a lot of SoCal natives." She picked up the laminated menu and stared at it.

He took her cue and did the same. "What do you recommend?"

"Tonkotsu Ramen. Extra pork, extra egg."

"Done. And an Asahi Dry," he said.

Renée pressed a small white button on the corner of the table. A chime sounded in the kitchen. The Japanese waitress materialized, smiling at Renée like an old friend. She took their order and handed the ticket to the chef.

The chef wore a black bandanna and a spotless white apron. He stood over a battery of ramen bowls, his hand swiftly moving over them as he barked instructions to the line cook overseeing the noodle station.

"The chef seems intense."

"Only when he's in the kitchen. Otherwise, he's soft-spoken, real nice. He helped us set up the taco truck. Working in a confined space, you need to be as efficient as possible." She poured water into the cups and took a sip from hers. "No compromises, always striving for perfection, which according to him, he will never achieve."

The waitress brought over the beers.

"Here's to . . . what?" Renée said, as she poured the beer.

"New beginnings," he said.

"New beginnings."

They both took healthy sips.

The chef barked a command. The waitress brought over two steaming bowls.

Andrew sat back and admired the contents of his bowl. He picked up an egg with his chopsticks, placed it on the spoon, and pried it open. The custardy yolk oozed over the edges and fell into the broth. He slurped it down whole, and then stirred the noodles with the chopsticks.

"Wait until you taste the pork," she said, as she grabbed a few strands of noodles with her chopsticks. He watched her suck them into her mouth, finishing with a loud slurp.

"Nice technique," he said.

"It's the only way," she said.

Andrew followed suit. The noodles were firm, yellow, and bouncy. They proceeded to loudly inhale more noodles. He was getting a kick out of watching her. She placed the egg on her spoon, mimicking Andrew, dunked it in the broth, and sucked it into her mouth, the yolk running down her chin.

"I'm such a mess," she giggled, and wiped her mouth with the napkin. Andrew felt his face flush.

She put her chopsticks down and sat back, satiated.

"Almost as good as your tacos," he said.

"Please," she said, "tacos are just—"

"Amazing."

"—an escape from a career in which I'd become disillusioned. You know the story."

"I know the story."

"Let's focus on the here and now," she said.

"Like how you got into tacos."

"Lina is my college roommate's sister. She was raising money to invest in her own food truck and had learned the ropes by working with her cousins in San Diego. Her Aunt, Tía Matilde, runs a great restaurant down the street from here. They're her recipes. It was supposed to be temporary for me. I helped Lina with the plan and scouted locations in LA. I was going to go back into management consulting or maybe into industry, financial services. Yep, *that's* what I did before tacos. It was interesting at first, but the weekly commutes to places like Madison, Wisconsin, took their toll. Every week, Sunday to Friday, eighteen months, for one client. Have you ever flown there in the winter?" She sighed. "Why am I going on about this?"

He could listen to her all day.

"Anyway, the taco truck was a way for me to take a break. Recharge. But I'm loving it, three years later."

He realized he was staring at her. He wanted to reach over and caress the mole above her lips, but instead he reached for the white button and the waitress came over, picked up the empty bowls, and placed the check on the table. The restaurant was now full, bustling with a young crowd and a line out the door, with the din of the customers making it hard to have an intimate conversation.

As Andrew reached for the check, a small boy broke away from the line and ran up to their booth, stopped, and stared at Renée. He smiled. Renée caressed the boy's head. He couldn't have been more than two. The boy ran back toward a waiting couple.

"He's a cutie," she said.

"They're all cute," Andrew said.

"As long as they're not mine."

"Why is that?"

She sighed. "There's too much anger in the world. And I don't want that responsibility. It wouldn't be fair—to them."

A moment passed. "Do you want to go for a walk?" Andrew asked.

They spent the rest of the afternoon in the nearby botanical garden, the conversation meandering. Andrew hadn't been on a date in seven years and wasn't sure about the protocols, what to do, or what he *could* do. Renée seemed content in learning more about Andrew, soaking up information on his diverse upbringing, the Italian side of his family, and his travels, while Andrew couldn't get any insight into Renée's personal life, as she deflected with questions of her own.

"I've had a great time," Renée said.

"We'll have to do this again," he said. He leaned over and kissed her. She held his hands and pressed into him.

CHAPTER 14

The phone rang. *5:00 a.m. Who the—*
"Álvaro is dead." It was Mike.

Andrew jumped out of bed. He put the phone on speaker.

"They found him this morning in the desert. Apple Valley. Fidel identified the body and said it was not an accident."

"Who's Fidel?"

"The brother of Álvaro."

"How does he know it wasn't an accident?"

"Because his head was crushed. Fidel recognized him because of the tattoos. The coroner said Álvaro died on Thursday morning. His body was dumped. He was killed somewhere else from where he was found."

Andrew walked to the window and stared at the moonlit mesquite.

"Are you still there?"

"Sorry, I'm processing. First the dead guy near the factory, now Álvaro? I show up and people drop dead?"

"Yes, this is not right. Even for Adelanto. I mean, bodies appear occasionally, that is common in this part of the Mojave, but it is usually drug- or gang-related, or some poor guy stuck in the desert with no water. It has never impacted the factory. I will talk to his wife and his brother, find out what we can about the circumstances."

"Find out the meaning of those snakes, scorpions, and crosses tattooed on his arms."

"Maybe it is a gang thing."

"He was the nicest guy. You said so yourself."

"Maybe he had a past, and it caught up to him. I do not know. I hired him from the agency. They do the background checks. He was one of the few people who learned fast." He paused and then said, "I mentored him. I want to know what happened."

"We'll need to tell the team now."

"I will call Ashlee, Kyle, the leads. News travels fast in Adelanto."

"Tell them it was an accident. I'll call Charlie." Andrew hung up, threw the phone on the bed, and then it rang again. Charlie.

"You heard?" Andrew asked.

"I just got off the phone with that fucking sheriff's detective."

"What the hell is going on?"

"I don't know. All I know is that she's coming to the factory today. Give her what she needs, then get her out. Keep the team focused."

"Second time in a week she's coming to the factory."

"Second time it's none of our business. *You* stay focused, Andy."

Andrew jumped in the shower, downed what was left of the cold, left-over coffee, then drove to Adelanto.

The protesters were out again with twice the number of people standing opposite the jail. There were more signs this time, not just for Porfirio but for Alexis, Ruben, Pedro, and other names that he couldn't make out. There was no bonfire, just kerosene stoves heating pots of coffee, maybe tea. The same megaphone woman, standing like a superhero, shrouded in the faint glow of yellow lights, led the call and response chants: "Queremos . . . Justicia! Queremos . . . Justicia!" He wondered whether they had found Alexis or Ruben or Pedro in the desert.

"How did they take it?" The workers on the packing line were filling tins at half their usual pace. The music was off.

"They're in shock," Mike said.

"Charlie called me. Detective Morales is coming over this morning."

Mike shook his head. "The cops are not going to do anything. Álvaro is just another 'dead immigrant' like the one last week. Did they ever figure out what happened to him? No. They never find anything if it's an immigrant."

"How's Álvaro's wife?"

"Fidel said she is not speaking. He is with her now."

"Nothing we can do until our sheriff friend gets here." He dropped his backpack. "What's the status on the depositor?"

"Out until Wednesday. I took the machine apart. The pistons have to be replaced."

"Was there debris in the pistons?"

"Red, sour cherry, from when the machine froze. It could not be anything else."

"And we can't use the new machine or replace the pistons ourselves?"

"I called the maintenance company. They are bringing the new parts. Easy fix, but they said not to swap parts, something to do with the configuration. Without their help, it would take a couple of days to set the parameters, so we wait."

"We can reverse the schedule and make the classics until Wednesday."

"We will need to juggle some inventories to make sure we do not stock out, but I think we will be OK."

Lost in thought, Andrew stared at the schedule on the white board. "How do pistons warp?" he finally asked Mike.

"A sudden temperature change, a blockage. Wear and tear. I could not tell what caused the seizure and whether or not we started the machine with them already bent."

"What would cause a sudden temperature change?"

"I do not know. There is a process that we follow to shut the machine down. Before we clean the pistons, we have to wait for them to cool down, below seventy degrees Fahrenheit. I will have to ask Ashlee, and we can also review the factory floor video recordings and check to see that operators followed standard operating procedures—SOPs—when they cleaned the machine."

"Assuming those cameras even work."

"Yes, good point."

Detective Morales and Deputy Buy-A-Vowel showed up just after 9:00 a.m. They interviewed some of the operators and ran through the video feeds. They watched Álvaro grab his wallet and mobile from his locker, don his jacket, walk out of the factory at 4:00 p.m., which according to Mike was late since Álvaro was always out the door by 2:30 p.m., get in his red '67 Mustang, and drive through the main gate, never to be seen again. The detective said they'd found the spotless, locked Mustang in a residential community by a public park about a mile down the road. Someone had called it in.

"The car keys were found on the victim," Detective Morales said.

"Maybe he was visiting someone," the deputy said. He'd been quiet until then. "Maybe that someone's husband wasn't happy about it and—"

"We don't know anything yet," the detective said, cutting him off.

"Álvaro was a dedicated husband," Mike said.

"You never know with these people," the deputy said.

Detective Morales glared at the deputy.

Mike said, "Álvaro was more passionate about cars than women."

The deputy donned his cap. A thin, sly smile appeared momentarily, and then it vanished.

"We're going to interview residents where the car was found—see if they have video cameras we can access." The detective then said to Andrew, "Speaking of cameras, get your offline ones fixed."

She walked out the door without acknowledging the deputy. The deputy followed without saying a word.

"Álvaro would never see another woman," Mike insisted.

"Maybe it has to do with cars. Maybe he was buying car parts, maybe he was buying a car, maybe he was selling a car and—"

"And what? They could not agree on a price?"

"Maybe some shit went down."

"Not with him."

"Maybe he got mixed up with the wrong people. It's not that hard around here, or so I've been told."

Andrew went to the lunchroom to get some work done. Ashlee was seated at one of the tables, sipping coffee and scrolling through her phone. "Do they know anything?" she asked him.

"We checked the video cameras. They show Álvaro leaving the facilities. Nothing unusual." He sat down and opened his laptop.

"God knows what he was mixed up in. We're in a prison town whose second major industry is weed. Add in the cartels, and you've got a helluva trifecta."

"Cartels? Here?"

"They own most of the illegal facilities around here: Apple Valley, Victorville, Adelanto, all the way to Baker, if not to the Nevada border."

"How do you know all this?"

"My boyfriend is a guard at FDN. Hears all sorts of stuff from the other deputies and the inmates."

"What does he have to say about the protests? Each time I drive by, they get bigger."

"He said they're fueled by pro-immigration groups, you know, liberals." The word "liberals" came out of her mouth as if she had just swallowed a whole lemon.

"They're asking for justice," Andrew said.

"No comment," Ashlee said.

"No comment? A dead immigrant was found in the desert last week."

"Hey, I work in Adelanto, I'm neutral when it comes to immigrants."

"There's a bunch of other names on those placards."

"If it wasn't for legal immigrants, we couldn't be doing what we're doing."

Andrew closed his laptop.

"Who else would be willing to work for thirteen dollars and fifty cents an hour? I'm all for the legal ones," she said.

"Álvaro is not an illegal immigrant. What the hell happened to him?"

"What can I say? Shit happens all the time out here."

"That seems to be the standard answer."

He picked up his laptop and walked out of the room.

"Whatever happened to Álvaro is none of our business," Charlie said.

"What about the depositor?"

"Pistons are warped. Wear and tear."

"Can we produce?"

"Wednesday."

"Fucking amateurs."

That was kind of harsh. "Charlie?"

No response.

"Charlie, what's up?"

"Did they find anything on the video feeds?"

"No. But the detective said we need to get the offline cameras fixed."

"The working cameras, I mean. Did they find anything?"

"Nothing out of the ordinary on the video. Don't blame the operators."

"If we can't run the machines, if we keep blowing them up, we're fucked."

Andrew pumped the brakes. "I'll work with Mike and fix the situation." They hung up.

He downshifted into third. Stop-and-go traffic in this heat wasn't good for the car. He reached over the steering wheel and tapped the temperature gauge. It didn't move. He wasn't ready to get stuck in the High Desert waiting for a tow truck driven by an ex-con salivating at the sight of the Porsche. *No, thank you.* He switched on the radio. Static. Neither the KROQ nor NPR signals reached over the mountains, his vintage antenna not helping. He fiddled with the tuner knob, but all he got was religious programs, irate talking heads, guitars, and trumpets. He killed the radio. After a half hour, the traffic let up and he stepped on the gas, careful to stay within reasonable range of the speed limit. If Deputy Buy-A-Vowel was doing his job, he shouldn't be around here anyway.

CHAPTER 15

The next morning, Andrew took the back roads through Palmdale to avoid the clogged freeways. The two-lane "highway" cut through swaths of dust, rocks, and moribund Joshua trees. He drove through neighborhoods filled with single-story ranch homes whose decrepit once-white wooden fences contained accumulating debris: rusted hulks of cars, wheelless tractors, motorcycle carcasses, cages teaming with chickens, and parched grass.

It was fast cruising once he reached the Antelope Valley until he merged with the 5 and was enmeshed in LA gridlock, with drivers putting on makeup or sipping coffee while staring at their phones, talking, texting, and watching videos mid-navigation. He maneuvered through the traffic avoiding distracted drivers, took the Hollywood Bowl exit, and reached his destination a few minutes later.

He'd booked an Airbnb after perusing the hotel options within walking distance of the Kannawerks office. The hotels were either too expensive, too run-down, too noisy—according to the reviews—or too far. The unit was located in a vintage apartment complex that reminded him of a Bogart movie he'd seen recently.

He parked on the street, grabbed his bags, and walked through a cavernous entryway that opened up into a communal courtyard.

Lawn chairs and tables were strewn about. Each wing of the complex had its own open staircase leading to the second floor. A vacuum cleaner hummed.

Andrew left his suitcase in the lightless, musty apartment, and headed out in search for coffee. He walked up to Santa Monica Boulevard and ignored the Blue Bottle Coffee on the corner, instead opting for a coffee shop a block farther down. Freeze Frame was housed in a small standalone, off-white, wooden shack. He ordered a large coffee that was handed to him before he paid the barista. Andrew had an aversion to coffee chains: stand in line, wait for hipsters to order a frothy, overpriced, bitter concoction that smelled and tasted like a wet dog soaked in gasoline, and in essence was just a caffeine-delivery mechanism. He wouldn't even bother going in to order an espresso, even if he was desperate, for fear of having to wait. It negated the whole point: *espresso*.

Coffee in hand, he checked the office address and took a left on Laurel Avenue. He walked past two- and three-story apartment complexes, a few small bungalows with nice yards, and larger more modern homes with minuscule gardens. Trees lined the avenue. He crossed Romaine Street and walked to the designated address. It wasn't an office building. It was a house, and an expensive one.

With a white armored truck parked out front.

He pocketed his phone. As he walked into the driveway, he was met by Ish straddling an Indian Scout, the same bike he had seen parked in Helendale. A passenger was on the back whose arms barely reached around Ish's frame.

"Yo, Andrew," Ish said. "Meet Rosie."

Andrew nodded at the passenger. She let go of Ish's heft and timidly waved. Her visor was up. She had large, black eyes, pale, white skin, and a shy smile.

"I'll be back in an hour. They'll keep you busy until then." Ish started the ignition and the bike rumbled to life. Rosie held onto Ish, and they rode off.

The house was surrounded by a white fence at least eight feet high. He walked up the driveway past a beige vintage Bronco of OJ fame and rang the buzzer. He heard a click and pushed the gate open. He was greeted by a large man blocking the front door. He was clad in a blue shirt, dark-gray pants, black combat boots, and a bulletproof vest. A semi-automatic bulged from a holster on his right hip.

Andrew wondered whether or not he was in the right place, even though it was the right address, and Ish was just here. But why was a SWAT commando standing guard, and what was an armored truck doing parked out front?

"How can I help you?" the man said.

Andrew hesitated. "I work here," he finally said.

"Wait," the man said calmly. He stepped inside and shut the door. Andrew waited less than a minute. "Go ahead," the man said, holding the door open. And what Andrew saw explained the reason for the guard and the armored truck: piles of cash. Bricks of US dollars. Greenbacks spread out on a large table. The sun's rays emanating through a skylight shrouded the scene in a surreal, angelic glow.

"Glove up," Ethan said to Andrew. He wore a surgical mask, as did everyone else.

Andrew stared aghast at the spectacle unfolding before him. Boris, the EVP of Risk Management, took prewrapped bricks of twenties out of cardboard file storage boxes and passed them to Orinda, the CFO, who carefully unwrapped the purple money band from the bricks and placed the bills in a sorter. The bills shuffled like cards in Vegas with red counters rapidly incrementing. Orinda took out the counted bills, replaced the money band around the brick, stacked it on the table, and typed the amount into a spreadsheet on a laptop. Two women who Andrew had never seen before sat quietly on opposite sides of the table staring at the events.

It was like a scene out of *Narcos*, or *Scarface*, except they weren't in Mexico, or Medellin, or Miami. They were in West Hollywood—a residential neighborhood populated with couples, families, students, actors, and models, with law enforcement patrolling the streets and open-air restaurants around the corner serving sushi, organic salads, and vegan fare.

"Just another Tuesday?" Andrew said.

"Grab a mask," Orinda said.

"For this?"

"The last time we had novices help us, they didn't mask or glove up. One of them ended up in the ER with a respiratory ailment, and the other was down for the count in less than a day. You wouldn't believe the crap that's on these bills."

"Where can I help?"

"Pair up with Ethan."

Andrew slipped on blue nitrile gloves and donned a mask. Ethan walked him through the instructions and introduced him to the auditors—the two quiet women—and then Andrew passed pre-wrapped bricks to Ethan, who unwrapped them, and placed them in another sorter. After the count was done, Ethan rewrapped them, placed them in the appropriate pile, and recorded the amount. Errant piles of fives and tens were counted and placed on the opposite side of the table.

"I thought we used a bank," Andrew said.

"We do," Orinda said, "but some retailers are still all-cash, and they're unbanked, so we collect the cash and sort, count, and deposit the cash ourselves. Before we banked, we stored everything in a vault and paid everyone in cash."

They continued the counting and stacking for the next hour. Not much was said.

"Fit ten bricks of twenties in a large plastic bag, seal it, and then stack them in the boxes," Orinda said when they were done.

They finished placing the bundled, counted cash back into the file storage boxes. Orinda synched with the auditors and signed the receipt, then they loaded the boxes onto the armored truck and watched half a million dollars drive away.

"We'll start with Bodhi," Ish said, as he lit an unfiltered cigarette.

"People still smoke those?" Andrew asked.

"I do," Ish said, pocketing the lighter.

"Open the window, man," Ethan said, waving the smoke away.

The handle creaked as the window slid open. "I like the ride," Andrew said, observing the vintage interior of the Bronco.

"It was my dad's," Ethan said. "He bought it off the lot in the early seventies. Took meticulous care of it." He put down the sun visor. "Fucked up what happened to Álvaro." He ran his hand along the dashboard. "He loved this car. I let him drive it the last time I was in Adelanto. He couldn't stop talking about it. He knew everything about the make and model. Said he was going to buy one and refurbish it."

They sat quietly, observing the crowds, suits, and casual attire lined up outside restaurants along Santa Monica Boulevard. Valets were busy collecting tips and parking Mercs, Jags, and Porsches.

Ethan made a right on La Brea, parked in an open lot, and paid the attendant. They footed it back up to Santa Monica past a packed diner and a vintage clothing store with bright dresses displayed in the window. The noon heat was bearable—not as oppressive in Hollywood as it was in the High Desert.

Ish pressed the buzzer on a single-story, bright-green, brick building. It was devoid of windows, an iron gate guarding the only door in the facade. The sign next to the door read, HOLLYWEED. A faint smell of pot hung in the air.

A middle-aged man sporting horn-rimmed glasses opened the door, his leathered face pierced with assorted ornaments. "Come on in, friends."

"Armaan Bodhi, budtender to the stars," Ish said. They stepped inside and walked by a uniformed security guard. Bodhi closed the door behind them.

"They're the bane of my existence. But they pay the bills."

The store was well lit, making up for the lack of direct sunlight. An air conditioner hummed, and soft spa music emanated from speakers arranged throughout the store. A few customers meandered past the glass displays. One of the displays was filled entirely with Kannawerks gummies.

"Nice layout," Ish said.

"You're our number one edible, mostly. Mostly." Bodhi gestured to competing displays one cabinet over. "This stuff sells well but doesn't taste as good as yours. Yours." He seemed to have a tic, a tendency to repeat himself.

Budtenders stood behind the displays and counters, providing advice to browsing customers on what strain, product, and form was best for a targeted mood, ailment mitigation, or entertainment goal.

After Ish explained the reason for the visit, Bodhi led them on a brief tour. "There's a spectrum, spectrum, on the cannabis effect scale," Bodhi said. "On one end of the scale, you've got relief—pain, PTSD, anxiety, depression. On the other end, you've got *get fucking high*. And *just chill* in-between. Unwind. Unwind."

"Take our products," Ethan said. "Our current lines span anxiety relief up to the unwind spectrum. With the new Sleep line, we're extending the anxiety relief even further, and making it fast-acting so that people can relieve stress or fall asleep faster. Alta will just get you high fast. No need to inhale."

"And," Bodhi said, "you're not worried about targeting the hardcore users—the weed veterans—with your products. Most of our volume comes from flower, pre-rolls, and concentrates, but edibles are the fastest growing sector, sector, for new cannabis users—first-time or occasional users, the equivalent of social smokers and casual drinkers, searching for an alternative to chilling out and having fun. In a social setting, setting. They try it, they like it, without the stigma of being labeled pot smokers. Edibles make weed socially acceptable."

"What about the whole vape backlash?" Andrew asked.

"All the more reason to regulate the market," Ethan said. "People died because they inhaled tainted cartridges—which was, unfortunately, good PR for legalized cannabis. If you buy from a regulated dispensary—buy tested product—there is no risk."

"There's still some risk," Ish said. "But it's manageable."

"Hey, Bridget!" Ethan said to a blond woman standing behind a pop-up display booth in a far corner of the dispensary. The entourage walked over. The woman was dressed in a tight-fitting blouse and miniskirt, standing next to a redhead with painted-on yoga pants and a loose sweater.

"What have we got here?" Ethan asked. On the desk were two bowls labeled "undosed," filled respectively with yellow and red gummies.

Ish plunged his hand into one of the bowls and brought out a handful.

"It's our new Chillah line, ten milligrams per pop," Bridget said.

Ish held them out to Andrew and Ethan.

"Guaranteed to get you high and keep you there longer," she said.

Ish put a few gummies in his mouth. "Apricot?"

"New recipe, new flavors," the redhead said.

"Undosed, you said." Andrew tentatively ate one.

"What makes them so special?" Ethan asked.

"The dosage, the strains, the terpenes," Bridget said. "Nothing else out there like it."

"In here, maybe. Out there," Bodhi gestured at the door, "get in line, line."

"We're having a get-together this evening," Ethan said. "Come by after nine. Tell your friends." He gave Bridget a hug.

"Those guys don't know what the fuck they're doing," Ish said under his breath as they walked to the exit. "I don't know how they're still in business."

"As soon as we raise money, I'm going to gut their entire sales-and-marketing team and bring them on board. Bridget's already in," Ethan said, waving at her.

"Bodhi, what did you mean by, 'Out there get in line?'" Andrew asked.

"The minute a new product is launched, you'll find a copycat on the illegal market within a week at less than half the price, if it's good."

"What about a copycat product that's on the illegal market before the launch of the legit one?"

"What do you mean?"

"Pink Dot. A gummy with a similar formulation to our new, yet-to-be-released lines is already out on the illegal market."

"I've heard of it. I didn't know it was similar to yours, yours."

"In a perfect world, the government would get their shit together and enforce the law. But we're in California. We live with the consequences and work through them," Ish said.

"And why we need to raise money so that we can outspend the competition," Ethan said. "That's why our products are front and center, the first thing you see when you walk in the door. We buy our way into the dispensaries' premium shelf space. Right, Bodhi?"

"Right on."

"And we provide incentives," Ethan continued. "A one-dollar spiff for every Kannawerks tin sold goes straight to the budtender."

"Jesus," Andrew said. "A dollar? That's ten, twelve margin points per tin."

"Don't worry about it," Ish said. "We compete through the budtender while we build consumer loyalty."

"It's not sustainable," Andrew said. "You're telling me that we take away the spiff and our product never makes it to the customer?"

"Our competitors would pick up the slack in no time."

"It's worth it," Ethan said.

"This is insane," Andrew said. "How can anyone compete? On one hand we buy ourselves prominence until the money runs out, on the other we have an illegal and competitive product—Pink Dot—that is a clone of the ones we're banking on for growth, which is cheaper and just as effective."

"Forget about the illegal—"

"Where can we get our hands on some Pink Dot?" Andrew asked Bodhi.

"Don't know."

"An underground bodega?"

"Dee may still have contacts," Bodhi said. "I don't interact with that world as much anymore."

"We're going there now," Andrew said.

"That's out of our way. We've got some other folks expecting us," Ish said.

"Change of plans. I've seen what I needed to see."

Ish nodded and said to Bodhi, "See you tonight?"

"Sorry, man. An actor wants to start his own line of weed products, and he's coming by with his entourage to do 'research.' I may not make it out of here tonight, tonight."

"Anything for free weed," Ish said.

The traffic slowed them down as they continued on Melrose, passing taco trucks, whose smell of recycled oil and burnt meat wafted into the car, hole-in-the-wall dives, and an assortment of tattoo and piercing parlors. Ethan was careful to avoid the occasional vagabond crossing the street with bags in tow.

After they passed under the buzzing Hollywood freeway, Ethan parked in front of a single-story gray building. An unlit Open sign hung askew. A cluster of cypress trees partially obscured an adjacent home that had pockmarked blue stucco walls and board-ed-up windows.

The door to the gray building was ajar.

"Balthazar," Ish said, as a man appeared. "What's going on?"

"Check it out," Balthazar said. He was a broad-shouldered, African-American man with a thick moustache, wearing a short-sleeved, white, button-down shirt tucked into pressed beige slacks.

Shattered display cases were everywhere. Glass littered the floor. A door in the back hung on one hinge, its handle and locking mech-anism pulverized.

"What the hell happened?"

"Smash-and-grab yesterday. Took all our product," a statuesque African-American woman said as she floated into the room. She gave Ish a hug. Her short, cropped hair was streaked with gray, contrast-ing with her glowing, youthful skin.

After introductions were made, Ish said to Dee, "We just came in to ask . . . we should leave," Ish said.

"Nonsense," Dee said. "We haven't seen you in a while. Plus we have something for you." She led them to the back of the store. Buzzing fluorescent lights cast a pale glow on the surroundings as they walked past the hanging door, with Andrew bringing up the rear. A tall safe stood in the corner, unopened.

"Second time in six months," Dee said.

"Seriously?" Ish said.

"Running an all-cash *legal* weed dispensary in this part of town means we have a bullseye on our back, and we can't compete with what's sold on the street. There's no enforcement out *there*, and cops don't give a damn in *here*. They still haven't shown up."

"I can relate to the cops," Ish said. "They've spent their entire career enforcing the law against drug possession, drug use, dealing, and now they're expected to protect the legal stuff. It ain't happening overnight."

"No, it ain't," Balthazar said.

"What about the insurance?" Ish asked.

"The agent had the gall to ask me if I was high and forgot to lock the door. Said maybe it wasn't a break-in," Balthazar said.

After a brief silence, Dee said, "You caught us on a bad day." She punched numbers on a keypad and pressed her thumb on a biometric reader. The safe popped open.

More piles of cash.

Dee grabbed two bricks held together by thick rubber bands, scribbled something on a ledger, and handed the cash and a receipt to Ish. "What's this?" Ish asked.

"What we owe you guys for the month. Couldn't get it to you yesterday, for obvious reasons."

Ish stared at the money in his hands. "I don't want to go around town with this. We'll swing by later to pick it up—"

"Take it now. We have to deal with this mess today. Who knows what's going to happen." She shut the safe.

Ish handed one of the bricks to Andrew.

Andrew hesitated, surprised.

"We'll be fine." Ish stuffed the cash in his pockets. Andrew did the same.

Ish glanced at Andrew and said, "The reason why we came . . . we're trying to find underground gummies called Pink Dot. Maybe you know of a bodega around here."

"I've never heard of Pink Dot. Have you?" Dee asked Balthazar, who shook his head.

"Have you tried Ray?" she asked Ish.

"I was hoping you wouldn't say that," Ish said.

"Ray would know."

"I know he would know."

"I thought you guys—"

Ish didn't wait for her to finish. "What are you going to do?"

"Give it one more try, if the insurance comes through," Dee said. "Otherwise, we're shutting it down. We'll find something else. We ain't going back. No matter what happens."

Ish hugged Dee and then Balthazar.

"It's a shame," Dee said, as she held the door open. "It was never like this at the beginning. There was respect for what we did, respect for patients, for customers."

As they walked back to the car, Andrew glanced over his shoulder to make sure no one was watching or waiting.

"Not much they can do," Ish said. "None of the guys with equity licenses are profitable. Most of the licenses were given to small guys to give them a chance to pull themselves out of the street and make a legitimate living. The intentions were there, but the bias is entrenched, and the system is structurally flawed."

CHAPTER 16

Gridlock. After several minutes of stop-and-go, Ethan veered off through Echo Park, taking surface streets before making his way down Bunker Hill. They parked in a lot on Spring Street just past Eighth.

There was some back-and-forth on what to do with Dee's cash. Walking around downtown LA with over two grand in his pocket did not seem like a wise idea to Andrew. Leave it in the car? Not safe, especially in a '70s Bronco.

"Be cool," Ish said. "We'll be fine."

They walked up to a multistory, windowless carcass, a sign advertising, LIVE IN THE HEART OF DTLA, ONE AND TWO BEDROOMS, NO FEES!

"Shit," Ish said. "It's gone."

"What's gone?" Andrew asked.

"Ray's place. I haven't been here in a couple of years. Progress, I guess." He lit a cigarette. "I'll make a few calls."

Andrew and Ethan crossed the street and entered a local roastery, passing a ragged self-talker at the entrance. He started to scream. At them. At someone. They ignored him and ordered drip coffees, a couple of blueberry muffins, and a slice of pound cake. They sat at a corner table and devoured the pastries as they watched Ish, the phone pressed between his shoulder and ear, throw down his half-smoked cigarette, and light another one. After several minutes, Ish waved for them to come out.

"Nothing. No one's talking. And I don't have Ray's new deets."

A scruffy, barefoot man wearing tattered jeans and a tank top stood on the corner. He smiled and motioned with his hand for a smoke. Ish walked over, offered the man a cigarette, and lit it. They talked for a while. And then the man pointed west. Ish handed him the pack of cigarettes.

"This way," Ish said. The pungent smell of urine and feces followed them as they passed storefronts, alternating between open for business and boarded up with plywood.

As they waited for the light, people started shouting across the street. A crowd huddled around a prostate body. A cry for help. A police car materialized with sirens blaring. A cop jumped out of the cruiser, shoved the crowd aside, crouched over the inert body, and jabbed a syringe into an exposed thigh. An ambulance rushed past, deafening them in the process.

Moving on, they walked past more storefronts in disarray and approached a black metal door inset into a two-story building. No locks or handles or knobs, just a video camera above the door. A tent city festered in a lot across the street. Other than the encampment, nobody was visible for several blocks.

"Shut off your phone and don't ask any questions," Ish said.

Andrew complied and nervously felt the cash in his pockets. Ethan checked his phone.

Ish rapped his knuckles on the door.

They waited.

A commotion developed in the lot. Andrew snapped to attention when the door opened.

A man wearing a beige, silk kaftan stood in the doorway. He was Andrew's height and had a trimmed beard, straight, shoulder-length brown hair, a strong, aquiline nose, and dark eyes.

"What are you doing here?" the man said.

"Hey, Ray," Ish said.

"Who's this chucker?" Ray said, glowering at Andrew.

"Can we come in?" Ish asked.

"He's too clean."

"He's cool, Ray."

"I'm expecting someone."

"It won't take long."

Ray hesitated, then stepped aside. They entered a small, dark foyer lit by a solitary light. Ray shut the door behind them, punched numbers on a keypad, and a second door clicked open.

They followed him into a long, low-ceilinged room. As Andrew's eyes adjusted to the soft amber light, the room took shape: red-and-green velvet couches, ottomans, and armchairs, ashtrays and vaporizers strewn on low tables that intermingled with standing brass hookahs, and an array of exotic bongs and pipes occupying shelves behind a long wooden counter. A large, hovering, all-seeing eye was painted on the far wall and presided over the room.

Ray sat in a plush armchair while the rest of the crew sank into one of the couches. A couple was asleep, spooning on a couch in a corner. A bald, thick man stood guard at the only other exit, whose door was obscured by a beaded curtain.

"You still fishing off Catalina?" Ish asked Ray without making eye contact.

"When I have the time."

"I thought that's all you had, nothing but time." Ish fidgeted in his seat.

"The boy," Ray said. "It's been a year now. With Irene."

A pause. Then Ish extended his hand at Ray. "Congrats, man."

The bald man took a step forward. Ray waved him off. Then he pulled out a vape pen from the folds of his robe, took a drag, and leaned back. "What are you doing here, Ish?" Ray asked again.

"I need a favor."

"Why should I do you a favor?"

"I need some intel, Ray," Ish said in a conciliatory tone. "I'm not connected to the market anymore."

Ray waved the bald man over and whispered something in his ear. The man parted the bead curtain and disappeared. "Go on."

"Pink Dot. Have you heard of it?"

"Who hasn't? Stuff's flying off the shelves."

"No shit," Ish said.

"The right price for the performance." He took another drag of his vape pen. "Why you asking?"

"It's the same as a new product we're releasing. We want to check it out, see how it compares to our stuff."

A brunette wearing a purple bikini top and matching miniskirt came in carrying a tray. She placed glasses filled with ice on the table and poured from a pitcher containing a red liquid. Ray leaned over, picked up a glass, and sipped.

Ish grabbed a glass and took a lengthy gulp.

Ethan picked up the two remaining glasses and handed one to Andrew. It smelled like spoiled cabbage with a hint of cranberry. They both pretended to take a sip.

"Do you have any left?" Ish asked.

"Yeah."

"I'd like to buy three, four bags."

Ray put the glass down, stood, and disappeared behind the curtain.

"What is this place?" Andrew whispered to Ish.

"Ray's at the higher end of the scale in terms of clientele and product quality."

"Clientele? There's no one here," Andrew said.

"It's early," Ish said. "See those two? I bet they've been here since yesterday."

The spooning couple hadn't budged.

"Day is night, and night is day in here. As long as guests don't cause trouble, Ray lets them hang. It's his style. You just have to gain his trust, become part of his network."

Ray sat down and placed four translucent stand-up pouch bags the size of a classic iPhone on the table. Pink Dot was printed in black, cursive letters on the small bags, with, "20 pink lemonade gummies that will get you high fast and keep you there," in small fluorescent green type below it. In the bottom corner was printed, "10 mg THC per gummy, oh my!" The round, pink, sugar-coated candies seemed to float in air.

"How much you selling these for?" Ish handed a bag to Andrew.

"Fifteen bucks a bag," Ray said.

"And how much do you pay?"

Ray took another hit from his vape pen. "Seven."

"What's the active in it?"

Ray paused and then with impassive eyes said, "Distillate."

Ish rubbed his beard and glanced at Andrew, who had already run the numbers in his head. Theo was right. One dose of Pink Dot costs less than a quarter of an equivalent Kannawerks dose.

It didn't make sense. How could these guys be making any money? Sure, the active ingredient was cheaper by at least half—if not less, given the glut of cannabis in the market—but add in labor, packaging, rent, distribution—*and how the hell did they make it fast-acting and long-lasting, assuming it was?*

A melodic chime interrupted Andrew's thoughts. The bald man checked the video monitor and shut the main door behind him.

"Where you getting this from?" Ish asked.

Ray frowned. "I can't tell you." He sipped his drink.

The bald man came back in and shut the door. Andrew watched him place two semi-automatic handguns on top of a tall metal safe next to the entrance. He unlocked the safe, placed the guns inside, locked it back up, and opened the main door. Two Asian men walked in. They wore identical gray suits over black T-shirts and gold chains around their thin necks. They sat on an empty couch. The bald man leaned over and again whispered into Ray's ear.

"How much do we owe?" Ish asked, as he picked up the remaining bags and put them in his pocket.

"It's on me. Next time don't come back unannounced." Ray walked them to the door. He checked the video monitor and pressed a button. The door clicked open. Andrew followed Ish and Ethan out into the blinding sun and heat.

"What the fuck was that all about?" Andrew asked, as they walked back to the car.

"Ray and I go way back. He stayed, I left."

Andrew was now curious. "Why'd you leave?"

Ish picked up his pace.

"You mentioned a network. What network?" Andrew continued.

They walked past a couple of slow-moving pedestrians. "Ray runs one of the top weed exchanges in LA," Ish finally said.

"As in market?"

"No, not a market. He controls access. Strictly weed, none of the hard stuff. He's a matchmaker between buyers and sellers at the wholesale level; that's his network. Ray takes a big cut, but he guarantees distribution. The retail is the small stuff. It's a front. Keeps the cops off his back. They leave the little guys alone. In their eyes, Ray's a little guy."

When they reached the car, Andrew said, "I'm beginning to wonder what we're doing here."

Ish glanced at Ethan.

"I still can't believe the scale and quality of the illegitimate stuff—you've got dirt cheap product that may or may not make you sick or kill you, but it's a risk users are willing to take. It's all about the price per high. And the packaging—the consistency," Andrew said.

"It's the cost of doing business."

"Tell me how that works, Ish. If this is really fast-acting and long-lasting like our stuff, how can we compete?"

"Andrew," Ish said. "We have the opportunity to do some good with this thing by providing a safe product, by working from the inside . . . especially by working from the inside, because there are still many issues with legal weed. On the one hand, the corporate suits hawk products to customers they don't understand and make marketing claims that are misleading, and on the other hand, there is weed's adverse impact on some of the people that need it the most—people like Rosie—who don't realize the potency of today's strains, which can cause all sorts of dependency problems for some users.

"Legalizing cannabis gave me and others who have been operating in the black market legitimacy and created the opportunity to educate and help. Its positive impact is undeniable: helping terminal cancer and AIDS patients deal with their final days; helping people manage chronic pain; enabling an army veteran to work again, raise a family, and help them deal with trauma." He lit a cigarette and exhaled. "Until legalization, few of the people who needed it most had access to safe weed. Now that it's regulated and tested, people know what they're getting, without having to hide in the shadows or rely on people who don't give a shit about anything other than money. We coexist with Pink Dot and everything else that's illegal because together with all the taxes, regs, and hype, it's part of the cost of doing business, and legal weed is still a good business."

"We'll see after we get these tested. Why don't you give me the bags?"

"I'll hold on to them for now and give them to you at the house." Ish patted his pockets. "And remember that regardless of all the bad shit, the legit market is still a multibillion-dollar market in California alone. Granted, you need to know what you're doing and execute. Which we are. Anyway, this is why we're here, to answer your question."

"If Pink Dot is crap, great," Andrew said, stepping in the car. "But if it's anywhere close to our product, then we have a big fucking problem."

CHAPTER 17

A few budtenders were already mingling with the Kannawerks team in the dining room when Andrew walked in. He continued past them through a pair of French doors and stepped out onto a raised wooden patio. A massive Buddha sat in the middle of a fountain, water cascading down its enlightened face. A manicured lawn extended outward with a white fence visible through a wall of flowering bougainvillea. Chill music played through the speakers sprinkled around the patio.

Not a bad setting for an "office."

The session started, as predicted by Ethan, after 7:00 p.m. Andrew sat to the side and wondered, after what he'd just seen and learned that day, if all of this was just a monumental waste of time and resources.

The budtenders were a mixed bunch, half female, half male, mirrored like they were getting ready to board the Ark. Together with the Kannawerks marketing-and-sales team, they sat in a circle around an unlit firepit spread out on couches, chairs, large pillows, and beanbags, throwing ideas back and forth. The budtenders tried some of the undosed new flavors, while Claire led a discussion on how to optimize positioning against the competition. She facilitated the session, engaging her audience and offering insights that the budtenders didn't seem to comprehend. Ethan chimed in occasionally to guide the meeting, as the budtenders had a difficult time staying focused, given how stoned most of them already were when they showed up. This was further augmented by generous helpings of complimentary Kannawerks gummies. Andrew even saw a couple of the budtenders down *whole tins* of dosed gummies. One takeaway from the session was that for many regular, long-time users, 100 mg was the minimum dose required to elicit a high. Ethan later provided context: he ate edibles regularly, but anything over 20 mg had him stuck to his couch for hours.

Andrew wasn't sure what the team was trying to achieve with the budtender session. There was more focus and preparation in kindergarten. This was a freeform "brainstorming session," manifesting as full-blown chaos.

"It's for us to develop relationships with budtenders and to learn what the competition is doing," a young woman said as she sat next to Andrew. She must have sensed his confusion. "Want some?" She held out an open tin of gummies.

"No, thanks," Andrew said.

"You sure? Makes the session go by faster," she said, popping one in her mouth.

"I'd rather have a drink," he said.

She moved closer. "I'm Laine."

"I'm Andrew," he said, nervously.

"I know."

"I'm still getting my bearings," he said. He stared at her bare feet whose symmetrical, manicured toes were ensconced in thin, silver rings.

"I'll get you that drink," she said.

"Vodka," he said.

"Soda?"

"Neat. Cold."

"Be right back," she said, and he watched her glide inside. She wore a long, flowing tank-top dress that hugged her body, skimmed her ankles, and accentuated her curves, long legs, and the thin outline of her thong.

A couple brought out candles and placed them on the tables, and the outdoor lights flickered on, which immersed the buddha in a colorful glow.

"Here you go," Laine said and handed the drink to Andrew. "Belvedere. Hope that's OK."

He took a sip. "Perfect."

She sat down next to him.

"Tell me, do you get actual intel from these sessions?" he asked.

Her leg touched his. He noticed her wide eyes, the high cheekbones, her full lips, and auburn hair cascading over her shoulders.

"It depends," she said. "In the last one, we found that a competitor was moving down the fast-acting path, which made us accelerate product development."

She smelled nice.

"Sometimes we get nothing out of it except a good time." She laughed a cute, lilting laugh.

Andrew smiled. "And you hold these, what, every two weeks?"

"Just about, yeah. It depends. It's hard to stick to a schedule." She giggled.

"How many have you had?" Andrew nodded at the tin on the table.

"Oh, just a couple," she said. "Just to get going. Like I said, makes the session more enjoyable. I don't like to smoke or vape. *Yech.*"

"Yep."

"You just have to be careful with gummies. They don't hit you right away."

"I heard."

"Our new lines are a game changer, though," she said, staring into his eyes, as if she'd found a lost treasure. "No idea how they work, but they *work.*"

She fell back on the couch and twirled her hair. Her hand found Andrew's knee.

She couldn't be more than twenty-five. Andrew cleared his throat. "So, how long have you been with Kannawerks?"

"Six months." She leaned into him again.

"What did you do before?" He could feel the sweat forming on his forehead.

"I was a bartender. You know the resort, Las Ventanas?"

"In Santa Monica?"

"I worked in the restaurant and the lobby bar. I met Claire there, and she introduced me to Kannawerks. I needed a change. I'm part of the field marketing team, you know, in store pop-ups, product give-aways, swag. It's fun!"

The doorbell rang. She patted Andrew on the knee and went inside. He wiped the sweat from his forehead with his hand and checked the time; it was just past 8:30. As if on cue, Laine walked out with pizza boxes in her arms followed by other young men and women carrying bulging paper bags. They set the items down on the table surrounding the firepit, and the budtender session terminated abruptly as everyone reached for a slice, a wing, a handful of fries, or a taco. Andrew waited for the press of bodies to disperse, then grabbed a slice.

"Don't spoil your appetite." Ethan brought his joint down and exhaled away from Andrew. "We're going to dinner after this, but I first need to chat with a few of these budtenders before I lose them for the night," he said.

"Where's Ish? I thought this was his thing?"

Ethan shrugged. "He disappears sometimes."

After the food had vaporized, a few of the budtenders left while the rest stuck around to party. A group had laid out yoga mats in one corner of the lawn. They sat in lotus pose, hands in prayer, their chanting a muted droning. Candles flickered around them. Another group had made themselves comfortable on the couches and chairs around the firepit, passing around joints and gummies. A couple started making out on the porch, while another couple, holding hands, meandered to one of the bedrooms and shut the door.

"Having fun?" Laine whispered in Andrew's ear. She had snuck up behind him.

"Sure, yeah," Andrew said. *How'd she find me?*

"It's just getting going."

"I can see that. Where's that vodka?"

She took his hand and led him past the couple, then through a throng of bodies into the kitchen. A few people were mingling by the stove with drinks and joints in hand. Laine opened the freezer and took out a bottle of Belvedere. She poured a generous amount into Andrew's glass.

She grabbed his arm and led him to the couch by the entrance. Someone had lit a fire, and the flames lapped the logs, embers glowing red. Andrew took a sip of his drink. They were alone.

"What'd you think of the session?" she asked.

"I'm not sure what to make of it, but I don't think we accomplished much."

"Yeah, this one wasn't such a good one." She flipped her hair over her shoulder and moved closer. "Where are you staying?"

"You mean tonight?"

"Yeah, I guess, that too." She smiled. "But I meant you moved from San Francisco, didn't you?"

"Came down a week ago. Staying near Adelanto, for now."

"I heard there's nothing there but prisons and weed factories."

"That's true. I'll figure out a long-term situation."

"You should move in here. There's always room; no one ever stays here."

"Sounds nice," he said. "But I need to be near the factory to make sure things stay on track with the new product launch."

She had a relaxed expression on her face, her eyes soft. *Must be the gummies kicking in*, Andrew thought.

"You're so all business," she said suddenly, as if coming out of a trance.

"What about you?" Andrew countered, "Where do you live?"

"Melrose, down the road." And then, as if seeing him for the first time, "You're cute." She leaned over and smelled the nape of his neck. Before Andrew could move, she lifted her head and licked his ear, pressing her breasts against him. Andrew shuddered, her scent ensnaring him. He wasn't sure what to do. She *was* gorgeous—hot actually, in that dress and with those lips—but this was an employee, grounds for dismissal and lawsuits. Ulrike came to mind. When he started to say something, she kissed him hard on the mouth, her tongue probing for his. Andrew tasted sour cherry. They kissed for what seemed like an eternity, Andrew trying to minimize bodily contact while Laine aggressively probed him with her hands. In one liquid movement, she threw one leg over his and straddled him. Now she was on top, grinding and pressing. She started to moan, softly at first, then louder, more forceful, with purpose. She grabbed his hand and pushed it under her dress. His fingers touched her soft skin, and as he moved his hand, he realized the thong had disappeared.

This is insane. He gently pushed her back and untangled his tongue. Her lips remained parted, eyes half-closed, and her breasts moved with the rhythm of her breathing and moaning. She stopped moving her hips.

"Laine, listen," Andrew said. She smiled and tried to kiss him again. "Laine," he said, more firmly this time. Rational Laine wasn't here right now. She was batshit stoned.

"Hi," she said, smiling.

"Laine, I can't—"

"What?"

"I shouldn't . . . we shouldn't."

"Why not?" she purred and lay her head on his shoulder.

"Laine," he said, lifting her head. Her eyes were starting to close, and he realized no matter what he said, it wouldn't register. He gently eased her off of him and laid her on the couch, pulling her dress down, and covering her legs. She giggled as he placed a pillow under her head. "Laine, I have to go now," he said.

"You're cute," she said again. She smiled and closed her eyes.

Andrew grabbed his drink and walked outside. The situation had degenerated. The would-be yogis had paired up and were helping each other reach and hold their asanas, using the weight of their bodies and hands to push, caress, and squeeze, heads nuzzling in necks, breasts, and crevices. Couples kissed and groped in the fountain, while others were entangled and contorted on the couches by the firepit, in the far corners of the yard, and on the porch. Revelers mingled with drinks and joints in hand, oblivious to what was happening around them. And the music wasn't loud enough to mask the moans, groans, and cries emanating from the bedroom windows.

"Come on, let's go." Ethan tapped Andrew on the shoulder.

"Is it always like this?" Andrew asked.

"It usually doesn't transform into a full-on orgy," Ethan said. "Laine seemed to get the better of you."

"She was higher than a weather balloon. What is *in* those gummies?"

"They say ingested cannabis works as an aphrodisiac, especially for women. I'll attest to that."

They found Ish in the driveway checking his phone. "Let's go, we're walking."

The restaurant, modeled on a 1920s New York speakeasy, was packed. Ish motioned to the bartender and said, "Another round."

Andrew asked the bartender for a recommendation. He was polishing a glass, and with his sculpted features, Andrew had him pegged as an actor, an aspiring actor, or a model-slash-actor, working the bar to make ends meet. A dime a dozen in Tinseltown.

"Sazerac."

Andrew motioned with his hand to bring one on. He stared past the bartender into the floor-to-ceiling mirror, the reflections of the dining patrons distorted by the bottles of rye, whiskey, and scotch stacked up to the ten-foot ceiling. All the clientele were tall, spectacular human specimens ranging from thin to voluptuous. The men and boys wore chinos and polos, some with bright, colorful shirts, and a few sportscoats. The women and girls were adorned in slinky, strapless dresses, tight jeans, and minimalist blouses. Blahniks, Louboutins, and Pradas rounded out some wardrobes. Welcome to Hollywood.

Andrew picked at a basket of fries, while Ish downed another old-fashioned. He said to Andrew, "I went to see some old friends. About Pink Dot. You got me going on this thing now. None of them had any left."

"Did you find out how long it's been around?"

"July. It appeared out of nowhere. And they all said no way this shit's getting made in a garage."

"Should we be worried?"

"I don't know."

"Why didn't we just go see Ray in the first place?"

Ish put down his drink and ordered another old-fashioned. He sat his large frame on the stool and waited until the drink arrived. He took a long sip.

"Why'd you leave?" Andrew asked.

Ish faced Andrew. "This shit stays here, OK?"

"OK," Andrew said.

"Like I told you, he stayed, and I left. Before rec weed became legit, he and I were in the thick of it. Ray and I ran the joint together. We were tight. And we were killing it. Ray sourced product, and I sold it to underground bodegas and medical weed dispensaries—co-ops. We managed to hold our own in a competitive and dangerous environment. Then two problems converged." He took another sip of his drink.

"The first was Irene—Ray's girlfriend, now the mother of his child. The second was the excess—money, drugs, alcohol: dangerous for someone like me. Irene came onto me strong one night. It wasn't the first time. I had deflected all her prior advances—and I'd told Ray, told him she got frisky past a certain drink/joint threshold. Anyway, that night I ended up banging her. I don't know how it happened. But it happened.

"I was already drinking heavily, taking a ton of shit, going on benders, and many times I would wake up and not remember anything—I'd find myself in unknown houses, apartments, and warehouses and in some cases, even outdoors without knowing how I got there. Often. Way too often. And one day I woke up in the ER, blood all over, unfamiliar faces staring down at me, a needle in my arm, a tube up my nose. They said I had taken a bad fall—they weren't sure how my head had split open." He rubbed the scar on his temple. "They found me face down in the gutter. Grade three concussion. It was fucked up. I was fucked up. One of the nurses sat with me all night, waking me up every two hours, making sure I didn't pass out or die.

"The minute I was conscious enough she lectured me. My blood-alcohol level had been twice the legal limit, she said, the rest of my bloodwork was of concern. She asked me whether I was on any meds. I said weed; she said no not that kind; I said I wasn't on any meds. She said I needed to be and that I had to stop drinking." He lifted his glass. "I haven't." He took a sip. "She was nice, and she took care of me for the rest of my stay. And when I was discharged, she asked me for my number, I gave it to her, and now I live with her. She saved my life. Deb's her name."

Andrew raised his Sazerac and drank.

"Ray and I parted ways soon after the incident. He bought out my share of the business for next to nothing—I had no leverage—but it was enough to tide me over while I went through rehab. Tone down the drinking. I couldn't stop, no way. Deb had me see a hypnotist. The weed helps."

The bartender came over and put a basket of pretzels in front of them. "You guys want anything else from the kitchen? Last call for food."

"We're good," Ethan said.

Andrew grabbed a pretzel. "And that's when you got involved with Kannawerks?"

"Yup."

"I heard Kannawerks was started in a garage and burned through millions in less than a year. Is that how this industry started, with cowboys and stoners who had nothing better to do than burn other people's money?"

Ish waved the bartender over. "Bring us two fries, one wings— large and hot—and a chicken liver toast." He said to Andrew, "You heard of Abe?"

"Max's grandson. I'm having dinner with Max and Charlie tomorrow night."

"I'd stay away from bringing up Abe to either of them."

Andrew shrugged.

"Abe did start the whole thing in his garage, and he did burn through the cash—maybe the only thing he was really good at," Ish said. "Abe barely made it out of high school, but his mom—a serial entrepreneur who made millions before she was thirty—managed to get him into one of the Ivy League schools; she's an alumna and on some board. He graduates and gets fired from his first job within a month. He drifts in and out of companies that Mother has connections with until she runs out of options, so he joins a cousin in California who works for a crypto startup."

Andrew polished off his cocktail. "How do you know all this?"

Ish put a hand in Andrew's face, motioning for silence. "Abe talks when he drinks. He moves to Silicon Valley, and the startup goes nowhere, but Abe learns all about crypto, and when the startup folds, he comes up with an idea for cannabis banking services built on the blockchain."

"Doesn't sound so dumb. That would solve a lot of problems."

"Wait," Ish said. "He comes up with the idea after an ayahuasca retreat in the Los Gatos hills where he bonds with a shaman. The shaman, Kai, complains to Abe about the need to carry wads of cash received as payment for his spiritual services and used to buy drugs for his ceremonies and other festivities. This was in 2016, when recreational cannabis was on the ballot in California.

"They say if you can dream it, you can do it, but to transform vision into reality you need money and the ability to execute. The money was the easy part; Mother funded junior's latest endeavor. But they couldn't execute—Kai was always high, and Abe had no grounding in reality." He sipped his drink. "They built a hell of a website, though."

"You know," Andrew said, "they should replace METRC with a system built on the blockchain, a distributed ledger, issue tokens to track cannabis, from seed to sale—"

"Don't get distracted. They pulled the plug on the crypto deal and started making edibles with the money they had left over, and it was a good thing they did, because Prop 64 passed and all of a sudden there was pent-up demand—legal pot for the masses. In the weed market today, first-mover advantage doesn't get you much, it's all about execution, but in 2018? The first to market with a quality, accurately dosed product that delivered on its promise to both the experienced and novice weed user was going to win."

Their food appeared.

"This is when I came into the picture." Ish grabbed a handful of fries and stuffed them in his mouth. "I got out of rehab and searched for something to do on the legal side. I met Abe and Kai at a weed conference in Santa Cruz in early 2017. They were peddling weed-in-fused gummies. I tasted them. They weren't bad, and they had a nice texture. I was impressed.

"I listened to their story, and I asked them basic questions: What actives are you using? Where are you sourcing your cannabis from? Where are you having it tested? What's the dosage variability in each batch? They answered the first one. Distillate. They figured, 'It's drugs, man. Who the fuck cares?'

"But the agencies were there to prove that they could regulate a federal Schedule 1 drug at the state, county, and city levels, collect their taxes, and ensure people wouldn't get sick, die, or skim off the top. They were not going to fuck around. And these guys were clue-less. Have some fries."

"I'm good."

Ish grabbed a liver toast. "Most of what I'd done prior to 2017 was on the dark side with Ray," he said, with his mouth full, crumbs flying. "But then I became somewhat clean, enjoyed my weed in moderation, and only wanted to deal with legal shit: product, people, dispensaries. Because I know the ins and outs of legal *and* illegal weed, Abe asked me to join the team. By the time New Year's Day 2018 came around, we were one of the few edible companies that had everything in order to sell recreational gummies through legally licensed retailers. More than half of the existing dispensaries had to shut down because they weren't in compliance with the new regs. And other edible manu-facturers couldn't get their products dosed accurately or get clean COAs. The shelves in the licensed dispensaries were basically empty; they had flower, pre-rolls, vapes, some chocolates, and a smattering of gummies that tasted like shit. Nothing was at scale in the edibles category. We filled in the gaps. Our product tasted great, it was dosed accurately enough—we figured out how to game the system with how we comprised batches—and became number one in California edibles in the first two months of recreational legalization. Abe was the new king of legalized weed. Riding the momentum, he raised thirty million dollars in the first quarter of 2018, with his mother leading the round, and alongside his grandfather, Max, brought in the other investors."

Ish downed his drink. "And in less than one year, Abe had burned through most of the money. Max—a ruthless fuck—fired his ass, family ties be damned." He slammed his empty glass on the table.

"It was . . . is . . . like the Wild West," Andrew said.

"We were the fucking posse riding into town. We were pioneers on the weed frontier like modern-day Gold Rush forty-niners."

The fries, wings, and chicken liver toasts were gone. Andrew stood up to make room for some of the dining patrons who had stayed behind and mingled at the bar. He was having a hard time focusing, and he perceived a faint throbbing behind his left eye.

"Could I get some water, please?"

The bartender placed a glass on the bar and filled it.

"Sit down. You'll feel better," Ish said. Andrew sat on the edge of the stool.

"Last call, guys," the bartender said. It was almost 2:00 a.m.

"One last round?" Ethan asked.

"Let's do it," Ish said.

"Hey, how do you guys—"

"What?" Ish said.

"Joints, gummies, old fashions . . . old fashioneds . . . don't you guys ever stop?"

Ish smiled, "When it's time."

"OK," Andrew said. "But last one."

"Where you staying?" Ish asked.

"Romaine and Orange something."

"Grove?"

"Grove. Yeah."

"Around the corner. We'll get you home," Ethan said.

The drinks materialized together with the check.

"I got this," Andrew said. He fumbled for his money clip.

"Sit down," Ish said. He threw his card on the check.

"You don't have to—"

"Drink up," Ish said.

They were the last to leave the bar.

Where was he? That's right. Romaine, like the lettuce. West Hollywood. "How the hell did I get back?" he said out loud. It slowly came to him: Ish and Ethan escorting him to the apartment, walking through the darkened courtyard, climbing an infinite staircase, fumbling for his iPhone, punching in the code, punching it in again, and Ethan and Ish carrying him to the bedroom.

He sat up. His head pounded as if clamped in a vise. He tasted bile. He lunged to the bathroom and hurled his dinner into the porcelain toilet. He braced himself with his hands on the sides of the bowl. His head hung below the rim, and he kneeled, hurled, and spat out remains of the burger, wings, and fries lodged in his teeth. He dry heaved violently, retching several times. He reached for the tap and splashed cold water on his head and face. He rinsed his mouth. He retched again, coughing, spitting, wondering if he was waking up the neighbors, his eyes staring into the dark pool below him, the awful, gripping nausea refusing to leave. He spit again. The acrid, sour smell enveloped him. When the impulse to vomit finally subsided, he lay on the cold floor for a while, relieved, waiting for the room to stabilize, not finding the strength to lift his head. He finally got up and drank some water. He grabbed the sink for support, and after a long pause, tried to lift himself to his feet. After several attempts, he gave up and crawled back to the bedroom on all fours, mustering enough strength to climb into bed, and as he did so he glanced at the alarm clock: 4:57 a.m. What was on the schedule today? He couldn't remember. Fuck it. He placed a foot on the floor to stop the spinning and closed his eyes.

CHAPTER 18

Andrew downed Advil and guzzled coffee and water all morning, knowing he should put something in his stomach, but the thought of food only induced dry heaves. He mustered enough strength to head back to the West Hollywood "office" in the early afternoon. It was not the day to delve into strategy and numbers—budgets and revenue by region, dispensary, sales rep, and product line—but he figured it was better to stimulate the few brain cells he had left before his dinner with Max than lie on the couch and watch classic movies while moaning in pain.

After pretending to pay attention to Ethan's growth plans—Ish hadn't shown up—he got in the car and called Charlie.

"You don't sound too good," Charlie said.

"I'll be fine."

"You better be. How was the ride-along?"

Andrew exhaled, the whiff of his own breath making him gag. "It generated more questions than answers about this industry, this Pink Dot—"

"Andy, come on, man. We talked about this."

"Charlie, the illegal side is more dominant than I had thought. There's no enforcement, and the incentives, or rather the disincentives, make it a challenge for people like us to succeed."

"You're not planning on sharing these insights with Max, are you?"

"No."

"Our numbers will go up with the new lines. There's room for all of us." A muffled woman's voice could be heard on the line.

"Charlie—"

"Don't fuck this up, Andy. Without Max leading the round, Kannawerks is fucked."

"No shit."

"Focus on the positives."

"I know how to handle investors." But by now the reality and scale of the illicit market was a constant presence hovering in the back of Andrew's mind.

Crossing Wilshire, he merged onto La Cienega and cut through the hills dotted with rhythmically bowing oil pumps. He briefly hit the inevitable crawl of the 405, then took the Rosecrans exit. As the car went over the hill, the ocean appeared before him, a vast mirror extending into the horizon, the sun inching its way down, the blinding rays reflecting off the sheen. He parked and checked into the hotel. It was just past 5:00 p.m., giving Andrew enough time to dump his bags in the room, pop two Advil instead of the usual four since his headache was subsiding, and walk to the restaurant.

The warm wind buffeted his back as he walked down Manhattan Beach Boulevard. He was early, so he continued past the restaurant to the beach, where the calm Pacific stretched below him. As he walked along the pier, he noticed something strange: the beaches were bare. The azure lifeguard towers and the beach volleyball courts stood solitary on the sand. No surfers were on the water. A lone paddle boarder, standing upright, headed south, and the crisp, clean ocean reflected the setting sun like a looking glass. He stopped on the pier and observed the seemingly endless beach extending to the Malibu coastline. And he noticed that the planes landing into LAX were approaching from the west, the first time in the two decades that he'd been coming to LA that he had seen this. Planes usually approached from the east and landed into the wind.

The Santa Anas were back.

CHAPTER 19

M ax Aurel extended a pale, skeletal hand. He had a narrow, almost fleshless bald head and a sliver of a moustache sitting atop thin gray lips. A cane leaned against the window with an intricately carved white pommel in the form of a Corinthian column seamlessly merging into a thick, ebony base.

"That's a beautiful cane," Andrew said.

"Narwhal," Max replied.

Andrew sat next to Max—forget the sweeping views of the Pacific behind them, Max seemed to prefer a clear view of the restaurant patrons before him, the bar and tables filled with products of the southern California lifestyle: tan, trim, fit bodies, mostly enhanced, and mostly for the better, wearing casual evening clothes that captivated a viewer's gaze.

But Andrew's gaze rested not on the patrons but on the guest seated across the table. Manuela, Charlie's fiancée: straight, black, cascading hair framed an elegant face with large, brown eyes, and a faint smile on her lips.

"*Sei Italiano*," she said to Andrew.

"*Si, a metá*," Andrew responded, giving Charlie a subtle nod.

The three of them already had cocktails before them. Andrew opted for water. The waiter brought over pre-ordered appetizers: a platter of oysters, crudo, and grilled octopus. Max squeezed a lemon over the oysters, and fighting a slightly rhythmic tremor in his hands, used a small fork to cradle the mollusk into his mouth, careful not to get any juices on his tie. As he ate, he held court, going on for a while about the dietary benefits of oysters and other seafood as long as it wasn't squid or shrimp. His diet, he said, was optimized to counter his many ailments. Which ones he didn't say.

They ordered entrees. After the sommelier brought over a bottle of Montrachet and filled the glasses, including Andrew's, Charlie asked Andrew to share his thoughts on Kannawerks.

Andrew adjusted his chair, folded his napkin, and opened his mouth to speak.

"How would you deploy the funds if we raise ten million?" Max asked.

Andrew glanced at Charlie in a manner that let him know he had this. "Our products are solid. And they're going to get better with the introduction of the new lines. What we need is scale, better distribution, more shelves, more retailers."

Max helped himself to the last piece of crudo.

"So how do we scale? How do we win over budtenders? This is where we'd deploy the capital. If we merge with a company that *already* has distribution and reach, we wouldn't need to raise as much and could focus on executing at the retailer level, blanket the state, and sell in all seven-hundred-plus dispensaries."

"What if we raise twenty?" Max said. "What else would you do?"

He wanted to say, *Get the factory the fuck out of Adelanto*, but instead took the indirect route. "Invest in innovation," he said. "Develop a product portfolio to target a broader set of need states. Target a high-end demographic that cares about the provenance of the strain they consume. Deliver at least one new product per quarter. Introduce a vegan formulation. And expand beyond gummies."

"Can't we innovate at that pace now?"

Charlie cradled his glass, staring at Andrew.

"No. We have neither the capacity nor the talent."

"But aren't we launching the new lines in a month?"

"We are, but from what I understand—"

"Why can't we build on that momentum, after the new products are out the door?" Max drummed his fingers on the table.

"That was a three-month effort," Charlie interjected.

"Which is not sustainable," Andrew added. "The whole process—performing the research, iterating on the formulation, testing the product—is single-threaded through one employee. Kyle."

"Hire more talent," Max said, irritated.

"That's the thing, Max. There is no talent in Adelanto, and no one wants to move there. It's not the most pleasant of locations to live and work in. And if we find someone that's any good, by the time we train them, they leave."

"Build an R and D center elsewhere," Max said. "In LA, close to the universities."

"We could, but it's more efficient, more agile, if the R and D team is co-located at the factory. That makes the process faster as we can test and iterate the new formulations at scale without having to duplicate facilities and equipment."

"So, you would scout out alternative locations for an all-in R and D and manufacturing facility."

"Yes."

Max said to Charlie, "He figured all this out in less than two weeks?"

"I told you he was good."

"Go on," Max said to Andrew.

"Relo options include Santa Barbara, Los Angeles, Long Beach, and Santa Rosa," Andrew said.

"Don't go north. Stick to Southern California. LA and Long Beach. Have you checked out Northridge, Palm Springs?"

"Not yet."

"You should."

Their entrees came. Max immediately sent back his plate, annoyed, berating the waiter for the overcooked salmon. He wasn't as infirm as he looked.

Andrew stared at the whole baked branzino before him, herbs and lemon rind protruding from its belly. They waited until the server replaced Max's entrée, and as they ate, listened to his lips smacking in either satisfaction or disgust, Andrew couldn't decipher.

Then Max asked Charlie for an update on the financing.

Charlie poured more wine as he went through the investor candidates—he was heading directly to LAX after dinner to catch a flight to San Francisco to meet yet another prospective investor. Max wanted to know how much had been verbally committed and whether an M and A event was realistic. They agreed that the M and A letter of intent, if that was an option, had to be in by the end of the year. That gave them two months.

They continued sparring, Max throwing financial questions and Charlie parrying before being pummeled with a follow-up. When dessert arrived—a soufflé for Manuela—it was like the bell had rung to end the round. But from the tone of the conversation, Andrew knew he had done his job, giving Max confidence that with him on the team, Kannawerks stood a chance even though he was a cannabis novice.

A flare was lit at the end of the pier. The light illuminated the night sky, and the swaying palm trees cast shadows on the Strand. They exchanged goodbyes. Charlie took off for the airport, Max left in his chauffeured, black Lincoln Navigator, and Andrew and Manuela stood alone on the street corner.

As they started walking, Andrew caught a flash of the Navigator in a darkened store window, the red taillights and the elongated reflection giving the illusion of a hearse floating above the pavement. He watched the SUV vanish over the hill.

"Charlie didn't say goodbye," Andrew said.

"He's like that," Manuela said. She took out a pack of cigarettes and lit one. "Want to grab a drink?" She offered him the pack.

He declined the pack and accepted the drink. He wasn't ready to head back to the hotel.

They crossed Highland and Manuela led him to a bar that wasn't too crowded. Andrew held the door open for Manuela, and as she entered, he observed her charcoal, tailored pant suit, the blazer unbuttoned to reveal an elegant white blouse exposing a thin silver and emerald necklace. He hadn't focused his full attention on her until now. They settled at a high table near the bar.

"Andrea is better, yes?" she asked.

"*Certo.*"

They ordered drinks—a Negroni and a vodka tonic—and fell immediately back to their native tongue. The world they came from. Italian childhoods, summers at the beach, weeks in the countryside, surrounded by cousins and aunts and uncles, flirting with the seaside neighbor, picking fruit off trees and bushes, helping in the kitchen. And after the Ferragosto holiday, the end of summer, dreading school, the downhill slide toward the monotony of fall, the extended family dispersed back to their respective towns and cities, and Andrew returning to the Far East.

When he asked her what had brought her to Los Angeles, she responded by motioning around the low-lit room with her glass. "Can you imagine a woman of my age doing this in the sexist patriarchy of Italy?"

By *this* she meant the room, the space; she'd designed it. Andrew had sensed the Italian influence when he walked in: the hanging Flos lights, the blue-gray slate floors, the Alessi cocktail glasses and cutlery. Simple and subtle elegance.

"I had no connections, and in a country where there's limited room for meritocracy—'Who do you know? Ah, you work with

so-and-so'—there's no way I could have a business of my own. I don't
have to answer to anyone. Most importantly, I don't have to answer
to a man."

"Leaving Italy saved my mother. She escaped the calcified norms."

"I don't remember my mother *ever* being happy." Manuela sipped
her Negroni. "She was stuck in a listless marriage in a small town
on the outskirts of the big city, in my case Florence, catering to her
husband and daughters, and never having time for herself. My first
vivid memory of her is her watching a film on TV. She was crying. I
even remember the film, it was *The Apartment*, you know, the one
with Jack Lemmon and . . . I forget—"

"Shirley MacLaine."

"Bravo. Yes, her. My mother did that often. Watch old movies
alone, when she wasn't running after me or my sister, that is. I didn't
want to end up like her, trapped in a relationship devoid of love, relegated to domestic help, and pretending that nothing was amiss with
the husband," she said. "Don't get me wrong. My father loved us. In
fact, I have him to thank for being here, but my mother suffered in
silence." She finished her drink and ordered another round. "Thanks
to contacts my father had in the United States, I spent my high school
junior year in Southern California as an exchange student, and I
swore that I would one day come here. I've been here for almost ten
years. California is home now."

"A land that's fair and bright, where the handouts grow on bushes,
and you sleep out every night."

"What's that?"

"It's a song I heard in a movie once. I don't think it's about
California. But it could be. A land where, 'the hens lay soft-boiled
eggs, the farmer's trees are full of fruit, and the barns are full of hay.'"

She studied him with a wry grin.

"How'd you meet Charlie?" he asked, finally.

"Max introduced us."

"All roads lead to Max."

"He comes across as an ornery man, but he's a good person. He helped me get started, introduced me to the right people early on, and helped me build a portfolio of clients. When I first met Charlie, I didn't think I'd have the time to take him on as a client. He came to my studio, told me about his new restaurant, La Closerie, and offered me a crazy amount of money. I said no. He called me the next day and offered me a compromise: Help him select the fixtures and the lighting and the furnishings, and he'd work with my schedule, and could we get together? You know how he is."

"Persistent."

"I said OK, and we went to visit showrooms in Beverly Hills, La Brea. He gave me a sense of the restaurant's theme, the clientele he wanted to attract, the food he would serve, the vision for the layout of the bar and the dining room, and the mood and the ambiance he was striving for. I was surprised at how well we complemented each other's styles. I told him he had exquisite taste, and he smiled that smile—"

"I know the smile," Andrew said.

"And we agreed to do it again, and after the third outing, he invited me to lunch and I said OK, and he said he wanted me to try something different. He took me to a Thai restaurant in the bowels of East Hollywood, which is not such a nice area. He said it was the closest thing to home that he had found in LA. The food was simple. Spectacular. And he's speaking Thai to the waitress, and she brings out a whole mango for dessert. Charlie proceeds to delicately peel it and offers me the fruit, and it was the sweetest mango I had ever tasted in my life."

"You'll have to give me the address."

"That's when I agreed to do his restaurant. We were together one week later." Her expression was as empty as her glass. "I need a cigarette," she said. "Be right back." She squeezed past the throng of bodies and walked out the door. Two minutes later, she was back. "They made me put my cigarette out. These fucking vigilantes. Let's get out of here."

They headed north along the Strand. She hooked her arm in his. They passed beachfront homes decorated for the holidays, with jack-o-lanterns, witches, graveyards, and ghouls dominating the scenery and a few timid Christmas decorations interspersed amongst the skeletons. After a few blocks she said, "He's living with me now. He gave up the rental in Beverly Hills."

Andrew wasn't sure if this was good or bad.

"In the beginning, it was electric, chaotic, unpredictable. We were both busy, him with the restaurant, me squeezing in one too many clients, but when we were together the attraction was magnetic. And then before I knew it, he was living with me." She lit another cigarette. "'Why live in two places when we're always together?' he had said. But that's just it. After he moved in, I barely saw him—he'd just started with Kannawerks. I didn't understand why. 'Kannawerks is the future,' he said, and 'La Closerie's on autopilot.' He'd spend days at the factory and at that house in the godforsaken desert." She shook her head. "In the beginning I tried to spend some time there to be with him. I lasted less than two weeks in the desert, then I said he was on his own."

She threw her hair back. The sound of her heels echoed up the alleys. "He was seeing someone."

She stopped, slipped off her heels, and they walked for several minutes in silence.

"I could sense it. A feeling," she said. "I confronted him; he denied it. I could never prove it. And although he did spend more time in LA after that, the feeling never went away." A gust of wind rustled the palm fronds above them.

"Here we are," she said. The glow of the streetlamps reflected off the red door of her darkened beach house. They climbed the front steps.

"You forgave him," Andrew said.

"We figured things out." She lit a cigarette and exhaled. "Are you heading back to the desert?"

"In the morning."

"Pity," she said, smiling. She was elegant, poised. "Pity that we meet now."

He took a step back, careful not to fall off the steps.

Andrew lay in the hotel bed—a motel really—his head resting on his folded hands, pillows doubled up. He couldn't sleep. His mind raced. Malinee. Long, straight, ebony hair, her round face, with soft features, Eurasian eyes, a ballerina's grace. Malinee was the most stunning girl he had ever seen. Finally seen. She had been there all along. But one day he *saw* her there, sitting next to him in biology class in tenth grade. Daughter of an American executive for one of the multinationals operating in Thailand, a Thai mother from a well-to-do family—not the stereotypical Thai secretary that destroyed many a farang marriage. Malinee was shy, kept to herself, and had few friends. He mustered enough courage to speak to her, make small talk. They had lunch together, casually, seemingly by chance. He couldn't stop thinking about her. Andrew had become obsessed.

"Just ask her out," Charlie had said, as they waded in their apartment's pool one afternoon.

"Ask her out where?"

"Take her to a movie. Take her to the shack at the end of the Soi and buy her a bag of sugar cane. Take her to a party. You know. Engage."

"And then what?"

"Jesus, Andy." Charlie dunked his head underwater. He came back up and vigorously shook his head, spraying Andrew. "Hold her hand, kiss her. It's not that hard. You're tall, handsome, you're smart. Hell, I'd go out with you if I was a chick."

"Well, you're shit out of luck." Andrew smiled and dove in, emerging on the other side of the shallow end.

Charlie splashed water in Andrew's direction and swam over. "Be yourself, Andy. Didn't you just spend hours telling me about your romantic adventures this summer? Weren't the girls lining up outside your door?"

"You've got the story the other way around. I was the one pursuing them."

"Whatever. The point is that you had balls."

"She's out of my league."

"No one is out of anyone's league. Don't hesitate. Be direct."

"Easy for you to say. You're the one with the revolving door."

Charlie grabbed a tennis ball floating in the water. "It's all about confidence. You have to believe in yourself." He threw the ball against the cabana wall and caught it.

"She'll say no."

"So what? If she does, you move on, but I don't think she will. Something is lurking under that shy facade of hers, I can sense it. Those ballerinas spend countless hours sequestered in practice, and she's probably itching to engage, socially and physically. I bet her parents lock her up at night knowing that if they don't, she'd be out on the prowl. I bet she's a repressed tiger." He let out a loud guffaw. "I never see her at parties." He threw the ball against the wall, this time at an angle, and Andrew dove and caught it.

A few weeks later, the Bromer brothers threw one of their legendary parties. They lived in a classic Thai villa: two stories with tall, thin windows on all sides to mitigate the humidity and heat and a front yard covered in lush grass dominated by a gigantic Bodhi tree. A shallow Japanese koi pond welcomed visitors as they approached the front door and entered into a cavernous living room devoid of furniture except for couches and a wide, circular staircase leading to the bedrooms, bathrooms, and the game room.

They had a foosball table, a ping pong table, and a billiard table, enough to keep the guests engaged when they weren't drinking, making out, or fucking.

Andrew and Charlie had planned to meet there, but first Charlie had a pre-party to go to with the varsity soccer team. The Bromers' villa wasn't far, a short tuk-tuk ride, *sahm sip* (thirty) baht, *khop khun khrap* (thank you very much). The party had already started when Andrew arrived: music blared, pot smoke hung in the air, discarded plastic cups littered the front yard, a flip-flop floated in the pond, and his shoes stuck to the puddled parquet floor. Couples made out on the couches, the chairs, and the floor.

He helped himself to a beer from the refrigerator, said hello to Dwight Bromer, walked back to the living room, and saw Charlie and Malinee holding hands as they came down the stairs.

He remembered the moment as if it were yesterday: Malinee's smile evaporating at the sight of Andrew; Andrew stepping back until the wall stopped him; Charlie's shameful, apologetic demeanor.

Malinee was grounded the next day. Rumors spread. Andrew and Charlie didn't speak for two weeks. And then one day, Charlie came down to his apartment, like he often did, and told Andrew it had just happened, he didn't mean to hurt Andrew, and he was sorry. Nothing could come between them.

Malinee didn't return to ISB after summer vacation. Her parents sent her to ballet school in the States, like a prisoner to a gulag to atone for her sins in isolation. He received a letter from her in September of that year postmarked from San Francisco.

"How's school and how are your classes and are you seeing any girls? Just kidding."

He never heard from Malinee again. He still had the letter.

A piercing car alarm startled Andrew from a dream. Malinee had vanished. He was in an auditorium, surrounded by anonymous faces, a man going on senselessly about Toyota, Taco Bell, Lexus, and

Jack in the Box. He sat up, felt around the sheets for the remote, and turned off the TV. He was pooled in sweat, and his head pounded. It was past 3:00 a.m., the room a sauna. He got up, braced himself on the wall until the dizzy spell dissipated, parted the blinds, and opened the sliding door. He stepped outside onto the small balcony and eyed the scenery: a few stragglers making their way home, Highland Avenue devoid of cars, and the moon's reflection a bright semi-orb on the flat ocean. He switched on the AC. Tepid air engulfed the room.

He popped four Advil, adjusted the trajectory of the AC vent, and fell back asleep, dreamless until the alarm sounded at 5:00 a.m.

CHAPTER 20

The traffic wasn't bad until he hit San Dimas, and then everything slowed to a crawl. It took him two hours to reach the exchange with the 15, and he soon saw why there was a slowdown: he counted five overturned semi-tractor trailers in the southbound lanes. It was as if a giant hand had picked them up and violently cast them down, scattering them like matchsticks. Containers were strewn across the highway, over the median, and on the embankments, while crushed cabins pressed against bent metal dividers. Firetrucks and ambulances were on both sides of the highway blocking the two left northbound lanes; add the rubberneckers and traffic flowed like molasses.

And then he understood the reason for the apocalyptic scene: sand smacked against his windshield, with a sharp *tic click tic click tic tic*, the impact's sound varying based on which gust of Santa Ana wind the particle happened to hitch a ride on. Even at a snail's pace with his car's center of mass low to the ground, Andrew had to squeeze the steering wheel to keep the car from swerving out of the lane.

He noticed multiple plumes of brown and black smoke as if emanating from giant smokestacks scattered throughout the countryside. The wind carried a floating river of soot west. Not a good day for California.

He passed a handful of protesters outside FDN with the same megaphone woman addressing the silent crowd, surprised to see them so subdued after the ferocity of the prior days.

It was past 10:00 a.m. when he rolled into the Kannawerks lot, exactly four hours from when he'd left Manhattan Beach. As he walked into the lobby, he stumbled into a dramatic scene with a crying woman. She stood in front of an open locker, Ashlee between her and the main entrance, and Mike in front of the door that led to the factory floor. The woman was saying something incomprehensible in between sobs, while throwing things into her backpack. She slammed the locker door, threw her keycard at Mike, gave Ashlee the finger, and walked out.

"We had to fire her," Ashlee said.

"She started working on the line today with those fake nails that you glue on," Mike said.

"We gave her three warnings," Ashlee said.

"Can you imagine if a customer finds a fingernail in a gummy tin?" Mike said.

"And good morning to you, too." Andrew grabbed some coffee and met Mike in his office. On his desk were the warped pistons. Andrew picked one up. "So, we still have no idea how this happened?"

"No," Mike said.

"This thing doesn't feel too solid. In fact, it's lighter than expected—flimsy."

"I thought so, too. Delicate. The maintenance guys say this happens once they reach a certain number of cycles."

"Ashlee did say we run them hard."

"Yeah, but they said that with this model, it should not happen before six months. Assuming three or four runs per day, that is about four hundred to five hundred runs. We have only been running the depositor for four months, with two, sometimes three runs per day. That is about two hundred runs, a lot less than when you would expect to see this."

"How many runs does the log say?"

"I have not checked."

"Do it now."

"OK, but why do we care?"

"Because these things *may* crash after six months, and we've been using it for four. Maybe they gave us a lemon. Maybe they gave us a refurbished model." Andrew put the piston back down, suddenly irritated. "Who the fuck knows?" He glowered at the video display. "Why haven't these cameras been fixed?"

"It is complicated."

"Meaning?"

"Meaning that Nett Security, the installers, are not returning my calls."

"So we sit here and do nothing? We keep violating the regs, risk a fine, and risk being shut down? This is not how to run a business. Why can't we fix it ourselves?"

"I do not have admin access."

"Get the credentials."

"They will not give them to me."

"Are you fucking kidding me? Was every day amateur hour before Charlie came in?"

"These Nett Security guys are a couple of *pendejos*. It is two cousins, Louis and Lou. They were recommended to Kannawerks by one of the original contractors, who himself was not reliable. We had to redo a lot of the electrical stuff a year ago." Mike fiddled with the mouse. "They cut corners building out the place and did the minimum required to get the license. We are still paying the price."

"Keep calling those guys at Nett. Tell them we demand admin access."

"OK."

Andrew dug into his backpack and took out the bags of Pink Dot.

"What is that?"

"Contraband. Pink Dot. I want to get it tested and to check the formulation. They say that it is fast-acting and long-lasting."

"*They?*"

"Everyone that's tried it."

"Not possible."

"What makes you so sure?"

"That is what all these guys say. 'Fast-acting, long-lasting, libido-enhancing,' but they do not know what they are talking about. They are high twenty-four hours a day. How can they possibly tell?"

"Let's make sure."

"Do you know how long it took us to develop that formulation? You do not just make it in a garage."

"Ish doesn't think these were made in a garage. They are professionally made, unlike other contraband on the market."

"What are you saying?"

"I'm saying that there is someone with sophisticated manufacturing capabilities that's making a high-quality product and selling it for a lot less than ours on the illegal market. And if we don't report this to the BCC and get them to do something about it, we'll continually be undercut, and you can kiss Kannawerks and the rest of the legal industry goodbye."

"The BCC will not do a thing. Illegal product is a fact of life in this business."

"Why are we busting our balls then? What's the fucking point of legalized weed?"

"It is a job, amigo, and the pie is big enough for all of us."

"Goddamn it! I wish you'd all stop fucking saying that to me!"

Mike shrank back into his chair. "Sorry, boss."

"No, I'm sorry." Andrew sighed. "This whole situation . . . *We* do the right thing and make sure *we're* in compliance, otherwise *we're* punished, lose our license, and get fined. Meanwhile others circumvent the law, and they're *not* punished. The illegal shit is probably going on right under our noses."

"There are known illegal operations in Apple Valley, and no one does anything about them," Mike said. "Or I should say, they did something about it and shut one of them down. It was in the local news. The Law rounded up the workers and emptied the warehouse. They had the press there and made sure the removal of the biomass was captured on TV. But a few weeks later, the *cabrones* were back at it in the same location."

"Get these tested, will you?"

Mike placed the bags of Pink Dot in a desk drawer. As Andrew walked to the door, he regretted his short tone. That was the cantankerous Silicon Valley Andrew, not the wiser, I'm-so-over-that-shit Andrew. He paused at the door. "It's Halloween tonight, right? What are your kids going to dress up as?"

"Raúl Jiménez and Elsa, the Ice Princess."

"Jiménez? As in the Mexican center forward?"

"Ángel is crazy about him."

"Elsa I can understand."

"I support my son one hundred percent," Mike said, smiling.

"I'll pick up some candy on the way home."

A dirt devil crossed his path as he approached the taco truck. The aroma of charred meat and spices enveloped him.

"You just caught us," Renée said, leaning out the window.

"It's been that kind of day."

"What'll you have?"

"You decide."

Andrew peeked inside the truck as Renée passed the ticket over. Lina was hunched over the prep section, murmuring to a woman who looked familiar, but he couldn't place her. After a few minutes, they stepped out of the truck.

"This is Olivia," Renée said. She was slightly taller than Lina and had her same complexion and oval eyes. The sister: Renée's college roommate.

"I passed by you and your megaphone this morning; the crowd was thin."

"Protest fatigue. And people are scared." She cleared her throat. "I'm losing my voice."

"What are they scared of?"

"Deportation."

"Olivia leads Border Justice, an immigration nonprofit advocacy group," Renée explained.

"We were getting a great turnout, but somebody must have said something or seen something. Many of these people are barely scraping by and can't afford to risk their livelihood." She adjusted her backpack.

"This zero tolerance crap is cruel," Andrew said.

"Compounding that policy is the incompetence of the authorities at multiple levels, with migrants disappearing. That's what we work on, recently anyway."

"You mean the dead migrant?"

"Not just him. Others are missing, too. One day they're at FDN, then the next day they're handed over to ICE and sent to the border to be repatriated and sent back home, but they never make it. They disappear in the system. Nobody knows where they are. It's gotten worse these last few months. Which reminds me, I have to go. I was on my way to file more Freedom of Information paperwork to force FDN to disclose more data. But I needed a break." She patted Renée on her shoulder.

"Take some of these with you." Renée handed Olivia a bag. "And get some rest, Liv."

Olivia unwrapped a taco and ate it as she walked to her car.

"She's passionate," Andrew said to Renée.

"I worry about her. It's consuming her." She glanced toward Olivia.

"It can't be easy, what she does."

"It's not, especially now, with the missing migrants. Sometimes I feel that it's too personal, for her."

"In what way?"

"Olivia and Lina are daughters of immigrants who clandestinely came across the border and made a life for themselves. They were amnestied under Reagan in eighty-six." Renée leaned against the truck.

"Imagine that."

"It gave them and their children the opportunity to succeed. Olivia is fighting to give the migrants the same opportunities her parents had."

"Through Border Justice."

"Now, yes. But three years ago, when the immigration issue escalated, she ran for the Adelanto city council on a platform to shut down the private prisons. Eradicate the enablers of migrant abuse. She was soundly defeated; no one was going to vote for a councilwoman intent on eliminating their livelihood. That's when she started Border Justice."

A gust of warm wind slapped the awning of the taco truck. Renée and Andrew instinctively turned toward the barren desert and observed a disheveled man materialize. His face was contorted in a grimace as if in great pain. He had matted hair and wore torn jeans caked in dust and held up by a piece of thick rope. A filthy, buttonless dress jacket exposed a ripped T-shirt. The man stank like an open sewer in the summer.

"Hey, Norbert," Renée said.

"Hiya," the man replied, waving his hands clumsily. The grimace disappeared.

"Andrew, meet Norbert. Let me get you something, Norbert."

Andrew faced the man, who swayed and eyed the door of the truck, a smile exposing black and yellow teeth. Renée handed the man a paper bag. "Haven't seen you in a while."

He opened the bag, took a deep breath, and started to cry. "Thank you," he said, the tears carving a path down his grime-covered face.

"I put a couple of bottles of water in there for you."

"Thank you," he said softly.

"Have you been to the shelter?"

"Thank you," he said, almost in a whisper.

"The shelter, Norbert."

He sniffled and wiped his nose with the back of his hand. "The shelter," he repeated.

She helped him sit down on the curb. "Your meds, Norbert. Did they give you your medication?"

He shook his head, then reached into the bag, took out a bottle of water, and drank.

"Wait here," Renée said.

Norbert took out a taco and shoved it in his mouth, his beard absorbing the leaking sauce. Renée handed him two more bottles of water.

Andrew and Renée stood to the side watching Norbert eat.

"He's a harmless desert walker," she said.

"A what?"

"Homeless people that live in the desert. We feed the regulars. We do what we can. I've never seen him this out of it, though. He'll stay at the shelter, get back on the meds, stabilize, have a relapse, and then he wanders the desert until he either goes back in of his own volition or gets picked up for vagrancy—hanging around strip malls, diving in dumpsters."

They watched Norbert devour his third taco. This time he used a napkin to wipe his mouth and beard.

"He's coherent when he's stable. Funny, too. Worked in aerospace for one of the big defense contractors. He said that when he was diagnosed, they relegated him to unclassified work, so he left. I met him about six months ago; he's always around this part of town."

Norbert had lined up three bottles of water on the ground and crushed the empty paper bag into a neat, compact ball. He handed it to Renée, and as if in a trance, said, "They're here." He pointed at the Kannawerks factory.

"Who's here, Norbert?" Renée asked.

"They are."

Renée eyed Andrew, who shrugged.

"Every night. They're here." Norbert leaned over, picked up the bottles, and put them in his pocket.

They watched him walk off into the desert and disappear behind a cluster of Joshua trees.

"I better go," she said.

"Hey, so . . ."

"Yes?"

"Do you want to meet up in LA on Saturday? If you're free that is. I understand if you're busy. I understand if—"

She touched his arm. "It's a date."

CHAPTER 21

"I need you in Vegas," Charlie said.

"When?"

"Now."

"I just got back from LA. Mike and I were going to—"

"Whatever it is, it can wait. The San Fran investor wants to visit our Nevada operation on Monday. He wants to expand multistate and envisions using Kannawerks's methods as a baseline to replicate the manufacturing process."

"What did you sell them on?"

"That we have a platform—a factory-in-a-box."

"Do we even have machines in Nevada?"

"There's one depositor, but it's not operational."

"Why don't you have him visit Adelanto?"

"He wants to see a satellite factory."

Andrew shut the office door and put his phone on speaker so Mike could hear.

Charlie continued. "The depositor doesn't need to be online. Just make sure it comes on, make some undosed gummies using the old process in the new molds, and let them touch, feel, and taste the product."

Andrew put Charlie on mute and asked Mike what he thought.

"They are good at making gummies in Vegas, they just do not show well—they messed up the last investor visit. I will call them and give them a heads up."

Andrew unmuted the phone. "I'll be on my way later today."

"They're in if they like what they see in Vegas, and they are one hundred percent behind the M and A strategy." Charlie hung up.

"Make sure you do not stay at the hotel near the factory in North Vegas. *Es una mierda*. Stay on the Strip," Mike said.

Andrew grabbed his backpack.

"And do not drive your car to the factory. Leave it at the hotel and take a taxi."

"Anything else?"

"Bronson is in charge," Mike said. "I hired him."

"Tell your kids I'll drop off the candy when I'm back." Andrew stepped outside and put on his sunglasses, shielding his eyes from the pelting dust.

Andrew stopped in Helendale to grab a fresh change of clothes and dump his suitcase. He wound his way around the golf course, proceeded down Camino del Celador, but when he drove up to the house, a black Cadillac Escalade blocked the garage. *Who the hell . . .* He drove around the cul-de-sac, parked on the street, and walked up to the Escalade: warm to the touch. Did Ish get a new ride? He punched the numbers into the lock and stepped inside the house. He was greeted by a faint, nauseating smell of sweet cologne like the kind his grandmother used to buy him. Before he could make any sense of it, a man appeared from the kitchen. Andrew dropped his bags and as he started to say something, another man materialized from the bedroom. This one carried a gun. And it was pointed at Andrew.

They wore black suits and over-starched white shirts with the top two buttons undone, exposing matching gold chains with a small crucifix and chests competing with each other in terms of hair density. The man with the gun was tall—at least six feet—and his hair was slicked back like in the moving pictures from the thirties, revealing a large diamond stud in his left ear.

"Come in," the other man said. He was shorter, and his dark hair was tied back in a ponytail.

"Who are—"

"Shut up," the short man said. Without warning, he pushed Andrew down onto the couch.

He started to sweat.

"Where's my money?" the short man said.

"What money?"

"My money."

"I don't know what you're talking about—"

Andrew felt a sudden, searing pain, as if he had been hit with a frying pan . . . not that he'd ever experienced that before. The violent force threw him sideways onto the couch. He gingerly sat back up and held his face. The tall man stood over him. He could make out the thick, knobby fingers of his raised left hand. The gun was still on him.

"You've got the wrong guy."

"That's what they all say," the short man said and nodded at the tall man. He hit Andrew again, harder. This time he stayed down. His ears were ringing, and his heartbeat pounded in his head.

"I'm telling you you've got the wrong guy," Andrew said forcefully. "Check my ID." He sat up slowly. His cheekbone throbbed.

"Where is it?" the short man asked.

"In my right front pocket."

"Stand up. Hands behind your head."

Andrew obeyed. The tall man reached into Andrew's pocket, took out the money clip, and handed it to the short man.

"Andrew Eastman. Who the fuck are you? Where the fuck is Charlie?" he yelled. "That rat fuck."

He paced the floor.

"We do have the wrong guy, Junior," the short man said, smiling. He threw Andrew's money clip and its contents on the floor. "You know Charlie?"

"Yes."

"This is where he lives?"

"Yes." He lied.

"Where is the fuck?"

"How the fuck would I know?"

"Bullshit."

"I swear, I don't know." The pain this time was sharper, crisper, like an electric shock that coursed through his body.

"San Francisco," Andrew mumbled. He stayed down.

"That cocksucker. What's he doing there?"

"Business."

"What business? My business?"

"I don't know what your business is."

"What business?" the short man yelled.

"Kannawerks." Andrew sat up, his hands raised. He couldn't feel his teeth.

"Kannawerks? What the fuck is that?"

"Cannabis—"

"I don't give a shit about cannabis! I want my money! The money we lent him for that cocksucking restaurant!"

"I know nothing about—"

"Shut the fuck up!" The short man paced the floor. "Junior, put the gun away. This pussy ain't doing shit." He came over and sat next to Andrew. "You can bring your hands down."

Andrew complied.

"I need you to get a message to that cocksucker. Can you do that for me?"

He nodded.

"Tell him Lorenzo wants his money. Tell him that if he doesn't have it by Monday at noon, he's fucking dead. Dead, that mother-fucker. You can tell him that?"

"Sure, Lorenzo."

"What did you just call me?" His face was a few inches from Andrew, the rotten stench of the man's breath mixing in with the cologne.

"Lorenzo."

"No, you dumb fuck, if I was Lorenzo, I would know what that cocksucker looks like. What a dumb motherfucker," he said, motion-ing at Andrew with his thumb. He patted the back of Andrew's head and stood up.

"What's the message?" the short man repeated.

"Money by Monday noon or else."

"He's dead. Good. Tell him to drop it off at Lorenzo's office. He knows where that is. Let's go, Junior."

As soon as the sound of the Escalade faded away, Andrew shut the front door and went to the kitchen. He rummaged through the drawers, found a large Ziploc bag, filled it with ice, and placed it on his face. He lay on the couch and started to shake.

CHAPTER 22

A sledgehammer echoed inside of his skull. He wiped the drool from his chin, squinted, and checked his watch. It was past four—he'd been out for two hours. He waited for his eyes to adjust to the light and then sat up. He touched his face and grimaced. He could feel the welt on his cheekbone where Junior's ring had made contact. He waited a few seconds to let the dizziness pass, then headed to the bathroom. He stood in front of the mirror. The right side of his face burned. He noticed a large bump forming below his eye. He found the bottle of Advil.

One step at a time. He dialed Charlie's number. Straight to voicemail. "Charlie, call me. It's urgent." He paused and then, "No, it's *fucking* urgent." He wanted to extend the string of expletives but held back. He texted Charlie to call him stat.

His vision was blurred. Probably not a good idea to drive, but sticking around this godforsaken place was not an option. He'd already driven four hours today, what was another three to Vegas? He replenished his backpack with a clean set of clothes and the Advil and headed north.

He followed Route 66 to Barstow and then merged onto the 15. Nothing but desert. The same landscape he had seen every day—the same Joshua trees, the same low-lying desert bushes, the same hills covered with red and yellow and brown and black rocks—only today they were lit pink by the setting sun as if on fire. Like his face. He zipped by road signs riddled with bullet holes—Cactus Gulch, Broken Rock Way, Rillito Trail—names out of classic westerns. He envisioned himself as part of a wagon train, stagecoaches racing through the barren plains, hightailing it from Apaches, or outlaws, or just making better time to the next town.

He fiddled with the radio, trying to find something to help him focus and stay awake, but it was no use. The ancient antenna picked up morsels of music, static, and preachers predicting the end of the world if everyone didn't embrace Jesus and guns and the Republican Party. Southbound traffic raced by him.

Andrew put down the visor and opened the slot exposing the mirror. The welt was getting bigger, redder, and a slight tinge of yellow was forming below his eye. He flipped up the visor. He reached over and sipped from the water bottle.

By the time he passed Baker, he had been driving an hour. Just over an hour to go. He tried to occupy himself with the scenery, but there was not much to see as even the Joshua trees had vanished. It was dark, anyway, with only a few stars visible in the infinite sky. He passed by a couple of slowing tractor trailers, and as the car started its descent down the mountain pass, he saw a fiery blaze of lights in the distance. He checked the time. It wasn't Vegas. Too soon, too small. As he approached the lights, a sign enlightened him: WELCOME TO NEVADA. Someone had built a gambling pueblo on the border with California to siphon away the stragglers arriving from LA. Why not stop here first, try your luck, lose some money, eat at the buffet, check out a revue, and then head on to Sin City? Like an appetizer before the main course.

The pueblo was called Primm. He stopped at the Flying V to fill up on gas—he was down to less than a quarter tank—and as he waited in the cold desert night, he took in the surroundings: a three-story,

multicolored flashing sign beckoned guests to Billy the Kid's Resort
and Casino; the Twisted Titty lounge, conveniently located near the
freeway exit ramp; a sign for the Whiskey Rose motel; a crumbling,
half-occupied outlet mall; and a smattering of taco, fried chicken,
and fast-food joints. It was a city completely conceived and planned
for transient gamblers, a spider's web catching errant travelers who
were desperate and weak.

Andrew topped off the tank, locked the car, and entered the con-
venience store for a caffeine boost; he still felt groggy. He grabbed a
Coke from the fridge and waited in the checkout line.

A woman was paying for a bottle of water, two packs of cigarettes,
and a box of orange Tic Tacs. She wore a slinky, green sequin dress,
a white faux-fur blazer, stiletto heels, and sported long, black, subtly
undulating curls that reached down to the small of her back. The
heels-hair combination made her almost as tall as Andrew.

As she picked up her merchandise and placed it in her leather
tote bag, she glanced back at Andrew. She stared as if she recognized
him. She was in her late fifties and wore just a touch more makeup
than necessary—a looker in her prime.

Without warning, she reached up and caressed his cheek. "That's
real fresh there, hon." Her touch was soft and the gesture second
nature . . . motherly. In her Texan drawl, words flowed like a slow-moving brook as it cascaded down the gentle slope of a mountain.

"I was on the wrong end of a fist."

She nodded in a way that said she knew all too well. "Let me put
something on that shiner. Wouldn't want the pretty girls in Vegas
to get the wrong impression—that's where you're headed to, isn't it?"

She didn't wait for an answer. "Come on, there's better light in
here."

"I don't think I—"

"I won't bite," she said.

He noticed her rousing, intelligent eyes. She waited for him to pay for his Coke, and then she took his hand and led him into the women's bathroom, a small vestibule of the roadhouse kind. She locked the door, reached into her tote bag, and pulled out a small beige tube.

"Look this way," she said. She tilted his face upward. She unscrewed the cap, squeezed a small amount of potion on her index finger, and applied the foundation to his cheek, gently smoothing it over the bruise and careful not to press too hard. When she was done, she took a step back and stared at her handiwork. "See? No one will ever know." She handed him the small tube. "Take it. I've got another one in the car."

"Are you always like this with strangers?" He put the tube in his pocket.

"Not always. You just look like you could use a friend."

They walked out of the store. Her drawl evolved from a gentle stream to a crashing waterfall as she called out, "Oh, Cooper, get away from that car before you drool all over it, for heaven's sake."

Wearing alligator boots, a bolo tie, and a white, ten-gallon cowboy hat, Cooper was bent over, inspecting the Porsche's wheels and brake pads as if he was a mechanic in the pit lane. He peered in through the driver's side window, and then walked around the car. He ran his hand gently along the rear spoiler as if caressing his prized mare.

"Now you've got your paw prints all over it."

"This your vehicle?" Cooper asked in a long, slow drawl. "Damn fine ride—the smoky blue, the beige leather. What's the year? How many miles?"

As the woman dragged the pawing cowboy away, he threw his arm over her shoulder—he seemed tipsy—pulled her in, and gave her a long kiss.

"Nice ride you got there yourself," Andrew said, as the man opened the door for the woman, who gave Andrew a sympathetic wave. Then the cowboy touched the brim of his hat in a salute, fell into his silver Dodge Viper, and sped north.

Andrew sat in the car for a few minutes, guzzling the Coke. He pulled down the visor and exposed the mirror—the color of the expanding welt was barely noticeable. But the makeup couldn't suppress the throbbing pain. He tossed the empty bottle on the floor and drove out of Primm, whose trailer park was the last remnant of civilization on the outskirts of town. The glow faded in the rearview mirror as the car was immersed in darkness.

This time the lights were brighter and extended outward like the arrows on a compass. Driving into the valley, Las Vegas hit with the force of a thousand volts. Andrew perked up with his hands tight on the wheel. As he approached, the lights brightened and became more intense, penetrating like laser beams, the silhouette of the Strip visible ahead. Incandescent lights extended in one uninterrupted line from the Luxor Pyramid to the Stratosphere Needle, while airplanes lined up to land into McCarran, ferrying the suckers into dens where the odds were stacked against them. Billboard after billboard invited visitors to partake in entertainment: come see the circus, the show, the magic act, the crooner. A smiling, sultry librarian with a stack of gummies on her desk beckoned: Kannawerks—Live the High Life.

He came upon a carcass that resembled a half-finished spaceship surrounded by cranes. The black enamel walls of the stadium glistened in the glare of spotlights. *We'll see how the Raiders do in Vegas.* That was a great combination: put overpaid, testosterone-laden, twenty-somethings in Sodom and Gomorrah and win a Super Bowl. Good luck.

Andrew took the next exit and made a right on Las Vegas Boulevard. He was now in the bowels of the Strip, amidst the lights with the cacophony of the revelers audible over the noise of the tight traffic. It took him several minutes to reach his destination, through eyes ogling his Porsche trying to discern who was at the wheel or in the passenger seat.

He pulled into the hotel and took a chance with the valet. He was tired, hungry, and thirsty. But most of all, he was in pain, his face pulsating like a subwoofer emanating house music. He walked past the check-in counter lines and entered the VIP room for platinum members only. The young trainee smiled as she upgraded Andrew to a higher floor, thanking him for his loyalty—perks from the Valley days. She walked through the available amenities while Andrew largely ignored her and perused the clientele in the room: a Lolita arm-in-arm with a septuagenarian and nuzzling his neck, while the tanned man smiled.

The first thing Andrew did when he reached the freezing room was walk over to the floor-to-ceiling windows. The Bellagio fountain had just started its spectacle. The rhythm, order, and synchronicity of the light and water comforted him. He liked the discipline. The show was hypnotizing. He relaxed, pressing his hands and forehead on the cold glass with his eyes mesmerized by the patterns. And then, as if waking from a dream, he pulled back from the window. His backpack slid off his shoulder and hit the floor. He checked his phone. Charlie hadn't called him back.

Why would Charlie resort to a loan shark if he had connections like Max? It didn't make sense. Or maybe it was part of the same pattern? Andrew thought back to his last encounter with Charlie—the lost weekend in Boston. He had said he had left Thailand for good, and that he would never return to the land of his birth. Andrew had asked him what kind of trouble he'd gotten himself into, but Charlie just deflected the questions.

"There was nothing to go back to," Charlie had said. "I'll hold on to the memories."

Andrew splashed cold water on his face, the yellow now more pronounced, expanding into a greenish hue. He reapplied some of the makeup. He wasn't sure whether or not it made any difference.

He changed his shirt, pocketed the phone, and headed to the elevator bank. He squeezed by hordes of tourists in their Halloween costumes. They were busy taking selfies, documenting every minute of their lives and posting for everyone to see. He ducked under a battery of camera phones capturing life-sized paintings of half-canine, half-human aristocrats. *What the fuck is everyone thinking?*

He checked in with the hostess and was shown to a seat at the L-shaped bar. He ordered a martini, very dry with one olive, and a small bowl of tsukemono, pickled vegetables that paired well with chilled vodka. Andrew took a long sip of his martini. The cool liquid soothed him. The pain in his face began to subside.

As he popped the last pickle in his mouth, the bartender placed a shot glass filled to the rim in front of him. "Compliments of the gentleman," the bartender said, motioning to the far end of the bar.

The man raised his shot glass and downed it. Andrew smiled and did the same, knowing it was Belvedere. He slammed the empty shot glass on the counter, walked over, and embraced the man with a warm hug.

DJ, the scion of a second-tier Korean chaebol, who instead of returning to his native country to run the family conglomerate once he'd "made his bones" in the United States like his compatriots of equivalent pedigree, had remained in California to run his own investment fund.

"What the fuck are you doing in Vegas?"

"I should be asking you that question," DJ replied. He was a couple of inches shorter than Andrew, with jet-black hair, a ready smile exposing a row of perfectly white teeth, and prominent jug ears—a symbol of Korean nobility, according to DJ. He sat down and grimaced. "What happened to your face, dude?"

"Slipped in the shower."

DJ wasn't convinced. "How the hell are you, man? Last time I saw you, all that shit was going down with your company."

"I've moved on."

He nodded. "Right. Let's not dwell on the past." He waved the bartender over, motioning for another round. "So why *are* you here?"

"Cannabis."

"You? Cannabis?"

"Where some people are high some of the time, and the rest are high all of the time."

DJ let out a high-pitched cackle. "Do you know anything about cannabis?"

"Absolutely nothing."

He cackled again. "What *do* you do?"

"A bit of everything. I'm here to meet the local team and get them ready for an investor visit."

"In this market? Dude, you've missed the cannabis train." DJ briskly rapped his knuckles on the counter. "The time to raise money was before the summer."

New shots appeared. They downed them together, slamming the glasses on the counter.

The shot didn't phase DJ. "We've written off most of our investments in the sector. It's the same situation as the dot-com days, you should know: a cratering sector, stocks at an irrationally high valuation, none of the companies making a dime in profit."

The bartender placed a plate of pork buns in front of them. "Have you eaten?" Andrew asked.

"I just sat down when I saw you."

Andrew pushed the plate towards DJ. "Help yourself."

"These never get old."

Andrew called the bartender over and ordered dishes he knew DJ would inhale: braised pork knuckle, smoked pork ramen with extra pork belly, spicy, stir-fried rice cakes, a mound of kimchi, an assortment of buns, and two Belvedere martinis, dry.

After some time was spent catching up on common acquaintances, Andrew asked, "Do you really think we missed the cannabis train?"

"Wake up, dude." And like a renaissance artist painting the Last Judgement, DJ described the end of days for cannabis: it was in a death spiral and descending into the Ninth Circle of the Inferno.

Andrew listened and sipped his martini. He shouldn't have been surprised. He knew the Silicon Valley playbook: the herd mentality, fear of missing out, fear of being one-upped by a nemesis—one of the criteria that drove people like Theo and DJ to invest in nebulous, nascent industries. And it was no surprise that they both loved to rant on how fucked up the cannabis market was *now*, in hindsight, as if it were a former spouse who had taken more than their share. They were onto the next shiny object anyway.

"You're not making this a career," DJ said. It was not a question.

"I don't know."

"Dude, you're a *tech* entrepreneur, what the fuck do you want to be in cannabis for?"

"Transition, DJ, separation. Maybe it's an opportunity to reinvent myself."

"I understand if it's temporary."

"It seemed like the perfect escape—think about it—out of the Bay Area, out of tech, shed the skin, and make a clean break."

"You sound like a self-help book."

"And then maybe one day when the scars have healed, I come back."

"Dude, please. *Scars*? You've had one shitty outcome. Don't you think you're being a bit dramatic? I'll show you some fucking scars. And yet here I am, raising funds and investing in the next fucking game changer."

"The last one is what stays with you, what defines you."

"That's bullshit—"

"It is for me," Andrew said. "For *me*. I'm the one that has to get up in the morning, recoil at myself in the mirror, replay the last five years, and wonder what I should have done differently. How do you do it, DJ? How do you survive after an epic fail?"

"I move on to the next opportunity, dude. But you were handicapped from the day you raised your second round."

"I know. I made the mistake of taking too much VC money when I should have held back and just stuck with angels. I think about this every fucking day. I'm reminded of it every time I check my bank account. I'm reminded of it every time I open TechCrunch and see the latest rounds of funding. I'm reminded of it when companies that I partnered with go public or get acquired at unicorn valuations and the founders make a fortune. And they all fucking deserve it."

They sat for a moment. Then DJ put his arm around Andrew's shoulder and pulled him close. "Dude, listen. We were roommates at Cal, for Christ's sake, so I can say this to you: you're overthinking it. Take a break. Have some fun in cannabis. If anything, you'll learn what *not* to do; you'll learn who *not* to work with. Then, when you're ready, call me, and I'll make some introductions. We've got some great companies in our portfolio, and this NFT thing is going to be massive."

"What's an NFT?"

"Non-fungible token. Crypto shit."

Andrew picked up his martini, careful not to spill any since his hands were shaking.

"Are you here tomorrow night?" DJ asked.

"I'm heading back to LA in the afternoon."

"No, you're not. You're staying one more night. For me. We're hosting a party for an investor conference, our portfolio companies are sharing insights, cross pollinating knowledge, finding synergies, you know, the usual VC stuff. I'll introduce you to some folks."

"I'm not ready."

"*Dude.*"

"We'll see."

"I said don't overthink this."

Just then the food appeared.

"Fuck it, let's eat."

Andrew watched DJ tear into the pork knuckle and slurp the noodles from the ramen bowl like a pro. Andrew picked at his food, lost in thought, focusing on his martini.

When the food was gone, DJ put down his chopsticks and said, "A toast." He raised his glass. "To not looking back." They drank. DJ was ready for another round and insisted Andrew not be a wuss.

There are no schedules in cannabis, after all.

CHAPTER 23

A shrill sound startled him awake. Was it the alarm going off or was someone calling? He rolled over and reached for his phone. The bedside clock read 5:15 a.m. His head felt heavy. Again.

"Hey, Andy," Charlie said. Andrew sensed a smile on Charlie's face; he was always upbeat, irrespective of the situation. A self-defense mechanism honed over the years.

"What took you so long?" Andrew jumped out of bed.

"Relax, Andy. I was with investors."

"Do you know what happened to me?"

"And dinner at this guy's house in Atherton, you should have seen—"

"Do you know what happened to me yesterday?"

The line fell silent.

Andrew opened the curtains. The dawn light illuminated the Strip, the buildings casting long shadows to the west. "Listen," he said, "this is important. Two goons were waiting for you in Helendale yesterday. They said you owe some Lorenzo guy money and that if you—"

"Those fuckers!"

"*Shut up*! They said if you don't pay him by Monday you're dead. He repeated this several times. *Dead*."

"Those fuckers," he said again, this time calmly.

"You should see my face."

He could hear one slow, deep breath after another on the other end of the line. "How badly did they rough you up?"

"I'll live." Like he'd care. "What the fuck is going on, Charlie?"

"It's a misunderstanding."

"Death threats? That's a *hell* of a misunderstanding."

"They'll get their money."

"Who are these people?"

"The less you know, the better."

"It's too late for that."

"I'll take care of it."

"Why not go to Max, other investors, a bank loan, something legit?"

"Nothing's legit, Andy. Not in the restaurant business, at least not in the circles I'm in. Try getting a loan from a bank with the track record I have. By the time they're done, you're left with nothing if they give you anything at all."

"And these guys offered you a better deal? What happened? I thought La Closerie was a winner."

"That place hemorrhages money. It did me in . . . *is* doing me in. It has nothing to do with Kannawerks. And not a word to anyone, including Manuela."

Andrew was starting to get worried. "Where are you, Charlie? We need to meet."

"I'm still in San Fran. You need to get Nevada ready."

"When are you getting here?"

"Monday morning, at the latest, to drive the investor visit. Have you met the team?"

"Headed there now."

"I'll explain everything the next time I see you. I need you with me on this, Andy."

"With you on what?"

"I gotta go. I'll be in touch."

Mike wasn't kidding about North Vegas. They passed a gas station with pumps out of order, a motel with a torn yellow awning and paint peeling off the doors, and a 7-Eleven with a posse guarding the door.

The car pulled up to a two-story building that had tinted glass windows and doors painted a metallic blue, with keypads and sensors the only means of access. Andrew walked over to Suite 4 and knocked.

He waited for over a minute. He checked the address and knocked again.

There was a click and the door opened.

Ashlee.

"What are you doing here?" Andrew asked, surprised.

"Setting up the depositor." She was in full PPE, minus the mask.

"We just need it for show."

"Charlie said he wants it running by Monday."

"As in making gummies?"

"Yep."

"That's not what he told me."

"Changed his mind."

"Who's going to operate the machine?"

"I am. I'll work the weekend if I have to."

She put on her mask and disappeared behind another door from which two young men simultaneously appeared. They introduced themselves after they shed their PPE: Bronson, the factory manager, and Travis, the lab technician. Andrew let the Ashlee situation go; he'd deal with it the next time he saw Charlie.

Andrew wasn't expecting much from the Vegas operation. But Vegas was a cash cow. Bronson had figured out how to win in this market where transient customers—tourists—made up 80 percent of the sales: develop relationships with key retailers, create joint marketing programs, buy premium shelf space, and invest in strategically placed billboards near the airport and on the Strip. Gambling, shows, restaurants, cannabis—the tourists came for all of it. While tourists were captive to the casino in their hotel, knew which show to attend, or knew which celebrity chef owned which restaurant, they were novices when it came to cannabis. They wanted to be educated, told what to ingest, smoke, and rub—and so Bronson obliged, spending his marketing dollars wisely.

When they were done with the investor visit preparations and the mock demo, Andrew said his goodbyes and headed back to the hotel. He came away impressed; maybe there *was* a way to make this crazy business work.

The bar was populated with guests who had just arrived for the weekend, some already wearing their Halloween costumes with Marvel and DC superheroes being the dominant theme. Andrew sat on a white leather couch while he savored his pre-party drink and observed guests entering and exiting the Tower Suites elevator bank. These were people going to exclusive rooms for high rollers and the rich and famous and those trying to impress their Tinder or Bumble date on a first escapade—those who could afford to spend a thousand bucks a night for a weekend in Sin City.

He watched a handsome couple walk past, headed to the elevators. A red-haired, goateed Aquaman was arm in arm with a voluptuous Wonder Woman. Her fishnet stockings led into heels too small for her feet, the red, blue, and gold one-piece suit accentuated her cleavage, and her tiara was resplendent against her blue hair.

Ashlee.

The couple disappeared into the elevator. *A factory supervisor making twenty-three fifty an hour staying in the Tower Suites?* One night in a suite is a week's pay, *with* overtime. And a prison guard couldn't be earning that much; there's a structural limit to how much one can make in Adelanto with very few exceptions. *And they were not exceptions.*

Andrew downed his drink, paid the bill, glanced one last time at the elevators, and headed to the party.

Andrew was greeted by dancing lights, thumping house music, and a petite Asian sporting a five-carat diamond ring and checking names off a list. As he walked into the cavernous space *he knew* from the demeanor of the crowd and their vestments: standard issue Allbirds, designer slacks and jeans, T-shirts, and button-down shirts in white, dark-blue, or azure. And the vests. The Silicon Valley uniform of choice: a sleeveless down or fleece vest, rain or shine, humid or dry, sweltering or freezing, it didn't matter. If you weren't wearing a sleeveless vest, you did not belong in the club. He'd never owned one and never would.

The majority of the attendees were men in their twenties and thirties, the entrepreneurs of today and tomorrow, but maybe not next year. White and Asian, with their fast talk, their crypto and AI and social media and trading plans, building the "platform of the future" because if it wasn't a platform or it didn't have the vision to become an immersive ecosystem, what was the point? How could anyone dominate without a platform, completely devoid of boundaries and rules? *Fail fast,* they said, *ignore the consequences.* It was all about the eyeballs—the engagement, stickiness, network, creation of a vast vortex that sucked you in and didn't let you out. Other than Asians, there was not one other person of color in the room.

The few women sprinkled in the crowd were multicultural Barbie clones of each other. Between five-two and five-eight, straight black, auburn, or predominantly blond hair, thin, and wearing tight-fitting jeans, a blouse or T-shirt, and a jacket. Automatons, as if they were dropped in for show to pad the numbers and demonstrate that the

Valley was becoming more inclusive, more "woman friendly." The five-carat diamond at the door was not alone tonight.

Most of the VCs were Andrew's age, and he could play the part for brief moments, but not for long, as it was tiring to smile, pretend, and bullshit, while listening to the latest idea for an app or a product—the boundaries were blurred these days—like the one about the pizza slice.

"Think about it," the young, bearded man said with beaming eyes, as if he'd discovered the cure for the common cold. "An app that aggregates all the pizza vendors in a city so that you can order a slice or more than one slice or a whole pie at any time of the day or night—you know, when you're in the middle of coding the next module and you're hungry and it's two in the morning."

"That's been done," Andrew said.

"What do you mean?"

"The one in New York. It's called Sliceapp."

"That'll never work."

"Why not?"

"It's in New York, first of all, and second, we're funded by DJ's fund and Sedonia Ventures, one of the top, most respected Sand Hill Road VCs."

"I heard Sliceapp is expanding."

"They'll never make it west of the Mississippi."

"They just launched in Kansas City." Now Andrew was fucking with the guy.

The bearded man huffed, annoyed. "They don't have our backers. They're funded by unknowns! *Our* VCs are mentors, advisors—they don't just provide the money, they're strategic, they give us insights. They're *smart money.*" The bearded man's eyes were now protruding from his skull. "Think Uber for Pizza."

Andrew suppressed a smile. The bearded man, armored in his sleeveless down vest, continued with his pitch. "Click on the app.

Order a slice and it gets delivered in less than fifteen minutes. Start focused. Don't spread yourself thin."

"What's the growth strategy?" Andrew asked.

"The vision is to expand beyond pizza," the bearded man said while extending his arms outward as if trying to embrace the world. "You know, wings. That's the hypergrowth, right there. And then smoothies. The opportunities are endless."

The VCs poured twenty million in his Series A round. *Good luck with that one buddy. At least you'll get pizza delivered until the money runs out.*

The mendacity was nauseating. In between the aroma of steamed dumplings, fried spring rolls, and glazed barbeque short ribs, Andrew smelled the bullshit—almost tasted it in every conversation.

"What do you do and what are you working on and you should come and see me and we can talk about your idea and it sounds great and it fits right into our sweet spot. Call me."

He'd seen the movie before—he'd *starred* in the movie—and he knew how it unfolded and ended.

He left before the coming attractions were over, escaping to the garage and opening the ride app and finding his way to the hotel. It was all there. The future. Food, transportation, news, fake news, money, fake money, gambling, entertainment, gaming, health, sex. All on one device. They had done something right; there were some good eggs in the VC basket, but most of these had been broken a long time ago. He knew; there was no going back.

CHAPTER 24

He called Charlie as soon as he reached Helendale. Straight to voicemail. Andrew had been up all night, wondering whether or not his friend was safe, if Charlie had taken care of the misunderstanding, and why the hell he hadn't told him that Ashlee was going to be in Vegas.

And there was another reason for his angst: Should he punt on staying at the house in Helendale, lest Junior and his pal decided to reappear?

"Of course, there's plenty of room," Renée said when he called and in un-Andrew-like fashion asked if he could crash on her couch. "Come by whenever you like."

"It's not too much?"

"No, no." Her voice had dropped to a whisper.

"I have to meet a guy about work stuff this morning, then I'll come by."

"On a Saturday? Sounds like trouble."

"It could be," he said.

Careful Andrew, you haven't dated in over seven years. The last relationship didn't end well. Renée was smart, independent, and attractive. He would play it by ear, take it one step at a time, not dive into something to later regret, and remain non-committal. And if they did end up sleeping together, so what? It was on his mind as he thought about a change of clothes, what toiletries to bring, what the weather would be in Claremont, and should he bring a sweater?

On the range, he duck-hooked his irons, sliced his woods, and chunked his wedges. It was hot, he hadn't slept, and his face was throbbing. A faint rainbow had appeared below his right eye, and the welt on his cheekbone had swelled to a subdued crimson. He applied an extra layer of sunscreen as Zeke drove up in the golf cart.

Zeke made everything within ten feet, and despite Andrew's heroics around the green, Zeke won the match with two closing pars.

"Iced tea and an IPA," Andrew said. He reached for some popcorn.

"I did some digging," Zeke said. He nodded at Andrew's eye. "Be careful."

"It may be too late but go on."

"Context first. Since this summer, cannabis companies that have spent money like it was going out of fashion can't go back to the well. It's dry. A lot of companies that are overextended are screwed. What happens when these companies fail? They can't declare bankruptcy. It's unavailable in the federal courts because cannabis companies, by definition, are in violation of federal law. So they are doubly screwed. Most people have just walked away after selling what hard assets they can."

"Kannawerks was in the same situation, but the investors re-upped."

"You guys were lucky. You had a brand worth salvaging. It was still early in California. Many of these other guys have nothing. Most of them are growers, extractors, or sell flower. Compound that with the price of cannabis getting cut in half over the past eighteen months because of overproduction relative to demand for legal cannabis, and you have a perfect storm."

"And Terence?"

"He's left with empty warehouses, empty grow houses, abandoned manufacturing facilities, and no recourse. His tenants are going bust, and he's left holding the bag with less than a fifty percent occupancy rate."

Zeke finally reached for his glass, swirled the ice with his finger, and took a long drink. "So now *he's* screwed. He lives the high life off of credit lines with properties as collateral. That's what he did when he was in data centers. He runs a shell game, obfuscating his financial position and misrepresenting his net worth. He hasn't changed. Why should he? It's worked for him in the past, until it's time to move on to the next sucker."

Andrew sat back, incredulous.

Zeke continued. "Whatever credit he has, it's in jeopardy. He doesn't have the cash flow that he had six months ago. I couldn't get the details on his loans, but I'm sure there are more stringent covenants on the debt and lines of credit relative to other less risky industries. He's in the same boat as his tenants—he can't declare bankruptcy, either, because he's also in violation of federal law."

"OK, so he goes under. Why does Kannawerks care? We keep paying rent to the new landlords and creditors."

"If they let you. It all depends on what's in the lease. A common rider that was included in early cannabis lease contracts gives the lessor's creditors the option to terminate the lease within sixty days and convert the facility to non-cannabis use if the lessor breaks the covenants on the loans. They convert the properties into logistics or warehouse facilities; I've seen it happen here in the Inland Empire. The rider was a reasonable hedge against the inherent risk of a nascent, federally illegal industry."

"Who the fuck wants to create a logistics hub in Adelanto?"

Zeke smiled and said, "You'd be surprised, Andrew, you'd be surprised. Anyway, I'm not saying that's the case with Kannawerks, but you should check the lease. Just in case. I don't want you getting dragged into any of the shit that scum is involved in."

"We're going to move out of Adelanto, once we raise a round or merge."

"Then make that a top priority. Losing your lease wouldn't sit well with either incoming investors or a merger partner during the due diligence."

"You're telling me that the viability of our manufacturing facility is predicated on the financial stability of our landlord? Jesus. Add another one to the cannabis shitshow." Andrew thought back to the night of the party. Terence seemed to be ensconced in wealth. Was it all show? "Sixty days won't be enough time to get out once the clock starts running. The minute Terence goes bust, and assuming the rider's in our contract . . . Assuming he does go bust."

"It's just a matter of time," Zeke said.

"How did you find all this out?"

"People owe me favors."

Andrew sipped his drink and gazed out at the golf course. The wind had picked up on cue as it had every afternoon.

"You don't look so good, Andrew," Zeke said.

"I don't feel so good." Andrew wanted to know more, but he was spent, and he got the feeling that now was not the time to ask.

"And given that shiner, you're going to want to get out of here as soon as you can."

CHAPTER 25

The debris had been cleared out of the southbound 15, and the weekend traffic was lighter than usual. He reached his destination, climbed the external stairs to the second floor, his golf clubs on his shoulder, backpack in hand, and knocked on the door. He found himself relieved to see Renée. She put her hand on his cheek.

"What happened?"

"I'll tell you later."

"Does it hurt?"

"A little."

She was standing close to him, close enough that he could smell the lemongrass and jasmine in her hair.

She stepped back and he realized that the clubs were still on his shoulder. "Sorry, bad habit, I take them with me, and I don't like to leave them in the car."

"Interesting."

"It is."

"Are you hungry?"

"Starving." His only food intake for the day had been popcorn.

"Tía's?"

"The aunt with the recipes?"

"It's a couple of blocks from here."

He was unsure about the sleeping arrangements; he'd not asked if she had a second room, and she'd not offered up the information. He dropped his bags, put on a light sweater, and they headed out. They walked past quaint, single-family homes, and two- and three-story apartment buildings before they entered a busy thoroughfare replete with individuals, couples, and families out for a stroll. The crowds seemed to be enjoying the evening with pleasant and dry air, while they stopped to gaze at well-lit storefront windows adorned with Christmas decorations or sat at the outdoor café and restaurant tables sipping cocktails or eating appetizers. Some were already on dessert. Compared to what he'd seen on his drive over, Claremont was an island of academia and peace amidst its chaotic and dilapidated surroundings.

Tía Matilde was on the corner. A middle-aged woman with dark, flowing hair greeted them at the door. She gave Renée a warm hug.

"*¿Cómo estás, querida?*"

She gave Andrew the same warm welcome, squeezing hard, her arms strong and her hands rough. She led the couple past the crowded bar and sat them at a table opposite the bustling open kitchen. Ranchera music filled the large, low-ceilinged room, whose walls were adorned with colorful drawings, paintings, and masks of skeletons, skulls, and other macabre effigies in celebration of Día de los Muertos. The tables, all of them occupied, were overflowing with baskets of tacos, chips, and salsa. And almost every table had a large, steaming bowl of braised meat and black beans that patrons were eagerly spooning into small tortillas.

"Mixiote," Renée said. "Lamb or pork wrapped in parchment. It's their signature dish."

"I'll let you do the ordering." Andrew smiled, pushing aside the menu.

Tía appeared with a tray holding two tumblers of margaritas on the rocks, a pair of small, ceramic cups filled with a clear liquid, a basket of chips, and a bowl of salsa. She placed the contents of the tray on the table and said, "The Mezcal came in yesterday."

Andrew picked up the small cup and brought it to his nose, careful not to spill the contents. The sharpness of the alcohol was mellowed by the scent of smoked leather and dirt. He took a sip and cringed. It tasted like a burnt bicycle inner tube blended with rotten lemons. His throat burned.

Tía laughed and went back to the hostess table.

"You can't buy this anywhere. They make it in her village," Renée said.

"I can tell."

Renée sipped from her cup. "Tell me what happened to your face."

"Do you want the innocuous answer or the truth?"

She furrowed her brow.

"Because I could just say that I slipped in the shower, but that would open up a whole other line of questioning, inevitably leading to you second-guessing my motor control and thinking I was going senile in my forties."

Her eyes narrowed further.

"On the other hand, if I told you that I was held at gunpoint and slapped around by a couple of goons, would you believe me?"

Renée's mouth fell open.

"It's like I'm Roger Thornhill in *North by Northwest*."

"What the—"

"Except this took place in a condo in Helendale surrounded by dust and rocks instead of an opulent villa in the shadow of Mount Rushmore. And this wasn't a Hitchcock flick, *I* was the star of a bad movie! Well-dressed thugs with gold chains and crucifixes, prominent chest hair, a gun, threats—the works. One of them was called *Junior*." He leaned back in his chair. "They were after Charlie, not me."

Renée's shocked expression hadn't changed.

"Looking back on it now, part of me wants to laugh."

"This isn't funny, Andrew." She leaned in.

"You're right, it isn't."

"Did you call the cops?"

"No cops. What's the point? Charlie borrowed money from the wrong people, that's what he said, and now the note's come due."

"For Kannawerks?"

"His restaurant." He picked up the tumbler.

"What are you going to do?"

"What is there *to* do?" He raised his glass. "Charlie's a survivor. He'll figure it out; he always does."

"You can't go back to Helendale."

He stared at his drink and for a moment they remained silent.

"This is a nice place," he said finally.

She watched him. "Where's your family, Andrew?"

"My mother passed away a few years ago. My father's retired in Tucson. He and I were never close until recently. We've been talking more these days." He took a sip. "You?"

She picked up her cup and downed the remains in one go.

"That was brave," he said.

"I haven't seen or spoken to my family in years." She fingered her cup and glanced around the restaurant. "Another round?"

"Sure," he said. "But hold the Mezcal."

She waved a server over and they exchanged words in Spanish.

He stared into her eyes and then lowered his gaze until it stopped on the imperceptible mole above her lip. "Do you keep in touch with them?"

She shrugged. "I hear about them from time to time from a cousin who left and never went back, like me." She turned the cup over. "I grew up in a small, isolated town. It was fine, I guess, until I got older and my breasts started showing and suddenly things were expected of me." She stared at her glass and sighed. "I saw what was beyond the perimeter walls of the town. So I left and came to LA. No regrets."

Another escapee making a go of it in SoCal. He wanted to know more but did not want to ask probing questions for now. He had caught a glimpse of what was behind the curtain. *Let the evening go by and take it as it comes.*

The server brought over the mixiote, tortillas, and a pitcher of margaritas. As Andrew refilled Renée's glass, she grabbed a tortilla, filled it with the steaming lamb and bean stew, and took a bite. Sauce dripped down her chin, and as he reached over to wipe it off with his finger, his phone rang. He ignored it.

"What if it's Charlie?"

"I'll deal with it later."

The restaurant was getting boisterous. Over the din of the patrons, they continued their absorbing conversation as they devoured the mixiote and polished off the pitcher.

When Andrew was done, he leaned back and pushed the plate away. Renée was staring at him.

"Is there something on my face?" She was making him nervous.

"I'm just wondering why someone like you isn't hitched?"

"I could ask you the same thing."

"I asked you first."

"I was with someone for seven years, then I moved here. She's still there."

"I see."

"Different priorities."

"I understand."

"I've never been married, if that's what you're asking."

"Sometimes it's good to be alone," she said. "To step away; take stock of oneself; re-evaluate."

"There were some good things." He took a sip of his margarita. "But I'm trying to move forward, embrace what's in front of me now."

"You mean like me?"

"Like you."

She laughed and then suddenly grew serious. "You know, Andrew, maybe you can't just 'try.' Maybe you have to completely wipe out the past and *go after* what's in front of you."

"That's a bit drastic."

"Sometimes you need to do drastic things."

"Like leaving twenty years of tech behind for cannabis in the High Desert?"

"What do you *really* want to do?"

He sighed. "I don't know."

"I did it more than once. I left home. And then, after college, I chose a path thinking I'd be on it for a while. But somewhere down the line, I realized it was the wrong one. Once you start cringing at the thought of another conference call or useless client meeting, you realize you're peddling intangible, unnecessary wares, like smoke from a chimney. After the consulting thing, I wandered for a while until I stumbled on the taco truck. I've never been happier than when working with Lina."

"I envy you."

"Whatever it is, go get it, Andrew."

He held her eyes.

"It's that simple," she said.

Andrew reached over and took Renée's hand. He stared into her eyes and caressed her cheek. It was warm to the touch.

Tía was standing by their table—it was unclear how long she'd been there—holding one serving of flan and two spoons. She placed it between them, cleared the empty plates, and left.

Renée picked up a spoon, scooped a piece of flan, and held it aloft. Andrew leaned in and let the custard fill his mouth. They took turns. He watched her swallow the dessert. She licked her lips, closed her eyes, and opened her mouth for more. Andrew hesitated ever so slightly, then slowly put the spoon in her mouth. She trapped the spoon, Andrew feeling the vibrations of her tongue swirling round and round, then letting go. She opened her eyes.

The bill was missing a variety of items. Andrew left a generous tip, and they stepped out into the cool night, the full, orange moon glowing above the horizon. They walked back to the apartment, hand in hand, without saying a word. At the first stoplight, Renée reached up and kissed Andrew, pulling him close to her. Her lips were soft, and her scent penetrating. "You smell good," he said, his nose grazing her neck.

She grabbed his hand and led him across the street. They climbed the outer stairs to her apartment, and as Renée fumbled for the keys, Andrew leaned over and kissed her. He held her tight, grabbing her and lifting her off her feet, pressing her against the wall. She wrapped her legs around his waist, her arms around his neck, pulling him in. She let out a soft moan. He let her down and she found the key, opening the door.

CHAPTER 26

He synchronized the dashboard clock. The first Sunday in November: daylight savings—*fall* back—an extra hour. He could use ten. He and Renée had spent the night exploring each other's bodies. Visions flashed: her tracing an invisible outline along his torso, finding its way down and back up again; him grabbing her and sliding her on her back, kissing her as he did so, the rising sun permeating the room and casting their silhouettes on the wall; their bodies pressing against each other, their hands touching, caressing, probing, squeezing; running his lips down her neck, taking in her smell, tasting the sweat on her breasts; throwing the sheets off the bed and making love again.

And so went his drive west on the 210, his thoughts running amuck with no sense or logic. He was tired yet euphoric. *Calm down there, buddy boy.* It was one night. They had just met. It was an infatuation, that was all. How many times had he felt this way after spending the night with a woman?

Now that he thought about it, not many. Not with this intensity, where the adrenaline clouded his thoughts, and his emotions got the better of him. *Shit.* These feelings had not been there when he started dating Diana, and that had been one of his more meaningful relationships. Why was this different? Was it a rebound? Not from Diana.

That flame had gone out a long time ago, even before the tryst with Ulrike. Maybe he was emotionally compensating for the professional chasm he had fallen into or the hole he had dug for himself. Maybe this was a reaction to a loss.

And then he felt afraid.

Afraid that it wasn't a reaction to any loss, personal or professional. He *liked* her. He liked being with her. She was funny. She had energy. She was smart. He liked talking to her; he felt comfortable. He liked how she smelled, he liked how she tasted, he liked to hover over her body and feel the soft, invisible hairs on her skin. He wanted to drive back to Claremont, climb the stairs, and open the door . . . and then what? He was afraid that this was a coup de foudre—struck by lightning. And he wasn't sure how long the effects would last.

One step at a time. What's the worst that could happen? A broken heart? He'd survived that before.

And all that could wait, because now he had to deal with the rider issue. Mike had gone back to the factory at Andrew's request and dug up the lease. Sure enough, the rider was there. So if Terence went under, Kannawerks *could* be fucked. Or maybe it was nothing. Maybe it was to be expected in cannabis. But if Andrew put himself in an investor's shoes, he'd want some guarantees that operations would not be interrupted or terminated and that the tenant was protected against the landlord's potential insolvency. He called Charlie again. No answer. He'd find out for himself. Andrew had called Terence that morning. He answered as if he had been sitting by the phone waiting for the call.

He exited the freeway and found the entrance to the club located in an exclusive, gated community in a small valley surrounded by low, undulating hills, scarred gray and black by a fire from the prior year. Andrew checked in with the gate attendant, who was adorned in a starched blue shirt and impeccably ironed brown pants. He held an iPad and wore an earpiece of the Secret Service kind.

The clubhouse pro was even friendlier than the gate attendant. "Mr. Kayne has already checked in and is on the range. And your green fee has been taken care of," he said.

Andrew thanked the pro, grabbed a scorecard, and headed to the range where his clubs were already waiting, along with Terence.

"Charlie tells me you're a scratch golfer."

"He exaggerates. I'm a three."

Terence let out a low whistle. "I'm a seven. We'll make it interesting."

Andrew's eyes landed on the titanium Richard Mille on Terence's right wrist as he scribbled something on the scorecard. The shirt he wore accentuated his taut upper body.

Terence smiled. "Fifty a side plus one hundred for the match?"

"I'll give you two strokes a side."

"Done." The round could get expensive, but Andrew wasn't planning on losing.

He lost the front nine by two strokes. Even though Andrew was operating on no sleep, there was no way Terence played to a seven handicap. He wasn't a long hitter—there were limits to the physics of the ball flight if you're five six and in your mid-fifties, but he hit every fairway and green, the ball below the hole more often than not. The alcohol from the cart girl seemed not to interfere. Terence provided guidance on where to aim from the tee, where to land the ball on the green, and what hidden hazards to avoid. But Andrew couldn't believe the accuracy of Terence's iron play, short game, and putting. This guy was a near scratch golfer. And a sandbagger.

By the time they reached the par five eighteenth, they were tied on the back nine, as Andrew had won two of the last three holes. He was still two down for the match. The alcohol was finally catching up to Terence, and a couple of errant irons found sand.

"Double the bet for the back nine?" Terence asked, as Andrew set his ball on the tee.

Is this guy for real? Andrew stepped back to line up his shot. "What's the worst that can happen? I'm out two-hundred and fifty bucks?"

Both drives found the fairway. Terence hit his second shot to within one hundred yards of the green, short of the waste area. One more swing and it was highly likely that Terence would have a chance at birdie.

"The question is should I go for it or lay up?" Andrew asked as he approached his ball.

"Sometimes you have to take a risk," Terence responded.

Andrew took out the five iron. He bent over, plucked a tuft of grass, and threw it in the air; it moved to the left. He choked down an inch on the grip and opened his stance ever so slightly. He took a couple of practice swings. He then addressed the ball, looked down the fairway at the target, focused back on the ball, and swung.

The ball bounced off the club face with the crack of a rifle shot. The projectile arched in the air, reached its apex, and began the downward descent. And as it fell, it floated to the right, the high cut imparted on the ball fighting against the right-to-left wind controlling the trajectory. The ball landed softly on the green, took a couple of hops, rolled a few feet to the right, and stopped.

"Bravo," Terence said, clapping.

"I know that swing is in there somewhere."

"You'll have to tell me where you got it."

"Thailand."

"The land of smiles," Terence said, a glint in his eyes. He hit a wedge to within six feet of the pin. "You're away, Andrew, and fortunately for you, I don't stroke on this hole."

No shit. Andrew nodded and smiled, and when they reached the green, he bent over, fixed his divot, and marked the ball. Ten feet. Now he just needed to make the putt as insurance against Terence's certain birdie. On his way to the green, he had thought about letting

Terence tie or even win the hole, putting Andrew out the entire $250. Stroke Terence's ego. Use that as a means to modify the rider. But as he crouched over his ball, he decided against it. The last thing Andrew could stand was losing, especially at something he was very good at.

He walked behind the hole and lined up the putt. He went through his routine, a couple of practice strokes to get the feel, slid the putter head behind the ball, adjusted his feet, and swung the putter. The ball bounced on the uneven surface. Did he hit it too hard? The ball rolled on, one revolution at a time, as if in slow motion. It found the edge of the cup, did a one-eighty, and dropped into the hole.

He was only out fifty bucks.

Terence picked up his ball and put his arm around Andrew. "It was wonderful playing with someone of your skills. You're so graceful, elegant, yet strong. Decisive." He continued with the adulations all the way to the valet. "Let's have another drink, shall we?"

It wasn't a question. Terence held Andrew's arm. "We'll go home. I'll message Lucian to get things ready."

Home? Andrew assumed they'd be going to the clubhouse. But he didn't have a choice; he hadn't yet gotten what he had come for. "Sounds good."

Their cars arrived. Terence and the valet watched in amusement as Andrew took out the driver and three wood from his bag and loaded the clubs across the back seat.

"You never cease to amaze me," Terence said. "Your car complements you perfectly."

Terence flew his British racing green DB9 down the winding roads of the complex, then up a steep incline where a solitary home was perched over the valley. It was a rush, Andrew had to admit, pushing hard to keep up, then letting her loose down the cypress-lined straightaway, downshifting, at last, as he approached the gate and saw the sprawling, single-story structure. It was in the style of a

Mediterranean Villa: burnt-red tiled roof reminiscent of the farm-houses in the Italian countryside, yellow-tending-to-orange stucco peppered with single- and double-paned windows, olive trees clustered along the perimeter, and a solitary fountain with the statue of a naked boy welcoming guests as they drove up to the main entrance.

Andrew parked behind the DB9. A four-car garage was to the right of the villa with the only visible vehicle a black Mercedes Roadster.

They stepped into a large hall with wood-beamed ceilings, a white marble floor overlaid with a smattering of tasteless rugs, and couches and armchairs that framed a fireplace large enough to hold a Volkswagen Beetle. A painting of a young, plain woman hung above the mantel. The woman was adorned in a white dress with a string of pearls around her short neck, her hands folded on her lap, and a faint smile on her thin lips. She sat on a simple wooden chair.

"That's my mum," Terence said, admiring the portrait. "Raised me on her own after my father passed when I was ten. She fell ill a few years after I brought her over from England. Mum was prescribed medical marijuana in her last months, which helped her with the pain—bloody miracle drug, if you ask me. She would have suffered immensely if it hadn't been for marijuana. Those bloody opioids . . . she was on those at the very end, you know, made her catatonic. If they had prescribed them earlier, she would have been dead a long time before. At least I got to enjoy her until the end. And every bit counted. She's the reason I'm in cannabis."

He gestured at a black-and-white picture in an ornate silver frame: a short, bare-chested man wore a cap and overalls, his face smeared black. Two small boys stood at his side. One stared forlornly at the camera. The other smiled at the man.

"That's me," he said, indicating the sad one, "and that's my dad and brother. Coal mining, the engine of the economy back then, until the Iron Lady came along."

Andrew sensed this was an initiation that all guests went through so Terence could show his roots sharply contrasting with the wealth that ensconced him today. A self-made man.

"Come, let's sit outside and enjoy the sunset." He took Andrew's arm and led him through a pair of French doors onto a covered patio in the style of a Florentine loggia, through a manicured lawn, and down a gravel path framed by red and white rose bushes, until they reached the infinity pool hanging over the valley below. They sat down at a table overflowing with nuts, chips, and other assorted snacks and adjusted their chairs to shield themselves from the setting sun. The view over the pool was breathtaking, as if they were standing on the peak of a mountain and the entire world lay at their feet with the valley and hills extending to the ocean in the distance.

"This was Mum's favorite thing to do in the afternoons. Sit out here, cocktail in hand, taking it all in."

"How long have you lived here?"

"Almost twenty years. This was my first residential purchase in California and still my favorite. Ah, Lucian." A young, lean, dark-haired man had appeared, wearing skin-tight, white pants, a loose, azure linen shirt, and red espadrilles, like a Club Med cabana boy. He carried a tray containing a pitcher, a couple of long-stemmed glasses, and a small bowl of green olives.

Terence said to Andrew, "Vodka martini, if that's all right with you."

"Whatever the house is offering, but I'll limit it to one."

"You can always stay here and leave in the morning," Terence said.

"I'm good," Andrew said.

Lucian disappeared. Terence stirred the contents of the pitcher, placed one olive in each glass, and poured. "Please," he said, gesturing to the glasses.

"Cheers," Andrew said.

"Cheers," Terence responded. He watched Andrew sip his martini. "Tell me more about that swing of yours."

"It's all thanks to Khun Archin, my golf pro in Bangkok. He preached the art of golf to us farangs—foreigners. He taught me the fundamentals of the swing and introduced me to the importance of playing in the now, one shot at a time. Keep the mind free of clutter. His mantras were: *mai pen rai*—it doesn't matter; *chai yen yen*—stay calm."

"A golf guru."

"You can say that."

"A wonderful place, Thailand."

"Yes, it is."

"I've had some good times in Pattaya. Have you been there?"

"Only once."

"*Everybody* goes to Pattaya."

"I went the other way, Hua Hin, quieter, less crowds. I'm not real fond of Pattaya."

Pattaya. High-school graduation, long weekend, coaxed by friends into one last road trip before they were off to college. He had walked the streets that first night, swarmed by nubile Thai girls, avoiding the locales where the pale-skinned, red-faced, whiskered, wife-beater-shirt-wearing men toyed with young girls and young boys on their laps. He had spent the rest of the weekend on the beach.

"Shepherd Dunes is a beautiful course," Andrew said, returning to the present. "Speaking of which, I owe you fifty dollars." He took out his money clip and placed the bills on the table.

Terence folded the bills and put them in his pocket. "We'll have to do it again soon."

Andrew set down his glass. "I had a question about the Kannawerks lease."

"I didn't think you'd come all this way just for a round of golf. What about the lease?"

Andrew explained the issue with the rider.

"That rider is standard practice in cannabis. And look around you. Does it seem like I'm going under?" He grabbed a chip and held it aloft, as if observing an expensive piece of jewelry. "I'd have to ask the bank to make the change. It's up to them."

"It may come up in the due diligence. I'm not saying that it's a showstopper, but it is a risk."

"And I'm not sure the banks would be willing to do so given the current cannabis climate." He swallowed the chip and picked up another one. "I don't think it's necessary to modify the contract."

"If I was an investor, I'd want to confirm the continuity of operations no matter what happens to the landlord."

"If I *were* an investor, I wouldn't worry about the landlord defaulting on his lease."

"That's not what I was implying."

"Isn't it?" He grabbed a couple of nuts and threw them in his mouth, chewing slowly and gazing at the setting sun. "Your lease runs out when? June 2021?"

"Yes."

"Given the market challenges, if I were to do this, and I'm not saying I will, I'd have to pull in some favors with the lender." He sat pensive for a moment. "Maybe the lender could be convinced to do so if you extend the lease."

"For how long?"

"Standard terms are three years. So, through 2024."

Another five years in Adelanto? *Fuck that shit.* "We're going to vacate Adelanto once the current lease expires, assuming that we raise money or merge."

"You want me to modify the contract without extending the lease. What's in it for me? What's the lender's incentive?"

"We'd commit to move to another one of your properties somewhere else: LA, Palm Springs, Santa Barbara. We'd work with you on the transition."

"The lender is going to balk at modifying the contract, Andrew, unless we give them something. Extending the lease is the best option. They'll want a commitment."

"Fine. We extend the lease, remove the rider, and add a termination clause. We'll give you six-month's notice if we vacate, with a contingency that we move into one of your other properties with a new three-year commitment."

Terence drummed his fingers on the table, searching Andrew's eyes until it became uncomfortable. "If this is so important, why hasn't Charlie brought this up to me before? He was here yesterday; the subject never came up."

Andrew feigned calm. "He's been busy."

"Busy indeed." He smirked.

"He's not the kind of guy that will read a contract at that level of detail."

"No, he isn't, is he? That's why he's got you." Terence sipped his martini. "I'm only willing to do this because I like you, Andrew. You're a breath of fresh air in this bloody industry."

Andrew picked up his glass and finished his martini. *Time to go.*

"Right, then. Shall we go for a swim?"

"I have to head back."

He touched Andrew's arm again. "Look at that sun." It *was* a majestic sight: the few clouds in the sky were streaked with fiery pink and red, undulating hills merged with the coast, and the sun was slowly disappearing behind the ocean.

"We'll get you trunks."

"Really, I'm fine."

"Then stay for one more drink. I'll be back in a jiff." Terence removed his hand from Andrew's arm and disappeared inside the house.

Andrew planned his exit. That stare, the faux chumminess, making him feel like something was expected of him, like Andrew owed him something. One more drink, that's it, if that's what it takes to get the rider eliminated. If Terence kept his word, called in favors with the lender—*What the hell was Charlie doing here yesterday?*

"Water's above eighty degrees, you sure you don't want to dip in?" Terence reappeared, holding plush towels and an extra pair of trunks. He wore tight yellow Speedo-like boxers that exposed his fit physique, which like his face was covered in a uniform, light tan.

Before Andrew could answer, a woman walked out of the house. She wore a white bikini with a transparent wrap around her waist, her bottom faintly visible through its thin folds.

"This is my friend, Rhonda," Terence said.

She extended her hand, adorned with blood-red talons; tight, corrugated flabs of skin wrapped around arms that were short for her frame. Her hand was as cold as a dead fish.

He noticed her earlobes: they were unnaturally attached to her face. Her cheeks were puffy and lifted, lips set in a permanent pout exposing bleached teeth and unable to fully close thanks to the generous injections of filler she must have recently received. Her eyes were wide, deep, and catlike, ensconced by long lashes, her hair jet-black and straight. And her breasts. The size of overripe cantaloupes. They burst through the small white triangles of cloth that were trying desperately to contain the volatile Jell-O. Albeit, she did have a perfectly symmetrical nose, as if it had been carved out of Carrara marble. She threw her wrap on a chair and waded into the pool.

"I'll get that drink now," Andrew said. But Lucian had beat him to it, refilling the pitcher with vodka, vermouth, and ice. He stirred the concoction, poured the martini, and placed two olives in a new glass.

"My pleasure," Lucian said.

As Andrew sipped the martini, his eyes met Rhonda's, her pout now a smile worthy of Jack's Joker.

Terence dove into the infinity pool, being mindful not to splash

Rhonda. "It's fabulous," he said, wading to the shallow end. "Lucian, mind bringing me one?"

Lucian poured the remains of the pitcher into a glass, garnished it with one olive, and brought it to the edge of the pool. He leaned over and handed the glass to Terence, who took a long sip. Terence placed the glass on the travertine edge, dove, and swam like a dolphin to the opposite side in one breath. Andrew nursed his martini and observed the sun's final dance, while Rhonda swam the length of the pool in an elegant breaststroke. Lucian disappeared into the house.

After several more laps Terence hopped out, dried himself off, and placed the towel around his waist. "Stay for dinner?"

Andrew felt woozy. "Thank you, I should go."

"Fine, but next time you'll stay, spend the weekend. There's plenty of room."

Andrew nodded. He tried to formulate a response. Nothing came out.

The sun compounded the throbbing. He was used to the pounding, but this felt different. He opened his eyes and sat up, startled. The sun was indeed finding its way through partially open curtains and onto the bed, a king-sized bed, with blue cotton sheets and too many pillows and—

What the fuck is going on?

Nausea set in. He examined his surroundings: charcoal outlines of copulating bodies, like the scenes depicted in the ancient frescoes of the brothels and the bath houses of Pompeii, were traced on a white wall and reflected in the floor-to-ceiling mirrors opposite the bed; a contoured black leather chaise lounge sat in the far corner; a massive LCD screen was embedded in the side wall; and one closed door. There was a familiar scent: sweet mandarin and geranium. He stood up and fell back down onto the bed. His head was spinning, and now on top of the nausea came panic and fear.

Why am I naked?

Out the window, he caught a glimpse of the courtyard. He had a sudden urge to run. He waited until the fog cleared and then stumbled over to the chaise lounge where his clothes were folded in a neat pile. As he started to dress, he tried to remember how he got here. His last memory was Terence diving into the pool.

And then he had a perverse thought. *I would feel it, I would know.* He held onto the headrest, steadying himself. They couldn't have. But he didn't remember a goddamn thing!

There was a golf round. Fucking sandbagger. He had a faint memory of a cabana boy pouring drinks. For some reason he thought of the Bride of Frankenstein. His visions of the day before were disjointed, as though they had happened years ago.

He felt his pockets. *Nothing. How am I going to get out of here?* He searched the room. *There they are*, on the night table—keys, money clip, phone.

6:00 a.m. Fuck. He cracked open the door and peered out into a carpeted hallway. Silence. He shut the door and sat back down. *I must be on the east side of the house. The main entrance has to be down the hall. I'll find the exit, hop into the car, and get the fuck out.*

But what if the car wasn't there? What if it was boxed in?

No way he was going to get stuck in this Hotel California. He opened the door, tiptoed down the hallway, walked by Mum's portrait without saying goodbye, and stepped out into the cold morning air, the sun illuminating the mocking smile on the naked boy's face. Andrew jumped in the car and floored it down the hill.

CHAPTER 27

"You're warm," Renée said.

"I'm fine," Andrew said, still groggy. He'd called Mike that morning, told him he wasn't coming in, and then proceeded to spend the day lying on Renée's couch, dozing in and out of foggy reveries, trying to piece together the prior afternoon, evening, and night.

"Did you get what you wanted, at least?"

"Who knows. How can I believe anything he says now?" He ambled slowly to the fridge, took out a couple of beers, and as he brought them back to the couch, the front door opened.

"I'll take one of those." Olivia threw her backpack on the chair and handed Renée a bulging plastic bag. Andrew passed Olivia a bottle, and she took a long swig.

"They found five bodies buried in the desert near Barstow."

"What the—"

"Five of the missing migrants. Kids found them; they were joyriding in their off-road vehicles—those dune buggies—and one of them flipped over. The kid who was driving found himself staring into a decaying face. They called the sheriff's department, who unearthed a shallow grave and then called the Border Justice hotline because we had reported several migrants missing, thinking that they had been sent back to Mexico. It's a mess."

"That's seven bodies now, on my count," Andrew said.

"The numbers are growing and will keep growing as more and more migrants continue disappearing. Contrary to what FDN tells us, they're not being sent back home, they're not being 'repatriated.' We know because our teams on the other side of the border can't find them."

"Maybe they escaped."

"FDN is run like a maximum-security prison. They're not escaping." She took another long sip. "They shouldn't be holding people in there for more than thirty days."

"How many are missing?"

"Forty, forty-five migrants, all of them lone wolves, ones that have no family in the United States, and who crossed the border alone. No spouses or children."

"When you say 'repatriated,' what exactly does that mean?"

"It means the migrants are sent to CBP holding stations and then bussed back across the border to Mexico."

"CBP?"

"Customs and Border Patrol. Sister agency of Immigration and Customs Enforcement— ICE; both fall under Homeland Security. ICE subcontracts their detention needs to FDN. CBP enforces immigration within one hundred miles of the borders, and ICE has jurisdiction everywhere else." She walked to the kitchen. "Talk about a messed-up organization. CBP's hired a massive number of agents to deal with the 'immigration problem' because the government sees immigration as a plague, a virus destroying white America. These agents who think they are hired and trained to stop terrorists at the US border, and see themselves as modern-day Rambos protecting the United States from the next Bin Laden, instead find themselves serving as humanitarian aid workers dealing with abandoned children, pregnant women, and starving and dehydrated human beings who survived trekking thousands of miles across the desert and now find themselves locked in cages like animals in a zoo."

She grabbed another beer from the fridge.

"A few years ago there was a period where the CBP had one of their officers or agents arrested on average every other day—*every other day*. For violence, corruption, misconduct, drug smuggling, and even murder." She fell onto the couch and blinked at Andrew.

"What happened to your face?"

"Long story."

"So what does this mean for you guys at Border Justice?" Renée asked.

"We have two goals," Olivia said. "The first is that we want to shut down private prisons, like FDN. The second is to help migrants receive adequate legal representation. We are protesting against the private prisons, contract extensions coming up for negotiation, and for justice, clarity, and compassion for the migrants. Some good laws are being passed. One goes into effect this coming January, which prohibits new private prisons from being built in California, but the existing ones get to run out their contracts. And guess what these prisons are doing? They are signing new, multiyear contracts with the cities before the deadline so that their revenues are guaranteed for another ten years."

"Sounds like the mob," Andrew said.

"It's perverse. They're perverse. They're all corrupt. Private prisons and cities have a nice and cozy relationship. The City of Adelanto gets paid pass-through fees for letting private contractors like FDN build prisons on their land. And do you know what the worst of it is?"

"Well, no, but—"

"They're a private equity-backed REIT—a real estate investment trust! A for-profit entity!" She paced the floor. "The incentives are all wrong. FDN makes money *per inmate*. Over a hundred dollars. Per inmate. Per day. A migrant is a good, a widget, an investment with a return! And these private prisons are protected. Congress passed a law that guarantees a minimum number of occupied beds per facility, a 'bed quota,' that ICE is *encouraged* to meet and exceed, as an incentive to cover the costs, whether the beds are full or not. Nobody checks how many people they are holding."

She guzzled her beer. "The more inmates, the more money FDN makes. It's all about revenue and profits, and with this racist, anti-immigrant, corrupt government, there's no hope for a change anytime soon." She violently threw the bottle into the recycling bin, causing it to detonate into shards. She stared at the broken pieces for a few seconds. "Sorry, I only came over to drop off some prep items for your tacos."

"The guy they found near our factory a few weeks ago. Is he on your missing list?"

"Yes. Why do you ask?"

"If he disappeared around the same time as the bodies buried in Barstow, there may be a connection. It may not bode well for the other missing people."

"I hope not," Olivia said, opening the door. "That would be an atrocity."

CHAPTER 28

A ndrew woke up after seven. Renée was gone. He pictured her driving over the Cajon Pass, making her way to Adelanto. He went into the kitchen. A spare key was on the counter. He stared at it for a long moment. Somehow it felt natural, without the implied burden of commitment that he had felt in past relationships. Maybe it had to do with age and experience. Or maybe it just had to do with Renée.

He slipped the key in his pocket and drove to the factory.

Fires still burned in the foothills, and smoke emanated from the San Bernardino National Forest. A brown-and-yellow haze hovered over the valley and abutted the hills, the Santa Anas having relented over the weekend. There was nowhere for the ash and soot to go, which created a suffocating dome, cloaking LA, and obscuring the sun.

"Your eye. What happened?" Mike asked.

"I hit my head on the side of a door." Andrew dropped his backpack on the floor. "Did you hear about the dead bodies buried near Barstow?"

"*¿Qué chingados?*"

"Five. From FDN. Might be related to the one they found around here a few weeks ago."

"¡*Ayyy guey!* I was hoping for better news to start the day. Because we may have another issue. The COA came in for Pink Dot." He shut the office door, picked up a sheaf of papers from the printer, and handed them to Andrew.

While Andrew tried to decipher the data, Mike brought over another set of papers. "These are the results for our Alta line, the fast-acting five mg THC gummies. The ones you are holding are the results for Pink Dot." He took the papers out of Andrew's hand and placed them next to the others on the desk. "Look," he said, running his fingers along a straight line from one set to the other. "The chemistry is *identical*. The active formulation is *identical*. The rest of the ingredients and quantities—the glucose, sugar, gelatin, pectin—are *exactly* the same. The only difference is that Pink Dot has ten mg THC per gummy and does not contain terpenes. The dosage in each gummy is within a tight range, plus or minus five percent. And no contaminants."

Mike sat down. "This recipe is *the same* as our formula: it was either stolen or someone gave it away. And Ish is right. These gummies were not made by hand. They were made in a machine. They are consistent in size, shape, and weight."

"Our instincts were right all along. Not only is Pink Dot a competitive threat, but it's also a clone."

"They could be using our depositor."

"That's impossible."

"Nothing is impossible, amigo."

Andrew considered the bustling operators through the large window.

"We shut down at two in the afternoon. No one is here past five, and the first shift arrives at five the next morning. Plenty of time to run a batch or two. Or three."

"But there's security, the guards," Andrew said.

"Maybe someone pays them off."

"The video cameras."

"Some of which are inactive." Mike didn't have to remind him.

"A camera system for which we have no admin access." Andrew drummed his fingers on the glass window. "But there's no one in the factory at night. We examined the feeds for the active cameras."

"It would explain the warped pistons and the excessive wear and tear on the depositor."

Andrew reviewed the printouts. "Let's take a step back. To be clear, you're saying that someone is using our Alta formulation to make Pink Dot? Couldn't someone have just reverse engineered our recipe?"

"No way, no," Mike said, shaking his head. "Our nano-molecular infusion is unique. I do not think you can reverse engineer it, even if the gummies were already on the market."

"We check the fucking video then."

"We did already."

"No, we get *all* the cameras working, and make sure they're recording twenty-four seven. Now."

"Good luck getting in."

Andrew swallowed the last dregs of his coffee, threw the cup in the trash, and walked over to the console.

"I need to go to the floor and monitor a few things; I will be back." Mike grabbed his lab coat and shut the door behind him.

Good luck getting in, my ass. It's a Linux system. Andrew had learned how to code on these things. He blew the dust off the keyboard, pressed a key, and the screen lit up, icons and folders scattered on the desktop.

He double-clicked on the camera icon and a window popped up with the administrator username already prefilled. *That solves one problem.* He opened the command line interface. He hadn't accessed one in a while, but it was second nature for him. He typed in the requisite commands to determine the operating system (OS) version: an antiquated Linux release, probably because the video software didn't run on later releases or was never upgraded. Who knew. *But the older the OS, the easier the hack.*

Next step: open a browser and type in a web address. No connection. *A standalone system.* He switched over to his laptop and scoured the web for password-cracking python scripts, downloaded and transferred them to a thumb drive, and uploaded them to the security system. He opened the scripts, made the necessary modifications, saved the files, typed the instructions on the command line, and pressed enter. He sat back and waited.

He was in within thirty minutes. The admin password was "ThE2Lous!" *What a bunch of dopes.*

He clicked on the option to check the status of the cameras and waited for the screen to load. He checked the monitor displaying the camera feeds and identified the zones that had inactive cameras. In the admin console, he selected Zone 2, wherein a cluster of cameras was pointed at the warehouse section in the back of the factory. He checked the corresponding camera numbers in the system. Half of them had been set to inactive. *What the fuck?* He switched them to active and all the dark feeds in Zone 2 popped up on the monitor, one after the other, until he could see the entire warehouse.

He checked the other zones, eight in total. Same thing: the inactive cameras had been manually set to inactive. He changed all the settings and the monitor lit up like a Christmas tree. All twenty-nine of the cameras were now active.

Mike came in and stared at the monitor in disbelief.

Andrew explained what he had found.

"You just flipped a switch?"

"Yes. But that's the problem. When was Nett here last?"

"I do not remember."

"Let's see what else we find." Andrew clicked on the camera

trained on the foyer, providing a clear view of the employee lockers and the main entrance to the factory. He went back to that morning and watched as he came in.

"The cameras that were active are recording fine. Let me check a few other things." He clicked on several other menu options and found the recording setting. Each camera had two recording options: twenty-four hours or custom.

"What the fuck?"

"What is wrong?"

"This setting should be twenty-four hours."

Mike leaned over Andrew's shoulder.

"It's custom for this camera." Andrew selected a handful of other cameras at random. All of them had the custom setting set to *not* record between 9:00 p.m. and 4:00 a.m.

"How is that possible? We saw the video during those timeframes when the deputies were here. An empty floor. No activity."

"Maybe these Nett guys aren't dopes after all." Andrew selected a camera with a view of the packing area. The live feed came through with the bright colors of the gummies contrasting with the light-blue gowns of the operators. The digital display hovered above the packing line. "That display is connected to the Internet?"

Mike nodded.

Andrew slid the cursor along the camera's timeline at the bottom of the screen, moving it to 8:59 p.m. of the night before. He pressed play and the timer at the bottom of the screen started. The image was grainy, black and white, and different shades of gray. Nothing moved on the screen.

"Here we go," Andrew said, leaning in.

The camera's timer flipped to 9:00 p.m. The image flickered and the movement was imperceptible. "Did you see that?" Andrew zoomed in on the factory's digital display on the video. "It jumped, from 8:59 p.m. to 10:00 p.m. Those Nett guys forgot about one thing."

Andrew slid the cursor to 3:59 a.m. "Pay attention," he said, pressing play. The factory digital display on the video switched to 5:00 a.m. for a millisecond and then jumped back to 4:00 a.m.

"Daylight savings."

Mike's face was now a pale shade of gray.

Andrew continued. "No one can see through that window, right?"

"It is a one-way mirror."

"*None* of the cameras record between 9:00 p.m. and 4:00 a.m. Yet all the active cameras show a continuous recording through the night, twenty-four seven. Right?"

"Right."

"But that can't be. The settings prove it. So how do they show a continuous recording? They must have taken recordings from the past where they recorded the factory at night with no activity and inserted the prerecorded segments from 9:00 p.m. to 4:00 a.m. into the feeds we're watching so that they show one continuous recording. You get it?"

"No."

"Think about it this way. You have twenty-four hours of tape, you unspool it, lay it out, cut out the segment from nine to four, and replace it with a prerecorded segment that never changes. You do this for every active camera, every day, programmatically, with software."

"But why were some of the cameras offline?"

"Because those are the ones they couldn't be sure would be consistent, day in and day out. Stacks of trays vary; the color of the gummies vary. All of the cameras on the curing stations, all of the cameras in shipping where boxes are stacked, they were all inactive. With daylight savings we *fall back*. They haven't updated the prerecorded video segments."

"*¿Qué chingados está pasando?*"

"Probably making Pink Dot like you hypothesized, right under our noses." Andrew manned the keyboard and proceeded to switch all the camera settings. "Now they're all recording twenty-four seven. Let's come back tomorrow and see what we find."

"What about this one?" Mike said, gesturing at the camera above his desk focused on them.

"Shit, hold on." Andrew found the camera in the admin console, switched it off, and deleted the last two hours showing him hacking into the system. "I'll have it record between 2:00 p.m. and 5:30 a.m. so that it stops recording when you get in. That way we can spy on them without worrying about them spying on us spying on them."

"Huh?"

"Only the paranoid survive." He logged out of the security system and placed the keyboard back on the console. Then he sat back, cradled his head in his hands, and stared at the ceiling.

If they were making illegal gummies in the factory between 9:00 p.m. and 4:00 a.m., who was driving it? Who was involved? How were they disabling the alarm? What about the guards? The inactive cameras meant that whoever *was* involved had intimate knowledge of the facility. Why Kannawerks? He needed to slow down and think rationally. And he wasn't ready to have a theoretical conversation with Mike. In the morning, they would have the footage from that night, and then they could discuss what to do.

Inform the BCC?

He needed to let Charlie know. "When do we produce the new lines?"

"One month. Ethan says we are expecting significant volumes. That should be good news."

"We need to deal with this shit first," Andrew said. He gestured at the video monitor, and as he did, he saw movement on one of the feeds—Charlie getting out of his M6 and walking to the back of the factory. His figure disappeared and reappeared in another frame.

And then he saw Ashlee.

They embraced, then she pulled out a pack and they lit each

other's cigarettes, cupping their hands to protect the flame from the wind. They leaned against the siding, talking. Suddenly Ashlee became animated, gesticulating with a cigarette in one hand and her phone in the other. Charlie motioned for her to calm down, but Ashlee walked away, disappearing and reappearing in different frames, while Charlie stood still, shaking his head. Then he threw his cigarette down and lit another one.

"Isn't that feed from the external camera that was inactive?" Andrew asked.

"It is. The one facing north."

"The one I just switched back on." He stared at the monitor and wondered if they met in that spot because they knew the camera was off. Something he wasn't going to say out loud, although Mike had probably figured it out. He jumped out of the chair and started typing.

"What are you doing?"

"Turning off the camera feeds to the video monitor, the same ones that were inactive, while leaving the cameras themselves on. The feeds need to appear like they're still inactive."

As his fingers flew across the keyboard, the designated feeds went dark, one by one.

"Hurry up!"

"Almost done."

The video monitor reverted to its pixelated form just as Charlie let himself in.

"Hey, guys." Charlie had a forced grin on his face. He ran his hands through his disheveled hair. "We're *rocking* in Vegas. I knew there was a reason I brought you here, Andy. The team had everything choreographed, nothing was out of place, the investor walked away impressed. I think we're almost there." He stared at Andrew's face. "How's your eye?"

"Colorful," Andrew said.

"Let's take a walk."

Charlie put his arm around Andrew's shoulder as they ambled through the parking lot. "I'm so fucking sorry about what happened," Charlie said.

"They wanted you dead."

"It's taken care of. Lorenzo likes to exaggerate." They walked quietly as warm, jarring gusts scattered dust along the ground and accentuated the skunk smell. Then Charlie said, "I heard that you went to see Terence. Did you have a good time?"

Andrew disentangled himself from Charlie. "I played a round of golf, lost some money, had a few drinks, and woke up without any clothes on. I wouldn't call that a good time."

Charlie remained quiet.

"I went to see him about the rider in the lease."

"Leave that alone. I've got it covered. And I wish you would have told me. I would have warned you to stay away from the guy. He's a bit weird."

"I'm not sure what happened—"

"Forget about it."

"If he's a *bit weird*, why did *you* go see him?"

Charlie lit a cigarette, the smoke dissipating in the dry wind. "He's helping me with the misunderstanding."

"You went to him for money? *Jesus*, Charlie."

Charlie stared at the gravel and nudged a stone with his foot. "I'm digging my way out of a hole. I'm almost there. Kannawerks is going to get me there. I fucked up with the restaurant; I'm making reparations. When we're done with Kannawerks, I'll be off the hook."

"Where the hell is *he* getting the money? I heard most of his properties are empty. He might go bankrupt. That's why I went to see him about the rider."

"Where did you hear that?"

"It's a small town."

Charlie smirked and then gestured at the vast expanse of the desert. "This is a godforsaken part of the world, a transitory place—to somewhere, or nowhere, depending on your point of view. It's my purgatory. I'm doing penance for past sins. One, two more quarters, and we're done."

One or two more quarters? Andrew wasn't sure he'd make it to the New Year given what he and Mike had just discovered. But he didn't say anything. He just stared at the parched San Bernardino mountains behind Charlie.

"If we do our job, this thing will run on its own, and as part of a larger entity, or with an infusion of cash, someone else can make this fly. And we pocket a nice chunk of change." Charlie tossed his cigarette to the ground. "I'm glad you're here, Andy. I really am. But do what I ask you to do—no more, no less. And stay away from Terence."

CHAPTER 29

When they were done for the day, Andrew drove by the FDN facility to see whether the protests were still ongoing and if they had grown in intensity. He was surprised to find not a single vehicle parked along the road, not a single person protesting, and not a single sign, probably due to the four sheriff's SUVs parked by the FDN entrance. Lights flashed and deputies stood ramrod straight by the open vehicle doors with crossed arms and holsters visible. He recognized Deputy Buy-A-Vowel's lanky frame and watched him track Andrew's car with his gaze. He wondered if the deputies' presence would deter the protesters for long. Having felt Olivia's passion, he doubted it.

He called Renée to let her know he was headed to Helendale to get his belongings. He downshifted into third, gunned the engine, and overtook a semi. He glided into the cul-de-sac, fumbled with his phone, and opened the garage.

Anxious and on edge, he half-expected Junior and his pal to materialize from behind a door. He felt dirty. Soiled. The way Charlie had said, "Stay away from Terence . . ." He tried not to think back to the prior Sunday night. He remained frozen in the middle of the living room, unable to move. He stared out the window at the undulating mesquite branches and the mottled fairway beyond the stucco wall.

Maybe if I hit the range. Disconnect. And then something occurred to him; he'd not washed his clubs after the round with Terence.

He went back out to the car and brought in his golf bag. He took the clubs and leaned them against the counter in numbered order. He started with the woods, then moved to the three iron and went down to the wedges, washing each club in the sink with warm soap and water, taking the abrasive side of the sponge and scrubbing the clubface, cleaning each groove individually, moving onto the shaft, and then the grip—as if disinfecting each club. He then dried each club with a kitchen towel and leaned them against the wall to let the remnant moisture evaporate in the desert air.

While waiting for them to dry, he opened one of Charlie's bottles of 2015 Bordeaux. He'd heard it was a good year. He didn't let it breathe and took his glass outside to the patio. The sunset was painting mystical patterns in the western sky, as the scent of mowed grass floated in the hot wind.

When the bottle was half gone, he found himself back inside on the couch with his laptop, searching the web for information on Terence Miller Kayne. He didn't find much. There was no mention of the reason for his exit from data centers, bankruptcy, court filings, and investigations that Zeke had told Andrew about. Nothing on social media, on LinkedIn, no memberships or donations to benevolent organizations or attempts at cementing his legacy. And lastly there was nothing from his time in New York or prior. Nothing. It was as though before his foray into commercial real estate, he hadn't existed. And like a ghost, he just appeared one day in Southern California with a prescient investment thesis and enough money to buy into a lucrative space before others had ventured into it. He took that model and applied it to cannabis. There was nothing on his current financial situation, no way for Andrew to determine whether Terence's tenants or properties were in distress or how many tenants had shut down. Maybe Zeke was full of shit and had an axe to grind? *Possible. But doubtful.*

Andrew checked the time. 7:00 p.m. He should be on his way to Claremont by now.

Instead, he shut his laptop, picked up his phone, and called his father, feeling guilty for not calling him sooner.

"You bought the house?"

"I did. On the eleventh fairway. There's a spare bedroom, for when you come and visit."

"I'll visit soon."

"I could use some help with my swing."

There was a hollow sound to his father's voice. Something Andrew would never get used to. Ever since his mom had passed away, ever since the current administration had made it impossible for his father to work in DC, and after the charlatans and sycophants had driven the career public servants away in hordes, his father finally had taken his pension. Only after he settled in Tucson had he and Andrew begun to connect on a somewhat regular basis—calls every other week or exactly two calls a month more than before he had retired—and it was on one of these calls that his father confided in Andrew what his activity had really been all those years in far-off lands, one of the reasons he had been a distant father and seldom spoke. The State Department had been a cover for the CIA. It had never come up in conversation after that.

"Do you remember Charlie? Lived above us at the Royal Garden Towers."

"Nice kid. Yes."

"I'm working with him now in LA."

"I don't know how he kept that smile with a father like that."

"Yeah, I know. He's expanding his business and is in talks with investors. We'd like to find out more about a particular individual, but there's not much out there that's publicly available. We want to make sure he's legit."

"If you don't trust him, don't take his money."

"It's complicated. You see, he's also our landlord."

"What does Charlie do?"

"He's in cannabis."

"Cannabis?"

"It's legal in California."

"What are you . . . I thought you were in tech?"

"We need to know if this individual is in financial trouble, if there's a risk he may default."

There was a brief silence. "What do you know about this person?"

Andrew gave his father what he had on Terence. "I've been told that he's had financial issues in the past, and we're not sure why he left New York. But it's all hearsay. Anything you can find out would help."

"I'll make some calls."

Andrew heard his father slide a door open.

"Andy, is everything OK?"

"I don't know to be honest with you."

"I'm worried about you. What happened with your company . . . you made out OK, right? You always seem to."

"I landed on my feet."

"Do you need money?"

"I don't need money, Dad. I'm fine."

"I'm sorry I couldn't be of much help."

"There was nothing you could have done."

"Come and visit. I have a spare bedroom."

"You mentioned that already. I'll come soon."

"My drives are all over the place."

"You need Khun Archin to help you with your swing."

"You're his proxy. He created yours."

Andrew smiled at the memory.

A moment passed, each of them searching for words.

"Dad?"

"Yes?"

"Do you miss Thailand?"

His father didn't answer.

"We should go back someday, together, get away from here."

"I'd like that, Andy." After a pause, his father said, "I'll see what I can find on Mr. Kayne."

"Thanks, Dad."

"Bye, Andy."

Andrew dropped the phone on the couch and stared at the inanimate object. He'd asked his father multiple times whether he'd like to go back with him to Thailand. He knew his father had loved it there, that it was the one place . . . and yet whenever Andrew asked, his father's response was always the same, "I'd like that, Andy." And nothing ever came of it.

He checked the time. *Shit*, it was past 8:00 p.m. One more hour and those fuckers would be cranking up the depositor. He wanted to hop in the car and—no, that wouldn't achieve anything. And he wasn't going to drive back to Claremont at this hour only to hoof it back over the Cajon Pass at 5:00 a.m. *Be patient.*

He rummaged through the cupboards and opened a can of cannellini beans, drained them in a strainer, and added salt, pepper, and olive oil. He ate standing over the kitchen counter. When he was done, he took the wine back with him to the couch.

He picked up the remote. A new lineup from the underground archives was on the Criterion Channel. He found an obscure film with Burt Lancaster, and savoring the dregs of the bottle, he stretched out on the couch and pressed play.

A warm, sunny afternoon. A tall, broad-shouldered, handsome man clad in nothing but a tight swimsuit appears at a small garden party, a friend's impromptu gathering to try to smother the prior day's hangover. The man decides that on such a beautiful day, he will swim home, from house to house, across the Connecticut suburbs, finding refuge in the pools of friends, acquaintances, and ex-lovers. As the day progresses and with every dive, a shard of illusion from the man's veneer dissolves. He speaks fondly of his doting wife and his daughters who are at school. He befriends their babysitter, and she accompanies him part of the way, until she runs away. He meets friends from whom he's borrowed money, he meets his former lover, and he talks of the memorable times they had together, until she recoils in horror and disgust at the mendacity of his recollection. He swims his way through a horde of people in a public pool, after having to borrow the fifty cents to access the complex. The day has become overcast, the swimmer is cold, and it starts to rain. He walks through the gate of his house whose sunbaked tennis court is cracked with weeds sprouting from the crevices, the torn net lying askew, and the garden unkempt and overgrown. He reaches the front door and tries the handle, but it's locked. He knocks on the door. The knocks intensify in a fierce crescendo. The camera pans to a window. There is a chandelier on the dusty floor. Cobwebs have overtaken the objects in the room. The furniture that's left is torn and decrepit. As the camera pans out, the swimmer is curled in a fetal position on the doorstep, crying, alone.

CHAPTER 30

When he awoke, it was dawn. He rubbed his eyes and felt his cheek, the fading pain a distant memory. He had slept straight through, without ominous thoughts meandering in his head, and with no reveries feeding on each other, one fueling the distress of the next.

There were a few texts from Renée:

Are you alive? I thought you were coming back tonight.

He'd been living with her for all of two days and was already fucking it up. He texted her and told her he'd fallen asleep on the couch, exhaustion catching up to him, *like she would believe him.* The strange thing is she did believe him.

I'm glad you're all right . . . I missed you last night.

He threw all his belongings in the car and drove to the factory, anxious about what they would find on the video. He tried to distract himself by observing the passing scenery, but there wasn't much to keep his mind occupied. Or there was, if he were a geologist.

He parked and pulled up the Brivo app on his phone. The door opened as soon as he pressed the button. He realized the app must keep a record of comings and goings, each key card access or phone access has to be logged—he should have thought about this before. But when Andrew stepped into the office and he and Mike checked the entrance logs, there was nothing out of the ordinary. The door to the factory floor had been offline since June, allowing unmonitored access. *But what about the door to Mike's office?* Someone had to trigger the magnetic lock on the door to get into the office because someone could only access the camera system *from* the office, as there was no way to manipulate the cameras remotely. But it was a dead end. There was nothing in the logs.

They waited until the end of the shift, and as soon as the last operator left the factory, Andrew switched the feeds on the large video monitor back on. He watched Mike dart in and out of the conference rooms, don PPE, and make one last foray on the floor.

"All clear," Mike said. He shed his hairnet and gown and shut the door.

Mike leaned against the wall, arms crossed, eyes expectant as Andrew logged into the security console. "Let's start from the back of the factory and move toward the shipping station." He selected one of the cameras that had been inactive in the warehouse area, opened the viewer, and slid the cursor back to 11:00 p.m. of the night before. The screen burst alive with activity.

"Holy shit!"

"*¡Qué chingados!*"

"Jesus, that's Kyle," Andrew said, staring intently at the screen.

"And Ashlee," Mike said flatly. "No one is wearing a mask."

"They're all wearing lab gowns."

"Who *are* all these people? And that door . . . it is always locked." The door was the one separating the Kannawerks factory from the adjoining building, the one that Terence had leased as a storage facility. The men were carrying trays filled with gummies from the

Kannawerks floor into that building and bringing empty trays back. Another tall figure, which was not Kyle, stood by the door, his back to the camera, arms waving and directing traffic.

Andrew selected a camera centered on the depositor. The pistons pumped up and down, a small spiral of steam emanating from the hopper. Ashlee manned the console as two unknown men pulled the molds off the conveyor and stacked them in the drying area, just as if they were Kannawerks gummies.

Except they were not Kannawerks gummies.

Andrew zoomed in. The slurry was pink, the mold shape nothing like they had seen before. But they had. They were making Pink Dot, right here, in their factory.

He stopped the playback and sat back, immobile.

The color had drained from Mike's face. "Check the outside camera, the one facing north," he said. "Go back to 9:30 p.m. and watch them come in."

Andrew switched cameras. The grainy feed, lit only by the spotlights on the side of the factory, showed a black van pulling up, sandwiched between black sedans. Two figures exited the cars and slid the van door open. A stream of men exited and disappeared behind the building.

"I count ten, twelve," Andrew said. "Not including the guys in the car."

"That is why the Brivo app shows nothing. They are not coming through the main entrance. They are coming through the other building."

"Terence's building," Andrew said. "What about the alarm?"

"They must shut off the alarm as soon as they come in, then have the rest of the crew arrive. They have thirty seconds to do it."

Andrew cycled through a handful of other cameras, those that provided alternate views of the manufacturing floor and the Kannawerks warehouse. The first signs of activity started right after

9:15 p.m. and continued unabated until 3:00 a.m., when the crew shut everything down and cleaned up and eliminated all traces of their presence. They must have produced at least two batches of gummies in one session, if not three batches, completing the curing and packing in the adjoining building—an efficient use of their time. Andrew ran the numbers in his head using Kannawerks as a reference and the wholesale numbers from Ray: *Two to three batches a day, four thousand bags per batch, seven dollars a bag. At this rate, they could take in between a million-two and a million-seven a month.*

"Who the fuck are these workers?"

"I do not recognize any of them," Mike said.

"They seem to know what they're doing."

"Anyone can do it, as long as you have someone like Ashlee and Kyle directing."

Andrew checked other cameras at random, those that were not trained on the manufacturing floor and warehouse: the conference rooms, shipping area, hallways. They were void of movement, with one exception: a man walked by a camera and entered the restroom. Andrew went back and played the video at normal speed.

"I recognize him," Andrew said, stopping the frame just as the man glanced at the camera. "That's the guy I saw with Ashlee in Vegas."

Mike stared at the screen. "Brody, the boyfriend," he said. "The beard, red hair, the nose. What was *he* doing in Vegas?"

"Going to see a show," Andrew deadpanned. "Shit, it's six-thirty."

They had been at it for almost four hours.

"We need to leave. What if they come early?" Mike grabbed his bag and started for the door.

"Let me download some of the footage. If they were in here last night, they'll be here again, and who knows when they'll figure out that they need to replace the inserted feeds."

"OK. But quickly."

Andrew took out a portable drive and copied the feeds from all cameras that showed the manufacturing and transportation of the gummies to the warehouse, with as many views as possible of the faces of those involved: Ashlee, Kyle, Brody, a couple of other white men that supervised the work, and the dozen or so workers.

Mike stood by the door. His hand choked the handle. "Come on!"

CHAPTER 31

"We have a problem on our hands," Andrew said, gulping his margarita.

"Amigo, I do not know what to say." Mike shook his head. "I cannot believe this was happening under my nose."

Andrew stared beyond Mike at a silent black-and-white movie projected on the wall. The camera panned to an open window. A couple embraced, stared into each other's eyes, and murmured words of love or goodbye. The camera then panned away from the couple to a close-up of a sneering, mustachioed pistolero waiting outside the casita.

"What clues did I miss? They must have deleted the access records to my office when they modified the cameras. It is crazy what they are doing."

"No shit."

Mike sipped his tequila. They sat in a corner booth, away from the crowded bar and tables filled with families, work gatherings, and couples. The screens hanging on the walls showed a college football game and the latest Mexican Clausura match.

"They could not have been doing this for long," Mike went on. "I would have found out eventually, video or no video. The use of the depositor, the alarm. It was just a matter of time. Everything is tracked."

"They're raking in the dough." Andrew pulled out a notebook and pen and began to write. "What do we know? We know Ashlee and Kyle are in cahoots with someone. They're not the take-charge type."

"I would not say that. They are smart."

"What I mean is they execute well, but someone's got to be directing them. But who?"

"Who knows." Mike put down his empty glass.

"And I didn't see anyone else that I recognized from the factory. No operators."

"No."

"We saw Brody and a couple of other guys directing traffic, Brody being from FDN. Can we assume the other two guys are also from FDN? They fit the type and build."

"Definitely. They are as Anglo as can be."

Andrew smirked. "I didn't see the security guards anywhere on the internal video feeds. They must have stayed outside manning the perimeter."

"Pendejos."

"And the men we saw carrying the trays, the workers—"

"Off the street—"

"Or from FDN." Andrew stopped writing and studied Mike. "Think about *this* hypothesis."

"Why do you say *hypothesis* again?"

"I'm an engineer. Listen. Someone decides to manufacture cannabis product clandestinely. Fine. It's happening everywhere, nothing new. They already have a core team—Ashlee, Kyle, Brody, and friends—call them the skilled labor. They need operators to carry product from the manufacturing line to the curing line to the packing line, pack it in plastic pouches, seal the pouches, pack the pouches into a box, and haul them away. And they need to be efficient. They only have seven hours . . . no six . . . to make the stuff and move it next door, where the work can continue uninterrupted, but probably also ends at the same time, as they don't want to risk exposure. So they need a large team to parallel process all of this. Hence the dozen or so operators. And where can they get cheap labor . . . *free* labor at that scale and *control* the labor so that no one talks about what they are doing?"

"*Impossible.*" Mike sat back. "From FDN? You are crazy. This place has gotten to you."

"Maybe I am crazy. But just think about it."

"Too risky. Why not just find people off the street and have them do the work?"

"Because this is about control. Leverage. The detainees have risked everything. They survived the trek across the desert. They got caught. They were sent to FDN. They're exhausted, hungry, disoriented, mistreated, and all of a sudden, they are offered a ticket out. Guys off the street can walk away and take their chances somewhere else."

"I do not think so."

Andrew grabbed his glass. "What about the connected warehouse? Do you know who's leasing it from Terence?"

"No. We can ask him."

"That's not a good idea." Andrew stared at the half-full glass in his hand. He'd not heard back from his dad. "I wonder if Álvaro figured it out. He found out what was happening, or suspected something was happening, and came back that Wednesday night to scope it out. Except he got caught."

"No way."

"It's a plausible scenario. The sheriff found his car a few miles away. Maybe he parked there and walked back to the factory. Maybe he got too close."

"He would have said something to me. I would have known. He trusted me."

"Maybe he didn't get a chance." Andrew put the glass down. "I'm going back to the factory to stake it out."

"Now I know you are crazy."

"It's the only way we'll know more. We've seen all we can from the cameras."

Mike pushed his plate away. "I am going with you."

"I don't want you involved."

"Too late, amigo."

"It goes without saying. This stays between us."

Andrew paid the check. On their way out, the projection showed the same film clip, but this time the pistolero palmed his revolver and entered the casita. The film must have been on a loop, like his mind was, spinning with visions of Charlie and Ashlee arguing, and Ashlee manning the depositor in the middle of the night.

CHAPTER 32

He texted Renée:

Factory issues, don't wait up.

Then they drove to Helendale, dropped off the Porsche, and drove back in Mike's black Prius. As they approached the factory, Mike switched off the headlights and proceeded in the non-dark of the night, the waning moon casting a pale blue glow on the surroundings, providing ample light for them to navigate. The hum of the hybrid engine and their breathing were the only sounds in the car.

Mike parked behind a cinder block wall of an abandoned and decaying scrap metal facility a few hundred yards from the factory. The facility was like the set of a film depicting the end of days, sustaining the last remnants of civilization, the survivors hiding in the carcass by day and prowling and feeding on desert critters at night.

They sat in the car and waited.

A soft glow of lights danced in the distance. "What are those?" Andrew whispered.

"Desert walkers, their camps. They live there."

"They must freeze to death in winter."

"Some, yes."

"This must be what Norbert was referring to when he said, 'They're here.' Hell, they must have seen it all, every night, witnessing the comings and goings. But do these bastards care about the desert walkers, or do they eliminate them if they get in the way, if they get too close, if they get too smart? Like the dead body found in the desert. But that was an FDN inmate. If that's who they're using."

"He probably tried to run and make an escape. What did he have to lose? These people have nothing to go home to."

"The risk-reward makes sense. And the five they found buried in Barstow, galvanized by the audacity of the lone escapee, probably thought that they had strength in numbers. There were only three men guarding them. But maybe it wasn't only the three."

"We should go to the authorities," Mike said.

Andrew shook his head. "I thought about it, but without more facts, the consequences would be dire for everyone. Kannawerks would be shut down. License revoked. We would all be under investigation, me, you, Charlie. You would have to go back to Mexico, and you don't want to, do you?"

"No, no. Not anytime soon."

"The authorities would make an example of us, of how they come down hard on a legitimate producer who flouts the laws and regulations. The regulators have to show muscle, show that they matter, and the way they do it is by coming after the legal producers who break the law. We would become a poster child for cannabis enforcement. We have to find out who's orchestrating this thing first and see if we can isolate the bad eggs from Kannawerks. If there's a way to show that Kannawerks was unaware of what was happening, that they're being taken advantage of—carve out the bad actors as acting independently under the direction of an outsider—then maybe we can keep the company out of it, including us."

"One thing is bothering me," Mike said. "If the workers are FDN inmates, how do they get them in and out of the facility without raising alarms? It is a whole production when they move detainees; they have to pass through multiple gates. There are escorts. A lot of people would know what was going on, inside and outside the facility."

Andrew shrugged. "It's almost nine. Let's go."

They stepped out of the car and moved toward the lights of the factory. It was cold, the night quiet except for the occasional wind gust. They were about one hundred yards from the factory gate. But there wasn't a clear view of the warehouse entrance.

"Should we go around?"

"We said we would stay here, near the car," Mike said.

"We won't be able to see anything from here."

"We'll see them drive up. Once they are inside, one of us can go around and get closer."

Andrew crouched behind a small pile of boulders, while Mike sat down, his back against the rocks, and zipped up his jacket. "Good thing I brought—" He stopped and grabbed Andrew's arm. "Did you hear that?"

Andrew listened. "I don't hear anything."

"Shhh."

Neither of them moved. "It's nothing," Andrew said.

Mike motioned for silence. And then they heard a shuffle, the sound of feet dragging in the dirt.

"Hiya."

They stared, stunned, at Norbert.

"Hiya," he repeated, a faint smile on his face.

This was not in the plan.

"Norbert, what are you doing here?" Andrew asked.

"I live over there, where the lights are."

"What do we do?" Mike whispered to Andrew.

"Why are you here?" Norbert asked.

Andrew motioned to Norbert to sit down. "We want to see if they're here, Norbert."

"They will be. They were here yesterday."

"We don't want them to know we're here."

"I don't want them to know I'm here, either."

"We don't want *anyone* to know we're here."

"I won't tell." Norbert averted his gaze, picked up a handful of dirt, and let it slide through his fingers.

"Norbert, they'll be here soon. It's better if you go. It's not safe."

Norbert picked up another handful of dirt. Then he said in a stern tone, "It's not safe for you, either."

Andrew hesitated. "We'll be fine, Norbert."

"You *must* be careful," Norbert said in a forceful whisper.

He was no longer out of it, as if he'd snapped out of a zombie trance.

"Those are bad people. Your friend was here, the other night. The bald one with the tattoos."

"Álvaro," Mike said.

"I told him to be careful. He didn't listen to me."

Andrew and Mike stared at the man.

"He tried to hide, but the guards walk around. They took him, threw him down. Kicked him. Put him in the van." He stood up. "I told you they were here." He let the dirt fall from his hand and then patted Andrew on the shoulder. "Don't worry. I won't tell anyone. And be careful."

He disappeared into the darkness, his scent following him, carried by the wind that had started gusting again.

They waited until he was out of sight, the shuffling out of range.

"Fuck me," Andrew said.

"Maybe this was not such a good idea," Mike said. "We should leave now."

"They'll be here any minute. We move now, and they'll see us."

Mike rubbed his hands. "Let us not do anything stupid."

They crouched down and waited. Coyotes cried in the distance, barks, yips, and whoops becoming long howls, the sound carrying across the plain in the thin air.

A convoy suddenly appeared, making its way down Rancho Road. Mike and Andrew watched the cars as they approached the factory. A van sandwiched between two black sedans, just like they'd seen in the video, entered the facility through the back gate on Commerce Way, avoiding the Kannawerks lot. It parked in front of the adjacent building's entrance. A man got out of the trailing sedan and opened the door of the van. A stream of men stumbled out and disappeared behind the building.

Mike and Andrew stayed motionless behind the boulders. They watched the security guards patrol the perimeter, while the man slid the door of the van shut.

The guards talked with one of the drivers, like work pals taking a break. The driver held out a pack of cigarettes, and the guards helped themselves and lit them.

"We will never get any closer," Mike said. "Not with those guys walking around."

"Let's wait and see." They sat down, their backs against the boulders, Mike occasionally peering over the rocks, making sure no one approached. They waited, stretched their legs, rubbed their hands to stay warm, and took turns keeping watch on the factory. No one had come out of the building since the convoy had arrived.

After a couple of hours, Mike nudged Andrew and whispered, "Remember what Norbert said? 'The guards walk around.' I have been watching, and they have a pattern. They walk around the building for ten minutes, then sit and have a cigarette, stare at their phones, and after ten minutes get up and do it again. They sit right under one of the lights."

"I'll go next time they light up."

They waited until the guards reappeared from behind the

building, sat down, lit their cigarettes, and took out their phones. Like clockwork.

"See you in ten minutes." Andrew kept low to the ground. He took an indirect route. He headed away from the factory and looped in from the left, where a cinder block perimeter wall protected him from view. The moon outlined obstacles for him with a faint glow, allowing Andrew to make his way around the rocks, cacti, and bushes. When he reached his destination, he sat on the ground with his back against the wall. He breathed fast, from exertion and fear.

He didn't wait long. He dashed forward and kept low and tight against the wall, until he reached the corner where the chain-link fence began. He peered around the corner. The cars were parked in front of the warehouse entrance. Now he just needed to get close, past the fence, and snap some pictures. He crouched and sprinted on his toes to the open gate, sat behind the first car, and kept the car between him and the entrance.

He snapped a picture of the first car's license plate. He then slid along the ground, the only sound the rustling of his clothes on the desert floor. He inched his way forward until he reached the van. A sharp burst of wind shrouded him in dust. He shielded his face with his arm until it was over. Then he wiped the sand from his face and snapped a picture of the van. As he lifted himself to snap the final picture, the warehouse door swung open.

He hit the ground and froze.

From under the van, he could see cowboy boots and jeans. He remained motionless. The boots shuffled away from Andrew and then stopped. A click, a strike, a long inhale, another click, and then a slow exhale.

Andrew slowed his breathing, hoping it would mask the sound of his pounding heart. The boots moved away and around the corner of the building.

Should he head back now? No. He was too far. Not worth the risk. He had to wait. And hope they didn't see him.

The boots reappeared. Another inhale, a longer exhale. The roach dropped to the ground. The left boot stepped on the embers, extinguishing the remnants. The warehouse door opened, and the boots disappeared inside.

Andrew slid forward and took a picture of the second car's plate. He slid the phone in his pocket and sprinted back the way he had come, the moon lighting the way, the wind drowning out the sounds of his steps in the desert dust.

"Did you get the pictures?"

Andrew nodded, hands on knees, panting.

"Are you OK, amigo?"

"I'm fine."

"What do we do now?"

"We wait until they're done," Andrew said between gasps. "And then we follow them."

"¿Estás loco?"

"We need to find out where they're taking the workers, FDN or not. We need to know."

"It is almost two."

Andrew sat down. "You get some sleep first. He gazed at the factory, where the guards were immersed in their phones and the orange light of the cigarettes glowed like a beacon. It was mesmerizing, the rhythmic flashing of the light—hypnotic almost—begging Andrew to close his eyes, him doing everything he could to stay awake, and observe the goings on.

The next thing he knew he was nudged awake.

"They are moving," Mike said.

Andrew's limbs were frozen, and it took him a moment to get his bearings. He finally shifted his weight and peeked over the boulders. The workers were filing back into the van under guidance from the cowboy. He slid the door shut, rapped his knuckles twice on the roof of the van, and got into the driver's seat of the lead sedan.

Mike and Andrew hustled back to the car. But when Mike pressed the start button on the Prius, the headlights came on unexpectedly, the beams bouncing off the cinder blocks, momentarily lighting the surroundings.

"*¡Puta madre!*" Mike hissed, shutting off the lights.

The convoy pulled out.

"Relax," Andrew said. "They can't see us."

Mike waited for the convoy to put some distance between them. Then he followed them on a parallel road.

With no headlights, they were able to navigate via the Prius's GPS, the display contrast turned down until it was barely visible. It was easy to keep track of the lights, three vehicles in the vast nothingness of the High Desert. Random cars could be seen on the horizon, solitary lights passing through the night. The sky was clear . . . infinite.

"And there they go—past FDN," Mike said. They followed the vehicles across the 15, past shuttered strip malls, through Victorville, and merged onto the 18.

"Where the hell are they taking them?"

"Apple Valley. Out here is where they found Álvaro," Mike said.

The convoy stopped at a traffic light. Mike slowed the Prius to a crawl. And when the light turned green, the convoy didn't move.

"*¡Muévanse güeyes!*" Mike said. "I am tired."

"Turn everything off," Andrew said.

"Do you think they saw us?"

"Wait." Flashing red-and-blue lights blazed across the intersection, seemingly at the speed of light. The convoy continued on its journey.

"*¡Chingada madre!*" Mike slapped the steering wheel. "I will die young."

They kept driving. The moon cast a macabre glow on the decaying neighborhoods. A decrepit children's playground stood between two houses, their windows boarded up.

The convoy slowed as it approached a complex of warehouses. Mike stopped the car. Tall chain-link fences with razor wire surrounded the gray buildings. Guards stood at the ready, with guns bulging in holsters. A large rottweiler, chained to the fence, barked at the incoming cars, each violent burst causing him to rise on his hind legs. The convoy went through the gate and stopped in front of the first building. Andrew noticed there were other vans, of the same make and model, parked in the complex. He counted five of them.

The lead driver—Andrew's cowboy friend—exited the car, walked to a black double door on the building, and punched numbers on a keypad. The workers filed out of the van, like prisoners in a chain gang, and proceeded through the open door.

CHAPTER 33

A ndrew opened his eyes. He sat up, disoriented. Back in Helendale. It was like he was in a circuitous loop, every time he tried to leave, he found himself here again. His own personal Groundhog Day.

The laptop lay on the mattress next to him. He had scoured commercial property databases and identified the owner of the warehouse complex in Apple Valley where the van had dropped off the workers as Yorkshire Holdings IV, an LLC registered in the British Virgin Islands. Quite a coincidence—the Kannawerks lease with Terence was executed with Yorkshire Holdings II. And Terence owned the adjacent facility to Kannawerks. He owned *all* the facilities that Andrew and Mike had identified as being used for illicit operations, manufacturing illegal cannabis and housing indentured labor. Slaves. Prisoners.

Olivia needed to see the videos. If they were FDN detainees, maybe she would recognize them.

He checked his phone—no messages from his dad. Nor from Renée. She'd probably given up on him. What the fuck was he doing?

He dragged himself out of bed and stepped in the shower. He let the warm water run down his head and back as he stretched and loosened his muscles and joints, the dust accumulated from sitting on the cold desert floor washing away.

He checked his email. Ethan wanted to know when he would

make it back to West Hollywood, meet with some new hires he was bringing on board. They would be lucky if any of them had jobs next week. And there was an email from Ish, asking Andrew what he'd found out about Pink Dot. Andrew closed his laptop.

What about Ish? Someone with his background and history, someone he barely knew? But Ish had reformed; he had found stability in a relationship; he had moved towards moderation; he had stopped the benders. He helped others "from the inside," as he'd said. He had left a lucrative underground opportunity behind by moving to the legit side. Could Ish deal with the pecuniary consequences of a Kannawerks shutdown? Andrew picked up the phone.

"You alone?"

"As a matter of fact—"

"They're making Pink Dot in our factory."

The line went silent.

"I have it all on video."

"How? When?"

"At night. And we ran the tests. The formulation is the same as Alta."

"What the fuck are you saying?"

"This is for real."

"Who? It has to be an inside job."

"Ashlee and Kyle."

"Ashlee doesn't surprise me. And I knew there was something about that other cocksucker. Gets kicked out of a graduate research program and ends up working for Akmana, the definition of a shitshow. Motherfuckers."

"I don't think they're the ones driving this. I'll fill you in on the details when I see you. Right now I need your help."

"Motherfuckers," he repeated.

"We have to tread lightly. We can't risk the BCC or anyone else finding out, not yet."

"They'll find out eventually."

"We need to find the source, the orchestrator, who's putting it on the market. Get enough evidence to take to the BCC and the authorities, show Kannawerks wasn't involved, that we're all patsies."

"You realize that whoever's involved is . . . we may be dealing with some serious shit here."

"What do you suggest we do? Leave town? Because I've thought of that. I've thought really hard about that."

"Don't do that, man—"

"Can Ray help?"

"What's he going to do?"

"Help us find out who's running this. Then we go to the BCC, the sheriff, and we take them down."

"Hold on there, cowboy." He paused. "Let me remind you, Andrew, that we're nobody. Plus, you report whoever's running this thing to the authorities, and Kannawerks *will* be done. And Ray's never going to rat anybody out."

"Kannawerks is done, anyway."

The click of a lighter broke the silence. A long slow drag, then an exhale. "Let me talk to Ray, if he'll even take my call. I'll see what I can find out. Then we can decide what to do, depending on who these fuckers are."

"What does that mean?"

"If they're amateurs, that's one thing, but I'm sensing that these may be people we aren't up to fucking with."

Andrew hung up. He had left out the parts about the workers, FDN, the warehouse lodgings, and that Terence owned all of the facilities. He'd wait until he had more evidence. He jumped in the car and drove off, saying goodbye to Helendale for good.

When he arrived at the factory, the workers were already gone. Mike was haggard: his usually neat, parted hair was unkempt, his eyes bloodshot, his chin covered in a thick stubble.

"Go home, Mike, get some rest."

"I was waiting for you."

They played back the video feeds from the night before. Everything they had seen and hadn't seen was captured: Ashlee and Kyle arriving just after nine; the convoy; the workers; the guards; the cowboy extending the joint to the guards; and the cleanup. The crew had managed to manufacture a significant volume of gummies during that shift, cranking the depositor to maximum output. If they had been doing this since July, it correlated with why the pistons had failed.

Andrew downloaded the feeds onto the external drive. "We should switch back all the settings to the way we found them, in case they come back to check or come back to replace the video inserts with the updated daylight savings ones."

"I think we should continue recording."

"Why? We have enough as it is."

"What if something happens to the workers?"

"Today's Wednesday . . . fine. We'll record twenty-four seven through the weekend, but Monday we reset and make selected cameras inactive again." He shouldered his backpack. "Go home, Mike, you're starting to worry me."

Andrew waited for Mike to set the alarm. Then they walked out together.

As Andrew sat in the car, he noticed something was missing. *Shit.* He'd left his driver and three wood behind; he could picture them back in Helendale, leaning against the wall, opposite from where his irons had been drying. No fucking way was he going back there. He headed out of the lot.

As he crossed the intersection with Palmdale Road, he noticed a pair of headlights approaching from behind, zigging and zagging, in and out of traffic, lifting up dust as the car drove along the embankment until it was on his tail. The red-and-blue lights came on, a metallic voice ordering him to pull over. *Are you fucking kidding me?* Andrew eased to the side of the road. He let the car idle in neutral, opened the glove compartment, and rolled down the window. Then he gripped the steering wheel and waited. Cold desert air permeated the interior; flecks of desert dust found their way on the polished dashboard. The clock read 6:00 p.m.

"License and registration." Andrew recognized the voice.

He grabbed the documents and handed them to Deputy Buy-A-Vowel.

"Wait here," he said. He'd left his cap in the patrol car.

In his rearview mirror, he watched the deputy slide behind the wheel. The light of a monitor illuminated his long, gaunt face, the narrow eyes focused on the paperwork, then back at the monitor. He sat there staring at the screen, fingers hitting an out-of-sight keyboard. Cars passed by, lifting dust into the night air, the roars of the engines and crunching tires drowning out any other sound or noise or thought.

The deputy now held a phone to his ear. He seemed agitated. After a long pause, he put the phone on the dashboard and continued typing. Andrew waited. Who knows what these idiots were capable of doing, of getting away with. If Andrew disappeared, no one would be able to trace him, not out here. Ashes to ashes, dust to dust. Buried in Barstow.

"You were texting while driving," Deputy Buy-A-Vowel said. He handed Andrew his license and registration and a yellow slip of paper. "No warning this time."

"Thank you, officer."

"You can go now," the officer said. He stepped to the side. Andrew threw the papers on the passenger seat and merged into the traffic. The officer hadn't moved, standing on the side of the road, watching Andrew drive away. *Texting my ass.*

He waited until the deputy was out of sight, then called Renée.

"Where *are* you? I was worried."

"It's a mess, Renée."

"Andrew—"

"Look, I'm on my way over. And I need to see Olivia, tonight. She's going to want to hear this."

"Can you tell me what it's about?"

"I'll tell you when I see you."

The traffic had thinned by the time he reached the 15. He was alone in the fast lane, passing by car after truck after pickup, but going no more than ten miles above the speed limit because that fucker Buy-A-Vowel was capable of following Andrew all the way to the Cajon Pass and dinging him again on another fabricated charge.

As he passed the Ranchero Road exit, Andrew noticed a red sedan in his rearview mirror, a pair of oval headlights mimicking the Porsche's every move, every lane change, every acceleration and deceleration since he'd been on the 15. It wasn't a sheriff's cruiser. Now he was being paranoid. He slowed down, he sped up. The headlights kept a constant distance. He thought about gunning it but held back lest there be other sheriff or police cruisers on the highway. Would they believe him if he told them he was trying to lose a tail? Maybe it was nothing, or maybe it was some goons following his midnight-blue vintage Porsche. Maybe if he kept going, he'd lose them once he crossed the Cajon Pass. Maybe if he pulled over, they'd fly by him.

Andrew wasn't going to wait to find out. He downshifted into third and cut across the lanes. He accelerated and squeezed onto the next exit. He checked his bearings and took a left over the highway overpass, then another immediate left onto the frontage road, parallel to the freeway, and headed in the opposite direction. He gunned it. No one followed.

After a few miles, he saw an isolated adobe structure, like a shrunken version of the Alamo, rising in the barren landscape. Cars streamed in and out of its parking lot. Red-and-blue neon letters flashed over the main entrance: Texas Chophouse. He entered the lot. It overflowed with vehicles, oversized couples, and families in their sweats, baggy cargo shorts, flip-flops, and sneakers waddling to and from their cars and pickups. Bright lights illuminated the scene. A Texas flag snapped in the wind. Country music blared from hidden speakers. The line was out the door. He drove past the entrance and backed into an empty spot in the far corner of the lot, giving him ample view of the comings and goings. He killed the engine and the lights and waited.

The aroma of roasted flesh floated across the parking lot, blending with hickory smoke and the gag-inducing scent of honey-barbeque sauce. He thought about the tequila he would soon be drinking with Renée as he observed the cars. He hadn't seen whether the tailgater had taken the same exit. *A few more minutes*, he said to himself. He glanced at his phone. Almost seven. He tried to call Renée again, but there was no signal. Not good.

And then he noticed a red sedan, a discolored Buick. It snaked its way through the lot, past empty spaces. Andrew turned on the engine. He watched as the driver stared straight ahead, while the passenger gawked left and right, his eyes intense, his head snapping to and fro, like a hawk hunting for prey. As the Buick came around the corner, he realized his mistake: there was no way out behind him. They could block his car and have their way. Andrew revved the engine. His right hand choked the gear shift, his left foot pressed on the clutch, and his right foot hovered over the accelerator.

The Buick inched closer, then abruptly stopped as a silver pickup pulled out in front of them and headed in Andrew's direction. Now was Andrew's moment to hightail it out of there, with the Buick blocked, while it was several car lengths away. But then he saw the line of cars waiting to get out of the lot, which killed the idea of a rapid egress. The silver pickup inched forward, the Buick right behind. Andrew sat back, his hands on the wheel, resigned to whatever came next.

When the Buick reached the Porsche, it stopped. The scrawny passenger, who couldn't have been more than eighteen, smiled a "fuck you" smirk, a *faccia da culo*, as they said in Italy, the kind that makes you want to slap them sideways. The passenger rolled down the window and made the motion kids made when they played cops and robbers or cowboys and Indians, in the pre-politically correct days. His hand mimicked a handgun going off, the dry smile immobile, the driver glowering over the passenger's shoulder. The gunslinger rolled up the window and the Buick slithered out of the parking lot.

Andrew's eyes followed the red sedan, watched it make a left and take the northbound 15 ramp. He stared at the pulsating Texas Chophouse sign illuminating the miniature Alamo. When the traffic thinned out, he drove out of the lot. As he merged onto the 15 South, he realized that he had seen the driver before: he was one of Brody's pals, a guard in the video. Which meant they knew, and they knew when and where to find him.

CHAPTER 34

"I can't believe what I'm seeing," Olivia said.

"It's fucked up." Andrew froze the footage and zoomed in on the warehouse feed of the operators as they first came in the door.

"It's hard to tell from that angle. Keep going."

He pressed play, and they watched the rest of the operators file in.

"Stop!"

"Where?"

"There!"

"Which one?"

"That one, second to last. That's Fidencio. Fidencio Guzman Cabrales. Keep going." Andrew fast-forwarded the video to where the operators were carrying the trays in and out of the warehouse. "Hold it," she said. "Go back. There. Stop. That's Gustavo Ubaldo Santamaría."

"You sure?"

"Gus, yeah, I'm sure."

Ashlee and Kyle came into the frame. "Those two work for Kannawerks. Our own Bonnie and Clyde," Andrew said.

They continued to scour the footage. Olivia was able to identify a half dozen of the operators. The rest she couldn't place. "Can you get me video stills of their faces?"

"No problem."

"I'll show them to my colleagues, see if anyone recognizes them." She sat back. "I've seen enough."

Andrew closed the laptop and refilled his glass.

"It's not surprising," Olivia said. "Everyone's involved. Probably even the deputy that stopped you on your way here."

She took her plate to the kitchen and grabbed a beer from the fridge. Renée stood next to her, where she was prepping for the next day's taco run. Olivia continued from the kitchen. "FDN has been fined for overcrowding. I know because we sued them. So they modify contracts, place riders on existing agreements between the US Marshals Service and local city and county jails to *extend* FDN's detention facilities. Now local jails, prisons and other private detention facilities become virtual FDN facilities, where the migrant overflow can be housed. Overcrowding in their primary facilities decreases, while the number of detainees increases, bringing in additional revenue." She threw up her hands. "And then they 'misplace' the inmates!"

"The warehouse in Apple Valley . . . you could call that an extension," Renée said, as she wiped the cutting board clean.

Andrew stepped into the crowded kitchen. "Couldn't Brody be doing this on his own with a few buddies to make some bucks on the side?"

"No. FDN knows. FDN exists to make money. They make money until the migrants are registered with CBP. The higher-ups know and let it happen. FDN and CBP blame each other, slowing the discovery process. FDN tells us CBP has the inmates, FDN shows us the paperwork, and CBP says they never received any paperwork or any detainee."

Renée started washing utensils in the sink. Andrew stared at the patterns on an abstract poster that reminded him of an expressionistic film circa 1920's Germany. The shades of gray merged into one another, culminating in a hypnotic vortex.

He was tired. And drunk.

"Gus went missing two months ago," Olivia said. "He was supposed to be 'repatriated' to Mexico. Problematic for him and everyone else because migrants are abused in Mexico—extortion, kidnapping, even killed; and he's from El Salvador. There's a good reason why he fled. He's from a small village and worked on a coffee plantation. His parents and brother disappeared. He said it was because they didn't pay their dues to be allowed to work on the plantation. He found his way here on his own, and as soon as he crossed the border, he was detained, thrown into a cell." Her gaze settled on Andrew. "His story is the same as everyone else's. We saw the repatriation paperwork, we tried to put a stop to his transfer back by requesting asylum, but we were denied. It's pointless. We thought he was sent back, and yet here he is in the surveillance video."

"Kidnapped and used as indentured labor," Renée said, corralling them all back to the couch with another bottle of tequila in hand.

"They know we know," Andrew asserted as he squeezed in between Renée and Olivia. He felt his eyelids growing heavy.

"What about the warehouse? Do you know who owns it?" Olivia asked.

"Terence, the same guy that owns our facility."

"Everyone's in this for money," Renée said.

"Why else?" Andrew said.

"We should follow the money," Renée said.

"Huh?"

"We know how FDN makes money. We know who owns the warehouses. But who's using them? And who's getting Pink Dot to the market?" Renée asked.

"Yeah, I've made inquiries with people." Andrew extracted himself from the couch, leaned against the wall, and stared at the vortex. He remembered something. "There were other vans at the warehouse in Apple Valley. Five or six."

"We counted twelve workers in the video," Olivia said, "but over forty are missing."

"Let's not get ahead of ourselves," Andrew said.

"I need to think this through," Olivia said. "I'll talk to Gene. He's familiar with the migrants' situation. And he has a good relationship with FDN."

"Who's Gene?" Andrew asked.

"Gene Walla, he's our immigration lawyer. We work with him on the asylum requests. You must have seen signs advertising his services."

"The sign on Rancho Road? Near the FDN entrance?"

"That's the one."

"What kind of a name is Walla anyway?"

"Indian."

"South Asian?"

"Yeah."

"What does he look like?"

"He's round and short. Interesting combover—I don't know how it stays set in the wind."

"What else?"

"He's got a prominent nose, like a hawk."

"I think I've seen him." The room was spinning. Or his mind was. "At a diner, with Ashlee—she's the Bonnie in the video."

"You've had too much to drink," Olivia said.

"I have."

"The guy's harmless. He's only ever tried to help us."

"I'm sure it's him. I haven't seen many other Indians since I got here."

Olivia frowned and glanced at Renée. "I'd better go."

After Olivia left, Renée locked the door and dimmed the lights. No more words. They stripped off their clothes as they stumbled to the bedroom, holding each other. They fell onto the bed and pressed close, skin to skin, Andrew taking in her scent as his face hovered above hers, then slowly finding his way down her body.

CHAPTER 35

"They know," Mike said.

"I know. I was followed last night, one of Brody's pals and some skinny Latino kid. Couldn't have been more than eighteen."

"*¡No mames!*" Mike said. "That is not good."

"Why?"

"Because in Mexico, they recruit kids as *sicarios*."

"They wouldn't attempt something on this side of the border."

"I would not be too sure."

"How do *you* know they know?"

"Ashlee and Kyle did not show up this morning. I called. They did not answer."

Andrew shut the office door. "They must have seen us in the car, when the lights came on, or when the cops drove by."

"Maybe," Mike said. "What is done is done. Anything on the license plates?"

"It's a dead end. They belong to an LLC headquartered in Encino, that's all I could find." Andrew logged into the security system. All of the camera settings were as he'd left them. "Let's see what they did last night." He selected one of the warehouse cameras.

There was no activity.

He selected the camera with the view of the digital clock. He dragged the cursor back to 3:59 a.m. and let the video run. The digital display hovering over the factory floor changed to 4:00 a.m. in sync with the computer's clock.

"They didn't come back to produce last night." Andrew backed away from the console. "They definitely know we know." He let out a long, slow exhale. Then he went to the window and stared out at the workers on the packing line, their heads bobbing to the rhythm of the music.

"I came here to help an old friend," Andrew said, absently. "I thought I was going to automate a few processes, fix some IT shit, and make a little cash while I figured out what to do next."

They stayed silent for a minute.

"I started looking for another job," Mike said.

"What about your work permit?"

"Tough to transfer if you work in cannabis. Any chance they get to send you back they will, especially now. But I cannot go back to Mexico. I mean I can, I know enough people to find something, but my kids, even here in Adelanto, their life is so much better."

"And it's not safe, you said." Andrew went back to the console and started typing.

"What are you doing now?"

"I'm resetting the video system to how we found it, adding back the inserts and deleting what happened a few nights ago. This way, anyone auditing the system will find nothing amiss."

"But the clock—"

"Let it jump back and forth. It's a small detail. I found it because I was looking for it."

"You are right, the BCC will only check for something on the floor, like a health or safety issue, something wrong with the documentation tracking the cannabis chain of custody. The BCC announces their intention to audit weeks in advance, and that gives us time to prep: deep clean the factory, update documented procedures, back-date logs—"

"And doctor the video." Andrew kept typing.

Mike watched him, despondent. "Now do we call the police?"

"Without the video, there's nothing to tell them. There's no trace of illegal activity at Kannawerks. The crew bring in their own raw materials. Our inventory audits proved that. As far as we know, only two of our employees are involved, and they've disappeared."

"What about the dead people? We need to tell the police of the connection—"

"Do you want your children to have a father?"

"Yes."

"Do you want to raise your kids here or not?"

"I do."

"Then we say nothing. Kannawerks has to stay clean. No video, no evidence."

"What if Brody and crew come back?"

"They won't."

"They followed you and threatened you. What if they come after you again? What if that skinny kid *is* a sicario?"

"Then tell me what to do, Mike!"

"Go back to where you came from! Leave this *pendejada*, this pile of *mierda* that is cannabis."

They sat there for a moment.

"I fought for my last company as it spiraled toward insolvency," Andrew said, breaking the silence. "They wanted to fire me. I wouldn't go. I stayed until the end and made sure my team was taken care of. I don't leave people behind. We've come this far. We eliminate the association between Kannawerks and Pink Dot. We help Charlie merge the company. Then I'll leave."

"Do you think Charlie knows?"

"I need a few more pieces of the puzzle, and then I'll be ready for my old friend Charlie."

The door was locked. GENE WALLA, IMMIGRATION ATTORNEY. SE HABLA ESPAÑOL! The office was sandwiched between Trudy's Laundromat and Yuki Sushi, in an otherwise abandoned strip mall.

Andrew rang the barely visible buzzer below the shingle and heard a loud click. He pressed the door and walked into the office where a young woman sat behind a desk, staring at a screen. Assorted chairs were spread across a stained maroon carpet, and a plant in dire need of water sat in the corner. No one else was around. The receptionist asked him to sign a register, then she pressed a hidden button and the only other visible door clicked open.

Gene Walla *was* a small man, and his combover really was immovable. A round, joyful face framed the prominent nose. He wore a rumpled, tan dress shirt with yellow stains seeping out around his armpits and a brown vest whose bottom two buttons were undone to allow room for his generous belly. Stacks of papers were piled every-where: on the desk, on a round table in the middle of the room, on a wall-to-wall bookshelf that contained a smattering of legal tomes, and on the floor accumulating dust. The AC was off and the window behind the desk cracked open letting in wisps of warm air that circu-lated aimlessly, the whirring ceiling fan combining it with the dank odor of stale cigarettes. Two diplomas awarded to Ganesh Doodwalla hung on the otherwise bare walls. Gene Walla picked up a bowl of nuts that was next to an overflowing ashtray and offered them to Andrew, who politely declined.

Gene set the bowl down. "How can I help you today, *sir*?" Andrew detected a familiar Indian cadence to his accent, pondering not only on his ability to *hablar Español*, but also whether anyone would com-prehend him when he did.

"Olivia suggested that I speak with you."

Gene scratched the inside of his nose and gave Andrew an opaque stare. Then he leaned forward, smiled, and said, "Livia! Yes, yes, sure, I know her. The asylum champion."

"She said you work with the detainees and compile the paperwork."

"Yes, I know them, know them all." He smiled, joining his hands in prayer. "I am the only game in town."

"She said several of these migrants held at FDN are being transferred to border stations where they are repatriated." Andrew wiped the sweat off his forehead. "It's dangerous for these people to be sent home. Border Justice thought that they had made headway with the asylum requests and were waiting for a final hearing."

"Today that is quite normal, given where we are with this administration."

"But you see, Mr. Walla—"

"Please call me Gene."

"Gene. The strange thing is, not only were the asylum requests denied, as you know, but also Olivia's organization has not heard from these people in quite some time. They've just disappeared." He wasn't going to let on that he saw a bunch of them making gummies.

"Oh no, no, no. Impossible," the lawyer said, lighting a cigarette. "Do you mind?" He held up the smoldering stub between his thumb and forefinger.

"No, fine."

"Impossible, Mr. Andrew, impossible." He took a deep drag and exhaled upward, the fan dispersing the smoke throughout the office. "You see, everything is documented. Your friend, Livia, Border Justice, along with others, are all vigilant to make sure migrants are treated fairly. And humanely. They cannot just *disappear*, my friend, no, no, no. Asylum being denied is one thing. I get that. What is probably happening is that they are still being processed in the system, and once they are back home, they will get in touch. I am sure of it. Positive."

"Doesn't seem like they are. Several have been missing for months, and from what I understand, they should be back across the border by now."

The lawyer pressed the cigarette in the ashtray, leaned back in his leather swivel chair, and crossed his arms. "Let me tell you, my friend. You don't know how much of a mess this administration is. This ICE. You know ICE?"

"Immigration."

"Yes, ICE. They are understaffed, and they have very, very incompetent people working there," he said, waggling his head. "You would be surprised that a government of this size cannot find good people to work." He threw his hands in the air. "It's amazing, the stupid bloody idiots working there. They lose paperwork all the time. Do you know how many times I have to resubmit the paperwork? If they lose it here, can you imagine what happens when they have to transfer someone?"

"You would assume that there is some sort of database to keep track of people."

"Hah! They are using very old technology. I heard that and I see that in what they send me: old printouts and dot-matrix printouts and crazy stuff like that." He was no longer making an effort to suppress his accent.

"You're saying that they'll be found. Eventually."

"Yes. That is right. They will be found. They always find them. They have a way. It just takes time." He lit another cigarette and inhaled deeply. "You must be patient. Livia must be patient."

Andrew was about to speak, but Gene Walla, gesturing with his cigarette at Andrew, said, "My friend, I am going to tell you my story." He flicked errant ashes from his vest. "I came here thirty years ago to go to university. I got my degree, I got a job, with the visa, you know,

F-1, H-1, that sort of thing. I got a green card in the lottery—back then they gave out *a lot*," he slammed his palm on the desk, making Andrew jump, "a lot of green cards." Cigarette ash floated in the air. "I went to master's school and got a law degree. I am still here, a US Citizen, helping the families, getting their relatives permits, finding work for these people, helping them start a new life here in the United States." He inhaled again. "I could not do this today. No way!" His voice rose to a high pitch as he stood up, his round frame obscuring the chair. "If I come to the United States an educated man now, today, I am treated like a criminal. An intruder. An alien. So you see, Mr. Andrew," he lowered his voice, "they are sending everyone back. Zero tolerance, you heard that? With very, very few exceptions." He sat down.

"I know about the zero-tolerance thing."

The head waggle again. "Your friend, Livia, and a few others are doing something, trying to do something. Very few people care." He lit another cigarette with the butt of the dying one. "Bad for business. For me. For everyone. Before 2017, it was good, fair, reasonable. Now, I have very few clients, I work with nonprofits. They have no money. I am creating useless paperwork, knowing it will be rejected. Everyone is being sent back. What is there left for me to do?"

Andrew wanted to feel sorry for the guy, but something inside held him back. "And what about the asylum seekers you processed for Border Justice? Did the authorities give you a reason why their requests were rejected?"

"No reason. They don't have to give me one. The burden is on me to prove the case."

"And there was nothing in the repatriation paperwork that was out of place that you could have used against them—a technicality?"

The lawyer laid the half-cigarette in the ashtray. He shuffled some papers on his desk, glanced at his computer screen, double-clicked the mouse, and studied Andrew. "Why are you asking this?"

"It's impacting my workers. That's also why I'm here." As good an excuse as any to further justify his presence.

"Your workers?" He picked up the still-lit cigarette and took a drag while maintaining eye contact.

"Kannawerks, down the road."

"Ah yes, *marijewana*. It's a good business."

Andrew shrugged and smiled.

"What is wrong with your workers, then?" Gene asked.

"They're afraid. Their relatives are in the same situation. The workers' families have legal grounds to remain in the United States, but they're being sent back. I thought that given your experience, you could shed some light on what to do to avoid the barriers that Border Justice has come up against," he lied.

"I can see if I can help," Gene said. "Although working for a marijewana company makes the case more difficult, especially now."

"I know, you never know where the line is between the legal and illegal stuff."

The phone on the lawyer's desk beeped twice. "Excuse me one moment, Mr. Andrew." He picked up the receiver. "Yes. Yes. Put him through," he said. He motioned to Andrew to wait. He lit another cigarette and swiveled his chair around to face the window.

Andrew sat back. He checked his phone. No messages. As he leaned forward to put the phone in his back pocket, he noticed a document protruding from a manila folder on the desk. A hand-scribbled date read October 30, 2019. Last week. The top half of the document was partially visible: I-589 Application for Asylum and . . . The checkbox in the header was filled in, but Andrew was unable to read the small print. He scanned the page. The first three fields were empty. The next three contained Santamaría, Gustavo, and Ubaldo. Last name, first name, middle name. Sounded familiar. Gustavo. Gus! What was a fresh asylum application doing on Gene Walla's desk? Olivia had said Gus's application had been denied two months ago, hence the repatriation and subsequent disappearance until he reappeared in the Kannawerks Pink Dot video. And now a fresh application for Gus was being processed. Or seemed to be in process. Andrew glanced over at the lawyer, his back to Andrew, his head waggling and nodding. Andrew slowly leaned forward and opened the folder. He lifted Gus's paperwork. There were at least three other similar forms, with the same fields filled in, the same date. He read the names but didn't recognize them. They didn't match any of the ones Olivia had identified on the video. Gene was still talking and waggling. Andrew made a mental note of the names. Were there other applications elsewhere on the desk? Too many stacks of folders and papers. Too much of a risk. As he put the papers back, Gene swiveled around and placed the phone down. Andrew snapped back in his chair.

Gene stared at Andrew, glanced at the manila folder, and put out the cigarette. He leaned forward and put his hands on the desk. "I have another appointment, Mr. Andrew. Thank you for coming." He extended his hand. Andrew grabbed the sweaty extremity. The lawyer's grip was weak, like a wilted flower. He grabbed a business card lying on the desk, blew cigarette ash off of it, and handed it to Andrew. "I am here. Send your workers here, and I can see what I can do about their families. But I cannot promise anything."

Andrew stepped into the waiting room and wiped his hand on his jeans as he shut the door. A young woman was cradling a baby, its piercing shrieks not disturbing the other child crawling on all fours. The receptionist pressed a hidden button, the door buzzed, and Andrew walked out into the heat and wind.

CHAPTER 36

"The workers are *all* migrants, every one of them." Olivia went through their names.

Andrew checked his rearview mirror. No red Buick, no Escalades, no deputies tailing him.

"They were detainees in the Adelanto FDN facility. We were told they had been sent home over the last four months, but there was no record of them being consigned to CBP or of them crossing into Mexico. They just vanished. And as I suspected, every one of them is a lone wolf. They came from multiple countries in Central and South America. If they disappeared, no one would notice or make a claim."

As he merged onto the 15, he passed a police cruiser and an ambulance, lights flashing, parked next to a car with its front end through the guardrail. The car's front tires hovered in midair over the ravine below.

"I'm calling Gene to resubmit their cases for asylum—"

"Don't trust him," Andrew said, braking suddenly in the slowing traffic.

"Why?"

"That's why I called. I was just there. I saw asylum paperwork for Gus on Gene's desk. The papers were dated October 2019."

"That's impossible. The asylum request for Gus was made in August."

"And there were others. Some of the names I saw match the missing migrants you just mentioned, what names I could see, anyway. When he saw me checking the papers, he clammed up and showed me the door."

"What is the guy doing? I'll make inquiries with FDN and ICE. I'll call the sheriff."

"I'd hold off on the sheriff."

"What do you mean?"

"If they come in now, Kannawerks is fucked."

"Who cares about a weed company when people's lives are at stake? What is wrong with you? I need to get these people help *now*! Not an hour from now, not tomorrow. *Now!*" She hung up.

He threw the phone on the passenger seat and flipped down the visor. No use. The sun still burned a hole in his retinas, his sunglasses and visor doing a poor job of shielding him from the rays as he made his way along the meandering highway through the Cajon Pass.

Suddenly his phone buzzed. His dad:

Call me.

* * *

"I need your public key."

"Signal?"

"Yes, I'll send the file on the same thread."

"One sec."

Andrew sent the key and sat back on the couch. He'd made it back to the Claremont apartment in twenty-five minutes from the time he had received the text. It usually took him forty from the Cajon Pass.

"Keep what I'm sending you offline. As soon as you receive it, copy it to an external drive. Access it there, never while you're online." His tone was stern, commanding. Good old Dad. "And keep it encrypted."

"Got it," he said. He plugged the external drive into the laptop and waited for the file to come through.

Neither of them spoke. There wasn't anything to say. His father never shared sensitive information and neither did Andrew. They operated on a need-to-know basis.

"Here it is." Andrew downloaded the file attachment from the Signal chat straight to the external drive and deleted the thread.

"Read it offline."

"I got it. Don't worry."

"Let me know what happens, Andy." They hung up.

Andrew skimmed through the file; it was over fifty pages long. It was comprised of scanned documents from various agencies across the government: IRS, Department of Homeland Security, Department of Justice (DOJ), and Department of Labor. Counties in New York and California. The FBI. He found redacted text. The clock on the mantel read 5:00 p.m. Renée was still on the truck; he had the place to himself. He got out his notebook and began jotting down the salient points.

The narrative he pieced together went as follows: Terence Miller Kayne, born 1964 in a small town in South Yorkshire, England. Emigrated to the United States as an employee of Lehman Brothers in 1995. He acquired a green card through said employer in early 1999. Multimillion-dollar compensation years in 1998 and 1999, with income dropping somewhat in 2000 and 2001, but still in the seven figures. The decrease made sense; when the bubble burst, few were spared, but Terence had kept his income levels above average.

In June 2000, he was investigated by the Securities and Exchange Commission (SEC) and the DOJ for suspicious trades made as part of Lehman's burgeoning, high-growth, e-commerce and technology desk, and had been suspended from trading for a three-month period. Trading privileges reinstated after no charges or convictions for insider trading were filed.

Some of the redacted documents alleged that Terence had engaged in unwanted sexual advances with multiple subordinates. Terence took a plea deal and was let go from Lehman with an iron-clad nondisclosure agreement (NDA).

Moved to California in December 2001, purchased multiple properties in the San Fernando and Simi Valleys, Thousand Oaks, and Santa Barbara. Flipped most of them in the next few years and exited the residential real estate business right before the bottom fell out in 2007. Prescient. Ironically, the fall was precipitated by his alma mater, Lehman Brothers. In 2008, he brought his mother over from England. Began to invest in data center properties in 2009. Grew the portfolio across Southern California. Investigations into his finances appeared. Accusations of overstating his net worth in order to borrow funds for future projects at favorable rates, in line with what Zeke had said. Main lender was a local California bank: the Manufacturing and Agricultural Bank of Encino: the MAAGIC bank. Liquidated several marquee properties over a six-month period until he depleted the data center portfolio in 2015. No criminal or civil charges were filed. Terence came out unscathed. 2016 tax returns showed substantial growth in assets. His mother died early 2017.

First investment in cannabis was in 2016, a cluster of canna-bis-licensed buildings in Long Beach. Then Adelanto, Palm Springs, Northridge, Apple Valley. Created separate LLCs for each cluster. Yorkshire Holdings I through XIII. Invested millions of dollars in grow, manufacturing, and distribution facilities. Tax returns in 2017 showed stagnant income and an increase in borrowing. Same California bank.

Who the fuck was lending him all this money? Andrew started typing. Manufacturing and Agricultural Bank . . . California, Encino. Incorporated in 1904 . . . manufacturing, commercial real estate, agricultural loans . . . board of directors . . . Max Aurel, Chairman Emeritus.

Charlie's buddy, Max. Fuck me.

He kept reading. Terence poured millions into the facilities that were not providing the expected return. Yet. 2018 financials showed an improvement. Kannawerks leased the facility in February 2018. There they are. Occupancy rates across the portfolio above 80 percent by early 2019.

Then the bottom fell out. Tenants defaulted on leases across multiple clusters. The loans associated with the vacant properties could not be covered without the tenants' cash flow. The property values plummeted. And yet, Terence remained solvent. He was not in breach of the loan covenants. He didn't default on one property despite an occupancy rate below 50 percent in his portfolio. Just like Zeke had said. Initiation of an IRS audit dated June 2019. One page. Andrew had reached present day.

He got up to grab some water when he noticed that there were two pages left to the dossier. A heavily redacted appendix.

He scrolled through the remainder of the document: the DOJ, while monitoring Nebula, a known cryptocurrency tumbler, identified transaction provenance from wallets they suspected were owned by members of a cartel, the name of which he didn't know because it was redacted. Near equivalent outbound payments from Nebula were traced to wallets belonging to entities associated with Terence Miller Kayne.

"Terence Miller Kayne traveled to Puerto Vallarta, Mexico on <redacted>. Met with <redacted>. Returned on <redacted>."

The report was dated June 2019.

And another one. "Subject was last seen crossing the US-Mexico border on <redacted>. Driver was identified as <redacted>, a known member of the <redacted> cartel. Recommend keeping under further observation."

September 2019.

CHAPTER 37

A ndrew opened the front door and let Ish into the apartment.
"It's bad," Ish began.

"I figured." Andrew grabbed a couple of beers from the fridge. He handed one to Ish.

Ish paced the floor like a caged bear waiting for his meal. "Ray didn't want to tell me anything at first. 'Why should I?' he had said. But eventually, he relented and gave me the scoop on Pink Dot.

"He'd first heard about Pink Dot in early July, when his customers started asking him for this new gummy. He reached out to his network, but no one wanted anything to do with it. He extended his reach and talked to people he hadn't worked with in a while, characters that dealt with the hard-core stuff. Ray has a line that he will not cross, but when so many were asking, he had no choice. He was able to get several boxes of Pink Dot from an old connection."

"Tell me something I don't already know."

"One of the cartels is behind it."

"Not a surprise, after what I've just read." Andrew summarized the dossier, culminating with Terence's alleged involvement with the cartel.

"Pink Dot is distributed through the cartel network, the same network that it distributes fentanyl, meth, heroin, and coke through.

That's why Ray couldn't get access to it at first." Ish downed his beer. "It's strange because cartels stick with raw material when it comes to weed—they don't go up the food chain to make gummies. They don't take this kind of risk. Why bother? Too many steps, too much overhead before it gets to market. Grow it, process it, or manufacture the hard stuff. Bring it over the border or grow it here and get rid of it. And yet here they are." He grabbed another beer from the fridge. "You don't fuck with the cartels. They'll take you out."

"But why does a cartel care about a gummy?" Andrew asked.

"I don't know. It doesn't make sense. But revenue is revenue."

"And they've got their hands in our factory."

"We don't know how far in they are. All Ray could tell me was that this one particular cartel has some sort of exclusive on the distribution of Pink Dot. But we know who's manufacturing it. Ashlee and Kyle—"

"With Terence in the driver's seat."

"Probably. The cartel's not going to deal with those other two."

"So what do we do?"

"We do nothing. They stopped using our facilities. Isn't that what we wanted?"

"This is bigger than I thought. And there's the migrants I haven't told you about."

"What migrants?"

"The detainees they're using as labor to manufacture Pink Dot."

"What the fuck?"

"We have the video to prove it, and a friend who works with the migrants identified several missing FDN inmates from the video." Andrew showed him the video and explained the situation.

When they were done, Ish put his empty bottle on the table, sat on the couch, clasped his hands behind his head, and stared at the ceiling. After an interminable pause, he said, "I went clean for many reasons, Andrew. Many fucking-good reasons. I wanted separation.

And here they are making contraband with slave labor under my fucking nose. In my factory."

Ish stood and when he reached the door said, "Maybe you're right. Maybe it's naive to think that the illegal and legal markets can coexist in parallel universes. Maybe they will always be intertwined, no matter what we do."

CHAPTER 38

The ocean came into view as he crested the hill on Rosecrans. This time the sea was dotted with surfers whose small black figures were dwarfed by the crashing waves. He drove through the light and continued until the road dead-ended at the Strand. He sat there, his car idling. Gray clouds obscured the noon sun with a ray occasionally breaking through and illuminating the white caps. The beach was filled with flying volleyballs, hovering seagulls, and ambling joggers. A lifeguard rushed into the water, a red buoy in hand, fighting the waves. He reached a bobbing object, arms flailing, disappearing and reappearing after each passing wave. The changing weather must have accentuated the riptides.

Andrew made his way back up to Highland, parked, and walked up the hill. The door was ajar.

"*Vieni, entra.*" Manuela stood in the vestibule, clad in black tights and a loose-fitting tank top, her hair in a ponytail. They spoke in Italian. "I'd give you a kiss but I'm completely wet." She took off her running shoes and kicked them into an open closet.

"Is he here?"

"He will be. He has to pick up his things. I made sure of that. Do you mind if I shower?"

"No, go ahead."

"Help yourself to a drink." She disappeared behind a door. Andrew went to the kitchen and grabbed an open bottle of white wine from the refrigerator.

He heard the shower as he walked past the bedroom, the door ajar. He perused the living room. On an antique chest sat a cluster of pictures in assorted frames. Parents, children, grandparents, and what must have been cousins, aunts, and uncles, sitting in lush gardens that reminded him of his summers in Rome. He found Manuela in a picture as a lanky teenager whose beauty was ready to blossom, standing next to a statuesque woman, the image of the adult Manuela. Neither of them was smiling.

Andrew heard the shower stop. Manuela appeared at the bedroom door wrapped in a towel, her wet hair splayed over her bare shoulders. "Did you find something?"

"Vernaccia," he said, trying not to make eye contact.

"That bottle's old. There's red in the pantry. Pour me a glass?" She leaned against the doorframe and stared out the window. "Look at those clouds." The sun was obscured by a dark mass ready to burst, a faraway mist forming on the horizon. She excused herself and disappeared into the bedroom.

Andrew opened a bottle of red and filled a couple of glasses. Manuela was making him uncomfortable. Was she flirting with him? He was here for one thing, and one thing only—Charlie—nothing else. *Stay focused.*

Manuela reappeared barefoot and clad in jeans and a sweatshirt that fell off one shoulder, her hair still wet. She took the glass from Andrew, touched it to his, and took a sip. "Let's go outside. We can watch the clouds roll in while we wait." They settled in matching rattan chairs.

"I left him," she said, reaching for a cigarette. "All this subterfuge these past few days. The tension rises the minute he enters the room. And we don't sleep together anymore. We don't . . . I know it's Ashlee."

"I thought you said you didn't know who it was."

"A woman can always tell. Him disappearing for days and then showing up as if nothing happened. 'I have to be at the factory,' he says. He was fucking her then, and he's fucking her now." She took a deep drag and exhaled, the smoke mixing with the heavy, sea-laden air. "I think something else is going on. He seems scared."

"He should be, look at what happened to me."

She leaned in and caressed his face, the color under his eye now barely visible. "Oh, *cazzo*. What happened?"

"Two guys roughed me up. They said Charlie owed them money."

"He owes me money. He owes everybody money."

There was silence for a moment and then she said, "You two are so different."

"We are."

"He never mentioned you until you got here."

"That's not surprising. We hadn't seen each other in over a decade."

She noticed him eyeing the pack of cigarettes. "Want one?"

"No, thanks." He cradled his wine glass.

"But you stayed friends."

"We were close, like brothers."

"He never talks about his family or parents."

"No." Andrew gazed at the ocean. "He never does."

"What were they like?"

"He could do no wrong by his mother, but his father . . . he was a believer in corporal punishment. If Charlie didn't do his homework, or get good grades, or was caught toking, or stayed out too long with friends, or disrespected his parents, which he never did with his mother, his father would beat the shit out of him."

"I never knew."

"He hid it well. My parents—especially my mother—were happy to have him. He was a charmer. He'd come over to spend the night and then stay for days."

He drained his glass, realizing that maybe his soft spot for Charlie was because he felt sorry for him and nothing else. Had they ever been friends? True friends?

And at that moment they saw Charlie walking up the hill, pausing at the sight of Andrew, at the sight of the two of them together with an empty bottle of wine between them. Charlie made his way across the small patch of brown lawn. Manuela went inside without saying a word.

"What are you doing here?"

"We need to talk."

"Can't it wait?"

Andrew braced himself against the patio railing, feeling lightheaded. "Let's walk."

"It's going to rain," Charlie said.

"We'll live."

They crossed Highland and walked down the hill. The waves pummeled the surfers as they braved the oncoming storm. Andrew zipped up his hoodie, as they were no longer protected from the biting wind once they reached the Strand, the path separating homes from the windswept beach. The sun had disappeared behind dense, black clouds.

They walked south, passing dog walkers, joggers, couples arm in arm, and surfers making their way back from the waves.

Charlie finally broke the silence. "Why'd you come here Andy?"

"To talk to you."

"No, I mean, why'd you come to SoCal?"

"Because you asked me to help."

"That's right, help." They kept walking without breaking their stride.

Then Charlie said, "Why didn't you come to me? When you found out what was going on."

"What *is* going on, Charlie?"

"For fuck's sake, Andy. You stuck your nose where it didn't belong, that's what's going on. And now we're at risk of losing everything."

"You're making illegal product in the factory, Charlie, risking our license."

"It was a risk worth taking."

"With indentured labor?"

Charlie stopped walking and glared at Andrew.

"The workers from FDN. I know, Charlie."

Charlie ran his hands through his hair. "Jesus, Andy. What *do* you know?"

"Someone is making Pink Dot gummies in our factory using people formerly detained at FDN. FDN makes money because their inmate population keeps growing, someone else makes money on the sale of Pink Dot, Terence is part of this, a cartel is involved, and there may be other operations elsewhere because there's over forty migrants missing, and we only saw a dozen in the videos."

"You're getting too wise, Andy." Charlie started walking again, lengthening his stride.

Andrew kept up the pace. "You still think I'm a little kid that will do anything you say, don't you? Well fuck you, Charlie. What did you think I was going to do when you asked me here to 'run the company'? You didn't think I would investigate the minute I suspected something was wrong?"

"And what's my role, Andy? Am I the mastermind or the victim?"

"You tell me."

"I don't have to tell you shit."

"I came here to help, Charlie, but you got me mixed up in this disaster. Come clean or shit's going to hit the fan."

They continued down the pier, and when they reached the end, they walked around the aquarium to get out of the cold, wet wind. A lone fisherman covered in a plastic poncho sat on a low stool. He fingered a rod secured to the railing. A bucket was by his side, brimming with shiny, immobile silvery fish.

"We stopped using the factory at night. That's over," Charlie finally said.

Andrew remained quiet, expressionless, which seemed to irritate Charlie.

"You need to stop sticking your nose where it doesn't belong! We merge, or sell this fucking company, we get the hell out." Charlie pulled out a pack of cigarettes and lit one, cupping his hands to protect the flame. He inhaled deeply, gazing at the horizon, the ocean merging with the slate-gray clouds. He offered the pack to Andrew, who declined them with a wave.

"These guys are serious, Andy. I had to go to bat for you. We're not dealing with amateurs." He squatted on his heels and pulled his jacket close. A few moments passed; the sound of detonating waves filled the void.

"Remember when we first met? We had each other's back. We had differences, but we never let each other down." He took a deep drag. "We run into each other in Beantown, and it's as if we'd seen each other the day before. You came here without hesitation to help a friend."

Andrew leaned against the railing, hands in pockets.

"It was all supposed to be temporary." Charlie gazed out at the ocean beyond Andrew, the Palos Verdes Peninsula shrouded in fog. "I needed the money for the restaurant. I was obsessed with making it a success. Every other restaurant venture I've ever started has either failed immediately or did OK in the first year and then collapsed. The restaurant in Boston, the one you saw, that lasted six months. Only perfection succeeds, and perfection is expensive. But I swore I'd get it right this time. La Closerie would prove that I had what it took to launch and manage a restaurant in one of the most competitive markets in the world. I put my own money in, and when that wasn't enough,

I borrowed from the investors that saw me as a winner, like Max, and when that wasn't enough, I took money from the wrong people, nine hundred grand from a hard money outfit that does non-collateralized deals on the side—Lorenzo. That's expensive, and dangerous, but I knew it going in. After we stabilized the restaurant and Max came to me with the Kannawerks opportunity, I took it, thinking it could help me generate extra cash flow that I could use to repay the loans—I had negotiated with the Kannawerks investors that I would receive dividend payments once we became profitable. But I was wrong. The net margins in cannabis are nonexistent, at Kannawerks, anyway." He flicked the cigarette butt into the ocean. "Then I met Ashlee."

He rubbed his head vigorously.

"We had just hired her and Kyle. One day we ended up in Helendale. She's wild and addictive. An animal. Her scent. I couldn't get enough, and neither could she. I loved Manuela, I really did, but I couldn't stop. So Ashlee and I spent lots of time together, and I confided in her. She told me there were ways to make money in cannabis outside of Kannawerks. Lots of money. She told me about Brody, his pals, and access to free labor. I thought it was fucked up, but I was desperate. The restaurant kept losing money, and I was still over eight hundred grand in the hole with Lorenzo. She said Akmana was selling expired vape cartridges *and* surplus gummies on the illegal market and someone had snitched. She and Kyle found themselves on the street. They got shut down for the cartridges, not the gummies. She was almost proud when she told me.

"She said the illegals were willing to work, to risk it all in exchange for papers. Papers that gave them legal status in the United States. 'Free labor plus automation is the golden ticket,' she had said. A dozen workers, in the middle of the night, the adjacent facility used for packing, storing, and distribution. We hired Brody and his pals to shuttle the workers back and forth and stand guard. Soon we're grossing around a million five a month."

"I know. I did the math."

Charlie glared at Andrew. "Fucking engineer."

"And that wasn't enough to cover your loan to Lorenzo?"

"By the time you take out the cost of the actives and everyone's paid off, I'm netting twenty percent of the proceeds; do the math on that." He ran his hand through his hair. "Ashlee recruited the Walla lawyer and got him to forge the paperwork. She created the model at Akmana and perfected it at Kannawerks. It was all her."

"And Terence?"

"Terence . . . he was more than happy to oblige with the ware-houses. For a big cut."

"You had those guys at Nett fix the video."

"The Louies'll do anything for a buck."

"When did this whole thing start?"

"July. We were going to do the Pink Dot thing until I paid off my loan, everyone else would make a nice sum, and then we'd shut the operations down. You are right, it was a risk, but it was a risk worth taking. Once we sold Kannawerks, there would be no trace. As if it never happened."

"Why the hell did you make it so obvious and use the Alta formulation for Pink Dot?"

"The BCC would never dig that deep! Why would anyone spend the time analyzing contraband formulations? *Everyone's* doing something on the side. We didn't think anyone would notice. Plus we had no choice—the illegal market is just as competitive as the legal one, and we had to differentiate and brand the product."

"This industry is more than fucked up," Andrew muttered under his breath. "Did you bring me here because you thought I was some blind, obedient fool? You don't know me at all, do you? You never fucking cared."

"I knew I could trust you. That's what I know about you. Cannabis is full of incompetent people: people who need direction, people who have zero business acumen, and people who are high all day. I brought you here to run the company while I raised money and found a home for Kannawerks, but I will admit, I did underestimate you, my friend." He lit another cigarette. "You getting wise has put us all in a precarious position."

"Why? You said it yourself. You shut down Pink Dot, and without the video, there's nothing to tie Pink Dot to Kannawerks. Kannawerks is clean."

"You poked the hornet's nest. This is much bigger than Pink Dot."

Thunder rumbled in the distance just as Andrew felt the first drops of rain.

"There's a reason why Terence's finances aren't in the gutter: more than half of his holdings are used by the cartel as storage facilities for hard drugs that come across the border and are waiting to be distributed, and for the manufacture of other contraband products. Pink Dot is one of many fleas on a large dog's ass."

"*Jesus*, Charlie."

"This thing is bigger than you can imagine. This whole cabal wouldn't happen without the cartel and Terence in cahoots. It's a quid pro quo: Terence leases the facilities to the cartel and thus maintains cash flow. The cartels give Terence protection and distribute his product. And the cartels have themselves a local logistics operation close to the border that no one would ever suspect."

"And what about FDN?"

"They're making a shit ton of money. And because they're politically connected, if the authorities find out, all FDN will get is a slap on the wrist. They'll just blame some rogue operators, pay a fine, and move on."

The rain picked up in intensity, and the scent of vapor mixed with the rancid grime and soot embedded in the asphalt wafted around them. They moved around the side of the aquarium, finding cover in the café entryway. A woman stood behind the counter flipping through a magazine. The place was empty.

"And Max?"

"Max is not a part of this. He would never put his legacy or reputation at risk, not in the twilight of his life."

"He's on the board of Terence's lender."

Charlie shook his head. "He's loaded. And he stands to make a lot more money, at least twenty million if we sell Kannawerks today. He wouldn't agree to a scheme that would jeopardize that, not to mention the upside if we wait, merge, and scale. And as long as Terence makes his payments, no one's the wiser."

"What about Álvaro and the dead migrants?"

"Álvaro was a mistake."

"A *mistake*? His head was reduced to a pulp."

"He stuck his nose where it didn't belong, Andy, just like you. They found him snooping around one night. Brody didn't know what to do with him, so he handed him over to the factory's security guards, who turned him over to their bosses."

"Our security guards work for the cartel! Are you fucking kidding me?"

"Shut up and listen! They wanted to send a message. 'Do what you're told and keep your mouth shut. And if you don't, this is how you'll end up.'"

"A message to whom?"

"To the other migrants, and to anyone else getting in the way."

"So the guy they found near our factory—"

"He tried to make a run for it. They had to stop him."

"And the five buried in Barstow?"

"Nothing to do with Pink Dot. That was someone else's operation. Let it go, Andy. I told you, we're done with Pink Dot. They, Terence, can keep doing what they're doing. But you stop. Right now. Just fucking stop."

"I can't."

Charlie grabbed his shoulders and leaned in. The stench of stale

cigarette smoke made Andrew gag. "They saw you Thursday morning following them from the factory. When you were pulled over by
JP and then followed, you're lucky you drove into that parking lot. If
it wasn't for me, *you'd* be buried in the desert by now—you, Mike,
and your girlfriend. I pleaded with Terence to tell them to leave you
alone. Back off, Andy, if not for your own sake, then for your friends."

"Leave them out of it."

"It isn't up to me, Andy. The cartels have a scorched earth policy."

"What the hell does that mean?"

"They go after you and anyone associated with you."

Andrew extricated himself from Charlie's grip and stepped back
against the aquarium wall. The amplified wind tugged at his hoodie;
the rain pelted him sideways. "Let me have one of those cigarettes."
Charlie handed him the pack. Andrew tapped the filtered end of a
cigarette on his watch, and Charlie reached over and cupped the
lighter in his hands. Andrew inhaled, hesitating. He exhaled and
took another deeper drag. He felt lightheaded and sat down on the
wet concrete. He rested his head against the wall; everything he saw
and heard merged into a chaotic blur: the surfers fighting the waves,
the solitary pelican hanging motionless above the shoreline, the rain
popping on the roof of the café.

"You know, Charlie," he said, "when you called me, it was a sign.
Or I interpreted it as a sign. I was at a stage in my career, in my life,
where I didn't think I could go any lower. I had never felt that down,
anxious at all hours of the night and day, struggling to get out of
bed. You wake up and you're staring into a dark tunnel. A feeling,
Charlie, where no matter what you do or say, a black cloud hangs
over you—there's a weight bearing down on you, and it gets heavier
every minute of every day. Nausea grips you, not just in your stomach. All over. You doubt yourself. You question all the decisions you
have made, the important ones, the menial ones, and trace a line
from one to the next, downward, and you think that maybe you're

the problem, maybe you're the one that can't figure it out, maybe you're the dumbass. It feeds on itself. So you lie, putting on a brave face so that others won't know what you're going through. You paint an idyllic picture. You spin it to your friends, what's left of them, to your girlfriend, before she leaves you. You drink more, hoping it will alleviate the pressure, and it does, for a brief moment, and then you wake up and your feet are anchored to lead weights and that feeling of oppression keeps you from getting up. You can't breathe. And then it starts over, and you feel like you're drowning." He flicked the ashes from the cigarette.

"And then you called, Charlie. *My brother* needed help. I was on my way to Thailand, disappear for a while, and instead I hopped in the car and drove to Adelanto, thinking, Where the fuck is Adelanto? But who cares? It was a lifeline. A way for me to start over. Whether it was temporary or the next big thing didn't matter. What mattered was there was a purpose I could commit myself to. To help you. It didn't matter that I knew nothing about cannabis, I'd figure it out. The self-doubts evaporated, the oppression and the weights lifted . . . and then I took that left on Rancho." He threw the cigarette over the railing and watched it as a sharp gust carried it into the ocean.

"Give me another one, will you?" This time Andrew lit the cigarette himself. "Purgatory. You said you are in purgatory. You're not alone. This was the way for me to make a fresh start. The first step in my rehabilitation. Help a friend in need. Help myself. Have something to show for instead of living off regret for what could have been, should have been. I've got nothing to show for the past twenty years. Nothing. Money? Gone. Legacy? A few co-founder credits for mediocre companies. No family, not that I ever wanted one." He took another drag.

After a few moments Charlie said, "You should leave, Andy, go back to where you came from. For your own sake. For everybody's sake."

Andrew inhaled from the lit stub and blew the smoke upward. "You want me to leave," he said calmly. "Pretend like nothing happened. Hope that nobody finds out. Sell the company and make a few bucks. Dead people on my conscience. You want me to live with this for the rest of my life."

"You're such a pussy," Charlie said, shaking his head. "Same old fucking Andy. That's exactly what you should do: nothing! Shut the fuck up, make some money, and walk away." Charlie stood over him and glared. "You're a privileged white boy, Andy. You've got your tech pedigree. You went to fucking Cal. Stop feeling sorry for yourself!"

Andrew avoided Charlie's stare. "Or I disclose the whole thing. Destroy Kannawerks. Free the migrants. Put Terence in jail, where he belongs. Make FDN pay. Shed light on the influence cartels have on illegal cannabis."

"You'd destroy me," Charlie said, stepping back. "And you'd be dead."

Andrew flicked the smoldering butt into the ocean. "You're not supposed to accumulate new sins in purgatory. There's only one path if that happens."

"Don't be stupid, Andy. Let it go."

Andrew remained quiet.

"I need to know what you're going to do, Andy."

"I'm going to think."

"There's nothing for you to think about!"

"I'll give you an answer tomorrow. Whatever decision I make, I'll deal with the consequences. Regardless of my decision, Charlie, the real issue for me is this: you used me. *My brother* used me."

He walked back up the pier through the rain.

CHAPTER 39

The steam from the shower purged his lungs of the tobacco, nicotine, and tar. He had arrived back at Renée's soaked, and when the shaking started, he wasn't sure whether it was because he was cold or angry. Or because of fear. Fear of what could happen, would happen, regardless of the decision he made. Fear of what the consequences would be. None of them good.

Renée came into the bathroom, took off her clothes, and stepped in the shower. She kissed him and held him close. He let the water run down her body while he reached for the soap and lathered her back, her head on his shoulder. They stood there a while and embraced until the hot water dwindled.

Afterward, she lay on top of him. She caressed his chest and ran her fingers down the scar on his abdomen.

"How'd you get this?"

"Fixed a genetic defect," he said.

She kissed it, then nuzzled her head on his chest. He ran his hand along her back, kissing her head, smelling her hair. He said that one day he'd take her to Thailand. He told her about a place he used to go, on the Gulf of Siam, when he lived in Bangkok.

"Hua Hin. A place where nobody knows you. You're just another farang, an outsider, hanging out with other farangs, the dregs of society, expelled willingly or unwillingly from their families, communities, countries, and society. A place to start over. I'd go on weekends, by myself, stay at the Railroad Hotel, play eighteen holes at the Royal, take long walks on the beach, swim in the green-and-blue water of the Gulf, the color dependent on the tide."

She rolled off him and onto her side. "I'll know where to find you."

There was a knock on the door. It startled him. "I'll get it," he said, throwing on jeans and a T-shirt.

It was Olivia.

"Why did you knock?" Renée asked.

Olivia glanced at Andrew.

Renée grinned sheepishly as she opened the refrigerator and took out catering trays overflowing with braised meat. She started to transfer the stew into Tupperware containers.

Olivia dropped her backpack on the floor. "You want to save your 'friend's' company, I want to free the migrants and make their suffering stop. Fine then, this is what we do."

"It's not about helping a friend, not anymore anyway. It's about getting everyone out of this mess," Andrew said.

"We threaten FDN with an audit," Olivia said to Andrew.

He almost laughed. "What does that even mean?"

"We know the migrants never made it to the border; we know where the migrants are being detained. We have the evidence as leverage. We'll show FDN the video of the migrants working in your factory at night and threaten to release it to the authorities. But I don't think we'll need to. If a request comes into the Inspector General to pursue an audit, they're obligated to investigate. An audit would show that FDN is making money off of phantom inmates."

Andrew started to say something. She cut him off. "FDN will not want to deal with the Inspector General. They're already having to deal with closing contract extensions before the January ban on construction of new facilities and with where and how to house a growing migrant population. They're dealing with lawsuits brought on by families of the prisoners, *and* by Border Justice due to the inadequate sanitary and health conditions—they treat the prisoners like caged animals. FDN will not want to deal with an audit and an investigation that will put a stop to these contract extensions and that may claw back millions of dollars in revenue, not to mention the fines they would incur. No. They'll make that problem go away. They'll get the detained migrants over the border, and they'll shut the operation down so other migrants don't suffer the same fate."

To Andrew it sounded like a precarious long shot. "Won't that risk exposing Kannawerks's indirect involvement, Pink Dot?"

"No, not if we compartmentalize the problem, focus on the plight of the migrants, and stay away from the specifics of the illegal cannabis operation. This approach excludes the involvement of the authorities, for now, as long as FDN does what I think they will, which is to get the migrants out of the warehouses, into CBP custody, and ensure Brody and his pals toe the line and keep their mouths shut."

"That could give me time to close the Kannawerks deal."

"I've already lined up a new lawyer. We will file the asylum paperwork as soon as FDN transfers them to the CBP."

She told them she'd heard that Gene had disappeared, his office deserted, void of papers and diplomas off the walls, just the legal tomes scattered throughout the office. Voicemail full. No trace of the receptionist.

"Won't the migrants talk?"

"They've probably been indoctrinated to lie, lest they end up buried in the desert."

"No, Olivia, I don't like this plan at all. What if FDN calls your bluff and goes through with the audit?" Renée stood in the kitchen doorway holding a ladle.

"They won't call my bluff. FDN will not want the Inspector

General to see the videos from the factory. They will not want to be implicated in the operation. They'll have no choice."

"No choice other than make you disappear," Renée said. "This just sounds crazy."

"They're not going to make me disappear," Olivia said. "I'll make sure they know the evidence will get to the proper authorities if something happens to me."

"There's too many assumptions. FDN may balk. The migrants may talk. You have to assume they will. You have to assume the worst-case scenario. Be realistic!"

"There's only one alternative, Renée," Andrew said. "You know what that is?"

She stayed quiet, still gripping the ladle.

"The alternative is we blow this whole thing up."

Renée didn't answer. She continued to transfer the meat from the trays into the containers.

Olivia joined Renée in the kitchen, and Andrew could hear them whisper-arguing while he paced back and forth in the living room. The streetlamp cast a sharp glow on the drawn blind, the occasional car driving over a loose manhole cover below providing a rhythmic counterbalance to his thoughts. Burn it all? Or lean into the audit threat to buy Kannawerks time to close a deal? As he ran through the plausible scenarios in his head, he'd go into the kitchen and debate each option with Olivia—Renée didn't want to engage with him—until he finally told Olivia to go ahead with the audit threat; he'd tell Charlie that he'd stay with Kannawerks through the merger. The goal would be to fast-track the transaction and sign a letter of intent before Thanksgiving. Charlie had already lined up two candidates—a multistate operator and a California-based grower specializing in resin products. The preference would be to merge with the grower, as that would allow Kannawerks to retain some independence and leverage the grower's distribution network. But in Andrew's mind the choice was simple: the only option was the one that offered the fastest path to closing a deal. And then after the merger, Andrew was done. That was one of the conditions he was going to put on the table when he met Charlie the next morning in West Hollywood.

Andrew was still pacing after Olivia had left. Renée had retreated to bed and was already under the covers, her back to him.

"Go to bed, Andrew."

"How can I sleep?"

She rolled onto her back, and he sat down beside her. He caressed her head for a minute. She closed her eyes. "Tell me more about Thailand," she said.

"When you first arrive, exit the airport, and walk outside into the humid air, you feel as if you're walking into an oven. But soon you become accustomed to the heat, and you welcome it. You begin to sweat, but it's not a bad thing, because you shed all the superfluous layers of clothes and you begin to relax. You take in the smells: the jasmine from the garlands hanging in the taxis, the inevitable exhaust from the cars and trucks and tuk tuk's, the meat skewers on the hot charcoal, the fish cakes in sizzling oil, the cilantro and lime in the fried rice. And the deep-fried pork and shrimp spring rolls. You have to eat them as soon as they come out of the wok."

She slid over and put her head on his lap. "What else?"

"You hear the lilting language, and if you hint at speaking it, the locals will assume you're fluent, even if you can barely understand a word. And no matter what situation you're in, everyone's always smiling."

He ran his fingers through her hair.

After several more sleepless minutes, Renée got out of bed and rummaged through a drawer. She handed him a tin.

He glanced at the label. "Wait seventy-five minutes for full effect? It'll be time for me to wake up when it kicks in."

She grabbed the tin, pressed down on the child-resistant lid, and popped a gummy in her mouth. She then placed two gummies on his tongue.

He chewed a few times and swallowed. "Tastes funky."

"Forget the taste. You'll sleep."

"I don't feel anything."

"You will."

CHAPTER 40

Andrew loaded the rest of the containers on the taco truck and shut the door. He rapped his knuckles on the window and waved. Renée smiled, their gazes lingering, and she and Lina drove off to a private gig. He watched the truck fade in the distance. A platoon of approaching clouds darkened the late morning sky.

He hopped in the car and headed to West Hollywood, flying for once, the only slowdown encountered while merging onto the 101 as he skirted downtown LA. When he arrived at the house on Laurel Avenue, he pulled the 993 alongside the Indian Scout and switched off the engine.

Ish was seated at the dining room table, scraping the remnants of scrambled eggs from a plate. No one else was around.

"I just spent my Saturday night formulating immigration policy. That wasn't on the job description," Andrew said. He tore a piece from a baguette lying on the table and brought Ish up to speed on Olivia's FDN audit plan and Andrew's mission to fast-track the merger. And he relayed the Charlie conversation.

"That fucker."

"Remind me again why *you* do this?" Before Ish could respond Andrew continued, "Maybe, like you said, it's because this stuff really works, and it helps people. There's a need. I didn't think I could fall asleep last night. I was resigned to my usual night of endless traumas, but I took two gummies and slept right through, no nightmares, anxiety, or headache. But is that enough of a reason to be in the business?"

Ish pushed the plate aside, pulled a couple of tins from his pocket, and handed them to Andrew. He walked into the kitchen and unlocked the pantry door next to the refrigerator. He stepped into a small, windowless room. A fluorescent light flickered on, casting a pale glow on colorful boxes stacked floor to ceiling. He reached up and pulled down a couple of open boxes, grabbed a dozen tins, and gave them to Andrew, who put them in his backpack.

Ish then locked the pantry door and picked up a leather jacket lying on the couch. "Come with me."

Andrew checked his watch and followed him to the driveway.

"Wear this," Ish said. He handed Andrew a matte-black helmet. He slipped it on and straddled the Indian Scout, careful to not touch the gleaming twin exhausts. He'd never been on a motorcycle before, and it showed. "Put your arms around my waist and hold tight." Andrew complied, leaning into Ish's thick frame.

The motorcycle roared, a loud, thundering rumble. They found Crescent Heights and proceeded up Laurel Canyon Boulevard. As they climbed into the Hollywood hills, Andrew's grip tightened around Ish at every turn and switchback. Towering eucalyptus, sprawling oaks, and skimpy palms bordered the boulevard, in some places creating a canopy that partially obscured the clouded sky. Thick chaparral and sage scrubs concealed mansions, ranch homes, and cabins interspersed with bare, brown vertical hillsides, where tufts of green occasionally appeared thanks to the recent rainfall.

Ish took a right on Mulholland Drive, snaked the bike around several more curves, and without warning, cut sharply onto a dirt path barely visible through the bushes and the weeds. Ish continued for a few yards then stopped. They dismounted and Andrew removed his helmet. They walked along a dusty trail until they reached a long, flat boulder and sat down. They remained silent, observing the San Fernando Valley extending before them, a cluster of buildings denoting Studio City, and the snaking Hollywood freeway choked in traffic.

"I come up here, sometimes, to think," Ish said. "Since getting out of rehab."

"Your Eden," Andrew said.

"You could call it that."

They sat awhile, taking in the sights and the sounds: the distant droning of the freeway, the wind rustling the bushes and branches and leaves, the occasional bird calling to its mate.

"You asked why I do this?" Ish picked up a couple of pebbles and cradled them in his palm. "I do it because people need help."

"I know. I get that part."

Ish threw the pebbles into the bushes below, lit a cigarette, and inhaled. "I don't think you do know, Andrew. I don't think you understand what I mean by *help*. The access that people have now to legal cannabis, it's a double-edged sword. People really believed that making it legal would not only fix the contamination issues but also help everyday people have access to a safer way to alleviate real physical and psychological pain." He scanned the valley below.

"Take Rosie. I got to know her after I got out of rehab."

"The girl on the bike."

Ish nodded. "I wanted to give back. So, I volunteered, counseling teens who were grappling with various forms of addiction. Rosie was a unique case. She had—has—a rare neurological disease. Causes excruciating pain, fatigue, and impedes motor skills. A deep brain stimulator was implanted when she was young to alleviate the symptoms, and that reduced some of the pain and allowed her to walk, but the pain never fully went away. It got worse over time. She tried various drug combinations, then she got a medical marijuana card—this was in 2016, pre-rec legalization—after both her psychoanalyst and doctor recommended it. But she had no clue what to take. She was seventeen at that time, and the budtenders had no idea what to recommend for her condition or any condition, for that matter. She tried different products—edibles, vapes, tinctures, topicals—some worked, some didn't, some made her sick. And then it started to get expensive—legal weed is not cheap. She contemplated ditching the dispensary channel and buying what she needed on the street, but she was advised against it. We know what's in the street stuff: rat poison, gasoline, pesticides, dog shit, E. coli.

"She was about to give up on the whole weed thing when she met a guy who manufactured CBD topicals and edibles in his garage. She apprenticed with him and then started to manufacture THC concoctions at home. At first, she thrived. She even started college." He stood and faced Andrew.

"And then the pain got worse. She took more weed. The pain increased. She was prescribed clonazepam to help with the anxiety and panic attacks. But the more weed she took, the more weed she needed to kill the pain. It feeds on itself—you told me you were surprised at how budtenders ate entire tins of gummies."

"Yeah, at the party. They downed it like candy."

"That's because they've ingested so much weed over their lifetime that they need more and more to feel the effect. Nothing seemed to work for her. And now she was high *all the time*. She dropped out of school." He let out a long exhale.

"And then one day she had a psychotic breakdown. Her mom called 911. The ambulance showed up, cop cars in tow, sirens blazing, as if they were there to corral a drug kingpin. This is a young girl who had taken too much weed with too many prescribed anti-anxiety meds, and they sent a fucking SWAT team. They tied Rosie down to a gurney with metal handcuffs, like a fucking criminal. Paranoia had set in. They rushed her to the ER, and she was put into an isolation ward. It was too late to pump Rosie's stomach, so they gave her not one, but *two* shots of Narcan."

"Jesus. That's insane."

"After two days, they moved Rosie to a behavioral health ward. They weaned her off weed and all prescription meds. She was observed by a team of 'super doctors.' They recommended she enter a two-tier outpatient rehab program for six months, to determine what she needed to cope with the pain and anxiety. That's when I met her.

"She's off weed now, and doctors have finally dialed in the right meds. I bring her up here sometimes."

Ish lit another cigarette. "Rosie, and people like her, are one of the reasons I stay involved. Because no one knows shit—budtenders, doctors, regulators. When they legalized recreational weed, they didn't think through the consequences. There was no planning, structure, or research. No one was trained; no one was warned. What strains are best for what affliction? Does weed have adverse interactions with other drugs? If taken with clonazepam? With antidepressants? With antipsychotics? Who the fuck knows. Budtenders sell you what they use or what they're paid to sell. Doctors don't know anything because there's no funding for research on the side effects of mixing a federally illegal Schedule 1 drug with prescription and over-the-counter meds. There is no accountability."

"It's the Wild West."

Ish gestured with his lit cigarette at Andrew. "There needs to be a standardized accreditation mechanism, just like you need a license to practice medicine, or become a nurse, or a pharmacist. You should require a license issued via a more rigorous process than what we have today to open, run, or work in a dispensary, if you're going to make weed recommendations. Marijuana legalization was an important step, but the Feds, the FDA, and the states have to step up, invest, add consistent infrastructure and frameworks and laws, instead of blindly collecting tax revenue. Put an end to the Wild West. And enforce the fucking laws."

"Right," Andrew said, sarcasm in his tone. "From what I've seen none of that's happening anytime soon."

Ish took one last drag. "And one more thing. You alluded to the fact that today's weed is not what we smoked and ingested in the eighties and nineties. And that's a problem. Weed has been bred to be up to five times more potent than it used to be, in some cases more. The cerebral cortex doesn't fully develop until age twenty-five—they teach you all this shit in rehab. So where in the past kids getting high may have moderately impacted them, today it's really going to fuck them up if they abuse the stuff. And, if a user already has latent issues, it can bring them out—schizophrenia, paranoia, depression, and suicidal tendencies." He crushed the spent stub of the cigarette with his heel.

"I know a lot of kids like Rosie, Andrew. They can't be left alone. That's why I do what I do. Until the government gets their shit together, it's up to people like me to help everyone navigate the cannabis swamp from the inside."

Thicker clouds were rolling in, starting to mask the sun. Andrew thought about what Ish had just said, putting it all in perspective: change doesn't happen overnight, especially if left unsupervised. Legalize cannabis, make money, let laissez faire reign, ignore the consequences, ignore the potency evolution, ignore its impact on users—users who now have unfettered access to the drug.

A sudden, cold wind gust rustled the leaves above them. Andrew wiped the dirt from his pants. "We should get back."

"I don't know what I'll do to Charlie if I see him," Ish said.

"Make yourself scarce then. He's showing up at the house at noon."

They walked back to the motorcycle.

"Do you trust me, Ish?" Andrew said, donning the helmet.

"I don't trust anyone."

They mounted the bike and wound their way down the canyon. This time Andrew didn't notice the green tufts of grass, the chapparal and sage scrubs, the mansions, the ranch homes or the cabins. Instead he perceived the vertical brown walls of the canyon closing in, the branches of the trees like skeletal hands, obscuring the road, as if he and Ish entered a lightless cave. He tightened his arms around Ish and took a deep breath, his mind now focused on one thought: complete the merger. And then leave.

That was the plan until his phone rang as they pulled back into the driveway.

CHAPTER 41

Andrew hung up. His mouth was dry. He walked in the house and grabbed his backpack.

"What's going on?" Ish asked.

Andrew froze for a moment. "Accident. Renée. Her truck went off the road. She's in the ICU." Andrew stared at his hands. An infinite moment passed. Ish sank to the floor.

Andrew pulled out his laptop.

"*They* did this," Ish said. "Not you."

"It's my fault," Andrew said.

"Charlie did this."

Andrew's fingers shook as he fumbled to open his email. Then he started typing and didn't stop, his fingers floating over the keyboard, the screen a blur as he composed a brief narrative. He then attached files that he had prepped the night before for Olivia, in case FDN blinked at the audit threat: the video; the Terence dossier; a list of the malefactors; the abuse of illegal migrants as indentured labor; the 'empty' warehouses used as dormitories; FDN's involvement. And the seven dead people, for now.

Recipients of the email: the Bureau of Cannabis Control and the San Bernardino Sheriff's Department, Attention Detective Morales. He'd make sure the law would do something with it. They would bring in the Feds: the Drug Enforcement Administration (DEA), the FBI. And who knows what they'd do. Arrest him? He didn't care.

Andrew pressed send and stared at the screen.

"Go," Ish said. "Go to the hospital. I'll deal with Charlie when he gets here."

Andrew closed the laptop.

"What should I tell everyone?"

"Tell them the truth. Tell them we were being used. Tell them to find another job." Andrew ran to the car, started the engine, and almost hit Charlie's M6 as it was pulling in.

Charlie rolled down his window. "Where are you going?"

"Get out of the way."

"What's going on?"

"Get the fuck out of the way."

"We're supposed to discuss—"

"There's nothing to discuss."

Charlie stepped out of the M6 and approached the 993. "Get out of the car, Andy."

Andrew choked the steering wheel.

"Andy! Get out!"

In one move, Andrew opened the door and lunged at Charlie. They crashed to the ground, rolling on the pavement, struggling to hold each other still. Andrew freed his right fist and hit Charlie hard across the face. The shock froze Charlie for a second, and Andrew took the opportunity to pin him down, sit on his chest, and hold his arms down with his knees.

"You bastard! You fucking bastard!" Andrew screamed in his face.

Charlie didn't move. He lay passive on the ground, a trickle of blood on his lips. Andrew stared at the blood, oozing in slow motion, one drip at a time. Was this the same man he knew, the one he grew up with, the one who would come down to apartment 8C for solace? He felt himself floating, slowly ascending above the scene, seeing himself hunched over the prostrate body of a man he once idolized. It all seemed so long ago. And all of a sudden Andrew really was lifted into the air: Ish bear-hugged him and threw him down.

"Calm the fuck down!" Ish yelled.

Charlie got up slowly. He touched his face and wiped the dirt off his clothes. Andrew stayed on the ground, head in his hands.

"What's going on?" Charlie asked.

"Best if you go, Andrew," Ish said.

"Move your car, Charlie," Andrew said, standing up.

"Andy—"

"Move your fucking car."

Charlie glanced at Ish, who nodded at the M6.

Andrew got in the Porsche and floored it.

CHAPTER 42

The emergency room was full of people waiting in various states of agony, boredom, and despair. It smelled like a musty cellar, mixed with bleach and alcohol. As he approached the triage desk, Olivia walked up. He hadn't seen her in the crowd. Her eyes were red, her cheeks streaked with dried tears.

"Any news?"

"Lina's been sedated. She has a broken arm and a few bruises, but no internal injuries."

"And Renée?"

"Renée's still in a coma."

His legs felt weak. They found empty chairs away from the din of the patients.

"The truck ran off the highway this morning just after the Cajon Pass on the way to the private gig. Fell into a ravine." She spoke in a monotone. In shock. "Burst tire, they say. They're interviewing witnesses down at the station. They'll talk to Lina when she wakes up."

"Can I see Renée?"

"They won't let anyone in." She reached up and wiped dirt off his cheek.

They sat in the stiff chairs breathing the antiseptic air and occasionally walked around the crowded waiting room to stretch their legs. After an interminable number of hours passed, Olivia was paged to the triage desk. A doctor waited for them. He told them Lina was still sedated and she needed to rest. They could see her tomorrow morning. Renée was in critical condition. Intubated. She had severe head trauma, a broken collarbone, and a shattered pelvis. Her right lung had collapsed. He paused, as if there was something else. But he just told them to come back tomorrow, there was nothing he or Olivia could do for her here.

They thanked the doctor, and as they walked through the parking lot, Andrew said, "I sent everything I had to the authorities. Kannawerks is done. Do what you have to do with FDN. Don't threaten with an audit. Go all in with the Inspector General."

She nodded.

When they reached her car, Olivia said, "Go home, Andrew, I'll see you here in the morning." He held the door open as she got in. He watched her drive off and then went back into the emergency room and waited.

Renée died just after 5:30 a.m.

Andrew got in the car and drove, finding himself in the thick commute of cars and trucks headed to Adelanto. He wasn't sure why he was going there. He just wanted to drive away.

As he approached Cajon Junction, he saw a thin layer of snow lining the freeway and sprinkled on isolated mountain ranges, the headlights casting dancing shadows on the red rock walls. He observed the snow blanketing the washes carved into the ravines, the snow thickening as the elevation increased, transforming the landscape of the once-barren desert into a Siberian tundra, as if he had been transported into a different dimension. He felt like a lone arctic explorer, struggling against new, unfamiliar elements.

The Mojave extended before him as he drove down into the valley, the traffic stop-and-go. The rising sun made the thinning snow glisten and exposed the same dust, pebbles, rocks, and boulders that had greeted him on his arrival almost one month ago. And as the freeway split, he drove by a couple of sheriff's cruisers, a fire engine, and an unmarked white van blocking the two right lanes to Adelanto.

He took the next exit and headed back to Claremont.

CHAPTER 43

A sharp knock on the door. As Andrew's eyes adjusted to the light, he saw open gummy tins scattered on the floor, an empty bottle of Belvedere, and crushed cigarette packs on the coffee table next to a small bowl full of spent stubs. Stale air filled the apartment. What day was it? He checked his phone. Wednesday. He'd been on the couch for two days. He sat up and steadied himself. Another knock. He grabbed a shirt on the armrest and pulled it over his head. He leaned over, picked up a pair of shorts lying on the floor, and slipped them on. Images of Rock Hudson dancing amongst naked women stomping grapes flickered on the screen.

As he approached the door, a sense of surrender engulfed him. He didn't care if they were going to come for him. *Let them.*

But it was Mike.

"You do not look so good."

Andrew left the door open and walked slowly to the kitchen. Mike followed. Andrew poured what remained of days-old coffee in a mug and placed it in the microwave.

"I am sorry about Renée."

The microwave dinged. Andrew grabbed the mug and sipped the bitter brew. He sat down on the couch and lit a cigarette. Mike sat down next to him. A few moments passed. "Detective Morales came to the factory today."

"I really don't care."

"You should care."

Andrew took a drag and exhaled slowly.

"And she wants to see you."

"What for?"

"To make a statement."

"I'll think about it."

"Amigo." He put his hand on Andrew's shoulder. "Do it for Renée."

Andrew put out the cigarette and rubbed his temples.

"And for the migrants. They found forty of them in the warehouses in Apple Valley. They were packed in like sardines, with those portable toilets overflowing with waste, only one shower, dirty mattresses, and not enough of them. Some people had to sleep on the hard floor."

Andrew lit another cigarette. "Are they OK?"

"Yes, fortunately. They all got a medical checkup."

"What's going to happen to them now?"

"The CBP already sent them to the border."

"Jesus. These bastards are relentless." Andrew shook his head. "What else did they find?"

"The warehouses were also used for storage. They found bags with fentanyl, a lot of it, in one of them. The rest had been emptied."

Andrew finished his coffee and faced Mike.

"What happened to those fuckers: Ashlee, Kyle, Terence?"

"Terence, I do not know. Ashlee was arrested at the Canadian border. Her mother was with her. They found two hundred and fifty thousand dollars in cash in the trunk of the car. Who knows what will happen to the daughter. And Kyle was last seen on a surveillance camera crossing into Tijuana. Cannot do anything about him now that he is in Mexico . . . And you would not believe what happened to the Walla guy!"

"Gene—"

"They found him dead in a motel near Vegas. The smell was bad; the neighbors called the authorities. The coroner said he died naturally. Apparently, there was a shredder in the room, with trash bags everywhere and forged asylum papers. The names on the papers were the same as the migrants in the warehouses."

"He was an enabler. He provided the carrot." Andrew now paced the room. "And no word on Charlie?"

"No."

"Did the detective say anything about Kannawerks?"

Mike reached into his backpack, pulled out a half-empty bottle of Cazadores Añejo, and placed it on the coffee table. "The license is suspended until they finish the investigation. Detective Morales said that Kannawerks was in a gray area because while the facilities were being used to manufacture Pink Dot, the company executives reported it, and the company did not profit from the sale of the illegal gummies."

"And?"

"She said there are two possible outcomes: the license is revoked permanently or it is reinstated with a fine."

"What do you think will happen?"

Mike went to the kitchen and came back with two glasses.

"It will be shut down. There is no way Kannawerks can survive— we cannot sell existing inventory, even what is already in the dispensaries, until the license is reinstated. If it is ever going to be. And if it is, the fine is going to be big."

Andrew lit another cigarette and exhaled. "What are you going to do, Mike?"

"I called my cousin in Tennessee. They have open positions." He poured the tequila and handed a glass to Andrew. "What about you?"

"I'll start with some of this."

They raised their glasses and downed their shots.

"I guess this is it, amigo."

"My condolences, Mr. Eastman." Detective Morales motioned toward an empty chair.

"Thank you."

She stood behind her desk, arms crossed. "Why didn't you come to me as soon as you knew what was going on?"

"I—"

"You had evidence. On video. Lives were at risk. You put the company before the wellbeing of the migrants."

"I wasn't sure—"

"We suspected something wasn't right after we found the first dead migrant in the desert. When we found the five bodies buried near Barstow, I knew there was a connection, but I didn't have any hard evidence, just a hunch. And I don't have the personnel to run this kind of an investigation effectively. Every bit of evidence would have helped resolve the situation sooner. And maybe even saved your friend." She sat down. "When we did get your evidence, everything came together. We confronted FDN, but of course they washed their hands of the entire thing, said it wasn't their responsibility, said they had handed over the migrants to the CBP. That it was not their problem anymore."

"What happens with FDN?"

"Nothing. They implicated a handful of rogue guards and one of my deputies, JP Wyjrczyk. They're all in custody."

"I knew he was involved." Andrew leaned forward. "How did you not know?"

Detective Morales let out a long sigh. "He's only been here for six months. He seemed all right, did good work, even though he's a prick."

"When you made the arrests, was a skinny kid with them? With a crew cut?" Andrew asked.

"No. Why?"

"I was driving home a few days ago and I was followed by one of those rogue guards and a skinny kid."

"Really?" She rummaged through some papers on her desk. "What kind of car were they in?"

"A red Buick."

She pulled out a document from the pile and handed it to Andrew. "That's Lina's statement."

Andrew scanned the document. He felt nauseous. He handed the paper back to the detective.

"You see what she says. The morning of the accident, a car pulled alongside the taco truck. Lina saw the passenger fire a gun at the vehicle just before it careened off the freeway. Your friend was driving. The windscreen shattered and she slumped over. Lina grabbed the wheel and tried to keep the truck from swerving. She heard a loud bang, and the truck went through the guardrail. She remembers seeing the valley floor approaching, she braced herself, and then everything went black."

She put the document back in the pile and said, "The car from where the shot was fired was a red Buick."

CHAPTER 44

Andrew called Olivia as he left the Victor Valley station to tell her he was leaving.

"I've been trying to reach you, Andrew, you didn't pick up."

"I couldn't."

"I know."

Neither spoke for a minute.

"What will you do, Andrew?"

A truck barreled by him, its horn blaring as a Hyundai scurried out of the way like a frightened rabbit.

"The funeral's in San Pedro tomorrow. We're spreading Renée's ashes in the ocean."

"I'll be there," he said.

Another pause.

"Andrew?"

"Text me the address," he said, and hung up.

He drove in a daze back to Renée's apartment, loaded his belongings into the 993, and placed the key under the doormat. Back in the car, he typed San Pedro into his phone and started driving. He now had a destination. He made his way through the lethargic freeway traffic. Instinctively he double declutched into third, shifted into the right lane, and passed a couple of turtles holding up traffic in the fast lane.

The air-cooled engine hummed as the car made its way over undulating hills. He reached the apex and shifted into sixth gear, the Porsche floating downhill, hovering over the black pavement. He passed a refinery, an abandoned quarry, and a church surrounded by fast-food joints. He wasn't going to miss this place. Billboards were everywhere: ads for personal injury lawyers, cars, better cars, car dealerships, The MAAGIC Bank. He passed a manicured golf course, the clubhouse opulent and lonely, an oasis surrounded by an industrial quagmire. Distracted, he fumbled for his phone to check the navigation and then he realized he'd missed the exit for San Pedro. *Fuck it, there's always the 405, always a freeway to take you somewhere in LA.*

He glanced at the rearview mirror. A pair of oval headlights moved closer. Was he being followed? Or was he being paranoid? It was only a matter of time before they found him. Why hadn't they? He downshifted into fourth and moved out of the fast lane. He kept his right hand on the gear shift and waited. The oval headlights sped by; it wasn't a red Buick. He shifted into sixth gear, and as he did so, he got a glimpse of the ocean in the distance as the car made its way down a gentle hill.

And then he remembered.

The MAAGIC Bank. Andrew thought back to what Charlie had said about Max: *He's not a part of this. He's not going to put his reputation at risk, not in the twilight of his life.* A frail old man with a razor-sharp mind. Andrew cursed under his breath. Charlie was naive, had always been. Terence had kept on making his loan payments, yes, but his lender, MAAGIC Bank, the bank Max was on the board of, would be aware of the catastrophes happening in the cannabis market—the asset sales and shutdowns. They would be monitoring it all and they would know that Terence was at risk of default. With the house of cards collapsing, Terence was solvent? No lender would ignore the situation. But they did because they were making their money, too. They knew. They *had* to know. Max *had* to know.

And now Andrew had to know.

He passed an exit for Manhattan Beach and a tall sign appeared in his field of vision, a giant gold-and-black-and-red shield on a stark-white background: a Porsche dealership. He skipped across four lanes of traffic and took the next exit.

Two hours later, Andrew was dragging his Tumi suitcase and golf clubs up the staircase of the same hotel he'd stayed at in Manhattan Beach. It was familiar territory, and it was close to LAX. He threw his belongings on the floor, lay on the bed, and called his dad.

The next morning before dawn, he took a cab to Cabrillo Marina. A charter boat was waiting, its gurgling motors the only sound besides the crying seagulls. Andrew took the bouquets from Olivia and extended his free hand to help her, Lina, and Tía Matilde on board.

They headed out on the calm waters, the chill sea air keeping everyone in the galley except Andrew. He sat on the bow bundled in a jacket with his gaze fixed on the peaks of Santa Catalina, the island partially obscured by a layer of fog. After a while, Olivia came outside and sat next to him. She was wrapped in a blanket, holding a steaming mug of coffee.

"Here," she said.

He took the mug and sipped.

She wrapped her arm around Andrew's shoulders, extending the blanket over him.

If Andrew had blown the whistle, it was Olivia who had unleashed the tempest. She'd gone after FDN with a vengeance. Border Justice had filed suit: negligence, wrongful detention, murder. The district attorney was involved. Until then, no one from any government agency had bothered to investigate. It was a sign of the times: migrants were guilty until proven innocent, according to the authorities, who also deemed them aliens, criminals, murderers, and rapists. The system and the culture were such that there were other priorities, like redirecting funds to build a border wall that was already breached; separating children from families; repatriating legitimate asylum seekers under the zero-tolerance policy; and maximizing profits off the backs of migrants.

"Did you resubmit the asylum paperwork?"

"We did. Nothing's happening. They're in limbo, trading warehouses for cages."

The engine stopped. The water was still. The smell of burnt oil mixed in with the scent of the ocean.

The captain came out on the bow and lowered the anchor. They were about four miles off Point Fermin, the striated cliffs visible in the distance, a solitary lighthouse beacon perceptible through the mist. A soft breeze picked up, forming gentle ripples on the blue ocean.

It was a simple ceremony. Few words were said. They gathered on the stern, the captain taking the urn and placing it in a metal contraption that extended outward. He stepped aside and nodded. Olivia pressed a button and the urn capsized. The ashes floated on the water, then sank to the bottom of the sea. Andrew handed out the bouquets, and they sprinkled the red-and-orange flowers on the ocean where they floated for a while, surrounding the boat in a fiery corona lit by the rising sun, before they, too, slipped down into the cold, undulating water.

CHAPTER 45

It was a short walk from the hotel. Her door was open, and she was in the kitchen filling a moka with water. He stood quietly in the doorway and watched her spoon espresso from a can, place the moka on the stove, and light the burner. She stared at it, waiting.

"Don't be afraid," he said.

Manuela gasped. "*Che cazzo*, Andrea."

"I didn't mean to startle you."

She came over and embraced him. "I'm glad you're here. I was worried about you."

He let go of her and stepped back. "Have you had any word from Charlie?"

"I saw him when you were here last week. I've not seen him since."

"Do you know where he might be?"

"I stopped guessing where he hides out."

He walked over to the stove and lowered the flame. "Do you think Max knows where he is?"

"I don't know."

"I'd like to ask him."

"OK, but . . . Andrea, what is going on?"

"Did you know?"

She didn't answer.

"Did you know what he was up to, Manuela?"

"That he borrowed money from everyone? Yes, I knew."

"That's not what I mean. You must have suspected something."

"I didn't know about the contraband."

The machine sputtered. She didn't move. He poured the coffee into espresso cups, while Manuela excused herself to get a pack of cigarettes. He took the cups out to the porch and sat there a while, watching surfers battle whitecaps. A light drizzle began to fall. After a few minutes she came out and offered him the pack. He lit one and exhaled.

"I just called Max. He hasn't heard from Charlie since our dinner."

She took a drag of her cigarette and then said, "Max wants to see you."

"I'm sure he does."

"He said he needs your help."

Andrew flicked the ashes from his cigarette, his gaze fixed on the ocean.

She nervously sipped her espresso. "Max is a good person, Andrea. Hear what he has to say."

The next morning, Andrew walked to the black Lincoln Navigator idling at the corner of Highland and Marine. The skeletal hand motioned from the back seat. Andrew climbed in and sat down opposite the old man. Max was dressed in a black suit and tie, a blue forget-me-not in his lapel, as if he were on his way to a gala. Or a funeral. His hands interlaced over the top of the narwhal pommel. Tinted windows subdued the light in the cabin, the driver separated from them by a thick partition.

The car started moving. As it passed a deserted gas station, Max said, "I spoke with the regulators about the Kannawerks license." He caressed his cane.

"That's not my business anymore."

"It's going to take some work to clear the license. Difficult, but not impossible. That's why I wanted to see you."

Andrew stayed silent.

"I want you to stay at the helm of Kannawerks. Work with the BCC, do what you have to do to get the license reinstated. Then follow through on the merger."

"I can't believe anyone would still be interested."

"Why shouldn't they be? I explained everything. A few bad apples, not the company's fault. We got rid of the rotten ones. You'll be the one in charge to see this through."

"I'm afraid that's impossible."

"Nonsense. You'll make a nice amount of money once we close on the transaction. I'll make sure of it." He smiled.

Andrew stared at the floor.

"Two million dollars. And that's not counting what's coming to you after we merge."

A moment passed.

"And I'll buy back that Porsche for you, the one you just sold."

This got Andrew's attention. His instincts had been right; they must have been following him.

"I heard the two of you were inseparable."

Andrew gazed out his window at the approaching rain showers cascading into the ocean. "I'm out," he finally said.

"But you must stay to save Kannawerks. There's a lot riding on this."

"What's riding—"

"*I* have a lot riding on this!" Max exploded. Then he started coughing uncontrollably. It took some time for him to calm down. "Forgive me." He wiped his mouth with a handkerchief. "My doctor said I shouldn't get too excited." He reached for a water bottle, but his hand shook too much to open it. Andrew leaned over and twisted the lid open.

"Why is it impossible?" Max said finally.

"The short version is I'm leaving. The long version . . . let me help you visualize: I was beat up by B-movie hoodlums; I was drugged unconscious, my body used for god knows what; my life was threatened; the woman I love was murdered; and I've lost a best friend or someone I thought was a friend. Nothing good has come out of this experience, Max. Nothing."

"Your *friend* let me down, too," he said. "But we're almost there. We're running a marathon, and I can see the finish line. Why give up on the last stretch, just as we enter the arena? We've come this far—"

"Where have *we* come, Max? Where? We'd be trying to resurrect a corpse."

The rain pelted the roof of the car with the intensity of machine gun fire. Andrew discerned the Manhattan Beach pier through the blurred windows. They were still heading south.

"Tell me something," Andrew said, leaning forward. "What's going to happen to Terence's properties now that they're in default?"

Max was quiet.

"You're on the board of directors of his lender. You must have an interest in what happens."

"That cockney turd," he sneered. "He's in the British Virgin Islands, fled like the coward that he is." Then he licked his thin lips like a rattlesnake probing his surroundings. His eyes narrowed. "You owe me, Andrew."

"I don't owe you anything."

He kept his eyes fixed on Andrew. "Yes, you do!"

The car made a sudden U-turn, throwing both of them against the door.

Max seemed unbothered by the move. He continued more softly, "You're too smart. I knew it the minute I met you. Digging around, sticking your nose where it didn't belong in an industry where everyone's either too stupid or too high to give a damn. You're a parasite, but instead of feeding off your host, you destroyed it. We had a good thing going. Charlie's Pink Dot fitting in nicely with the engine

Terence had created. With all the cannabis companies shutting down, Terence was in quite a pickle. But that cockroach is a survivor, and when he came to me to renegotiate the loans, instead of shutting him down or restructuring the debt, I did a simple thing."

"You introduced him to the cartel."

"I prefer to call him Héctor."

"You connected the dots and made this whole thing happen."

"I facilitated it. Everybody's interests were met: Héctor had access to warehouses for his products . . . cartels are in the logistics business after all; Terence kept making his payments, and we kept making money; Pink Dot had an exclusive and protected distribution channel; and Charlie could repay his debts to that lunatic."

"You've got your hands in everything."

"I said I *facilitated*. I wasn't *in it*. There's a *difference*."

"You knew they were putting Kannawerks at risk. You knew about the migrants locked in warehouses. You knew about the *dead* migrants. And you knew that Charlie had taken money from Lorenzo."

"I don't give a damn about migrants. And Lorenzo is scum."

"If you knew, why didn't you do anything to help Charlie with the restaurant? Let Terence do what he had to do but leave Kannawerks out of it?"

"Charlie didn't come to me for the money. After all I'd done for him. That restaurant would never have happened without *me*. When the opportunity at Kannawerks came along, I did *him* a favor. I did him a favor by giving him an out from that money pit of a restaurant. By the time I found out about Lorenzo and Pink Dot, it was too late for me to do anything about it. So I let it ride." He leaned back and let out a long sigh. "Charlie betrayed my trust and confidence. He betrayed me. And now he's still in the hole with that psychopath." He coughed into his handkerchief and took another sip of water. "And you, Andrew. You *do* owe me. I have a reputation to uphold. I have an investment to recoup. It's your obligation. You are the reason we're in this mess." He licked his lips again.

"Find someone else. You don't need me."

"Two million dollars, Andrew."

"Like I said."

"You bring cachet, gravitas, and legitimacy to an industry that lacks it. Just a few more months."

"I don't want your blood money."

"Héctor doesn't like it when his operations are thwarted!" He swatted the cane abruptly on the leather seat, making Andrew jump. "You've single-handedly shut down major delivery routes. Terence's warehouses had become essential to Héctor's distribution. I've held him off as long as I can, Andrew."

"You didn't hold off shit."

"The girl was a mistake. An overzealous henchman trying to impress his superiors. He's been taken care of."

"You're on your own."

"There's more where he came from." His tone softened into a macabre purr. "I can only do so much, Andrew. My business interests and Héctor's are intertwined." His pale fingers met again over the cane. "Don't let me down. I'm the only reason you're still alive."

"Stop the car."

The car kept moving.

"I won't ask you again," Max said.

Andrew reached for the handle. Max tapped his cane twice against the partition and the car stopped. The driver sat impassively, staring ahead. Andrew stepped out of the car, pulled the hood over his head, and walked to the hotel in the rain.

The black SUV floated past and disappeared over a hill. Andrew stepped up his pace. There were no other cars on Highland, too early on a rainswept Sunday morning in Manhattan Beach. The cafés were just opening up. The hooded workers were hunched over, like apathetic ghosts, sweeping the sidewalks, bringing in empty trash bins, yawning as they brewed the morning's first coffee.

When Andrew reached the hotel, he stopped as if expecting someone. And instead of climbing the stairs to his room, he crossed Highland and ran down to an alley, where a gray Toyota Camry sat idling.

"Did you get it?" his dad asked as Andrew sat down.

Andrew pulled out his iPhone, dragged the cursor back and pressed play: "There's more where he came from. I can only do so much, Andrew. My business interests and Héctor's are intertwined."

"Good," his dad said. He headed down the alley. "I almost lost you there when he made the U-turn."

They remained quiet until they reached Vista del Mar. The ocean raged to their left, and the clouds shed rain like a cascading waterfall.

"Send me the recording on Signal," he said. "Hold on to a copy offline."

"OK," Andrew said. He compressed the file and sent it.

"I've got this from here, Andy. Now I just have to get you to the airport."

They sat in silence until they reached Imperial Highway.

"You'll want to change out of those wet clothes."

"I will."

"I think I got everything out of the room. By the way, what happened to your woods?"

"I left them in the desert. I need a new set anyway."

"You can go to the pro shop at Springfield."

"I prefer the one at Royal Hua Hin. They know me there. They'll give me a discount."

"I'll see you in a few weeks. Where are you going to stay?"

"I'll find a room."

They had reached the labyrinth of LAX surrounded by cars snaking their way along the pavement. The Camry stopped just after terminal three. Andrew grabbed his bags from the trunk, hugged his dad, and disappeared into the crowd.

ACKNOWLEDGMENTS

I would like to thank Lauren Claire Smith and Beca Erickson for reading multiple drafts of the novel, for their advice on all matters cannabis, for their invaluable editing insights, and for their patience in working with me. *Left on Rancho* would not have been possible without them.

I would like to thank Sandra for sharing her experiences in dealing with the (legal and illegal) marijuana ecosystem and its deleterious influence on teenagers; my family: Angiola, Camilla, Giuliana, and Margherita for reading the early drafts and for their encouragement; Stan for sharing his law enforcement experience from his days in the High Desert; Teresa and Alberto for ensuring that the Spanish language and idioms were grammatically correct and used appropriately; Catherine for sharing new insights; and Lorraine, my copyeditor, for pushing me to cut the superfluous, tighten the narrative, and simplify the dialogue.

A special thank you to Brooke Warner from SparkPress for taking me on as a debut author and giving me the opportunity to share my story; to Addison for facilitating the editorial process; and to Crystal and the entire team at BookSparks for driving the marketing and PR, and for securing the exposure the novel deserves.

This book would never have happened if I hadn't taken a two-year detour from tech into California cannabis. A shout out to all those who toil, slog, and try to make a living in legal weed, despite the market, economic, and regulatory challenges. The day will dawn when the Federal Government comes to its senses and legalizes (and properly regulates) marijuana at the federal level. Until then, all the best.

ABOUT THE AUTHOR

photo credit: Tommy Rizzoli

Francesco Paola was born in Turin, Italy, and was raised in Italy, Thailand, and Australia before moving to the US, where he earned an engineering degree from MIT and an MBA from the Haas School of Business at UC Berkeley. He is an accomplished technology entrepreneur, and from 2019 to 2021 worked at a legal cannabis startup in California while on a sabbatical from tech. He has written technical blogs, white papers, and articles for over twenty-five years as an executive in the tech-startup ecosystem. He and his wife Jackie have called New York City home since 1999.

Looking for your next great read?

We can help!

Visit www.gosparkpress.com/next-read
or scan the QR code below for a list
of our recommended titles.

SparkPress is an independent boutique publisher
delivering high-quality, entertaining, and engaging
content that enhances readers' lives, with a special
focus on commercial and genre fiction.